big NATE
THIS MEANS WAR!

Complete Your *Big Nate* Collection

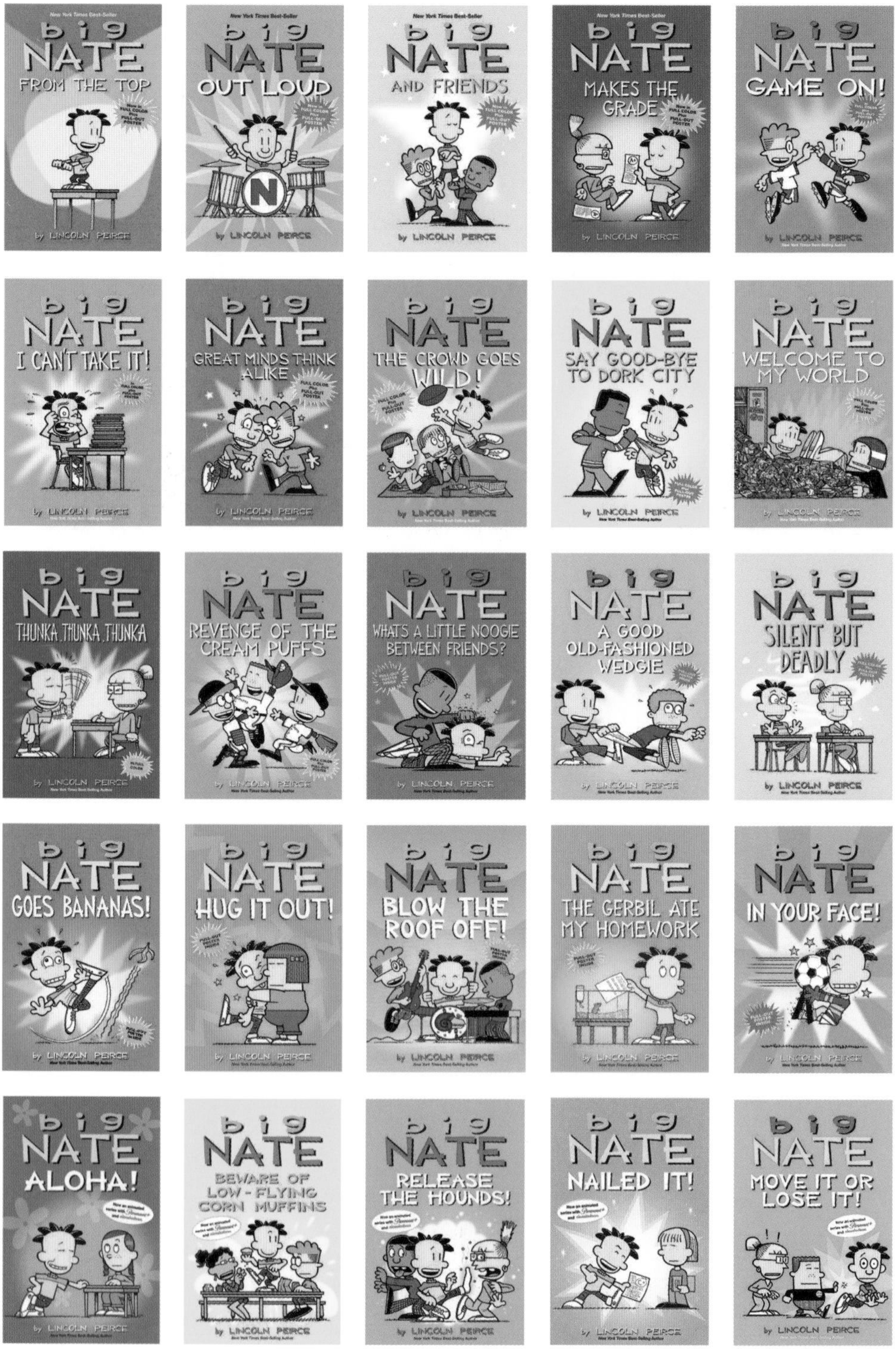

big NATE FROM THE TOP
by LINCOLN PEIRCE
big NATE OUT LOUD
by LINCOLN PEIRCE
big NATE AND FRIENDS
by LINCOLN PEIRCE
big NATE MAKES THE GRADE
by LINCOLN PEIRCE
big NATE GAME ON!
by LINCOLN PEIRCE
big NATE I CAN'T TAKE IT!
by LINCOLN PEIRCE
big NATE GREAT MINDS THINK ALIKE
by LINCOLN PEIRCE
big NATE THE CROWD GOES WILD!
by LINCOLN PEIRCE
big NATE SAY GOOD-BYE TO DORK CITY
by LINCOLN PEIRCE
big NATE WELCOME TO MY WORLD
by LINCOLN PEIRCE
big NATE THUNKA, THUNKA, THUNKA
by LINCOLN PEIRCE
big NATE REVENGE OF THE CREAM PUFFS
by LINCOLN PEIRCE
big NATE WHAT'S A LITTLE NOOGIE BETWEEN FRIENDS?
by LINCOLN PEIRCE
big NATE A GOOD OLD-FASHIONED WEDGIE
by LINCOLN PEIRCE
big NATE SILENT BUT DEADLY
by LINCOLN PEIRCE
big NATE GOES BANANAS!
by LINCOLN PEIRCE
big NATE HUG IT OUT!
by LINCOLN PEIRCE
big NATE BLOW THE ROOF OFF!
by LINCOLN PEIRCE
big NATE THE GERBIL ATE MY HOMEWORK
by LINCOLN PEIRCE
big NATE IN YOUR FACE!
by LINCOLN PEIRCE
big NATE ALOHA!
by LINCOLN PEIRCE
big NATE BEWARE OF LOW-FLYING CORN MUFFINS
by LINCOLN PEIRCE
big NATE RELEASE THE HOUNDS!
by LINCOLN PEIRCE
big NATE NAILED IT!
by LINCOLN PEIRCE
big NATE MOVE IT OR LOSE IT!
by LINCOLN PEIRCE

big NATE

THIS MEANS WAR!

by LINCOLN PEIRCE

Andrews McMeel
PUBLISHING®

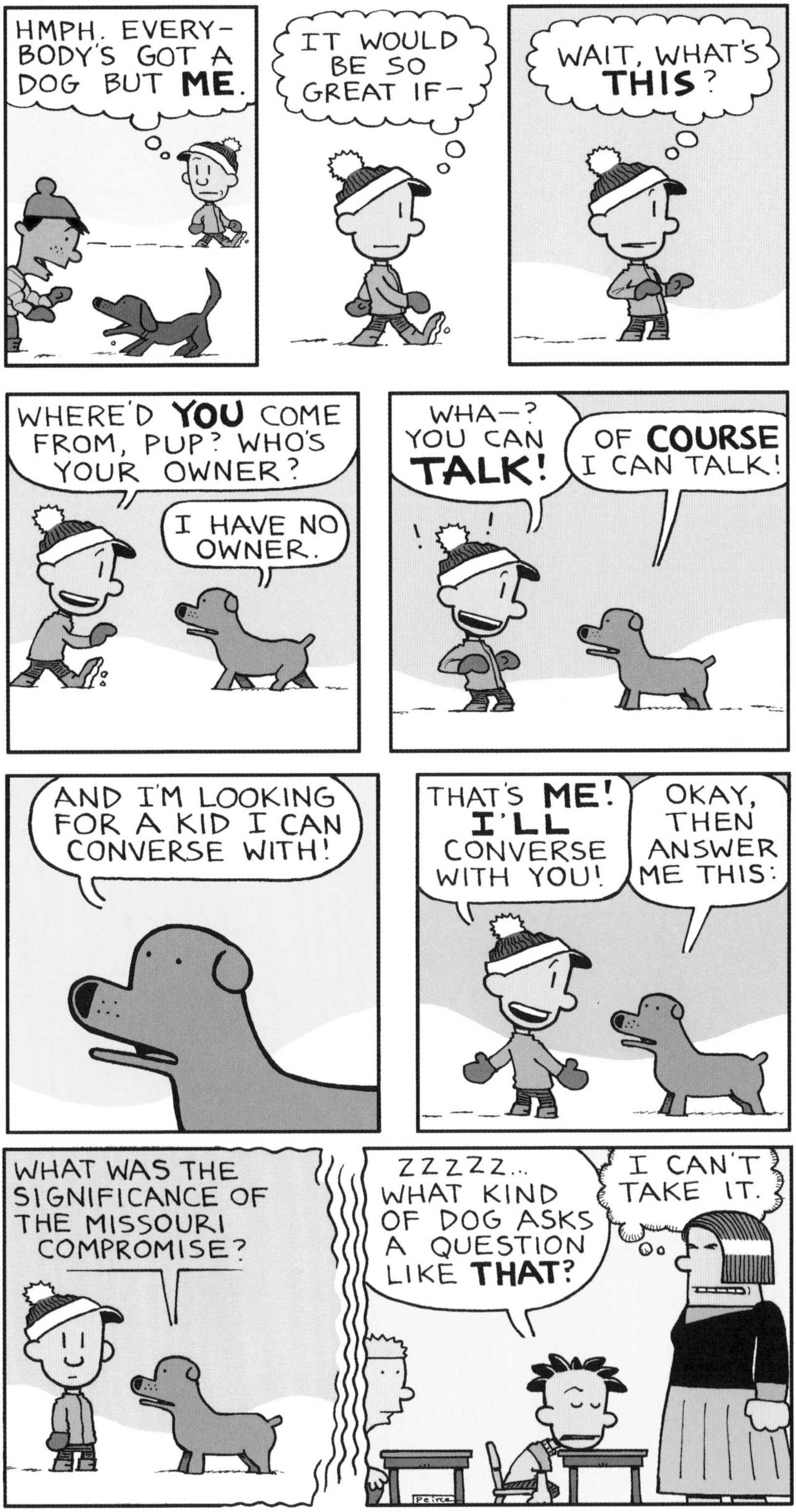
HMPH. EVERY-BODY'S GOT A DOG BUT **ME**.
IT WOULD BE SO GREAT IF–
WAIT, WHAT'S **THIS**?
WHERE'D **YOU** COME FROM, PUP? WHO'S YOUR OWNER?
I HAVE NO OWNER.
WHA–? YOU CAN **TALK**!
! !
OF **COURSE** I CAN TALK!
AND I'M LOOKING FOR A KID I CAN CONVERSE WITH!
THAT'S **ME**! **I'LL** CONVERSE WITH YOU!
OKAY, THEN ANSWER ME THIS:
WHAT WAS THE SIGNIFICANCE OF THE MISSOURI COMPROMISE?
ZZZZZ... WHAT KIND OF DOG ASKS A QUESTION LIKE **THAT**?
I CAN'T TAKE IT.
Peirce

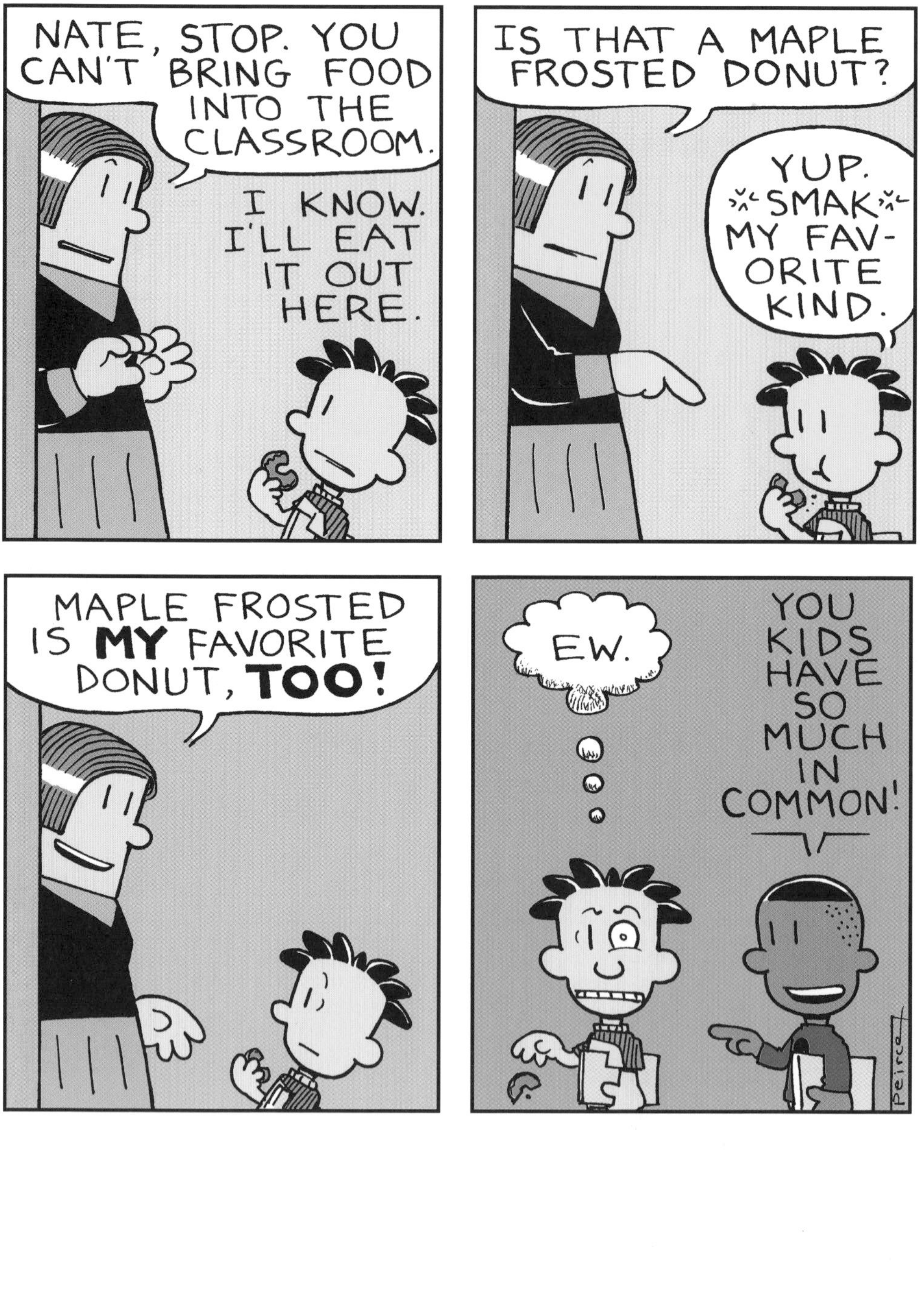
NATE, STOP. YOU CAN'T BRING FOOD INTO THE CLASSROOM.
I KNOW. I'LL EAT IT OUT HERE.
IS THAT A MAPLE FROSTED DONUT?
YUP. SMAK MY FAV-ORITE KIND.
MAPLE FROSTED IS MY FAVORITE DONUT, TOO!
EW.
YOU KIDS HAVE SO MUCH IN COMMON!
peirce

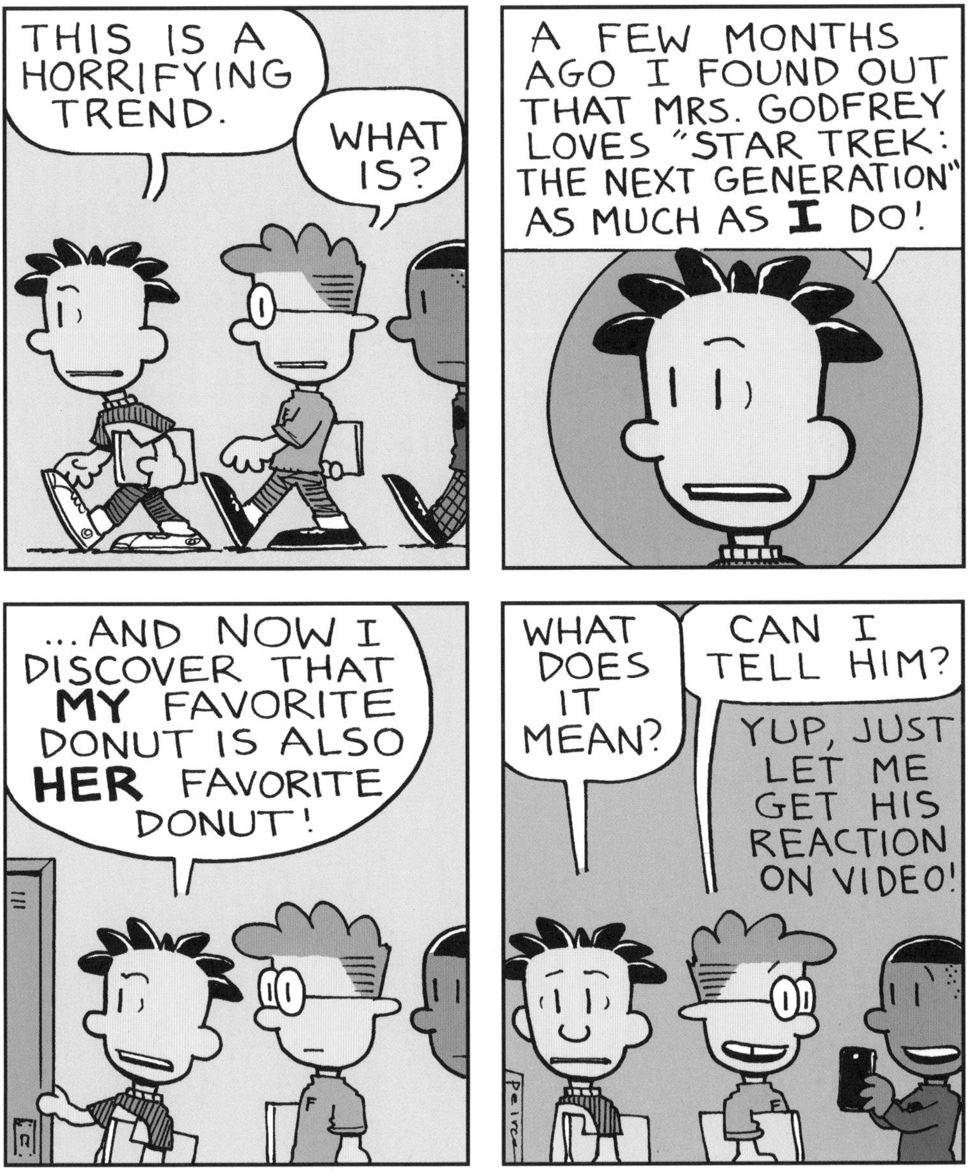
THIS IS A HORRIFYING TREND.
WHAT IS?
A FEW MONTHS AGO I FOUND OUT THAT MRS. GODFREY LOVES "STAR TREK: THE NEXT GENERATION" AS MUCH AS I DO!
...AND NOW I DISCOVER THAT MY FAVORITE DONUT IS ALSO HER FAVORITE DONUT!
WHAT DOES IT MEAN?
CAN I TELL HIM?
YUP, JUST LET ME GET HIS REACTION ON VIDEO!

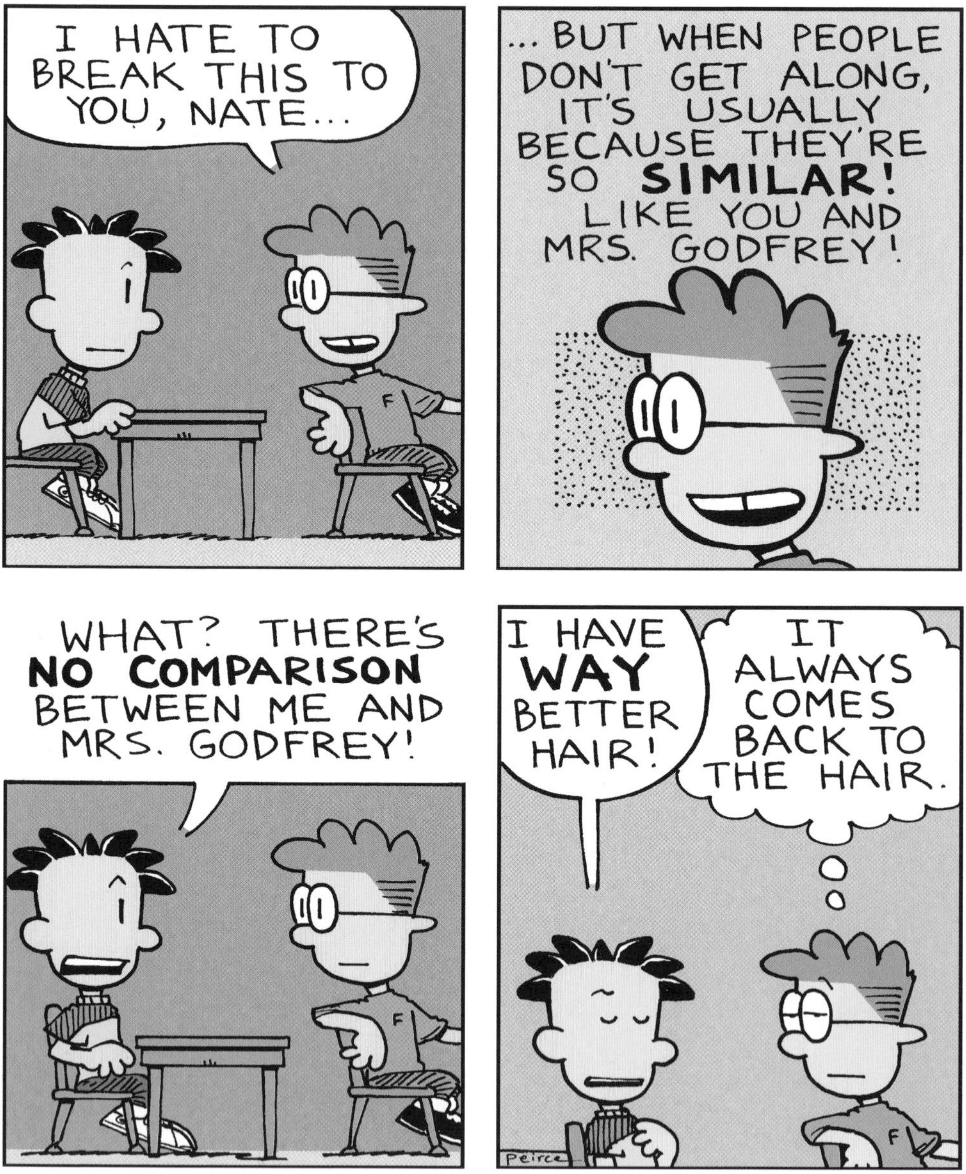
I HATE TO BREAK THIS TO YOU, NATE...
... BUT WHEN PEOPLE DON'T GET ALONG, IT'S USUALLY BECAUSE THEY'RE SO SIMILAR! LIKE YOU AND MRS. GODFREY!
WHAT? THERE'S NO COMPARISON BETWEEN ME AND MRS. GODFREY!
I HAVE WAY BETTER HAIR!
IT ALWAYS COMES BACK TO THE HAIR.
peirce

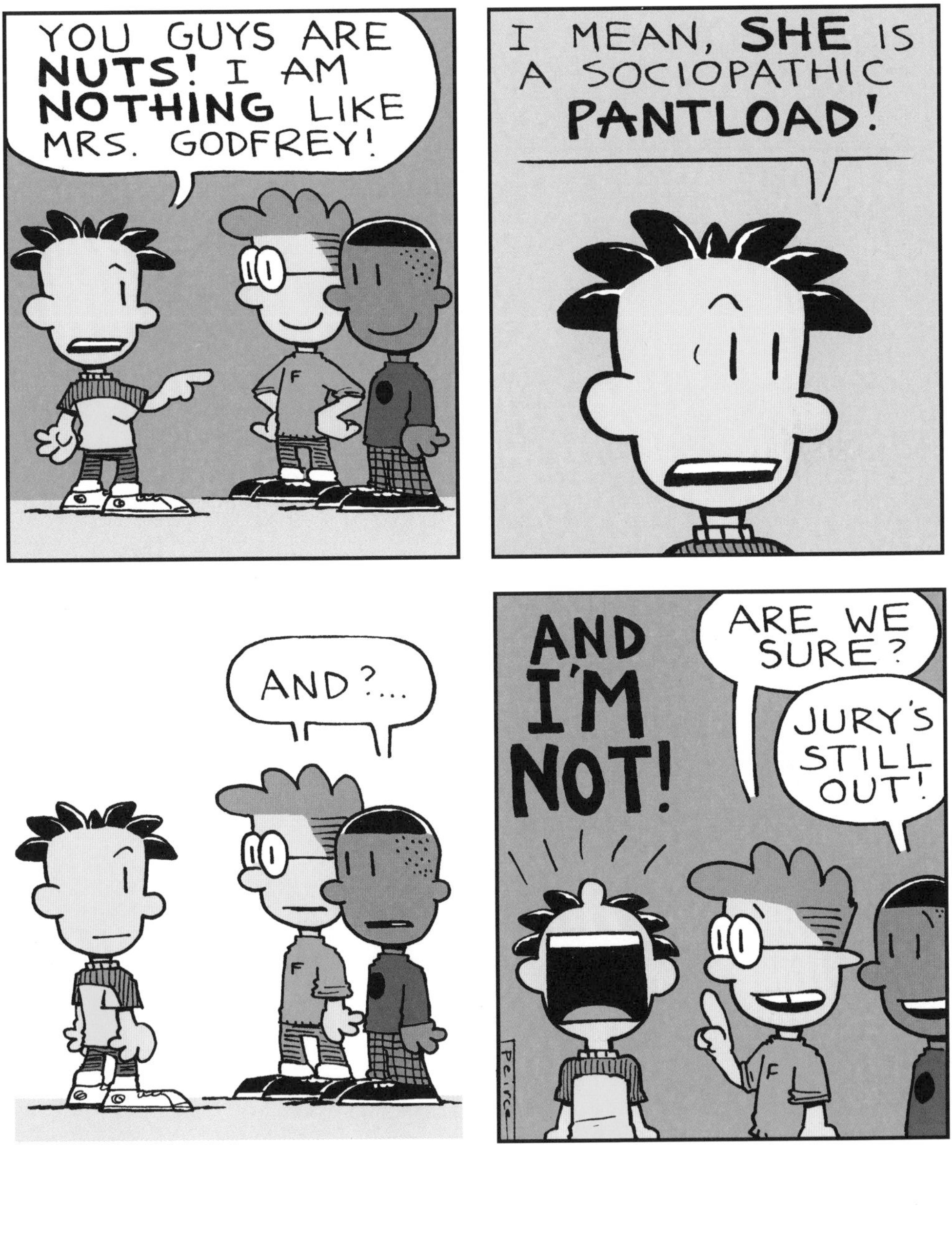
YOU GUYS ARE **NUTS!** I AM **NOTHING** LIKE MRS. GODFREY!
I MEAN, **SHE** IS A SOCIOPATHIC **PANTLOAD!**
AND?...
AND I'M NOT!
ARE WE SURE?
JURY'S STILL OUT!
peirce

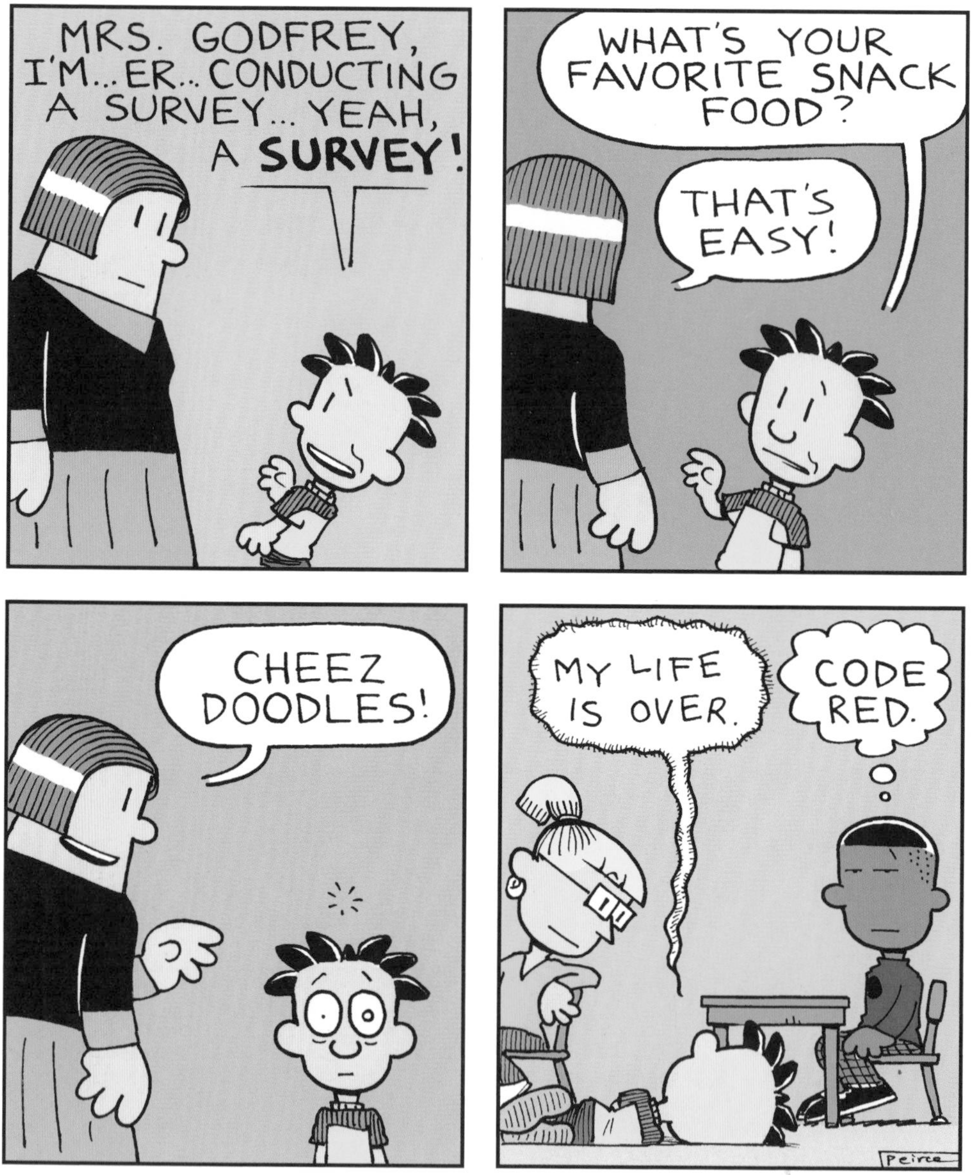
MRS. GODFREY, I'M... ER... CONDUCTING A SURVEY... YEAH, A **SURVEY**!
WHAT'S YOUR FAVORITE SNACK FOOD?
THAT'S EASY!
CHEEZ DOODLES!
MY LIFE IS OVER.
CODE RED.
peirce

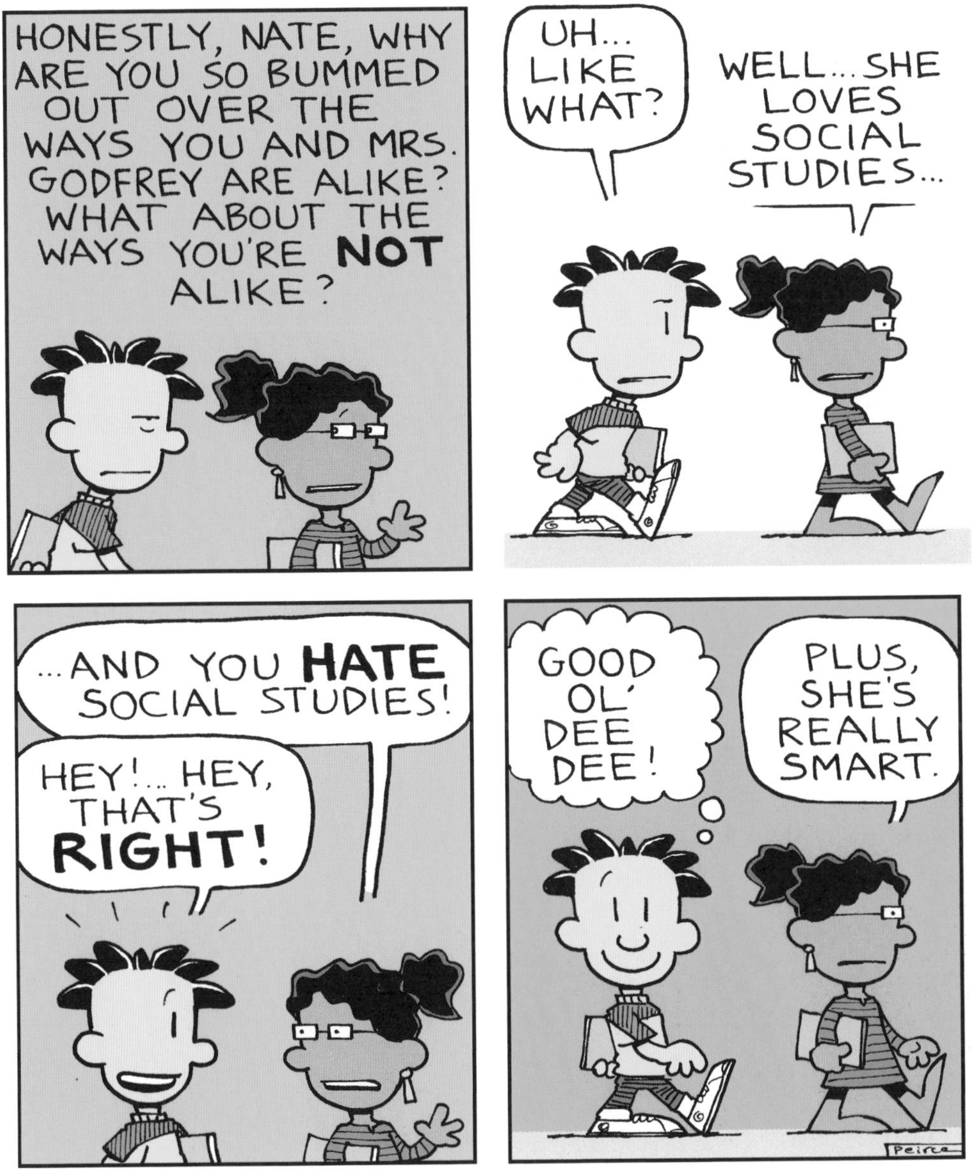
HONESTLY, NATE, WHY ARE YOU SO BUMMED OUT OVER THE WAYS YOU AND MRS. GODFREY ARE ALIKE? WHAT ABOUT THE WAYS YOU'RE **NOT** ALIKE?
UH... LIKE WHAT?
WELL... SHE LOVES SOCIAL STUDIES...
...AND YOU **HATE** SOCIAL STUDIES!
HEY!... HEY, THAT'S **RIGHT!**
GOOD OL' DEE DEE!
PLUS, SHE'S REALLY SMART.
Peirce

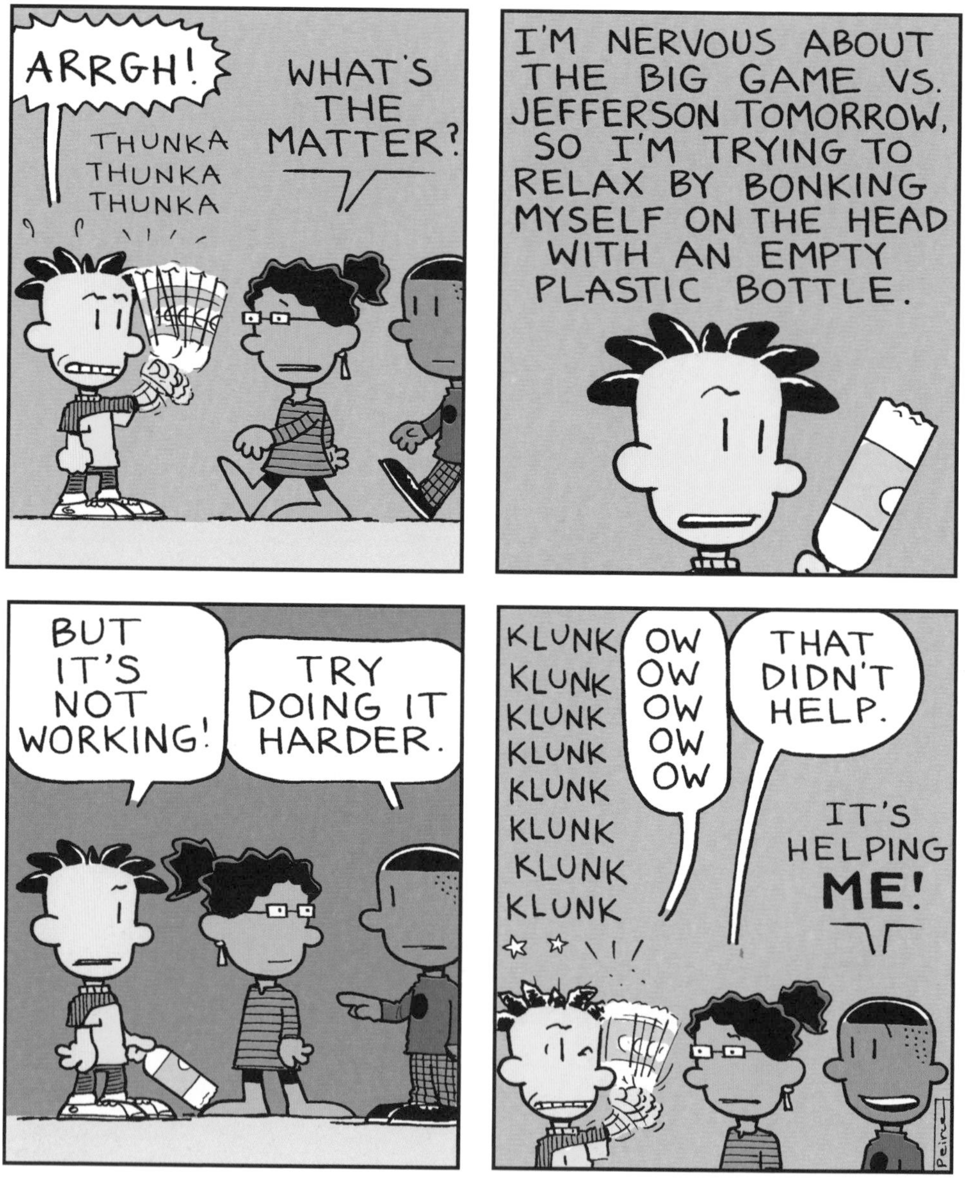
ARRGH!
THUNKA THUNKA THUNKA
WHAT'S THE MATTER?
I'M NERVOUS ABOUT THE BIG GAME VS. JEFFERSON TOMORROW, SO I'M TRYING TO RELAX BY BONKING MYSELF ON THE HEAD WITH AN EMPTY PLASTIC BOTTLE.
BUT IT'S NOT WORKING!
TRY DOING IT HARDER.
KLUNK KLUNK KLUNK KLUNK KLUNK KLUNK KLUNK KLUNK
OW OW OW OW OW
THAT DIDN'T HELP.
IT'S HELPING **ME**!
Peirce

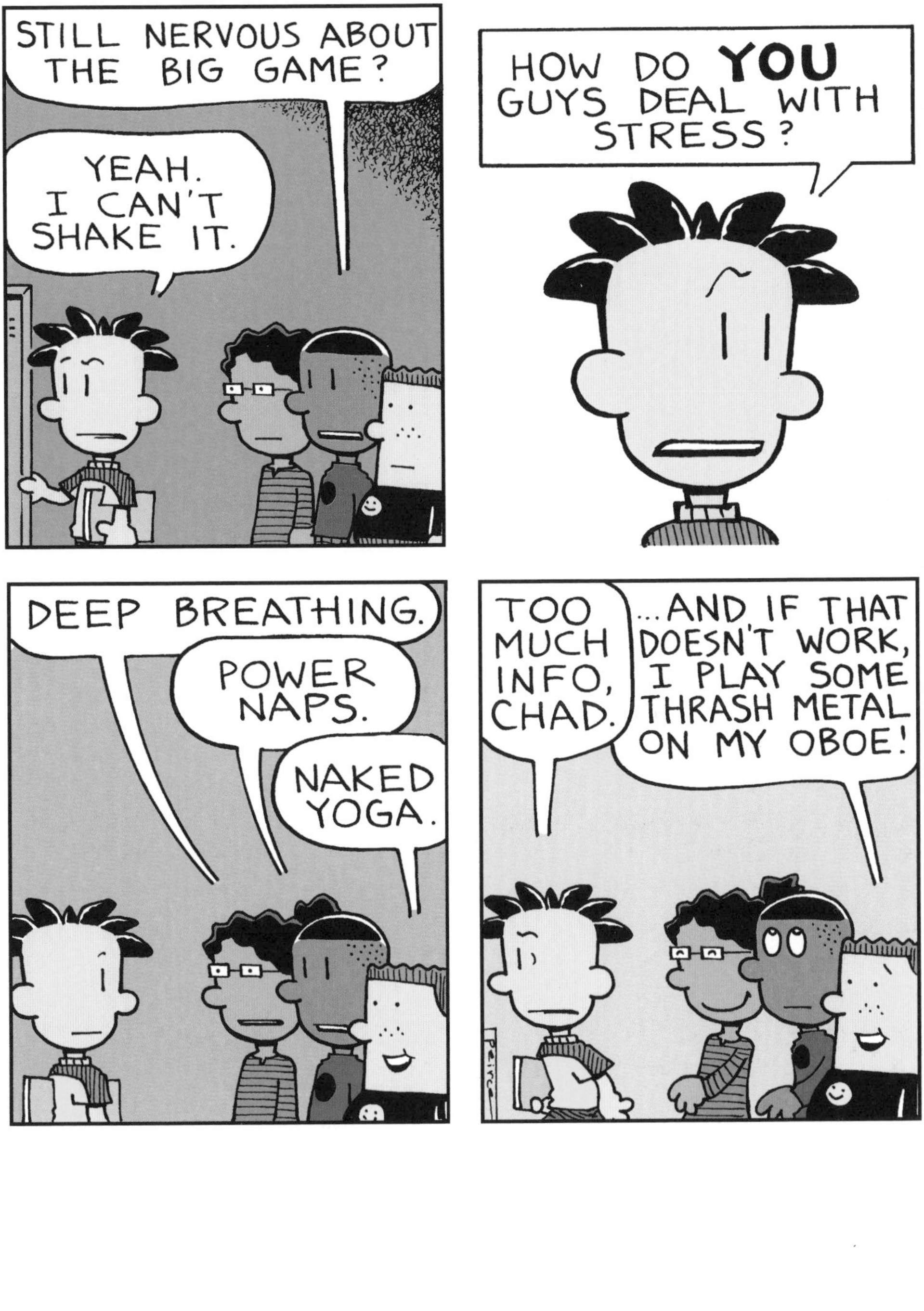
STILL NERVOUS ABOUT THE BIG GAME?
YEAH. I CAN'T SHAKE IT.
HOW DO **YOU** GUYS DEAL WITH STRESS?
DEEP BREATHING.
POWER NAPS.
NAKED YOGA.
...AND IF THAT DOESN'T WORK, I PLAY SOME THRASH METAL ON MY OBOE!
TOO MUCH INFO, CHAD.
Peirce

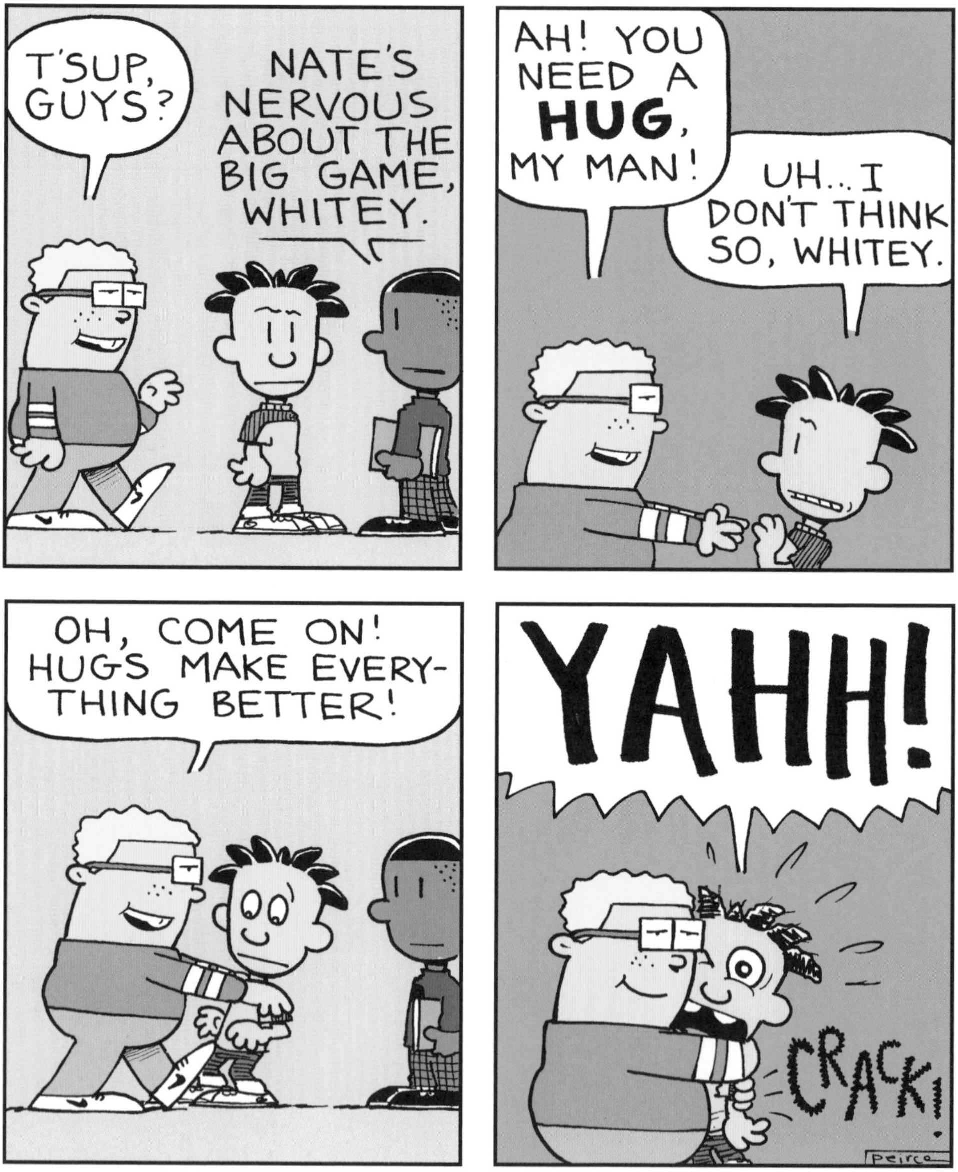
T'SUP, GUYS?
NATE'S NERVOUS ABOUT THE BIG GAME, WHITEY.
AH! YOU NEED A **HUG**, MY MAN!
UH... I DON'T THINK SO, WHITEY.
OH, COME ON! HUGS MAKE EVERY-THING BETTER!
YAHH!
CRACK!
peirce

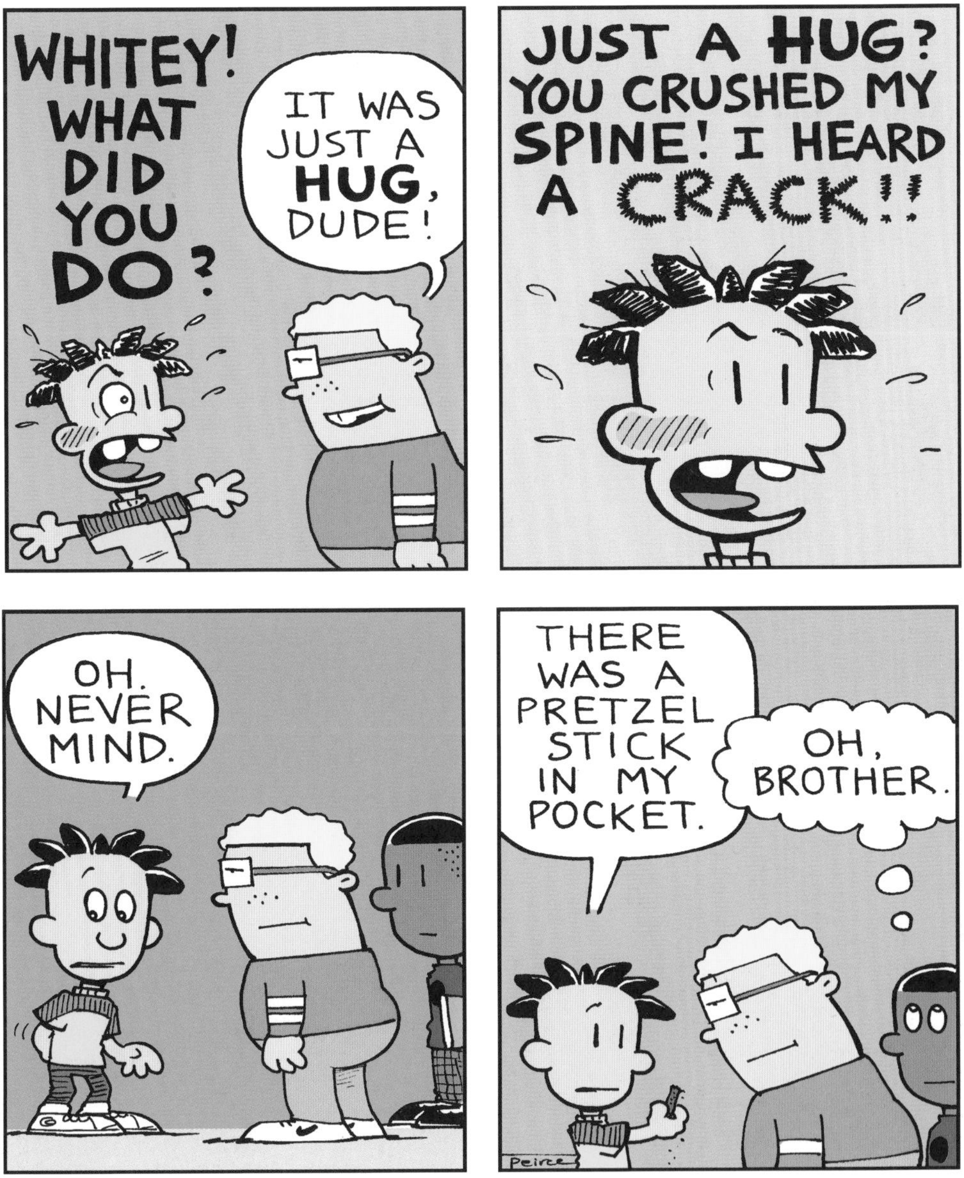
WHITEY! WHAT DID YOU DO?
IT WAS JUST A HUG, DUDE!
JUST A HUG? YOU CRUSHED MY SPINE! I HEARD A CRACK!!
OH. NEVER MIND.
THERE WAS A PRETZEL STICK IN MY POCKET.
OH, BROTHER.
Peirce

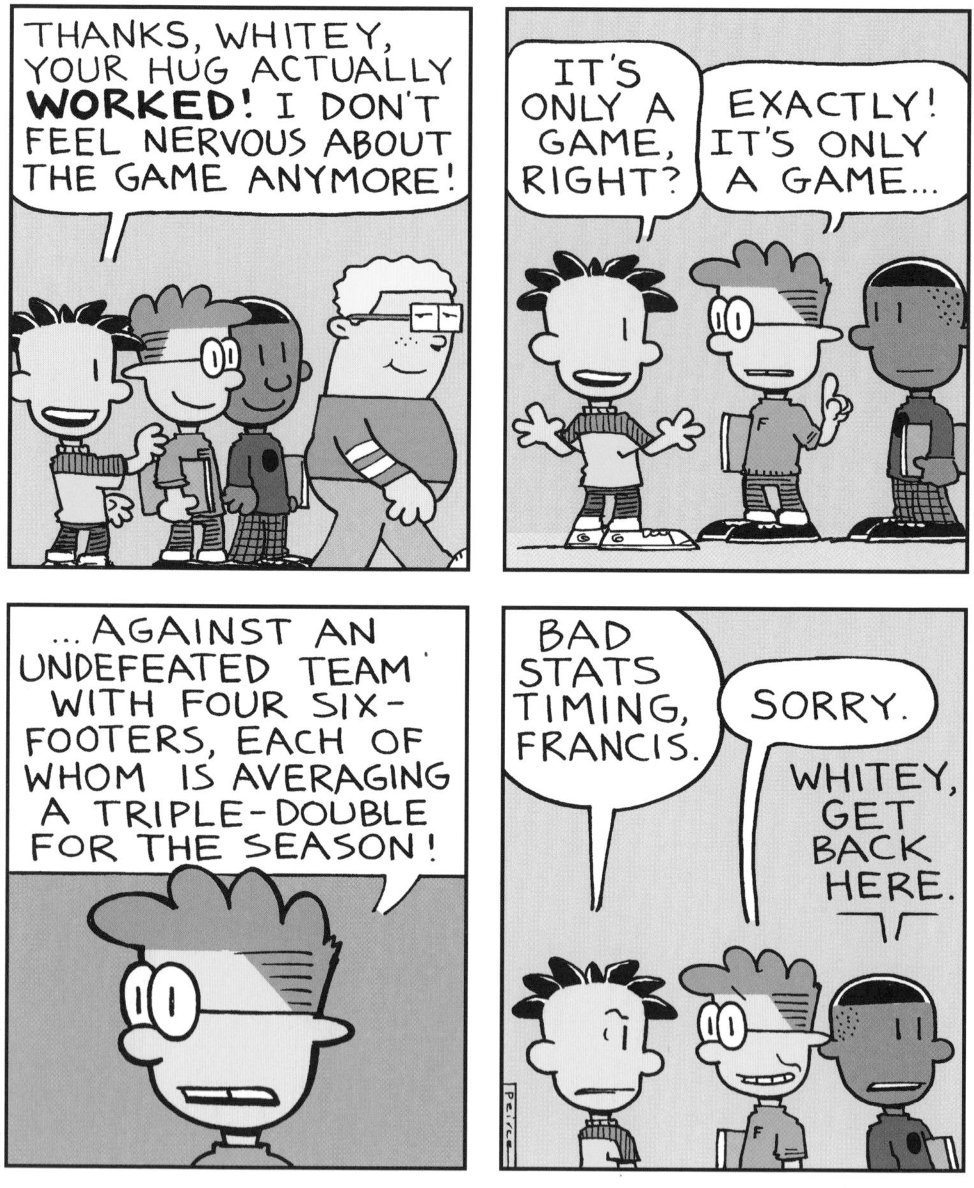
THANKS, WHITEY, YOUR HUG ACTUALLY **WORKED!** I DON'T FEEL NERVOUS ABOUT THE GAME ANYMORE!
IT'S ONLY A GAME, RIGHT?
EXACTLY! IT'S ONLY A GAME...
...AGAINST AN UNDEFEATED TEAM WITH FOUR SIX-FOOTERS, EACH OF WHOM IS AVERAGING A TRIPLE-DOUBLE FOR THE SEASON!
BAD STATS TIMING, FRANCIS.
SORRY.
WHITEY, GET BACK HERE.
PEIRCE

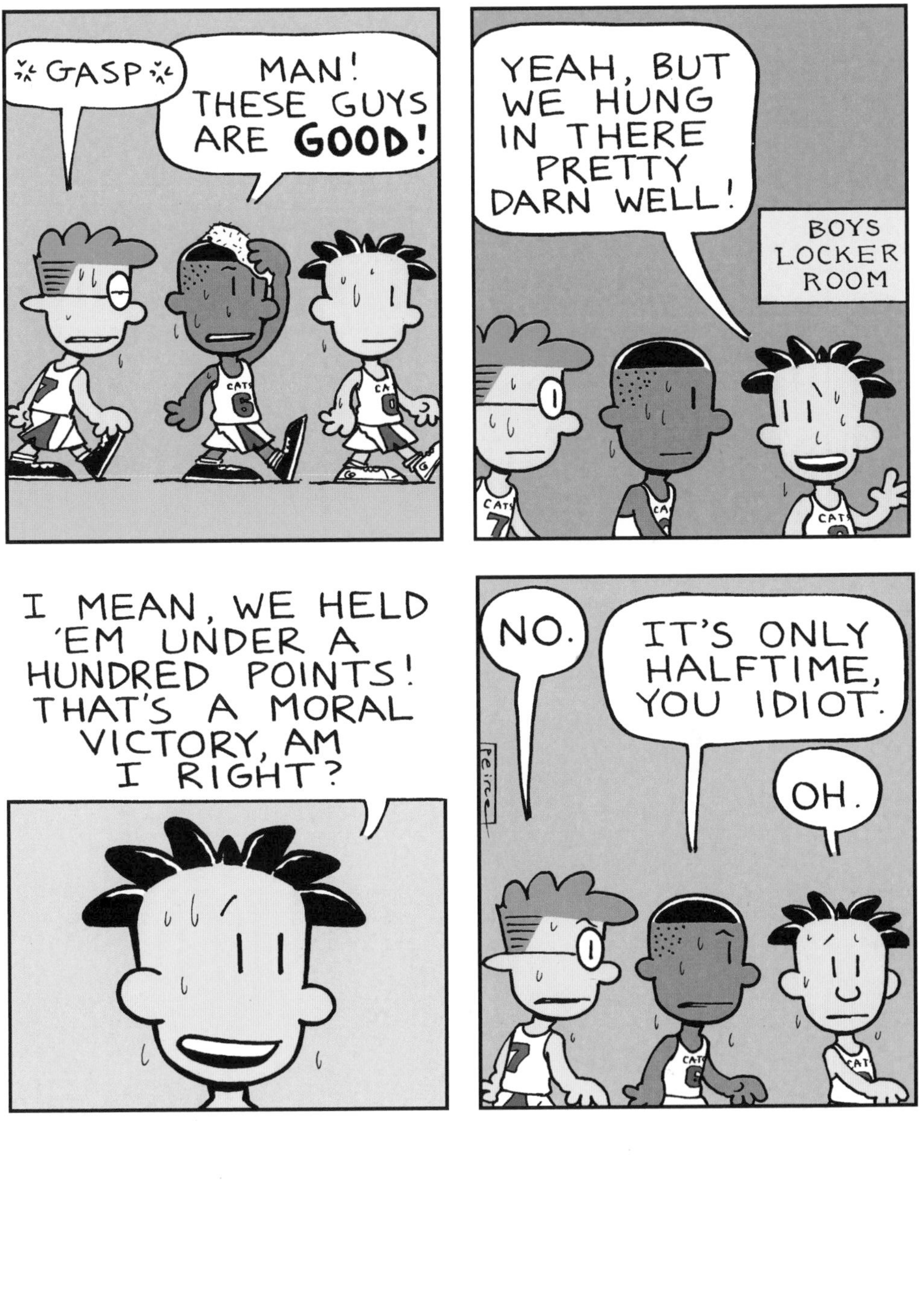
GASP
MAN! THESE GUYS ARE **GOOD**!
YEAH, BUT WE HUNG IN THERE PRETTY DARN WELL!
BOYS LOCKER ROOM
I MEAN, WE HELD 'EM UNDER A HUNDRED POINTS! THAT'S A MORAL VICTORY, AM I RIGHT?
NO.
IT'S ONLY HALFTIME, YOU IDIOT.
OH.

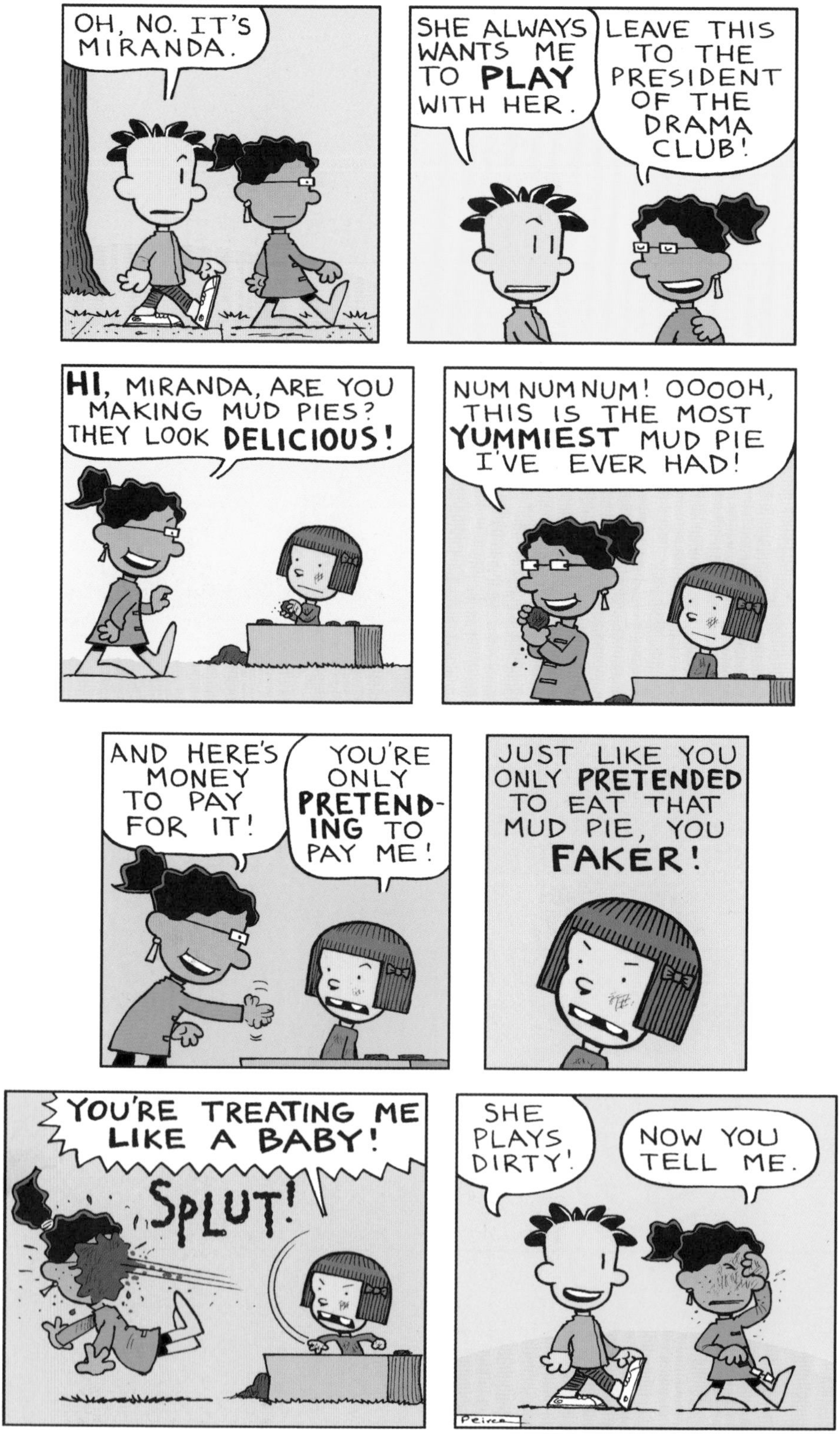
OH, NO. IT'S MIRANDA.
SHE ALWAYS WANTS ME TO **PLAY** WITH HER.
LEAVE THIS TO THE PRESIDENT OF THE DRAMA CLUB!
HI, MIRANDA, ARE YOU MAKING MUD PIES? THEY LOOK **DELICIOUS**!
NUM NUM NUM! OOOOH, THIS IS THE MOST **YUMMIEST** MUD PIE I'VE EVER HAD!
AND HERE'S MONEY TO PAY FOR IT!
YOU'RE ONLY **PRETEND-ING** TO PAY ME!
JUST LIKE YOU ONLY **PRETENDED** TO EAT THAT MUD PIE, YOU **FAKER**!
YOU'RE TREATING ME LIKE A BABY!
SPLUT!
SHE PLAYS DIRTY!
NOW YOU TELL ME.
Peirce

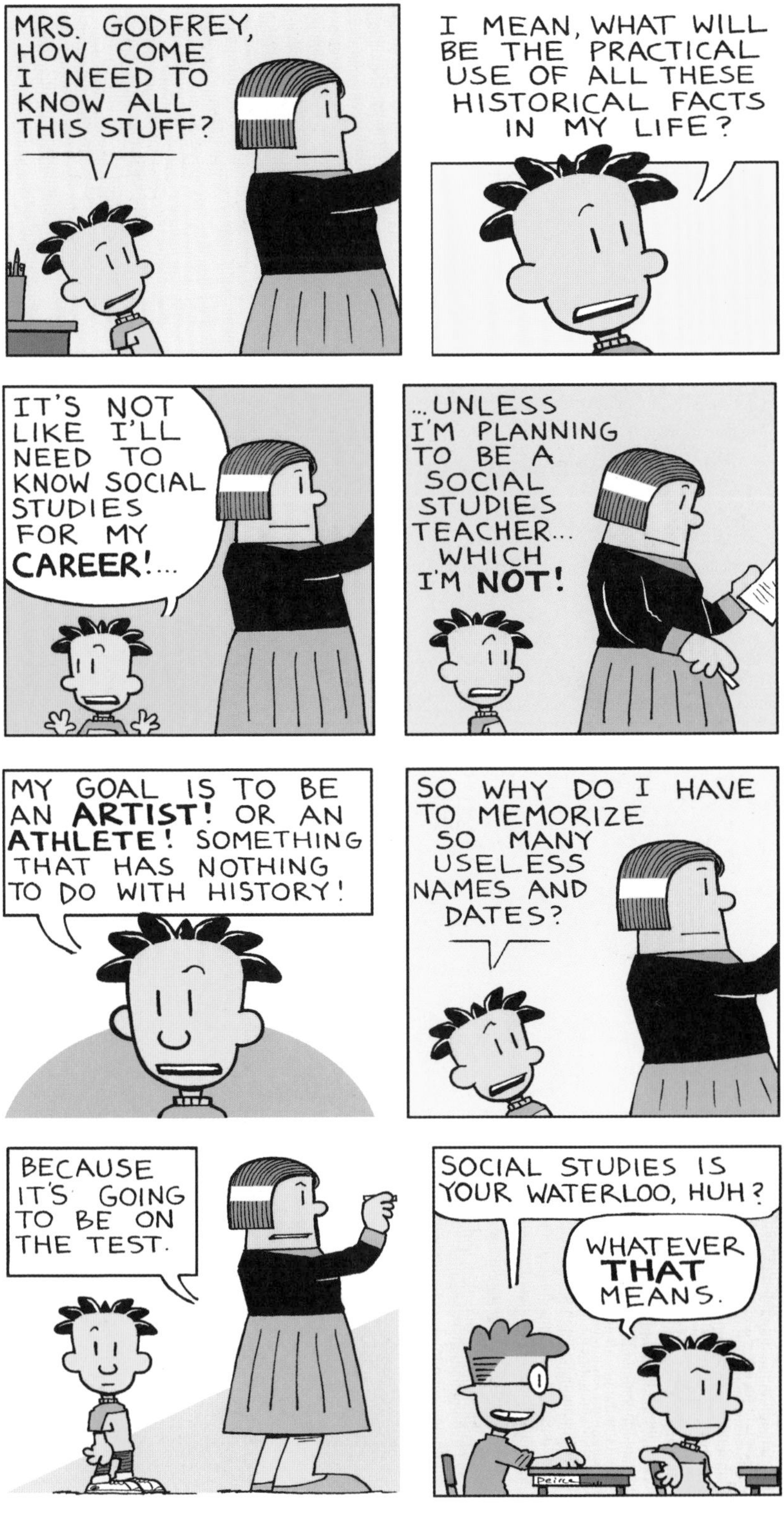
MRS. GODFREY, HOW COME I NEED TO KNOW ALL THIS STUFF?
I MEAN, WHAT WILL BE THE PRACTICAL USE OF ALL THESE HISTORICAL FACTS IN MY LIFE?
IT'S NOT LIKE I'LL NEED TO KNOW SOCIAL STUDIES FOR MY **CAREER**!...
...UNLESS I'M PLANNING TO BE A SOCIAL STUDIES TEACHER... WHICH I'M **NOT**!
MY GOAL IS TO BE AN **ARTIST**! OR AN **ATHLETE**! SOMETHING THAT HAS NOTHING TO DO WITH HISTORY!
SO WHY DO I HAVE TO MEMORIZE SO MANY USELESS NAMES AND DATES?
BECAUSE IT'S GOING TO BE ON THE TEST.
SOCIAL STUDIES IS YOUR WATERLOO, HUH?
WHATEVER **THAT** MEANS.
Peirce

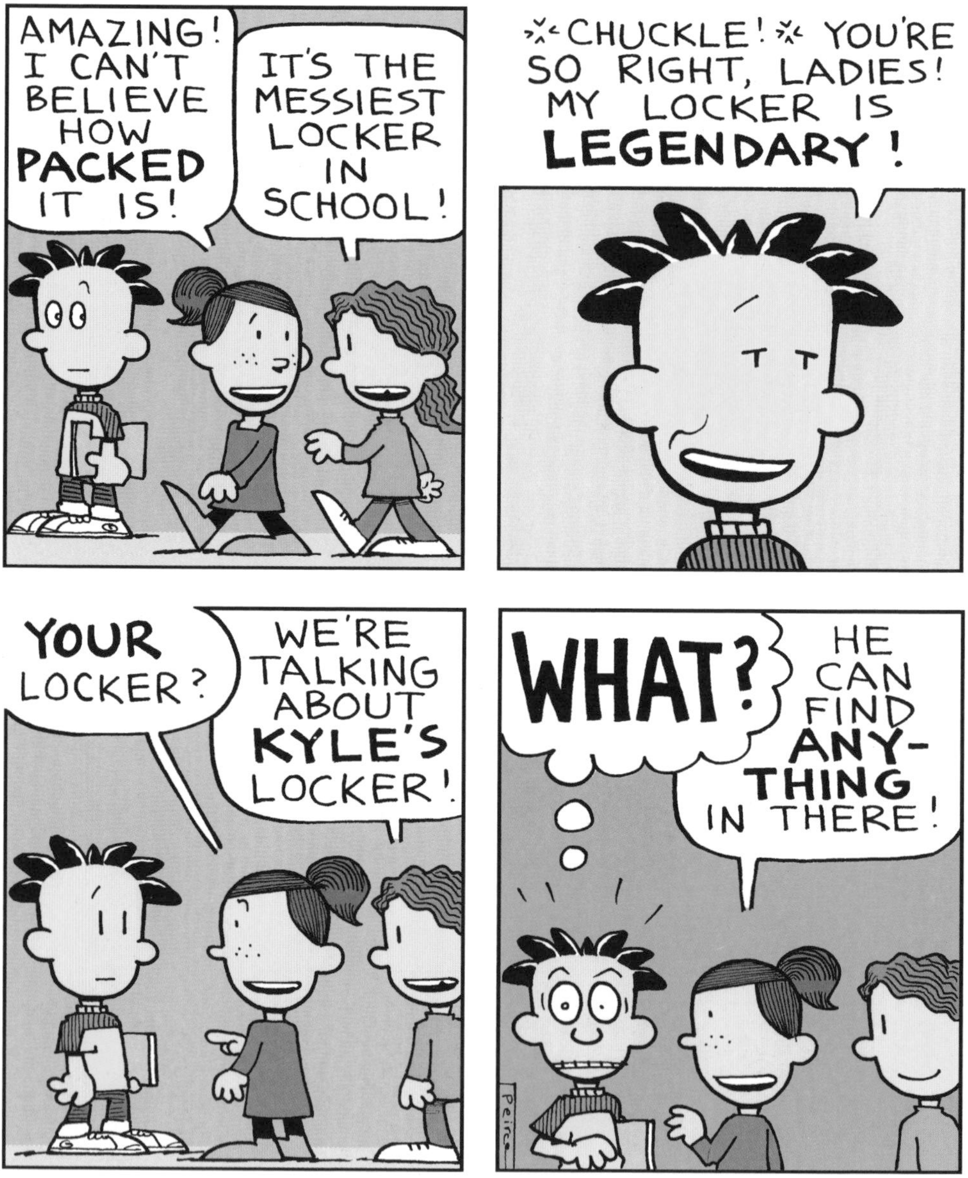
AMAZING! I CAN'T BELIEVE HOW PACKED IT IS!
IT'S THE MESSIEST LOCKER IN SCHOOL!
CHUCKLE! YOU'RE SO RIGHT, LADIES! MY LOCKER IS LEGENDARY!
YOUR LOCKER?
WE'RE TALKING ABOUT KYLE'S LOCKER!
WHAT?
HE CAN FIND ANY-THING IN THERE!
Peirce

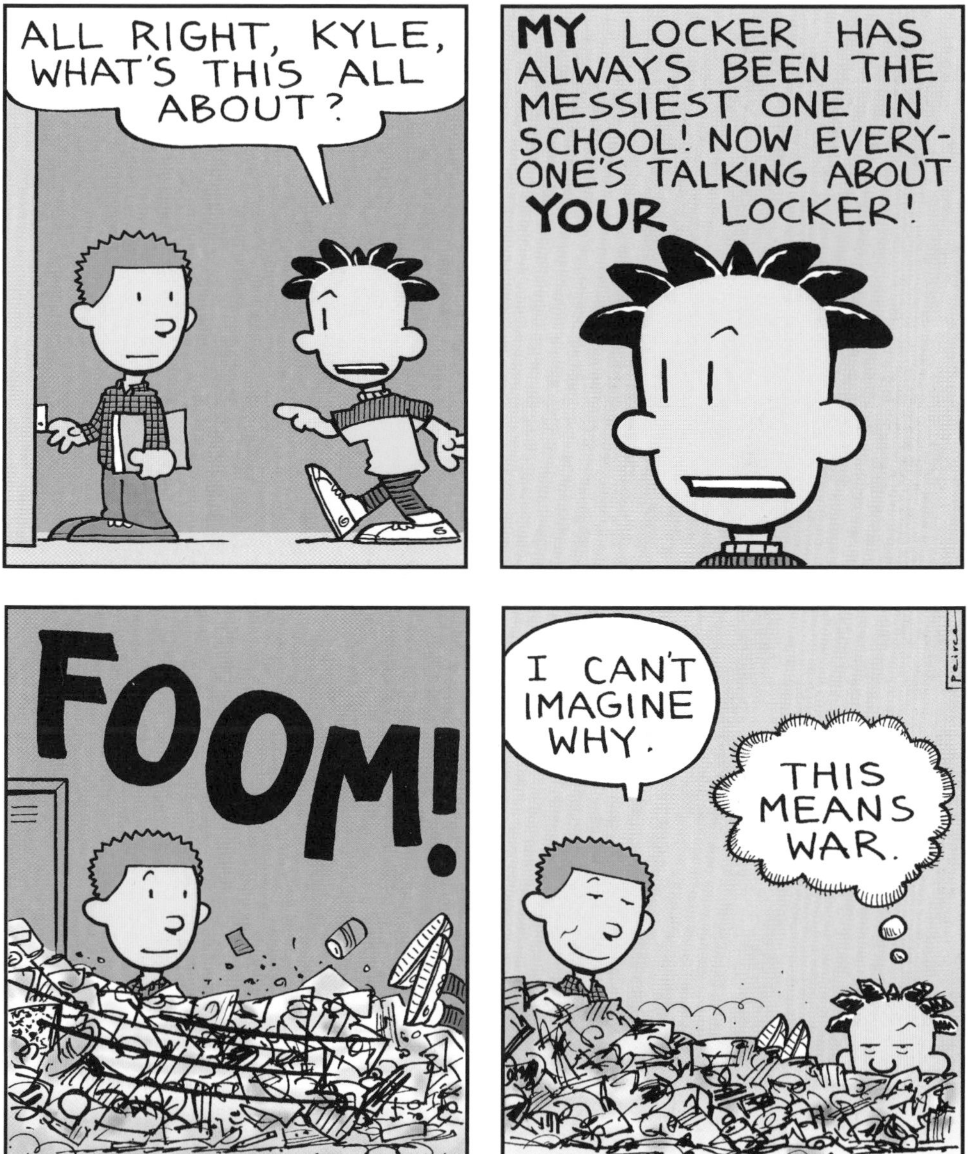
ALL RIGHT, KYLE, WHAT'S THIS ALL ABOUT?
MY LOCKER HAS ALWAYS BEEN THE MESSIEST ONE IN SCHOOL! NOW EVERYONE'S TALKING ABOUT YOUR LOCKER!
FOOM!
I CAN'T IMAGINE WHY.
THIS MEANS WAR.
Peirce

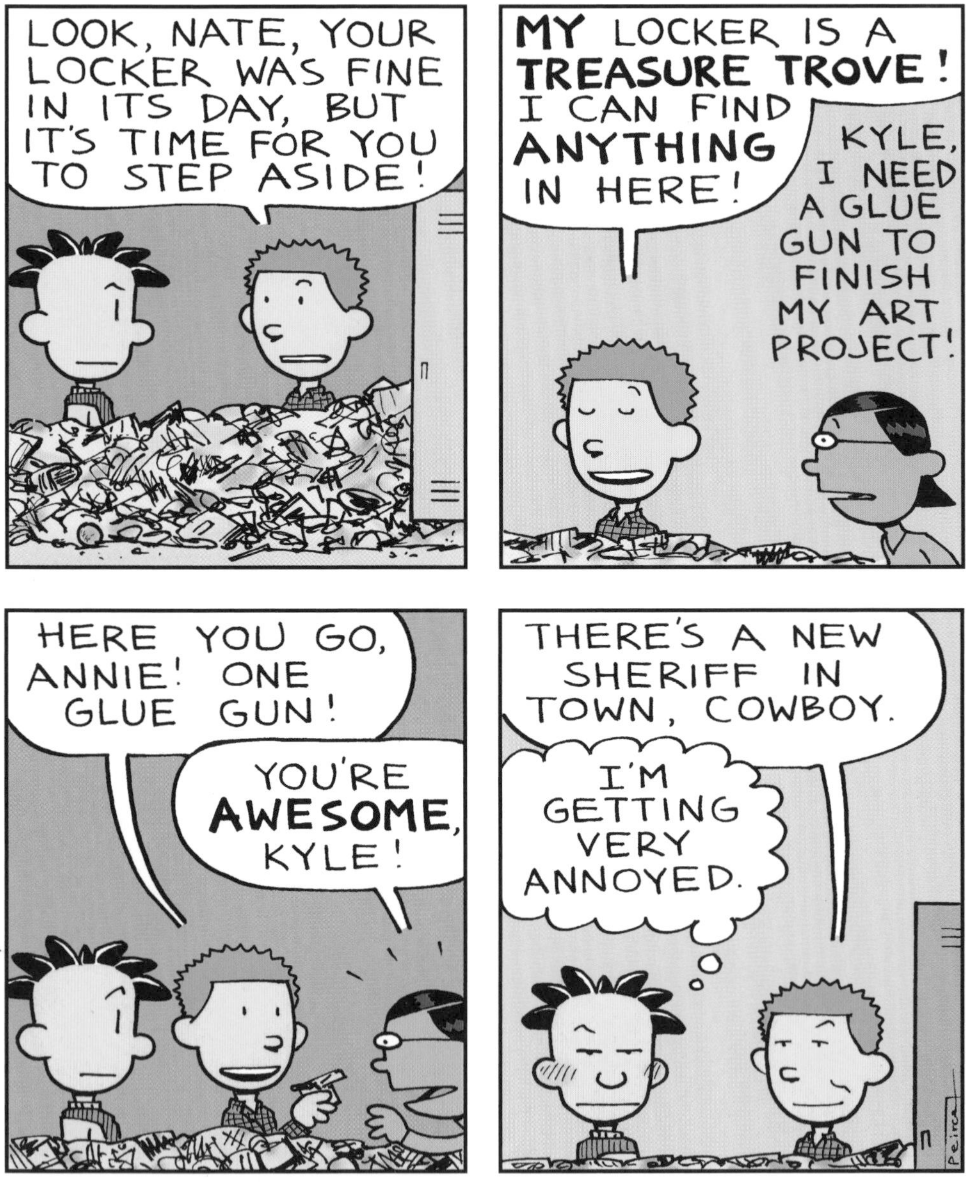
LOOK, NATE, YOUR LOCKER WAS FINE IN ITS DAY, BUT IT'S TIME FOR YOU TO STEP ASIDE!
MY LOCKER IS A TREASURE TROVE! I CAN FIND ANYTHING IN HERE!
KYLE, I NEED A GLUE GUN TO FINISH MY ART PROJECT!
HERE YOU GO, ANNIE! ONE GLUE GUN!
YOU'RE AWESOME, KYLE!
THERE'S A NEW SHERIFF IN TOWN, COWBOY.
I'M GETTING VERY ANNOYED.
Peirce

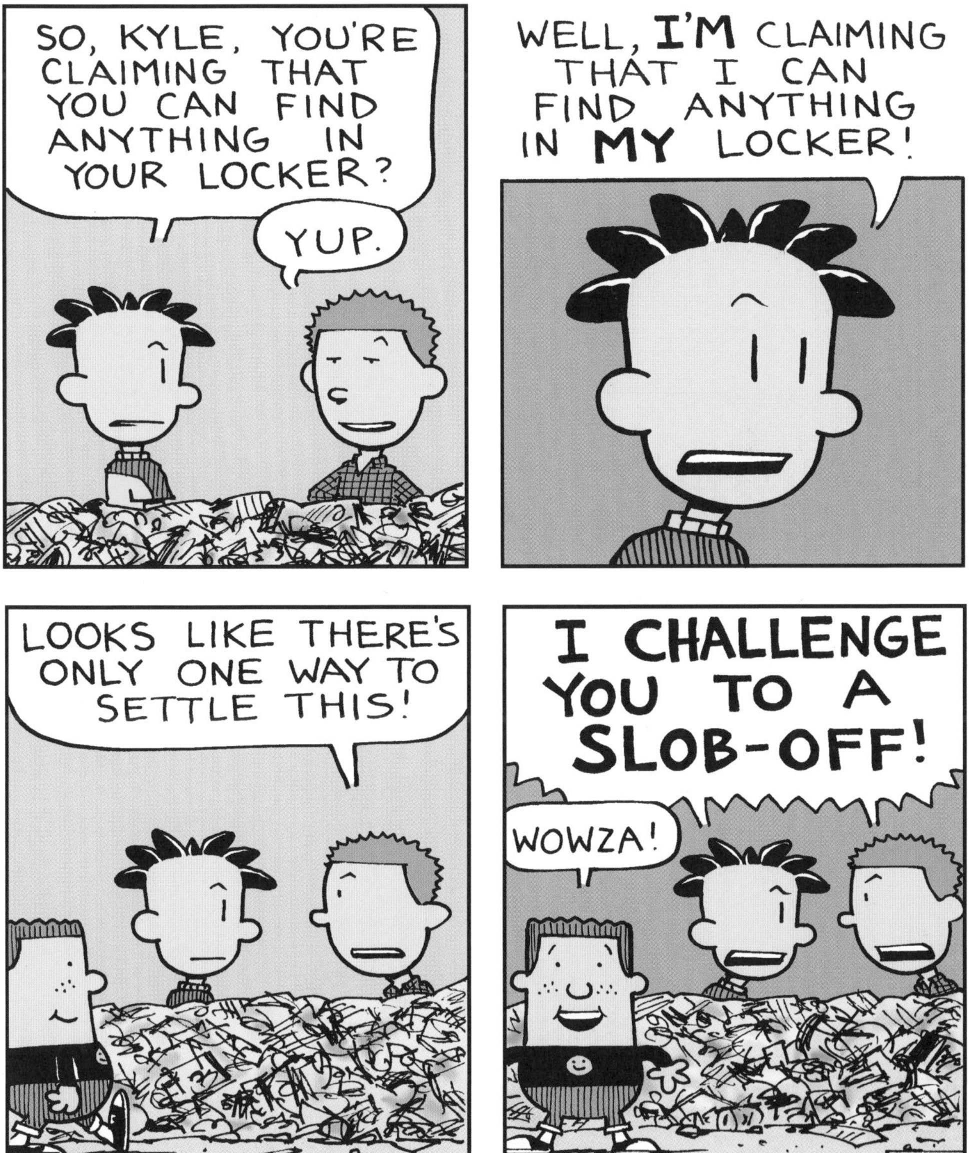
SO, KYLE, YOU'RE CLAIMING THAT YOU CAN FIND ANYTHING IN YOUR LOCKER?
YUP.
WELL, I'M CLAIMING THAT I CAN FIND ANYTHING IN MY LOCKER!
LOOKS LIKE THERE'S ONLY ONE WAY TO SETTLE THIS!
I CHALLENGE YOU TO A SLOB-OFF!
WOWZA!
peirce

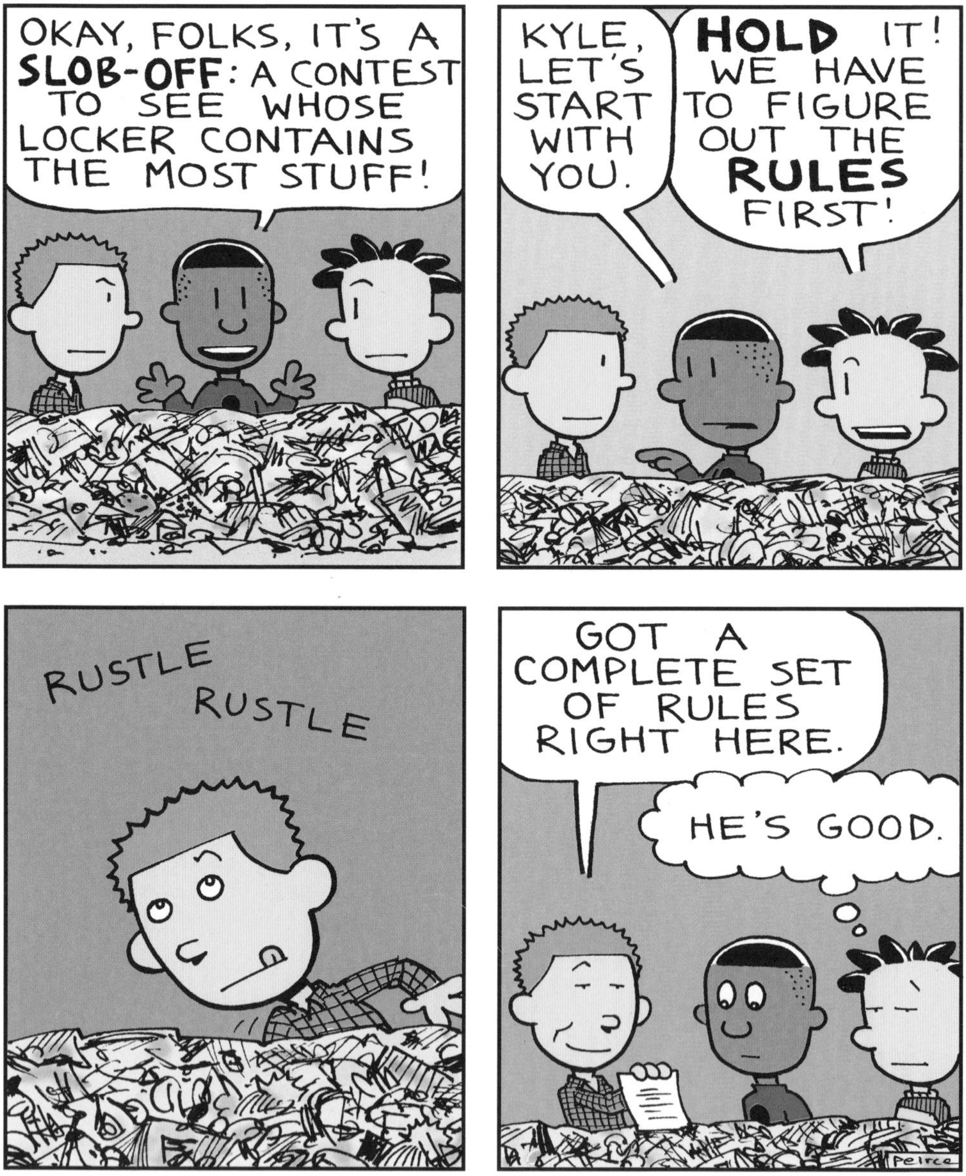
OKAY, FOLKS, IT'S A **SLOB-OFF**: A CONTEST TO SEE WHOSE LOCKER CONTAINS THE MOST STUFF!
KYLE, LET'S START WITH YOU.
HOLD IT! WE HAVE TO FIGURE OUT THE **RULES** FIRST!
RUSTLE
RUSTLE
GOT A COMPLETE SET OF RULES RIGHT HERE.
HE'S GOOD.
Peirce

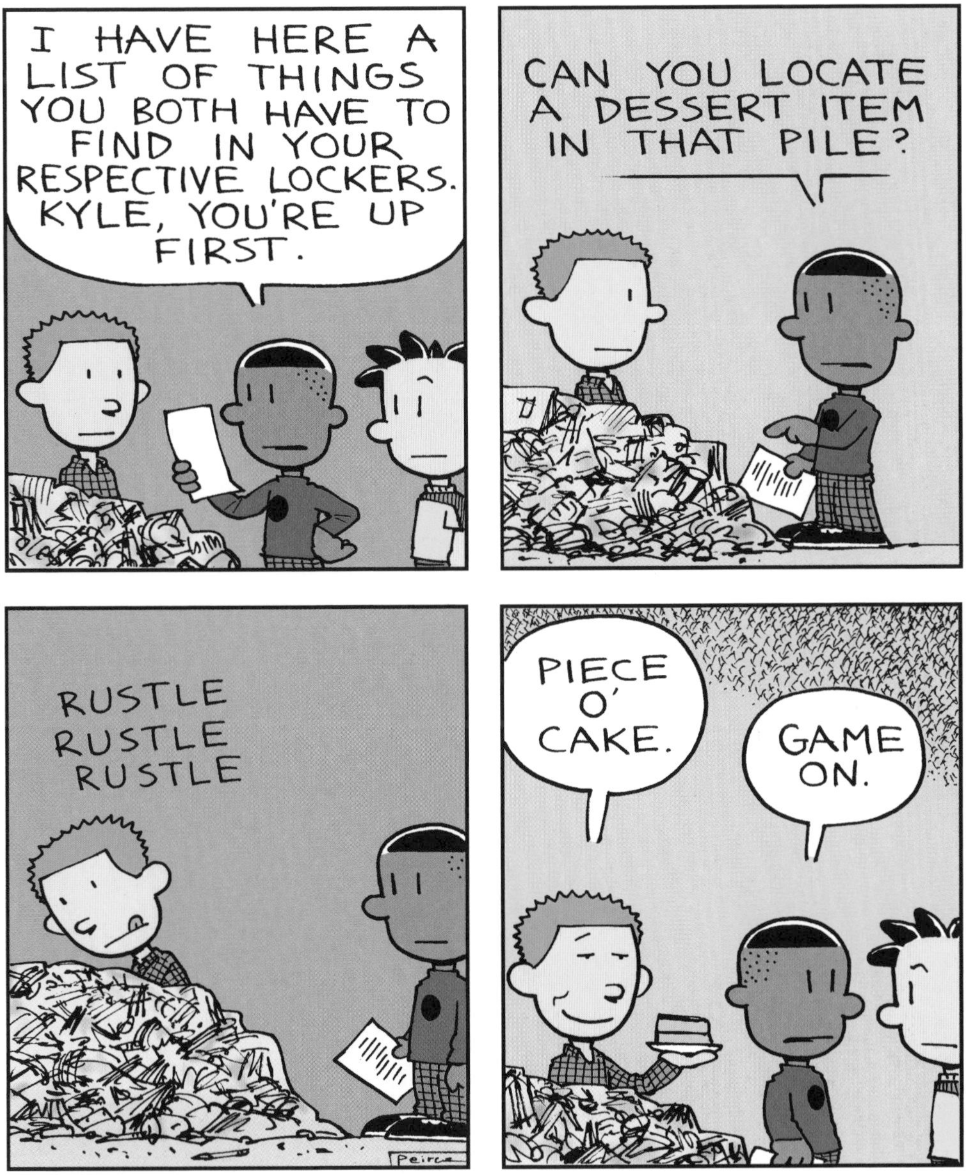
I HAVE HERE A LIST OF THINGS YOU BOTH HAVE TO FIND IN YOUR RESPECTIVE LOCKERS. KYLE, YOU'RE UP FIRST.
CAN YOU LOCATE A DESSERT ITEM IN THAT PILE?
RUSTLE RUSTLE RUSTLE
Peirce
PIECE O' CAKE.
GAME ON.

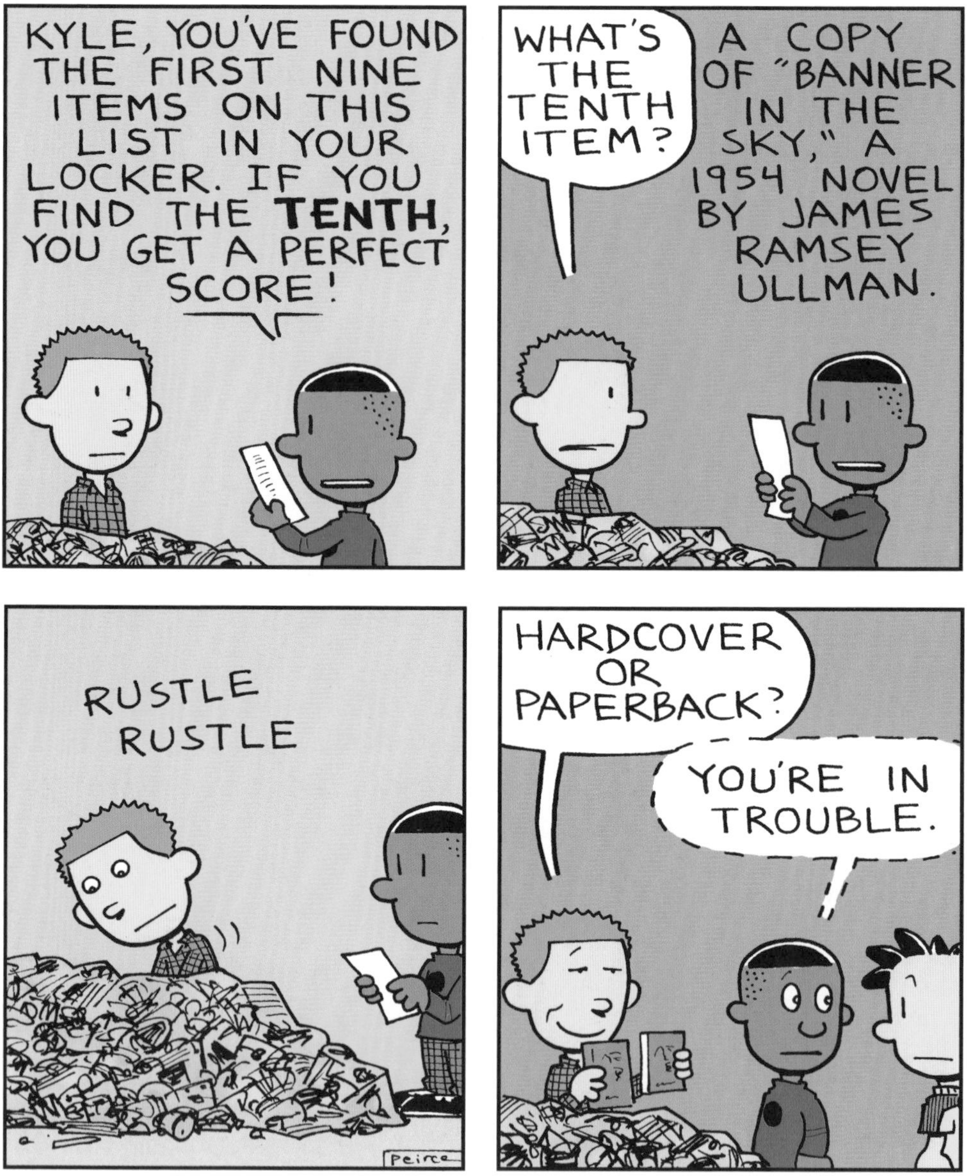
KYLE, YOU'VE FOUND THE FIRST NINE ITEMS ON THIS LIST IN YOUR LOCKER. IF YOU FIND THE **TENTH**, YOU GET A PERFECT SCORE!
WHAT'S THE TENTH ITEM?
A COPY OF "BANNER IN THE SKY," A 1954 NOVEL BY JAMES RAMSEY ULLMAN.
RUSTLE RUSTLE
HARDCOVER OR PAPERBACK?
YOU'RE IN TROUBLE.
Peirce

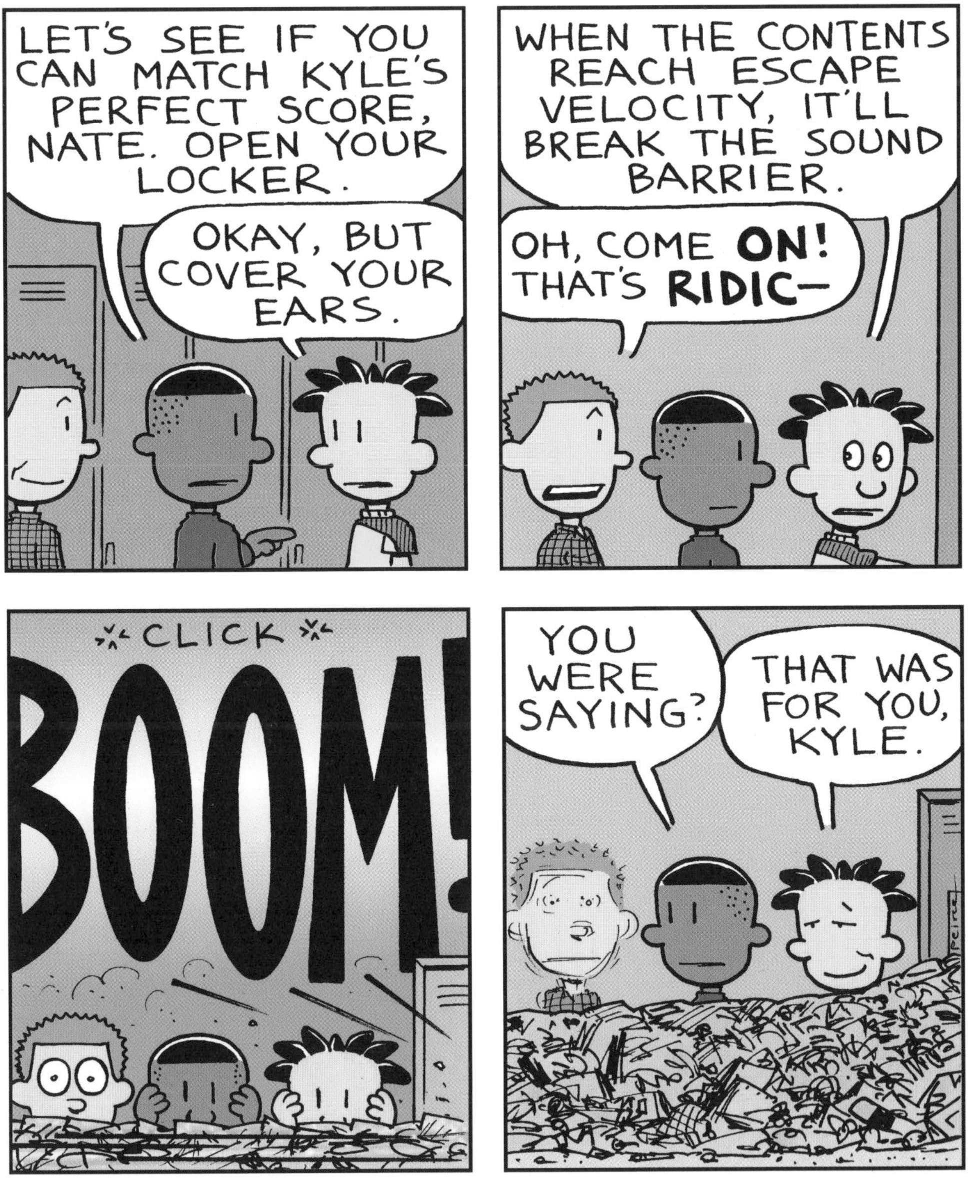
LET'S SEE IF YOU CAN MATCH KYLE'S PERFECT SCORE, NATE. OPEN YOUR LOCKER.
OKAY, BUT COVER YOUR EARS.
WHEN THE CONTENTS REACH ESCAPE VELOCITY, IT'LL BREAK THE SOUND BARRIER.
OH, COME **ON!** THAT'S **RIDIC—**
CLICK
BOOM!
YOU WERE SAYING?
THAT WAS FOR YOU, KYLE.

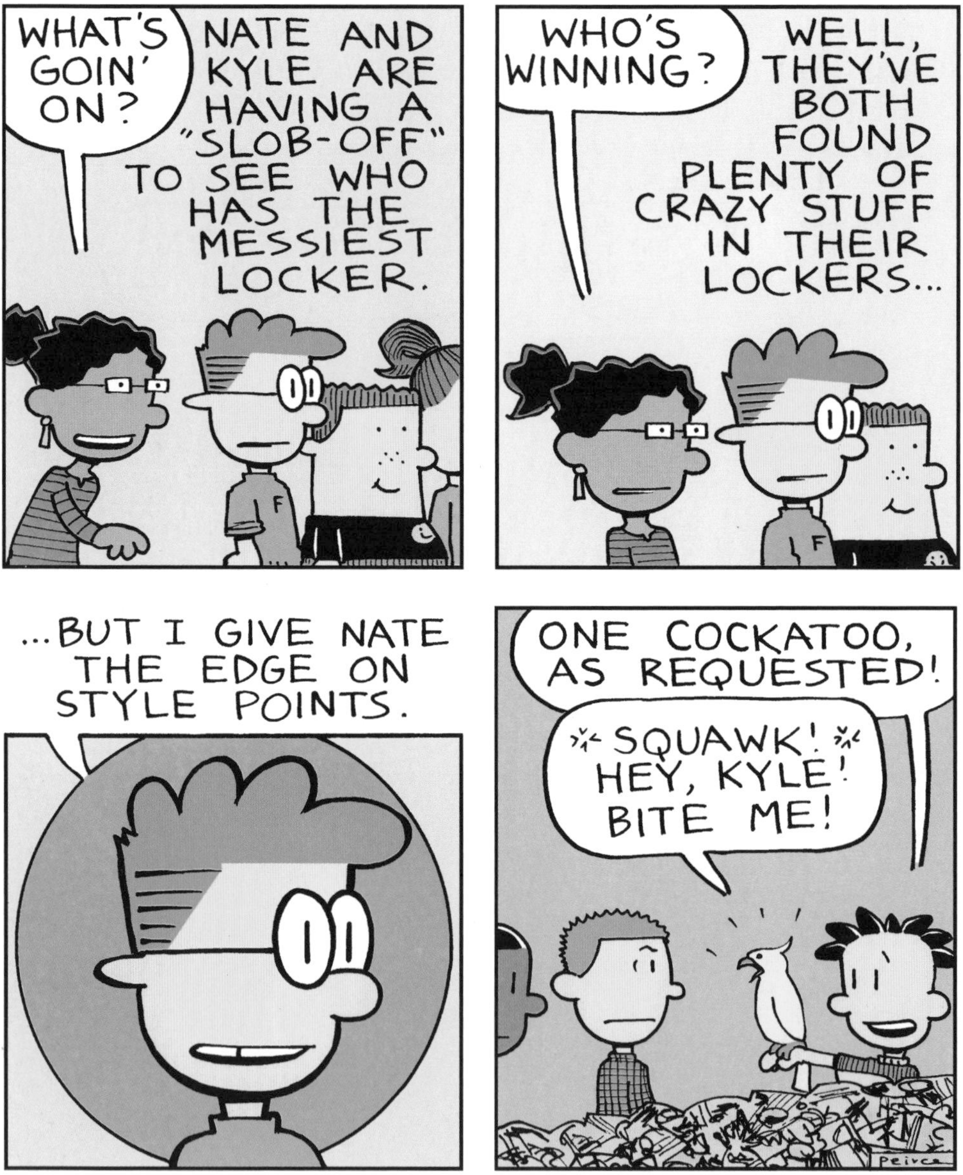
WHAT'S GOIN' ON?
NATE AND KYLE ARE HAVING A "SLOB-OFF" TO SEE WHO HAS THE MESSIEST LOCKER.
WHO'S WINNING?
WELL, THEY'VE BOTH FOUND PLENTY OF CRAZY STUFF IN THEIR LOCKERS...
...BUT I GIVE NATE THE EDGE ON STYLE POINTS.
ONE COCKATOO, AS REQUESTED!
SQUAWK! HEY, KYLE! BITE ME!
peirce

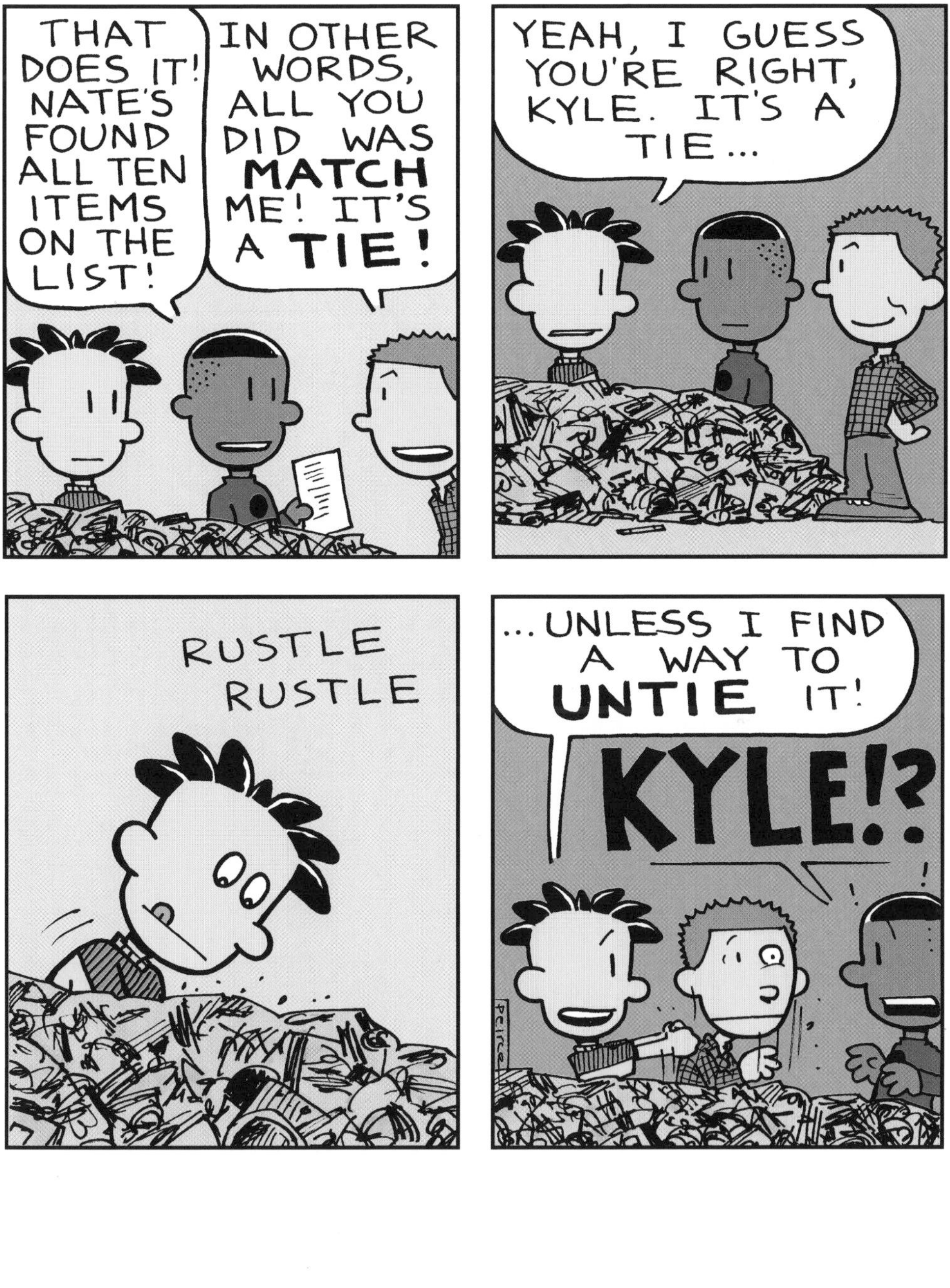
THAT DOES IT! NATE'S FOUND ALL TEN ITEMS ON THE LIST!
IN OTHER WORDS, ALL YOU DID WAS MATCH ME! IT'S A TIE!
YEAH, I GUESS YOU'RE RIGHT, KYLE. IT'S A TIE...
RUSTLE RUSTLE
...UNLESS I FIND A WAY TO UNTIE IT!
KYLE!?
!
!
PEIRCE

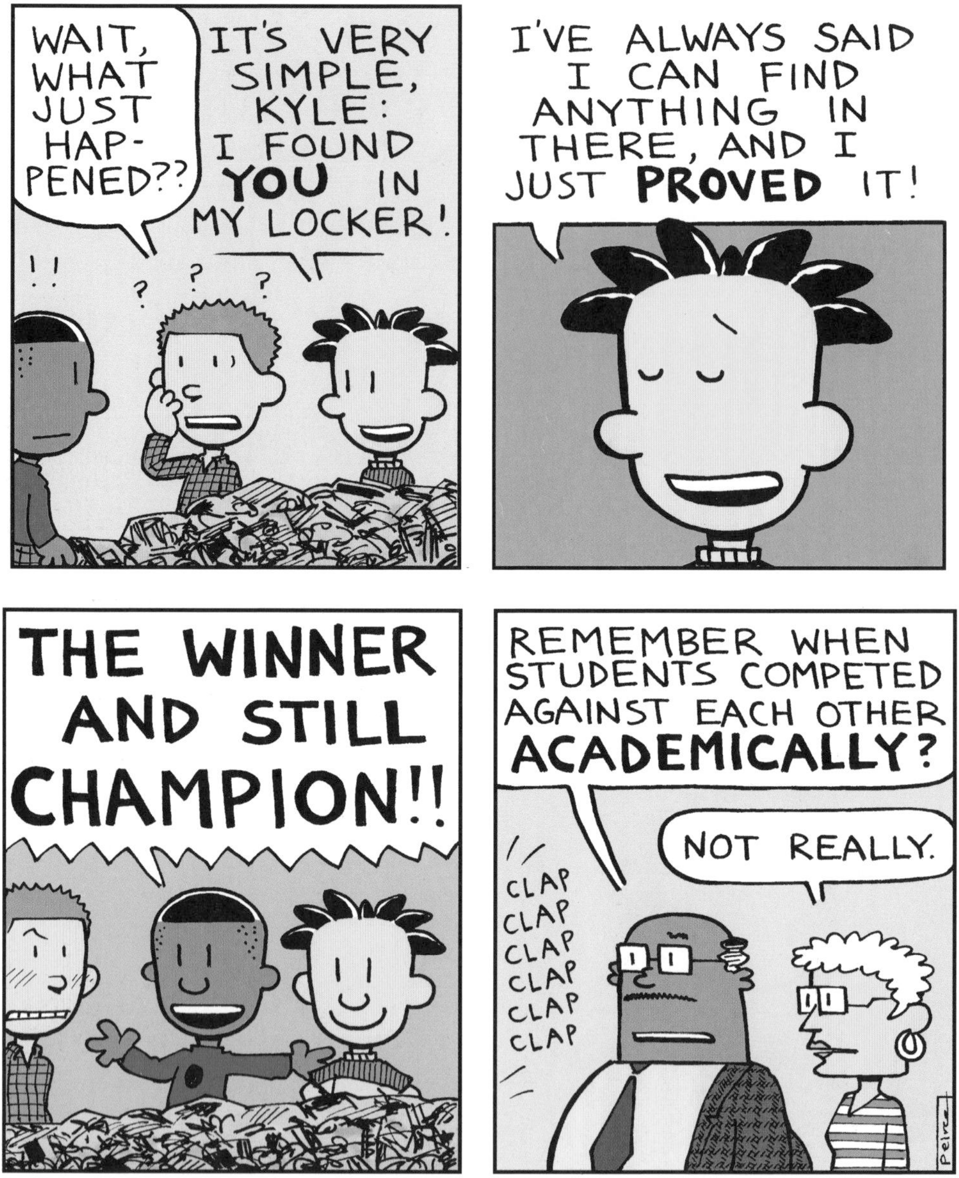
WAIT, WHAT JUST HAP-PENED??
IT'S VERY SIMPLE, KYLE: I FOUND **YOU** IN MY LOCKER!
I'VE ALWAYS SAID I CAN FIND ANYTHING IN THERE, AND I JUST **PROVED** IT!
THE WINNER AND STILL CHAMPION!!
REMEMBER WHEN STUDENTS COMPETED AGAINST EACH OTHER **ACADEMICALLY**?
NOT REALLY.
CLAP CLAP CLAP CLAP CLAP CLAP

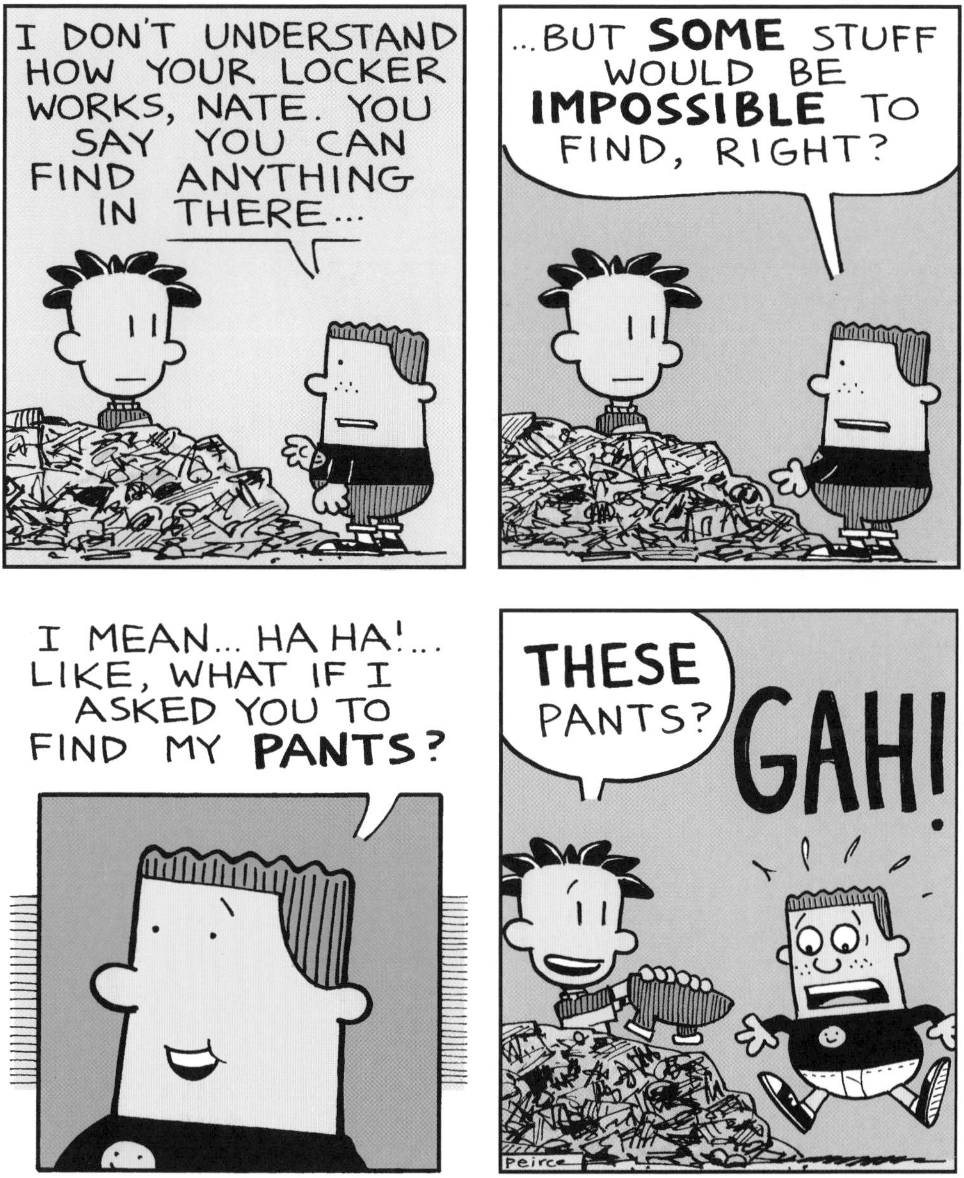
I DON'T UNDERSTAND HOW YOUR LOCKER WORKS, NATE. YOU SAY YOU CAN FIND ANYTHING IN THERE...
...BUT SOME STUFF WOULD BE IMPOSSIBLE TO FIND, RIGHT?
I MEAN... HA HA!... LIKE, WHAT IF I ASKED YOU TO FIND MY PANTS?
THESE PANTS?
GAH!
peirce

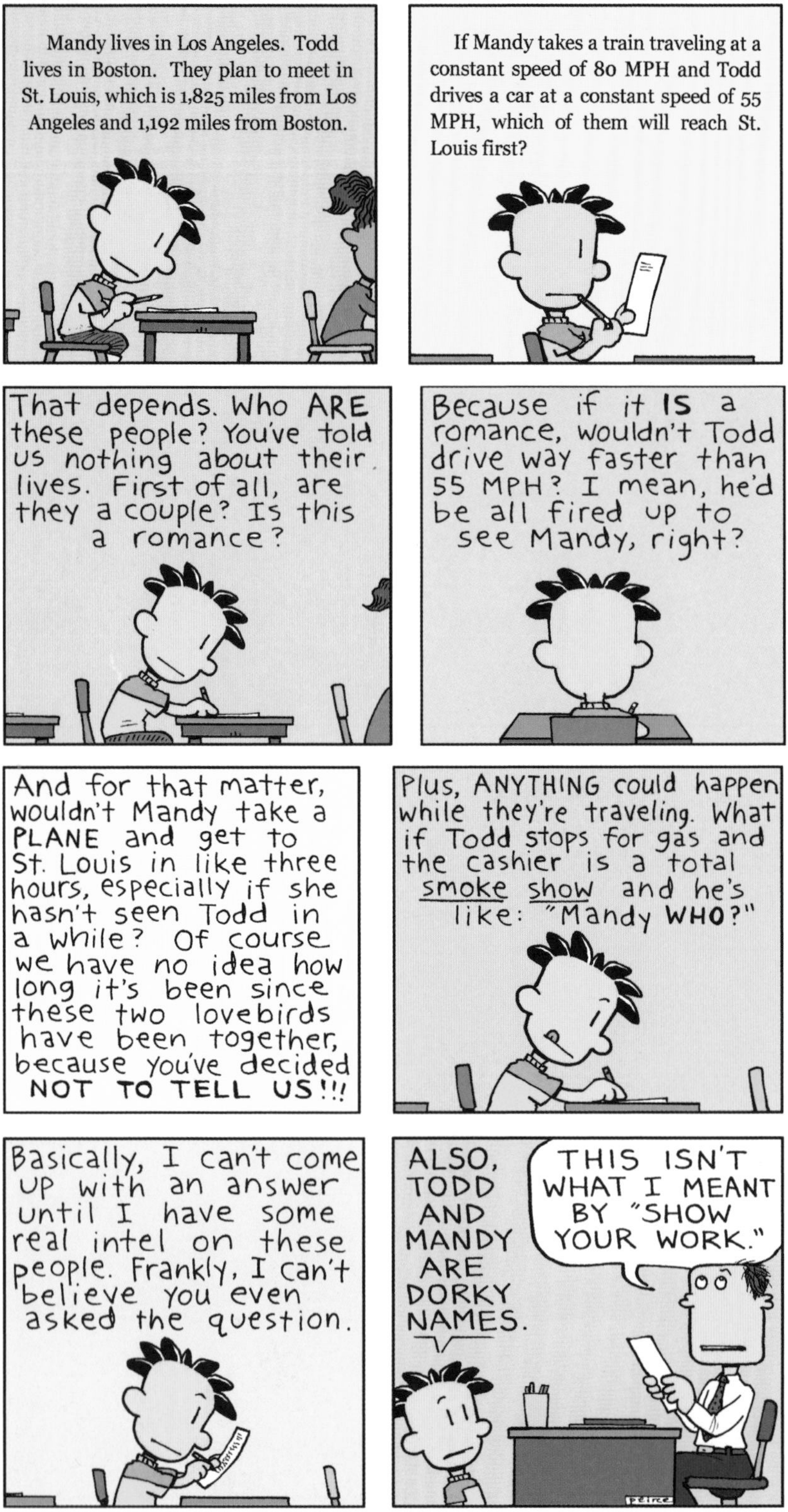

Mandy lives in Los Angeles. Todd lives in Boston. They plan to meet in St. Louis, which is 1,825 miles from Los Angeles and 1,192 miles from Boston.
If Mandy takes a train traveling at a constant speed of 80 MPH and Todd drives a car at a constant speed of 55 MPH, which of them will reach St. Louis first?
That depends. Who ARE these people? You've told us nothing about their lives. First of all, are they a couple? Is this a romance?
Because if it IS a romance, wouldn't Todd drive way faster than 55 MPH? I mean, he'd be all fired up to see Mandy, right?
And for that matter, wouldn't Mandy take a PLANE and get to St. Louis in like three hours, especially if she hasn't seen Todd in a while? Of course we have no idea how long it's been since these two lovebirds have been together, because you've decided NOT TO TELL US!!!
Plus, ANYTHING could happen while they're traveling. What if Todd stops for gas and the cashier is a total smoke show and he's like: "Mandy WHO?"
Basically, I can't come up with an answer until I have some real intel on these people. Frankly, I can't believe you even asked the question.
THIS ISN'T WHAT I MEANT BY "SHOW YOUR WORK."
ALSO, TODD AND MANDY ARE DORKY NAMES.

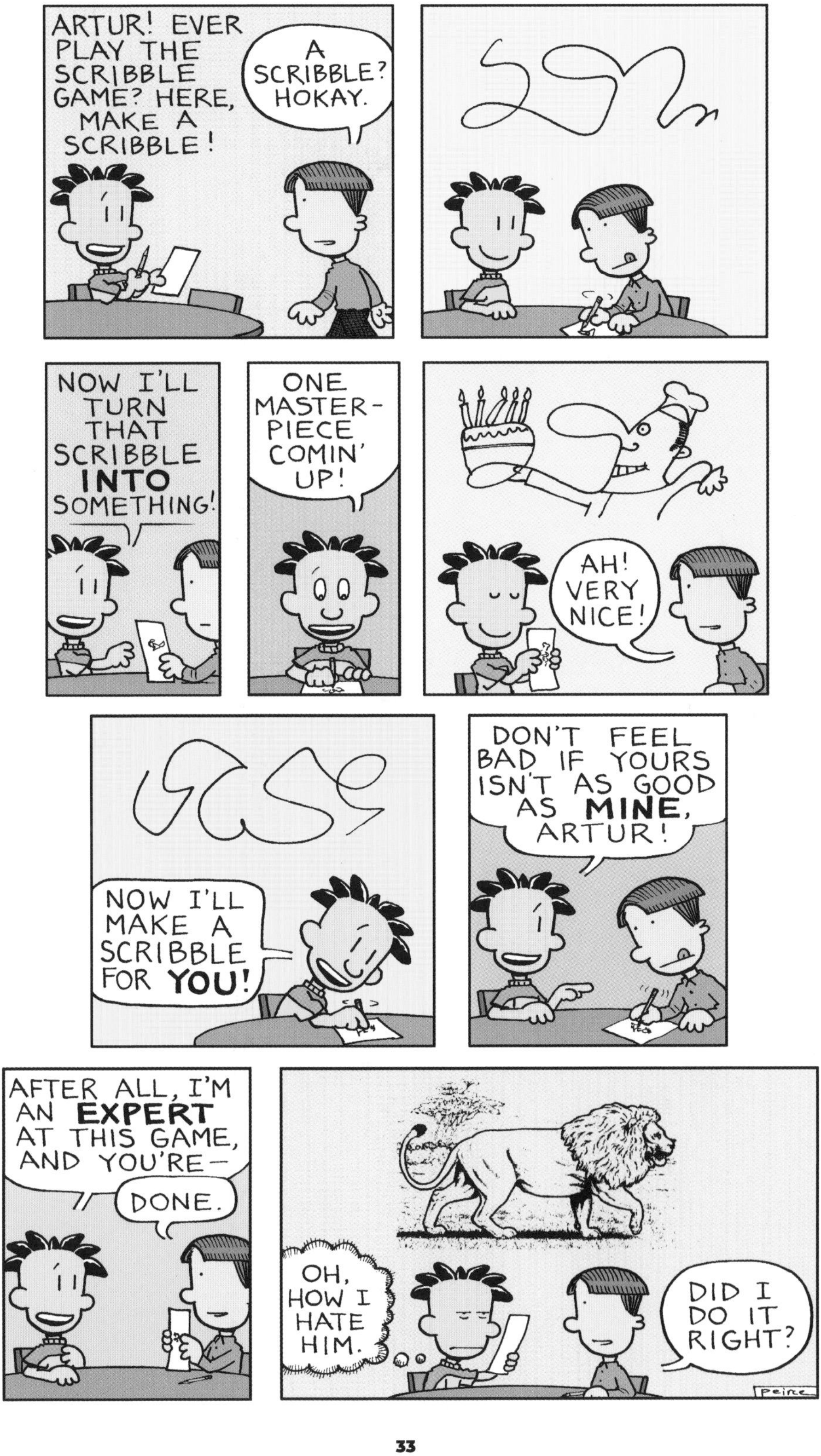
ARTUR! EVER PLAY THE SCRIBBLE GAME? HERE, MAKE A SCRIBBLE!
A SCRIBBLE? HOKAY.
NOW I'LL TURN THAT SCRIBBLE INTO SOMETHING!
ONE MASTER-PIECE COMIN' UP!
AH! VERY NICE!
NOW I'LL MAKE A SCRIBBLE FOR YOU!
DON'T FEEL BAD IF YOURS ISN'T AS GOOD AS MINE, ARTUR!
AFTER ALL, I'M AN EXPERT AT THIS GAME, AND YOU'RE—
DONE.
OH, HOW I HATE HIM.
DID I DO IT RIGHT?
peirce

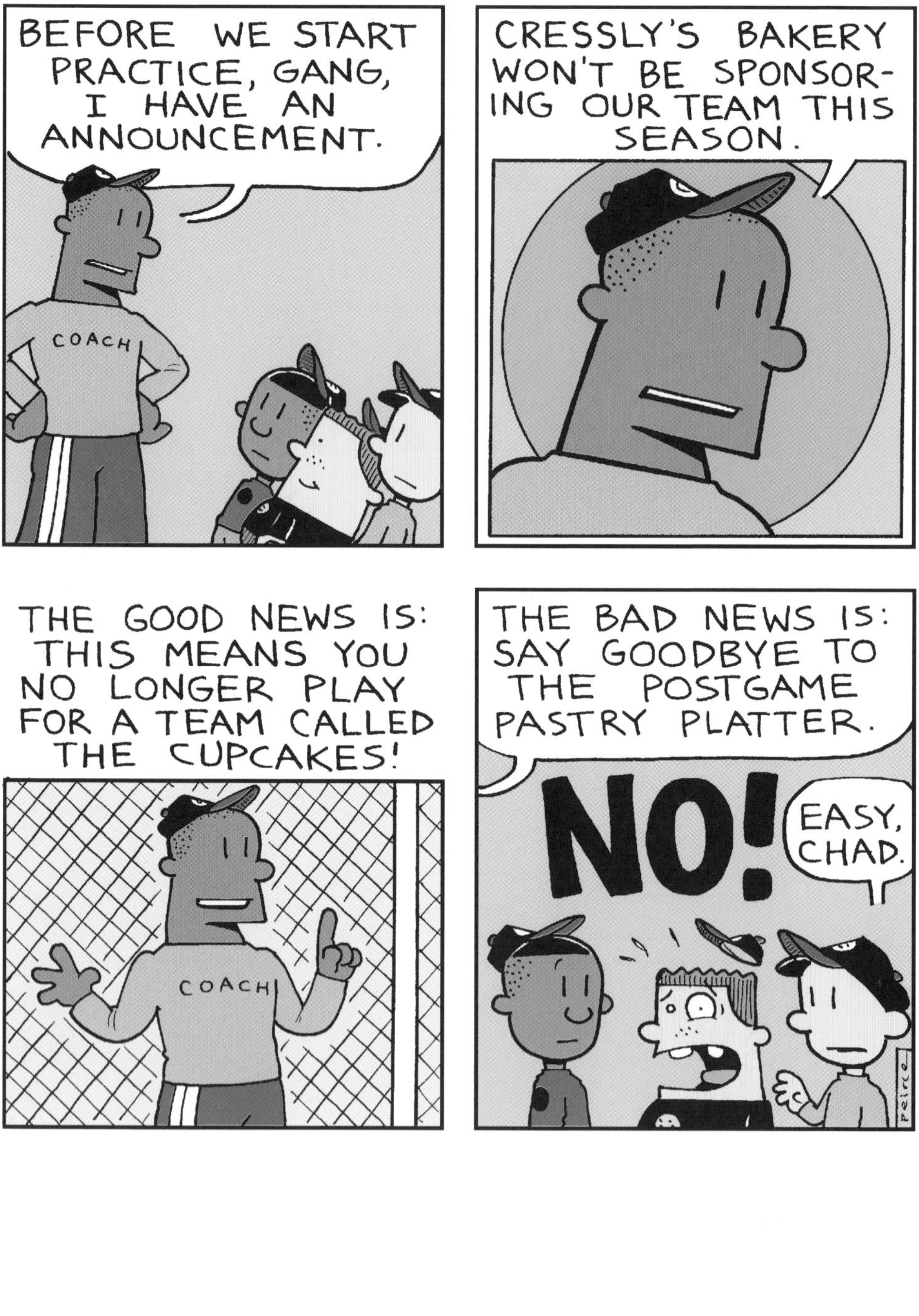
BEFORE WE START PRACTICE, GANG, I HAVE AN ANNOUNCEMENT.
COACH
CRESSLY'S BAKERY WON'T BE SPONSORING OUR TEAM THIS SEASON.
THE GOOD NEWS IS: THIS MEANS YOU NO LONGER PLAY FOR A TEAM CALLED THE CUPCAKES!
COACH
THE BAD NEWS IS: SAY GOODBYE TO THE POSTGAME PASTRY PLATTER.
NO!
EASY, CHAD.
peirce

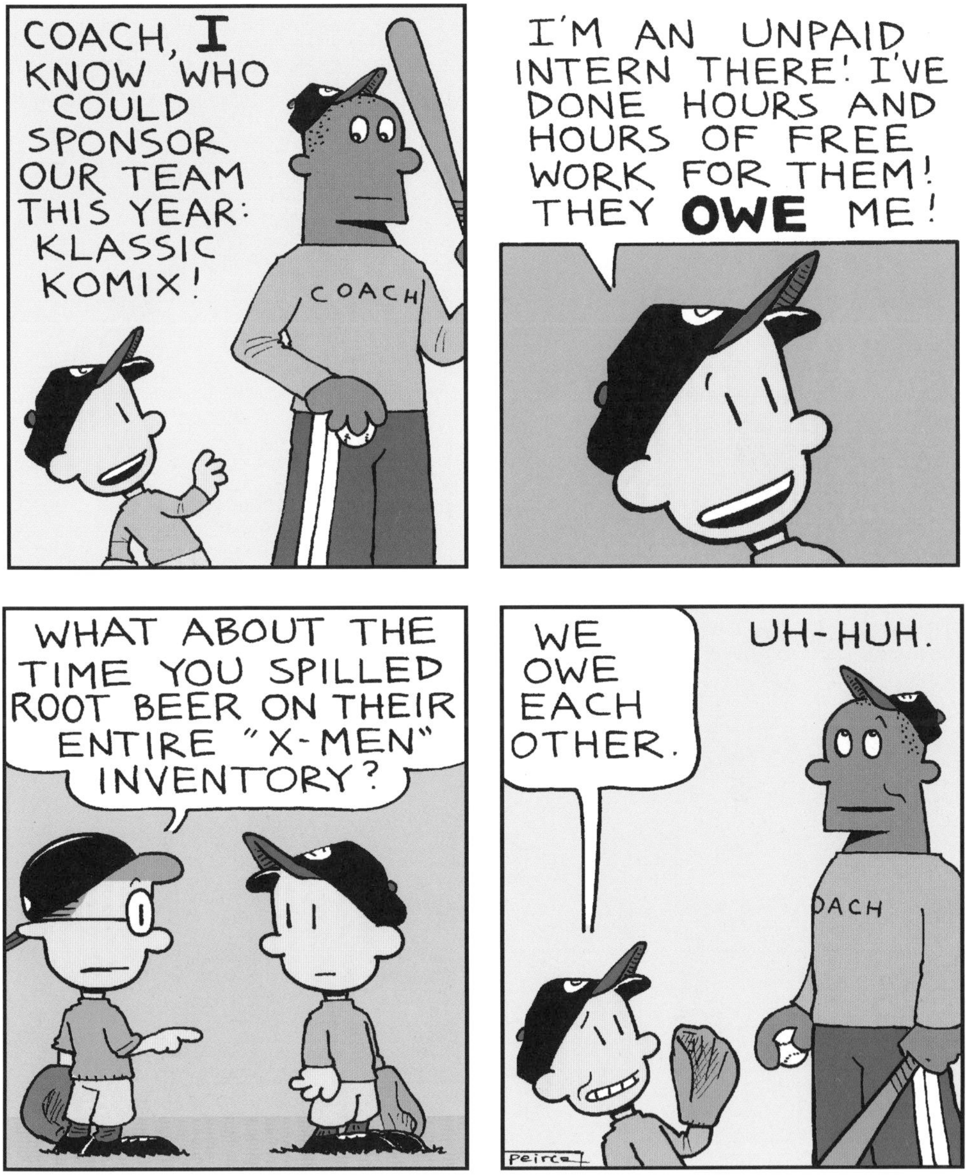
COACH, I KNOW WHO COULD SPONSOR OUR TEAM THIS YEAR: KLASSIC KOMIX!
COACH
I'M AN UNPAID INTERN THERE! I'VE DONE HOURS AND HOURS OF FREE WORK FOR THEM! THEY OWE ME!
WHAT ABOUT THE TIME YOU SPILLED ROOT BEER ON THEIR ENTIRE "X-MEN" INVENTORY?
WE OWE EACH OTHER.
UH-HUH.
peirce

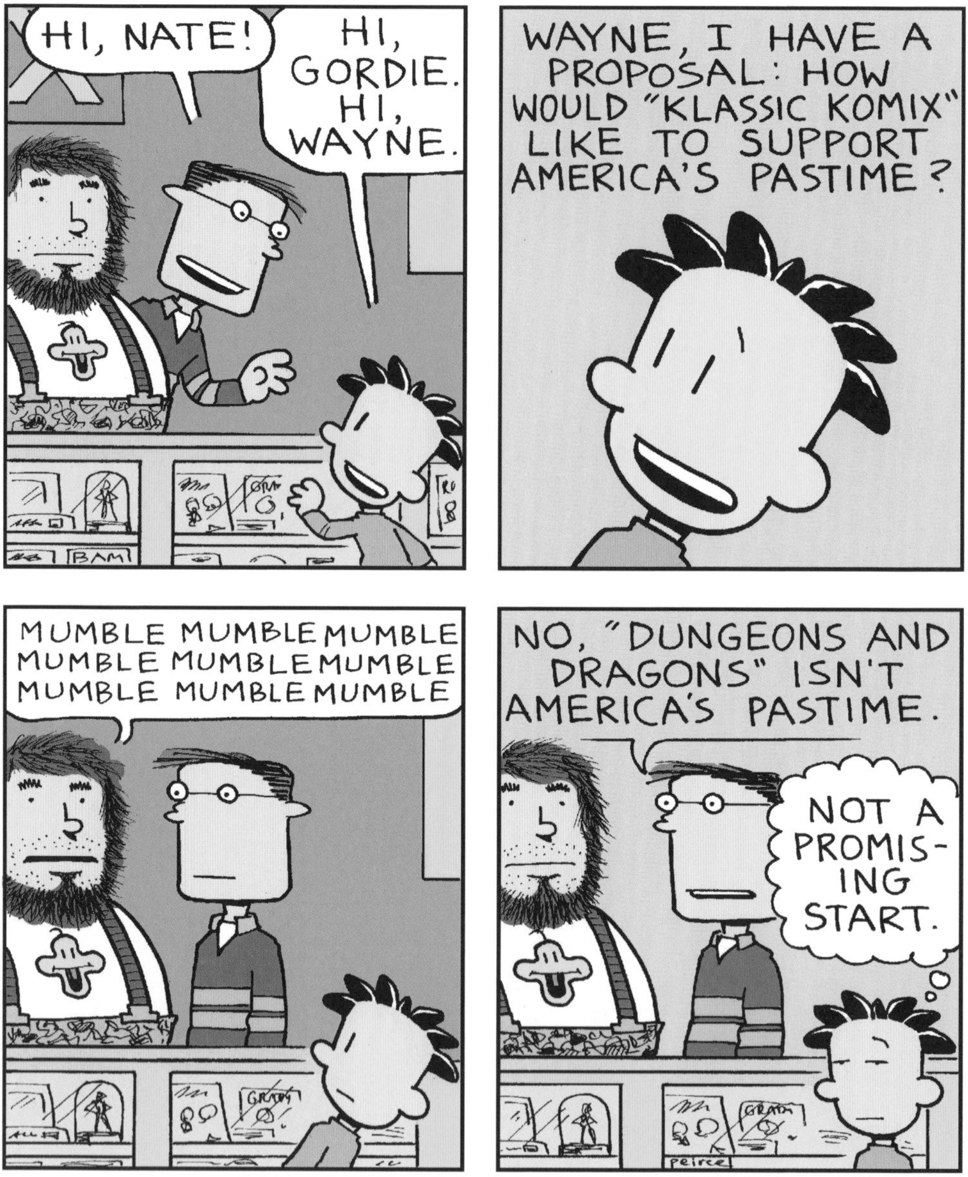
HI, NATE!
HI, GORDIE. HI, WAYNE.
WAYNE, I HAVE A PROPOSAL: HOW WOULD "KLASSIC KOMIX" LIKE TO SUPPORT AMERICA'S PASTIME?
MUMBLE MUMBLE MUMBLE MUMBLE MUMBLE MUMBLE MUMBLE MUMBLE MUMBLE
NO, "DUNGEONS AND DRAGONS" ISN'T AMERICA'S PASTIME.
NOT A PROMIS-ING START.
BAM
peirce

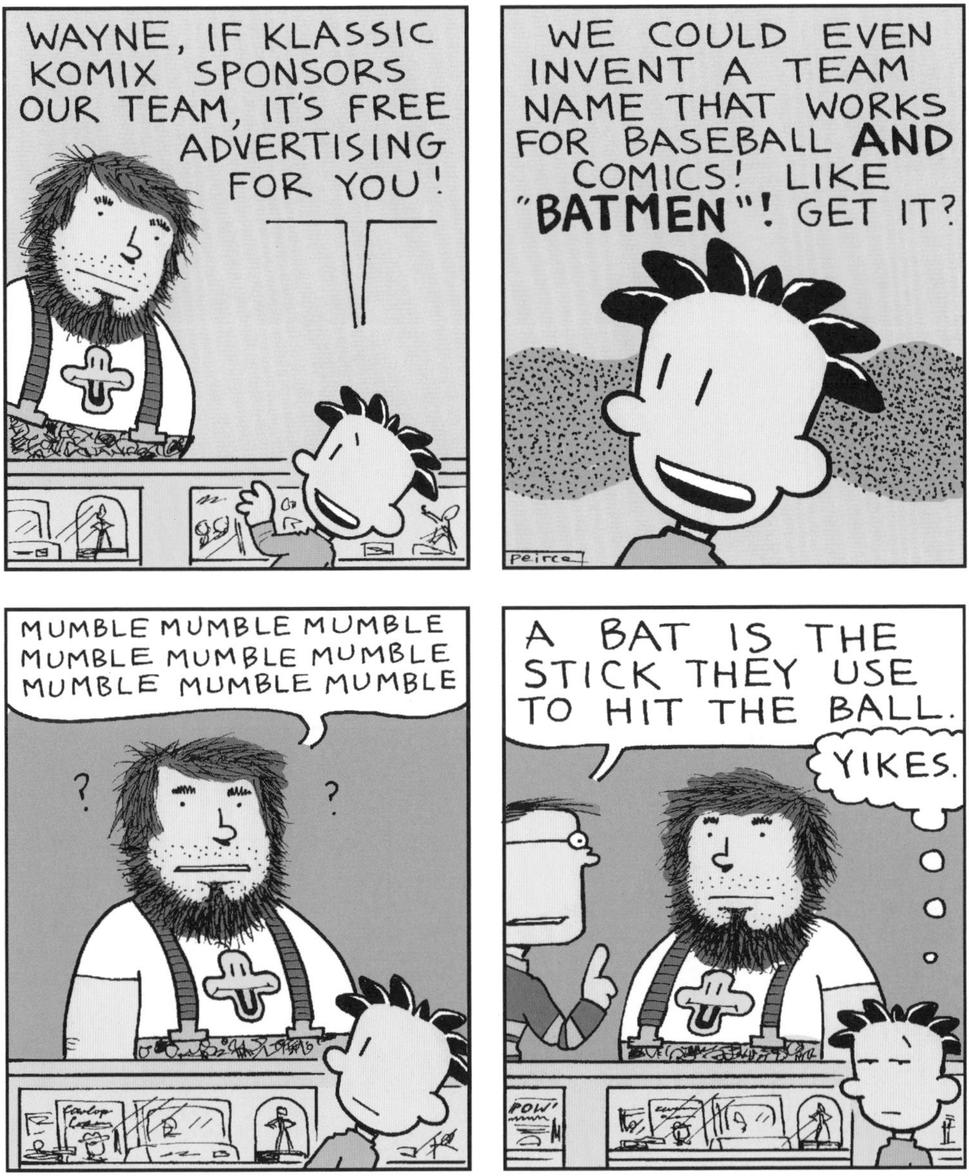
WAYNE, IF KLASSIC KOMIX SPONSORS OUR TEAM, IT'S FREE ADVERTISING FOR YOU!
WE COULD EVEN INVENT A TEAM NAME THAT WORKS FOR BASEBALL AND COMICS! LIKE "BATMEN"! GET IT?
peirce
MUMBLE MUMBLE MUMBLE MUMBLE MUMBLE MUMBLE MUMBLE MUMBLE MUMBLE
? ?
A BAT IS THE STICK THEY USE TO HIT THE BALL.
YIKES.
POW!

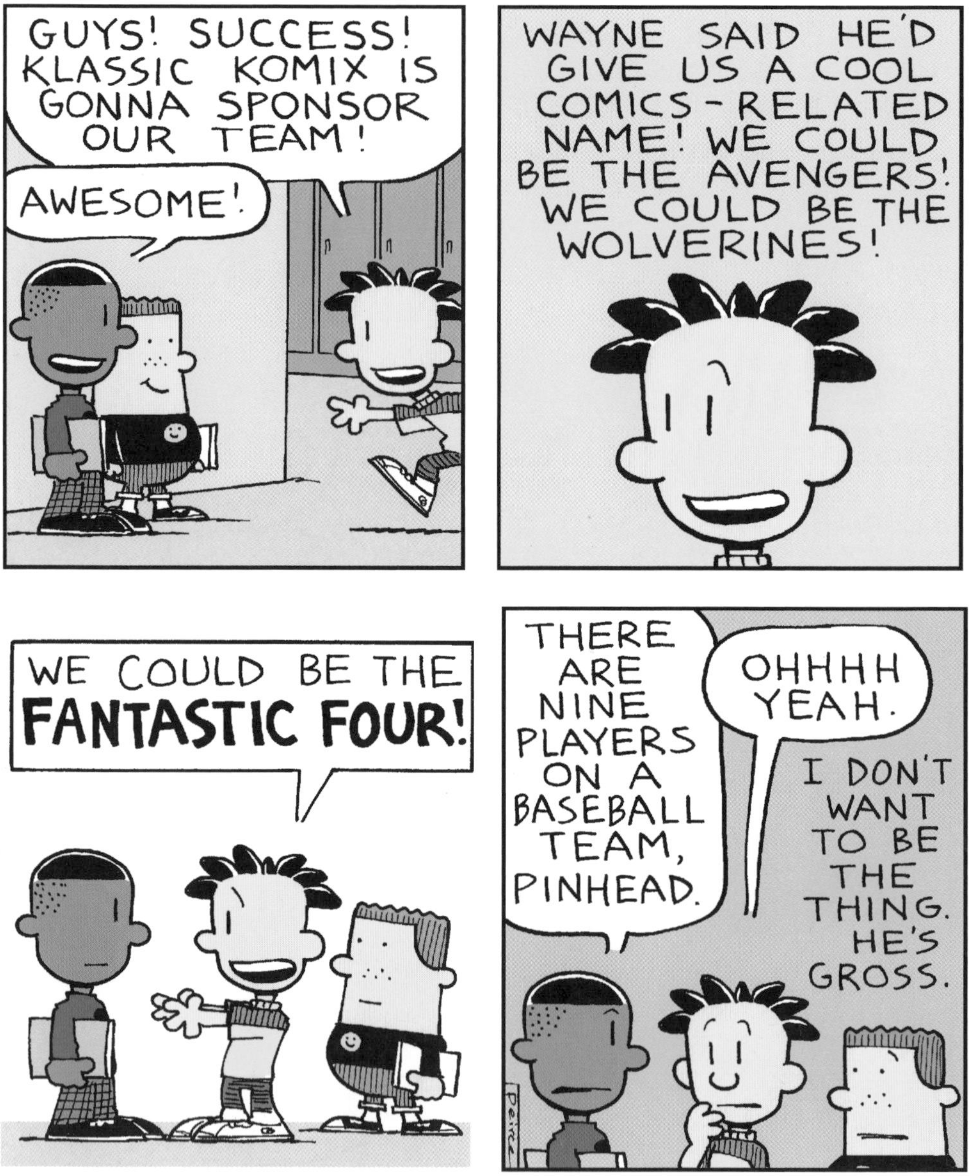
GUYS! SUCCESS! KLASSIC KOMIX IS GONNA SPONSOR OUR TEAM!
AWESOME!
WAYNE SAID HE'D GIVE US A COOL COMICS-RELATED NAME! WE COULD BE THE AVENGERS! WE COULD BE THE WOLVERINES!
WE COULD BE THE **FANTASTIC FOUR!**
THERE ARE NINE PLAYERS ON A BASEBALL TEAM, PINHEAD.
OHHHH YEAH.
I DON'T WANT TO BE THE THING. HE'S GROSS.
Peirce

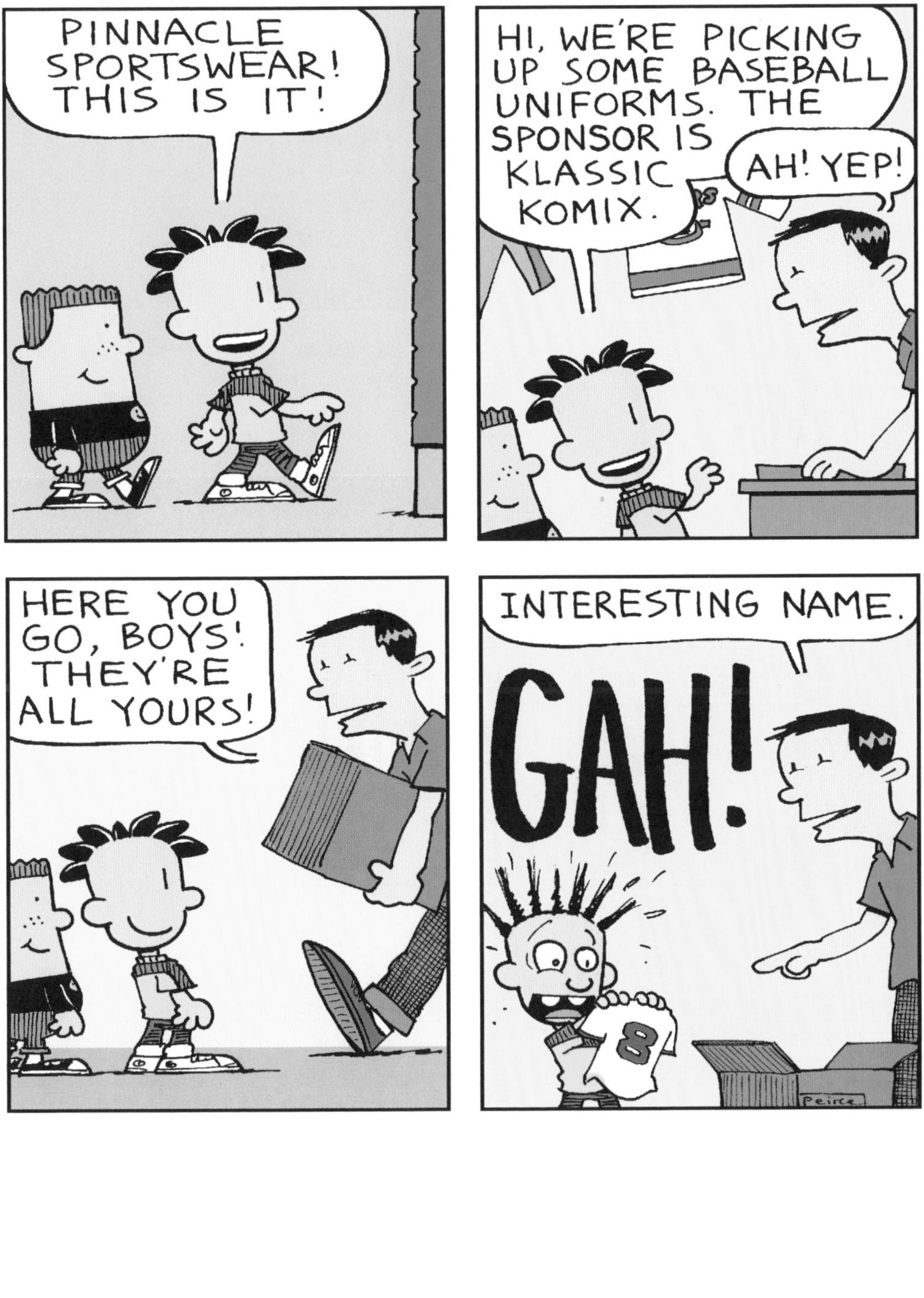
PINNACLE SPORTSWEAR! THIS IS IT!
HI, WE'RE PICKING UP SOME BASEBALL UNIFORMS. THE SPONSOR IS KLASSIC KOMIX.
AH! YEP!
HERE YOU GO, BOYS! THEY'RE ALL YOURS!
INTERESTING NAME.
GAH!
8
Peirce

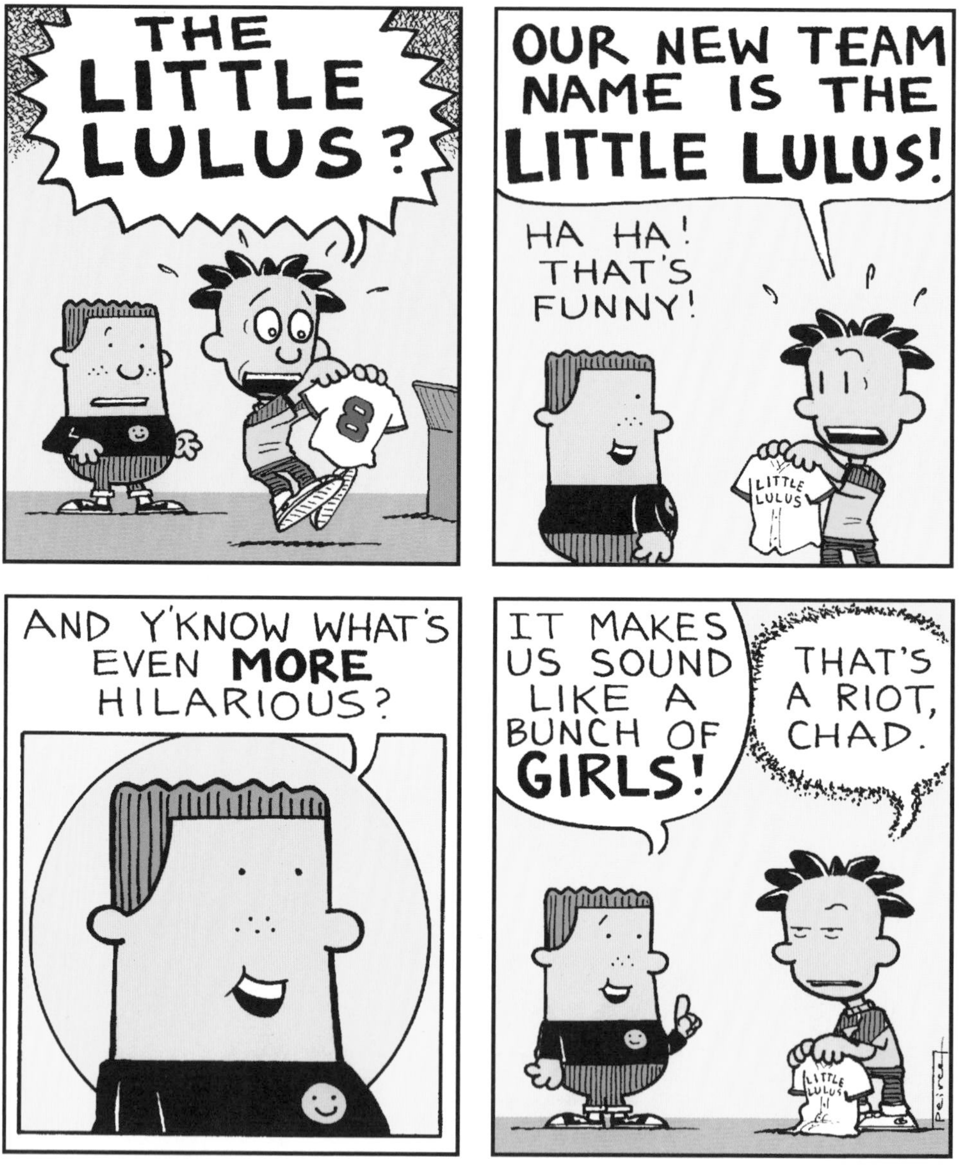
THE LITTLE LULUS?
OUR NEW TEAM NAME IS THE LITTLE LULUS!
HA HA! THAT'S FUNNY!
LITTLE LULUS
AND Y'KNOW WHAT'S EVEN **MORE** HILARIOUS?
IT MAKES US SOUND LIKE A BUNCH OF **GIRLS!**
THAT'S A RIOT, CHAD.
LITTLE LULUS
Peirce

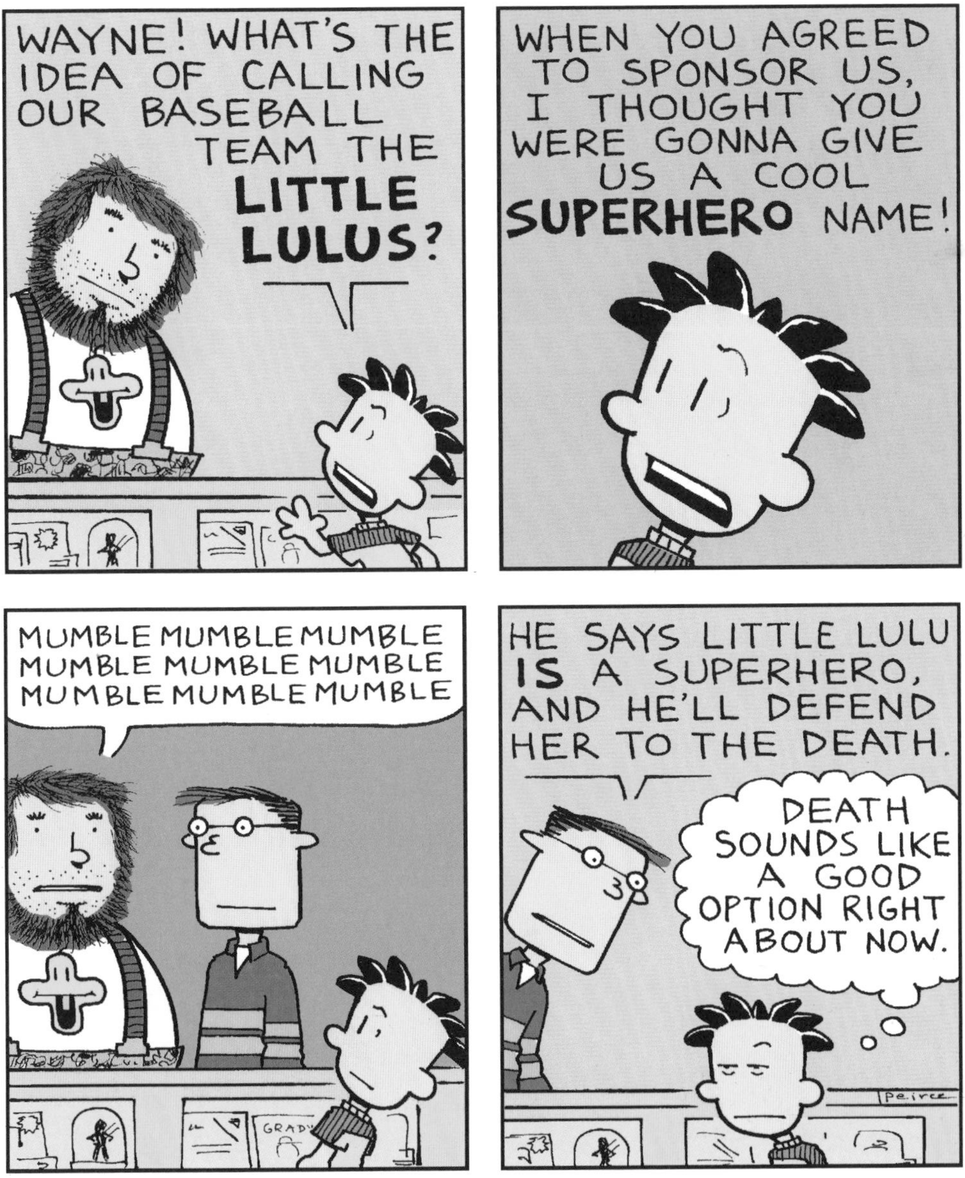
WAYNE! WHAT'S THE IDEA OF CALLING OUR BASEBALL TEAM THE **LITTLE LULUS**?
WHEN YOU AGREED TO SPONSOR US, I THOUGHT YOU WERE GONNA GIVE US A COOL **SUPERHERO** NAME!
MUMBLE MUMBLE MUMBLE MUMBLE MUMBLE MUMBLE MUMBLE MUMBLE MUMBLE
HE SAYS LITTLE LULU **IS** A SUPERHERO, AND HE'LL DEFEND HER TO THE DEATH.
DEATH SOUNDS LIKE A GOOD OPTION RIGHT ABOUT NOW.
Peirce

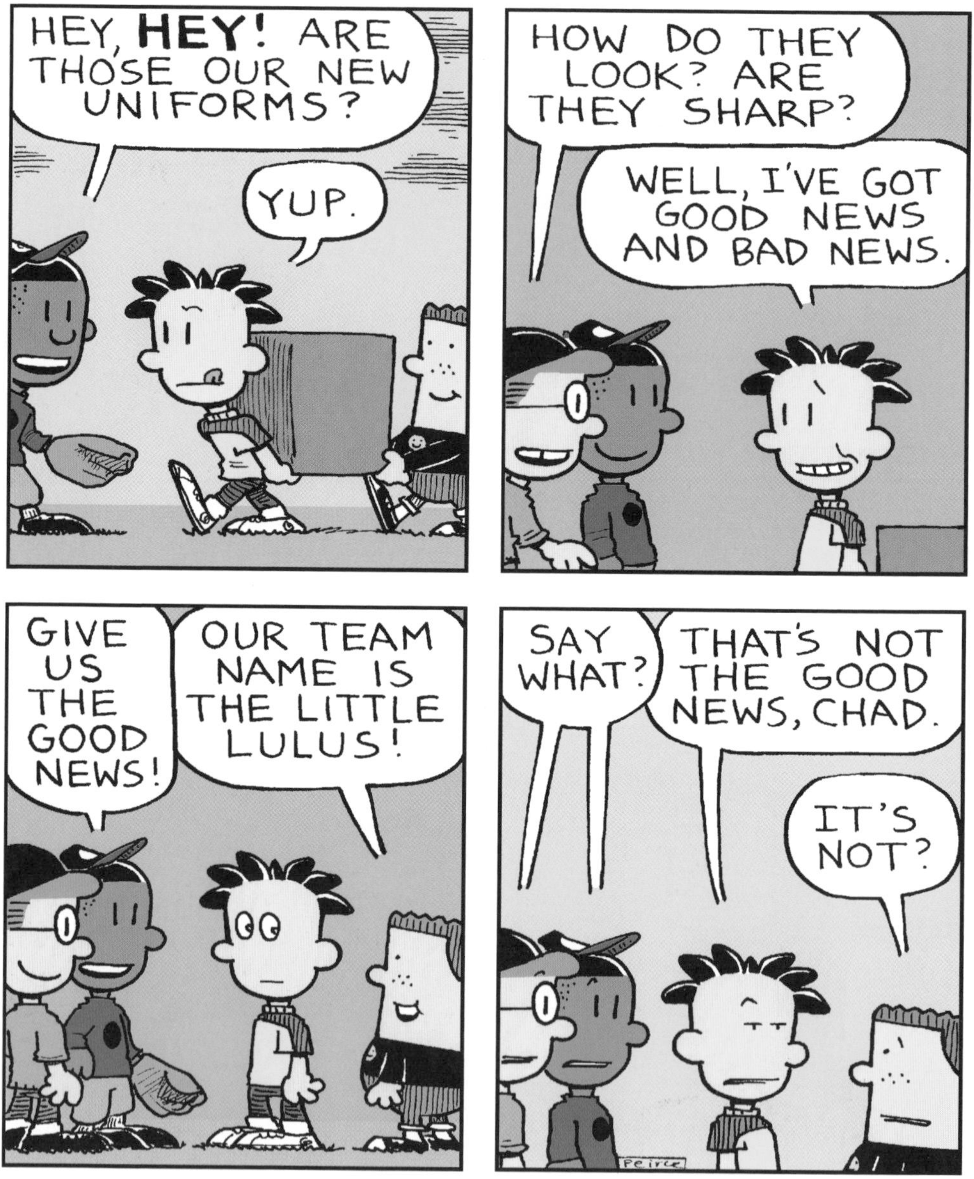
HEY, **HEY!** ARE THOSE OUR NEW UNIFORMS?
YUP.
HOW DO THEY LOOK? ARE THEY SHARP?
WELL, I'VE GOT GOOD NEWS AND BAD NEWS.
GIVE US THE GOOD NEWS!
OUR TEAM NAME IS THE LITTLE LULUS!
SAY WHAT?
THAT'S NOT THE GOOD NEWS, CHAD.
IT'S NOT?
PEIRCE

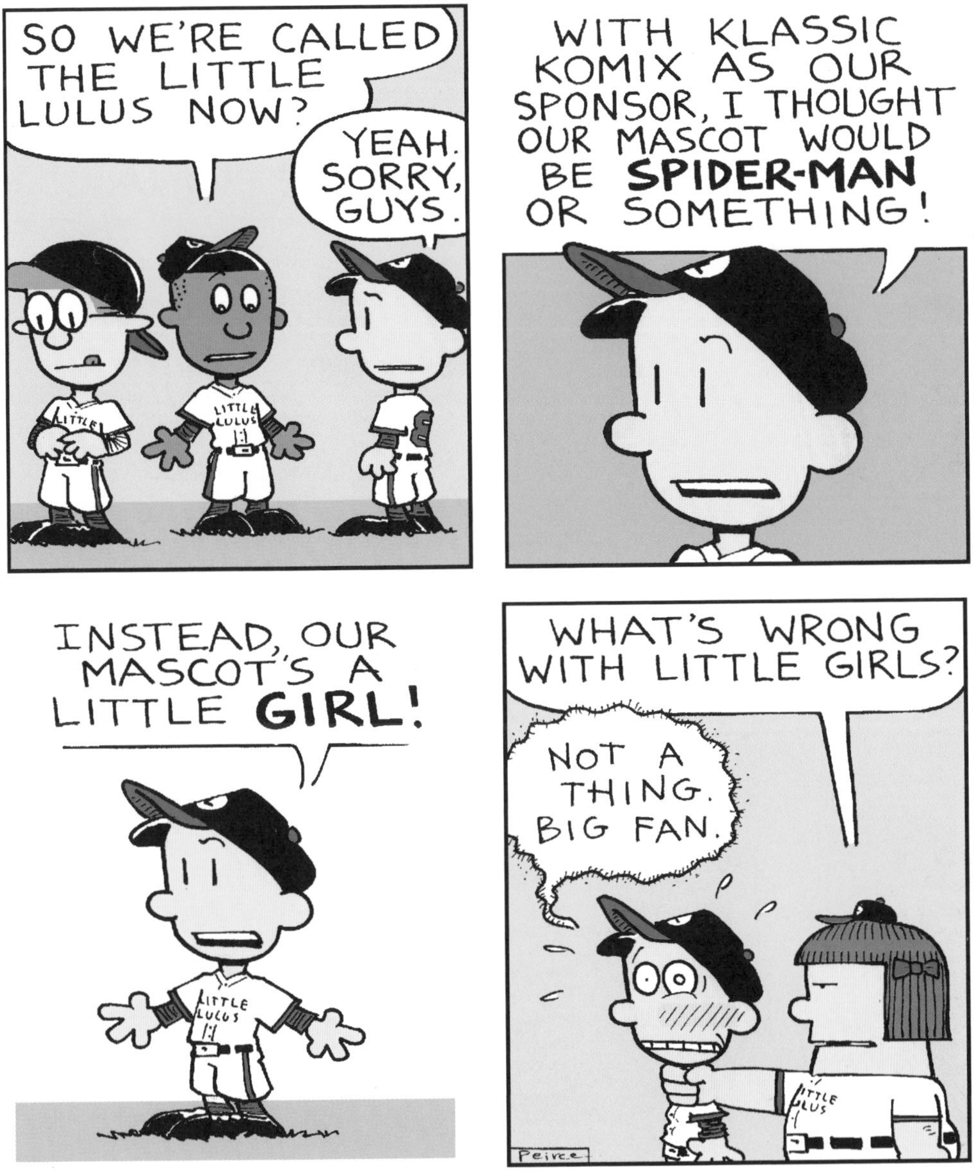
SO WE'RE CALLED THE LITTLE LULUS NOW?
YEAH. SORRY, GUYS.
WITH KLASSIC KOMIX AS OUR SPONSOR, I THOUGHT OUR MASCOT WOULD BE **SPIDER-MAN** OR SOMETHING!
INSTEAD, OUR MASCOT'S A LITTLE **GIRL**!
WHAT'S WRONG WITH LITTLE GIRLS?
NOT A THING. BIG FAN.
Peirce

NATE, BEING NAMED THE LITTLE LULUS ISN'T THE END OF THE WORLD!

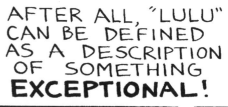

AFTER ALL, "LULU" CAN BE DEFINED AS A DESCRIPTION OF SOMETHING **EXCEPTIONAL!**

WE CAN USE THE WORD TO CHEER EACH OTHER ON!

LIKE: "GET A HIT, CHAD, AND MAKE IT A LULU!"

HA HA! I'LL TRY!

MY HEAD IS ABOUT TO EXPLODE.

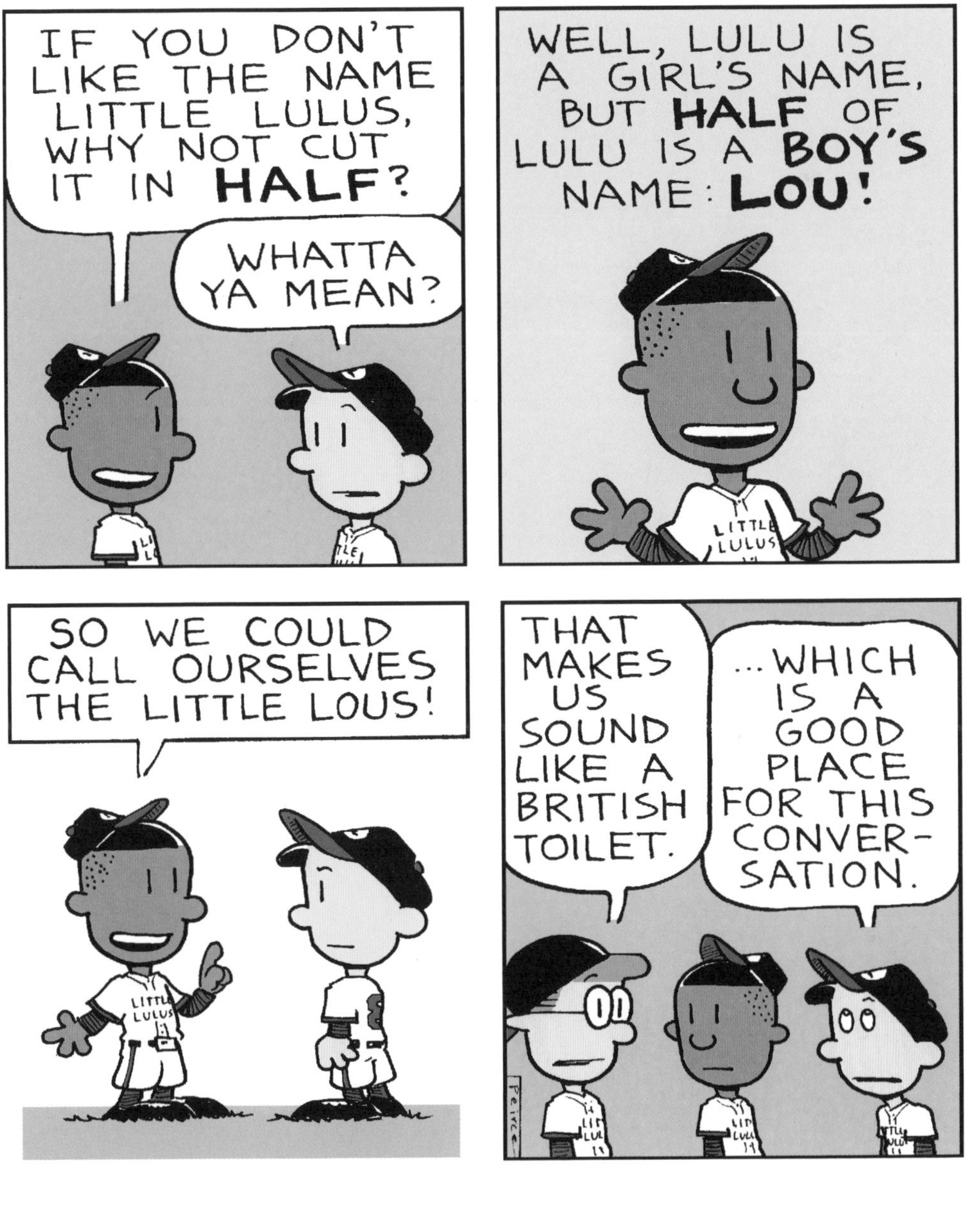
IF YOU DON'T LIKE THE NAME LITTLE LULUS, WHY NOT CUT IT IN **HALF**?
WHATTA YA MEAN?
WELL, LULU IS A GIRL'S NAME, BUT **HALF** OF LULU IS A **BOY'S** NAME: **LOU!**
LITTLE LULUS
SO WE COULD CALL OURSELVES THE LITTLE LOUS!
LITTLE LULUS
THAT MAKES US SOUND LIKE A BRITISH TOILET.
...WHICH IS A GOOD PLACE FOR THIS CONVER-SATION.
peirce

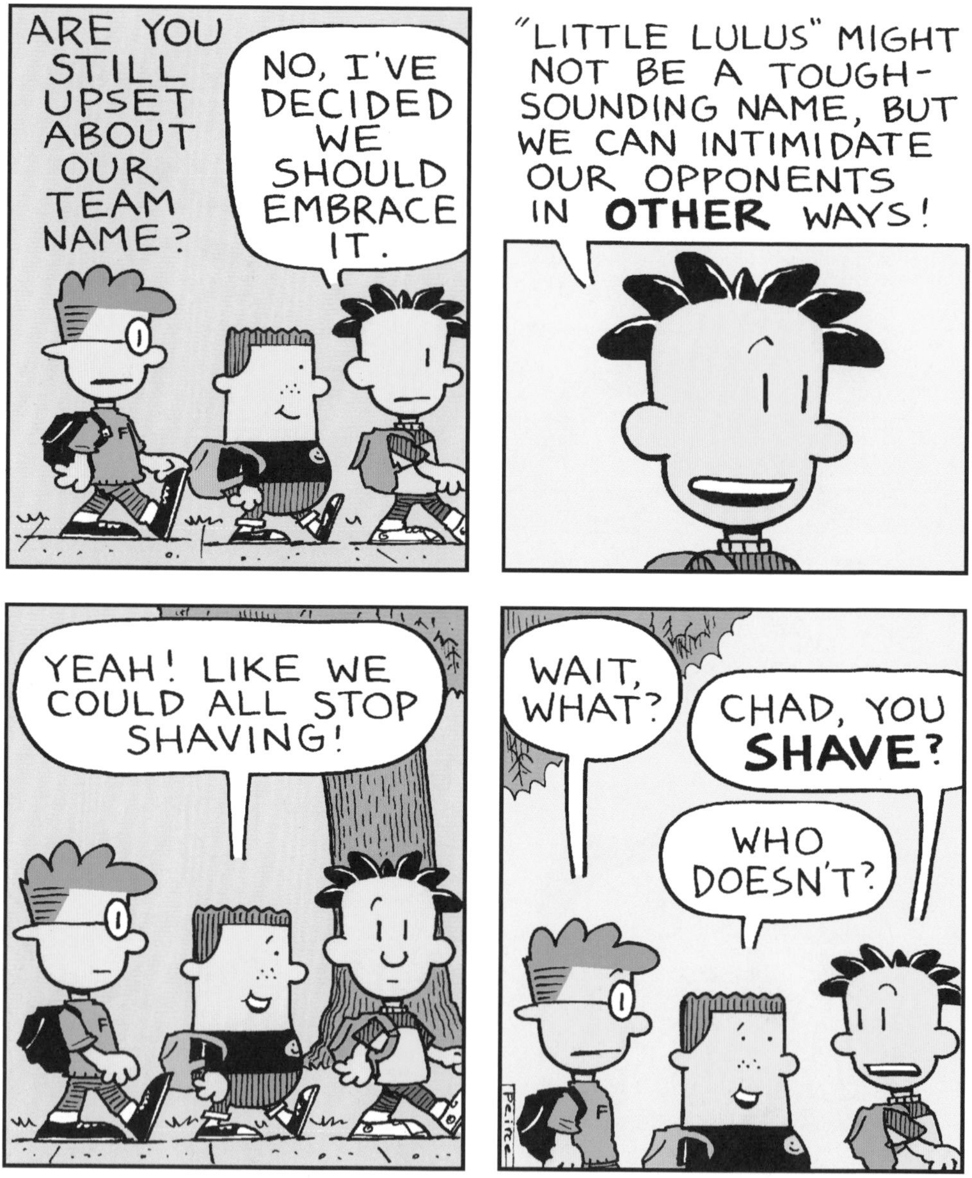
ARE YOU STILL UPSET ABOUT OUR TEAM NAME?
NO, I'VE DECIDED WE SHOULD EMBRACE IT.
"LITTLE LULUS" MIGHT NOT BE A TOUGH-SOUNDING NAME, BUT WE CAN INTIMIDATE OUR OPPONENTS IN **OTHER** WAYS!
YEAH! LIKE WE COULD ALL STOP SHAVING!
WAIT, WHAT?
CHAD, YOU **SHAVE**?
WHO DOESN'T?
PEIRCE

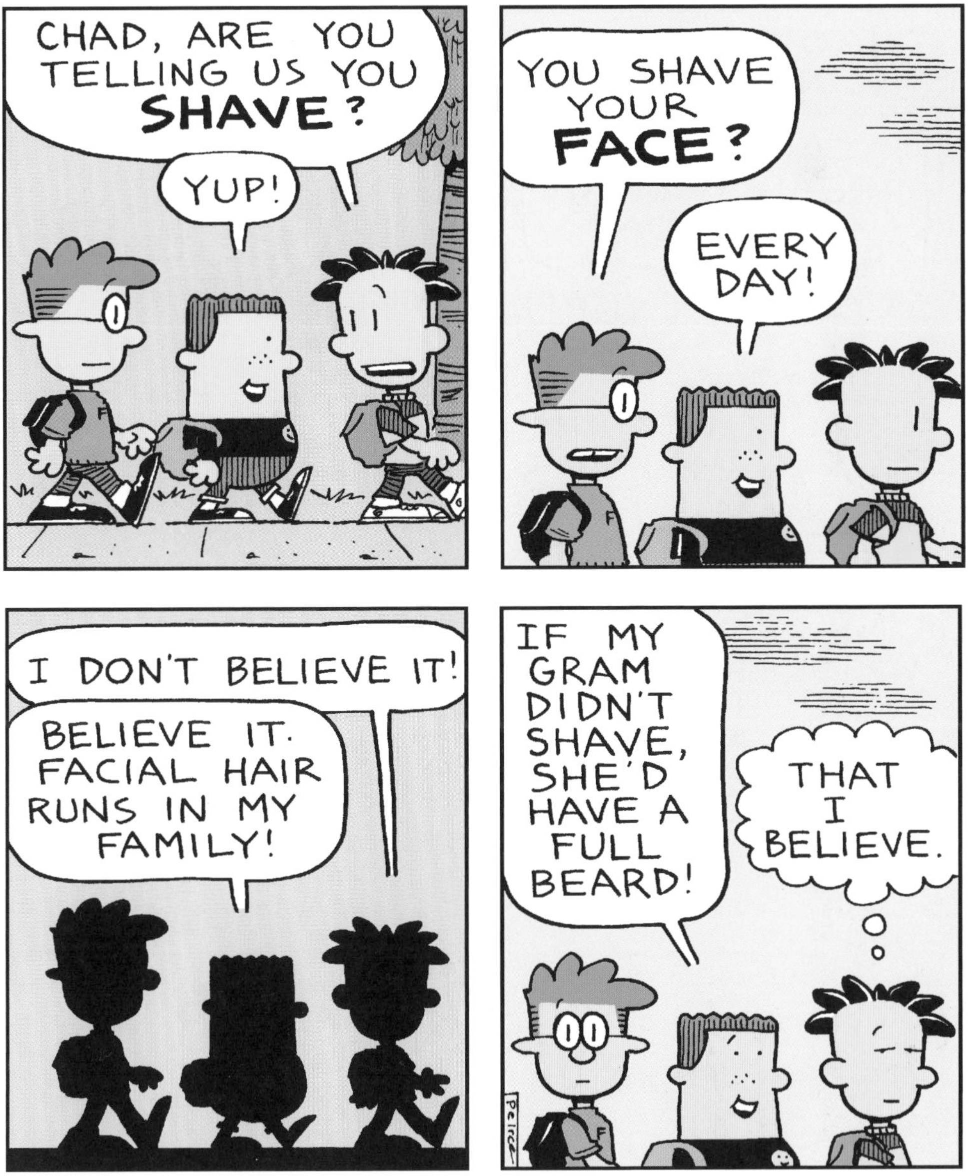
CHAD, ARE YOU TELLING US YOU SHAVE?
YUP!
YOU SHAVE YOUR FACE?
EVERY DAY!
I DON'T BELIEVE IT!
BELIEVE IT. FACIAL HAIR RUNS IN MY FAMILY!
IF MY GRAM DIDN'T SHAVE, SHE'D HAVE A FULL BEARD!
THAT I BELIEVE.
PEIRCE

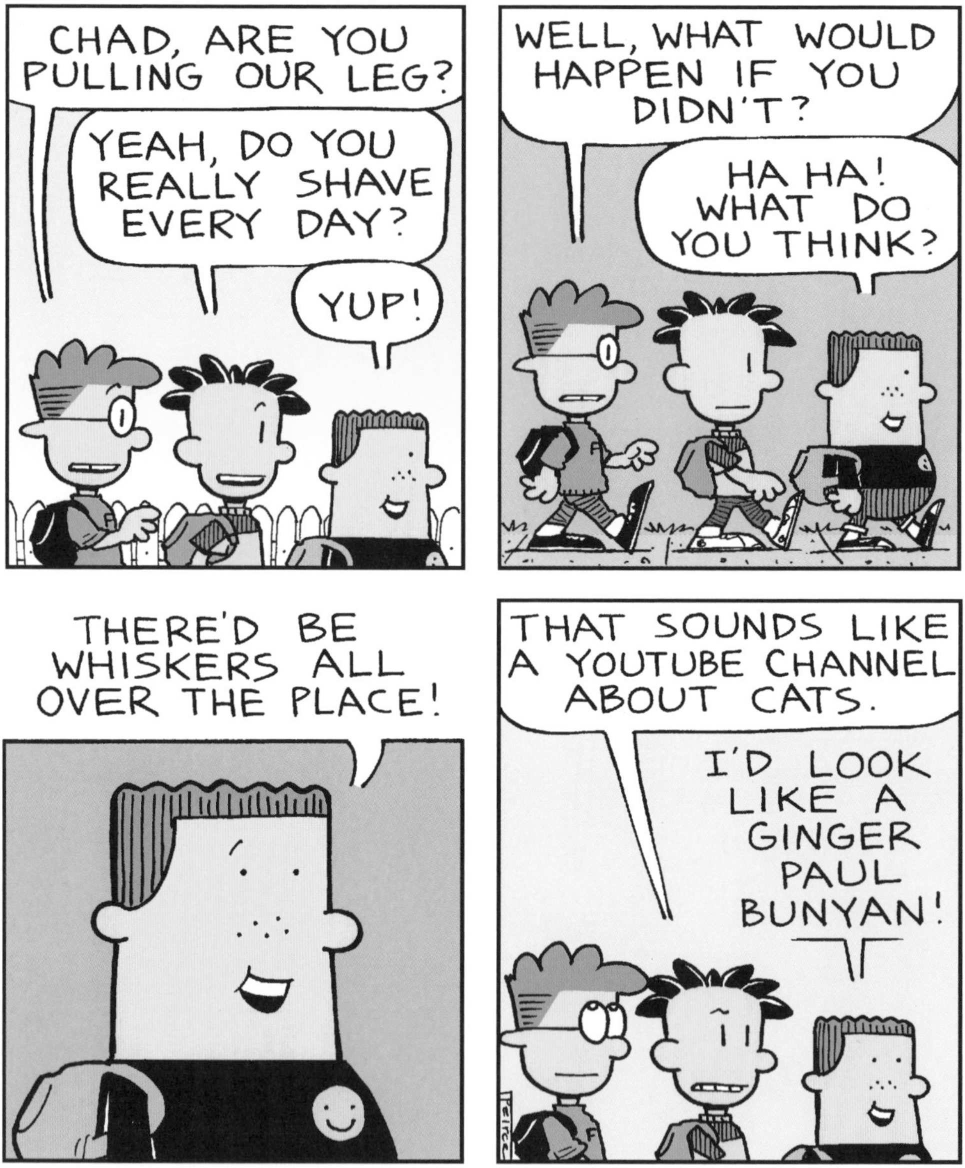
CHAD, ARE YOU PULLING OUR LEG?
YEAH, DO YOU REALLY SHAVE EVERY DAY?
YUP!
WELL, WHAT WOULD HAPPEN IF YOU DIDN'T?
HA HA! WHAT DO YOU THINK?
THERE'D BE WHISKERS ALL OVER THE PLACE!
THAT SOUNDS LIKE A YOUTUBE CHANNEL ABOUT CATS.
I'D LOOK LIKE A GINGER PAUL BUNYAN!

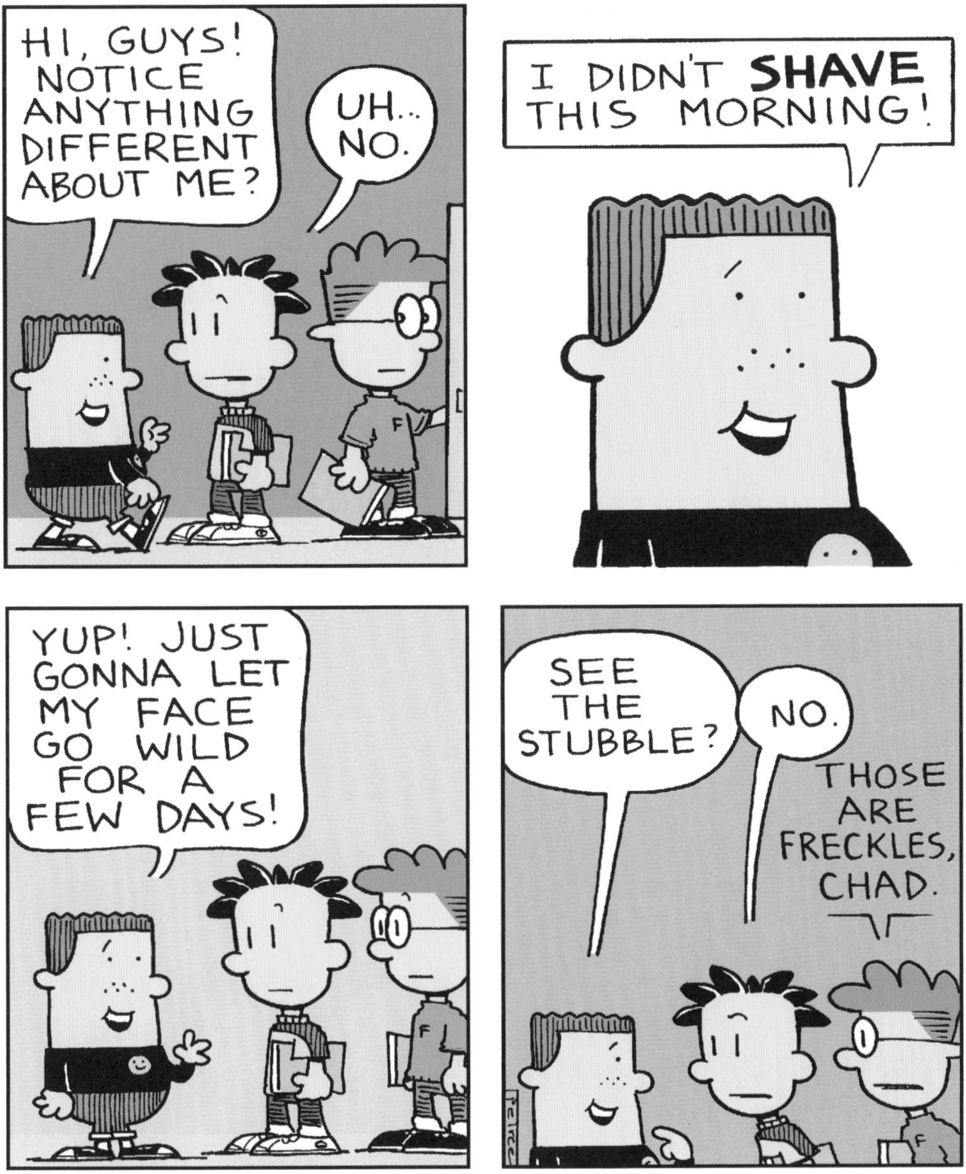
HI, GUYS! NOTICE ANYTHING DIFFERENT ABOUT ME?
UH... NO.
I DIDN'T **SHAVE** THIS MORNING!
YUP! JUST GONNA LET MY FACE GO WILD FOR A FEW DAYS!
SEE THE STUBBLE?
NO.
THOSE ARE FRECKLES, CHAD.
PEIRCE

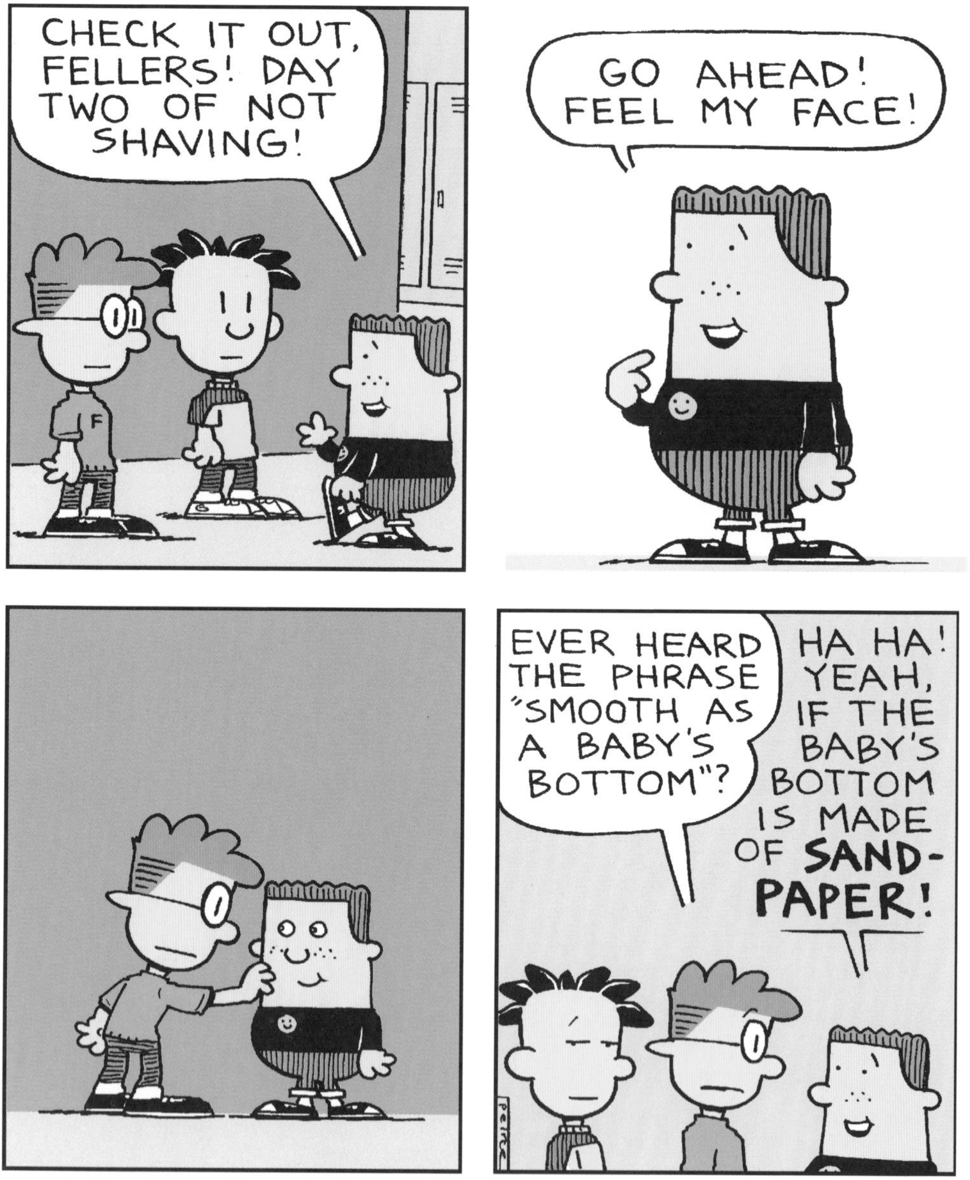
CHECK IT OUT, FELLERS! DAY TWO OF NOT SHAVING!
GO AHEAD! FEEL MY FACE!
EVER HEARD THE PHRASE "SMOOTH AS A BABY'S BOTTOM"?
HA HA! YEAH, IF THE BABY'S BOTTOM IS MADE OF **SAND-PAPER!**
PEIRCE

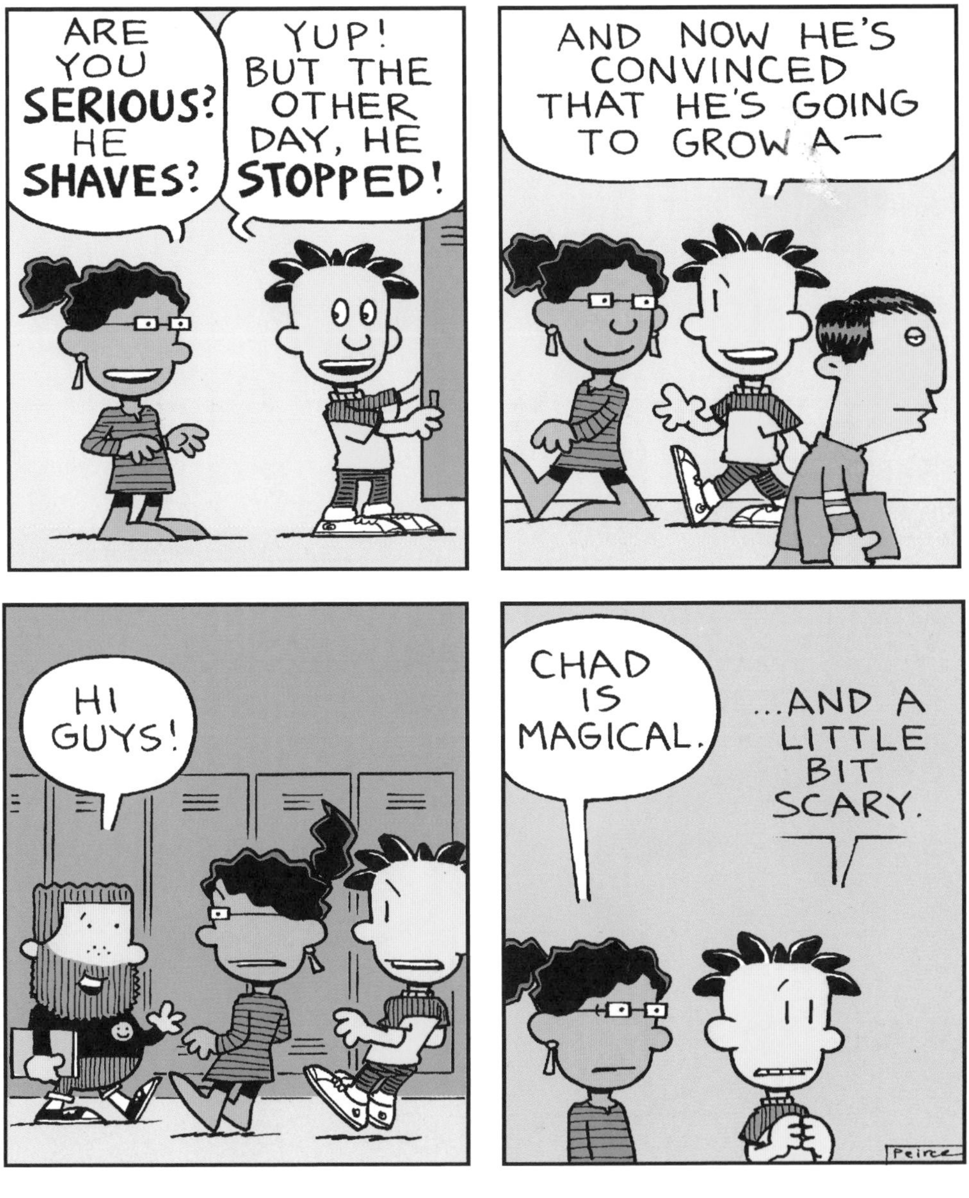
ARE YOU **SERIOUS**? HE **SHAVES**?
YUP! BUT THE OTHER DAY, HE **STOPPED**!
AND NOW HE'S CONVINCED THAT HE'S GOING TO GROW A—
HI GUYS!
CHAD IS MAGICAL.
...AND A LITTLE BIT SCARY.
Peirce

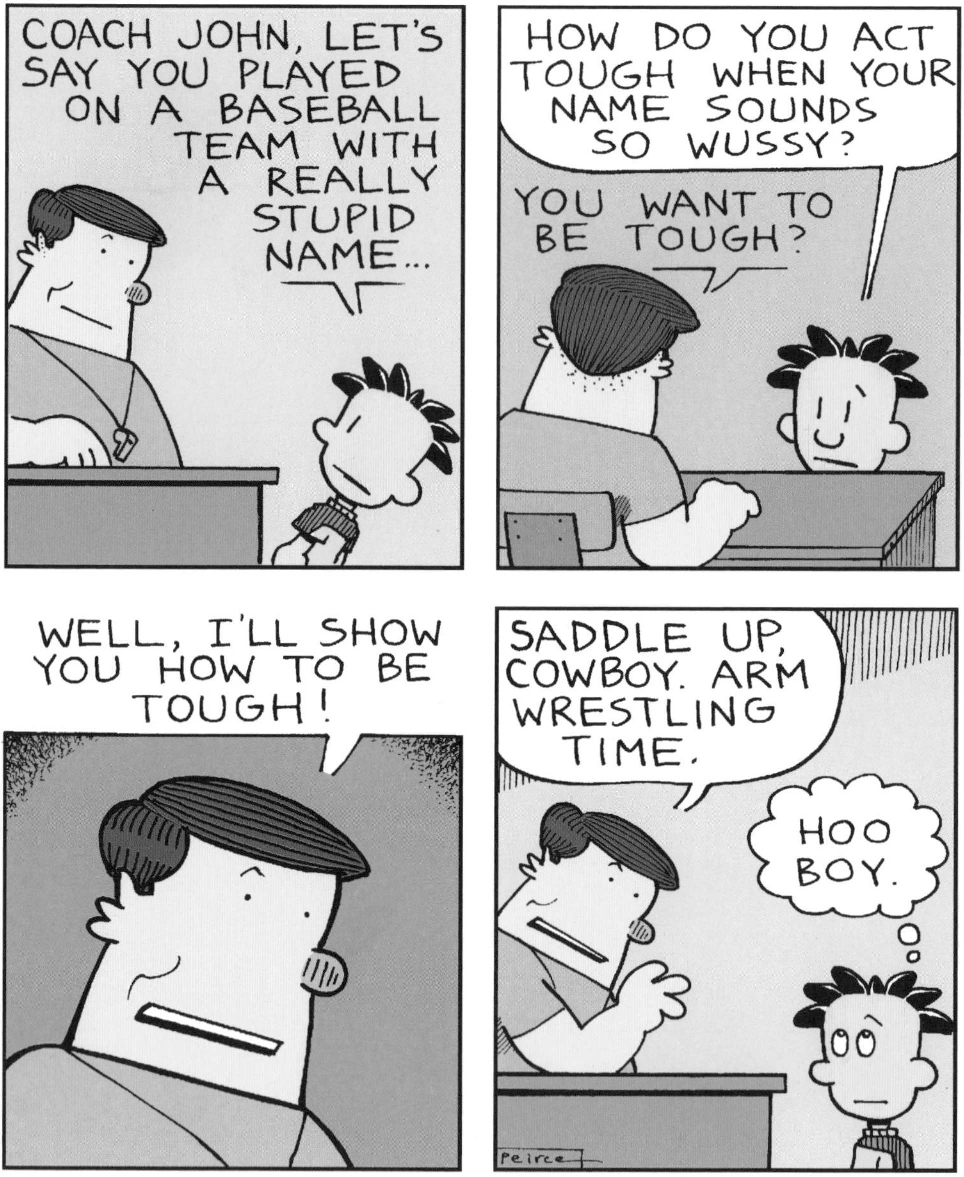
COACH JOHN, LET'S SAY YOU PLAYED ON A BASEBALL TEAM WITH A REALLY STUPID NAME...
HOW DO YOU ACT TOUGH WHEN YOUR NAME SOUNDS SO WUSSY?
YOU WANT TO BE TOUGH?
WELL, I'LL SHOW YOU HOW TO BE TOUGH!
SADDLE UP, COWBOY. ARM WRESTLING TIME.
HOO BOY.
PEIRCE

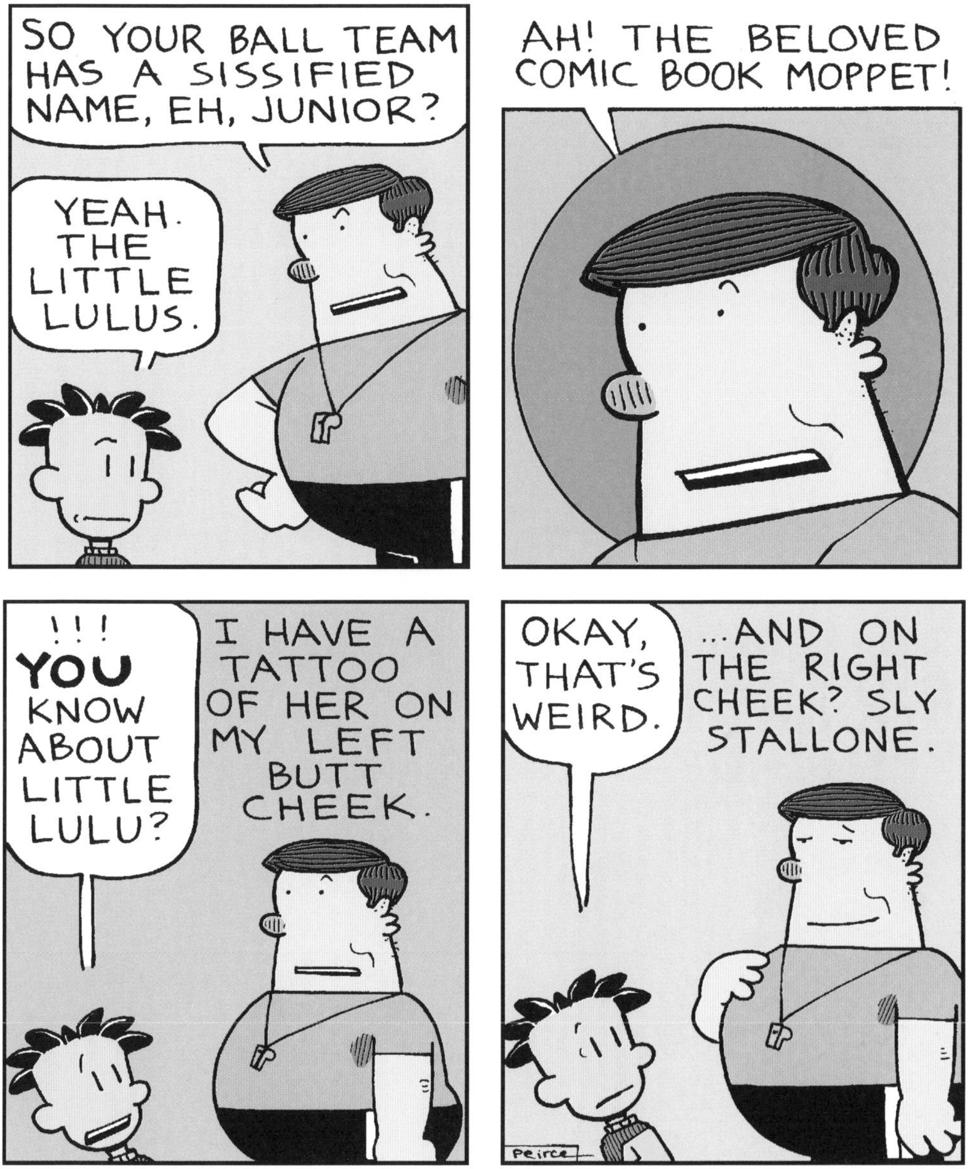
SO YOUR BALL TEAM HAS A SISSIFIED NAME, EH, JUNIOR?
YEAH. THE LITTLE LULUS.
AH! THE BELOVED COMIC BOOK MOPPET!
!!! YOU KNOW ABOUT LITTLE LULU?
I HAVE A TATTOO OF HER ON MY LEFT BUTT CHEEK.
OKAY, THAT'S WEIRD.
...AND ON THE RIGHT CHEEK? SLY STALLONE.
Peirce

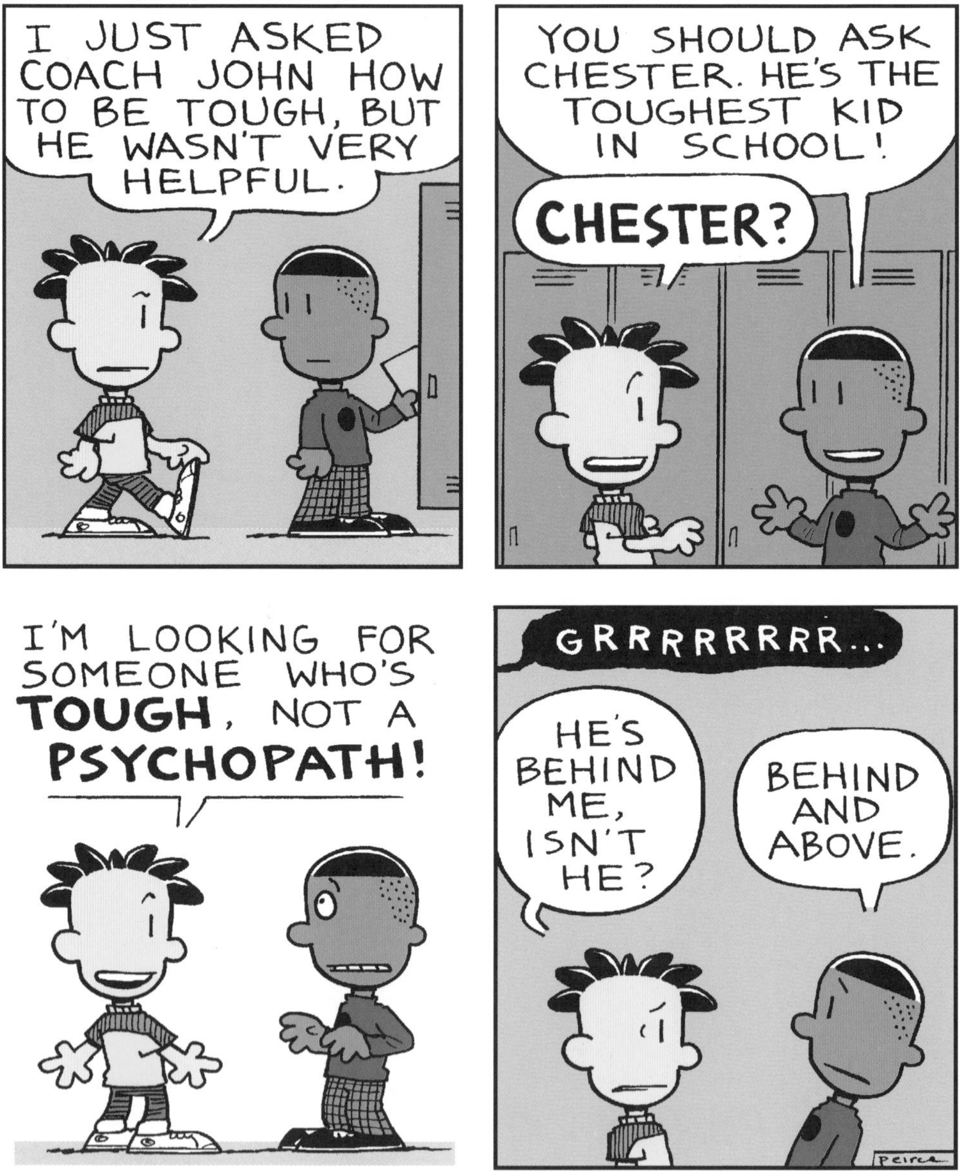
I JUST ASKED COACH JOHN HOW TO BE TOUGH, BUT HE WASN'T VERY HELPFUL.
YOU SHOULD ASK CHESTER. HE'S THE TOUGHEST KID IN SCHOOL!
CHESTER?
I'M LOOKING FOR SOMEONE WHO'S **TOUGH**, NOT A **PSYCHOPATH**!
GRRRRRRRR...
HE'S BEHIND ME, ISN'T HE?
BEHIND AND ABOVE.
peirce

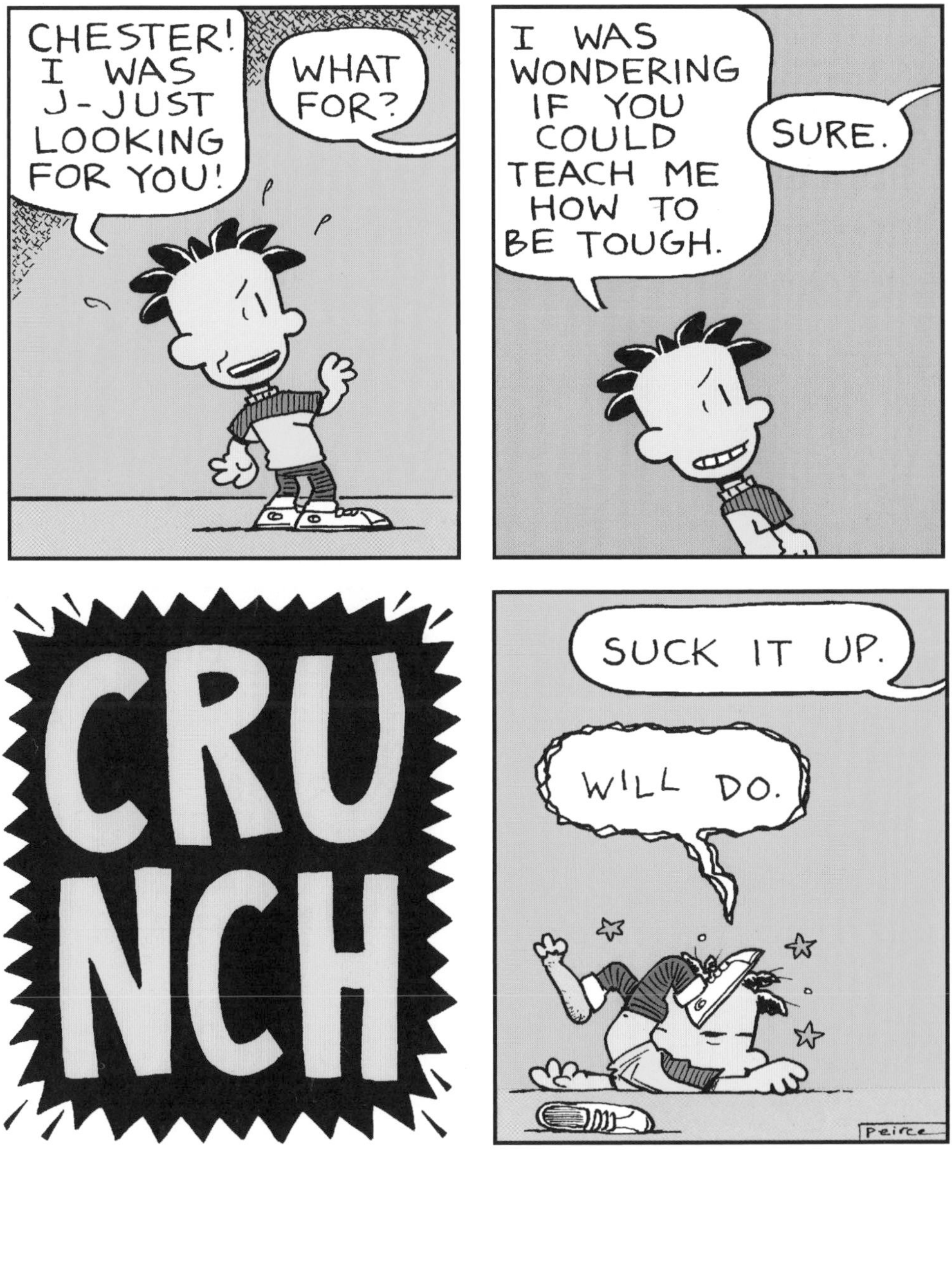
CHESTER! I WAS J-JUST LOOKING FOR YOU!
WHAT FOR?
I WAS WONDERING IF YOU COULD TEACH ME HOW TO BE TOUGH.
SURE.
CRUNCH
SUCK IT UP.
WILL DO.
Peirce

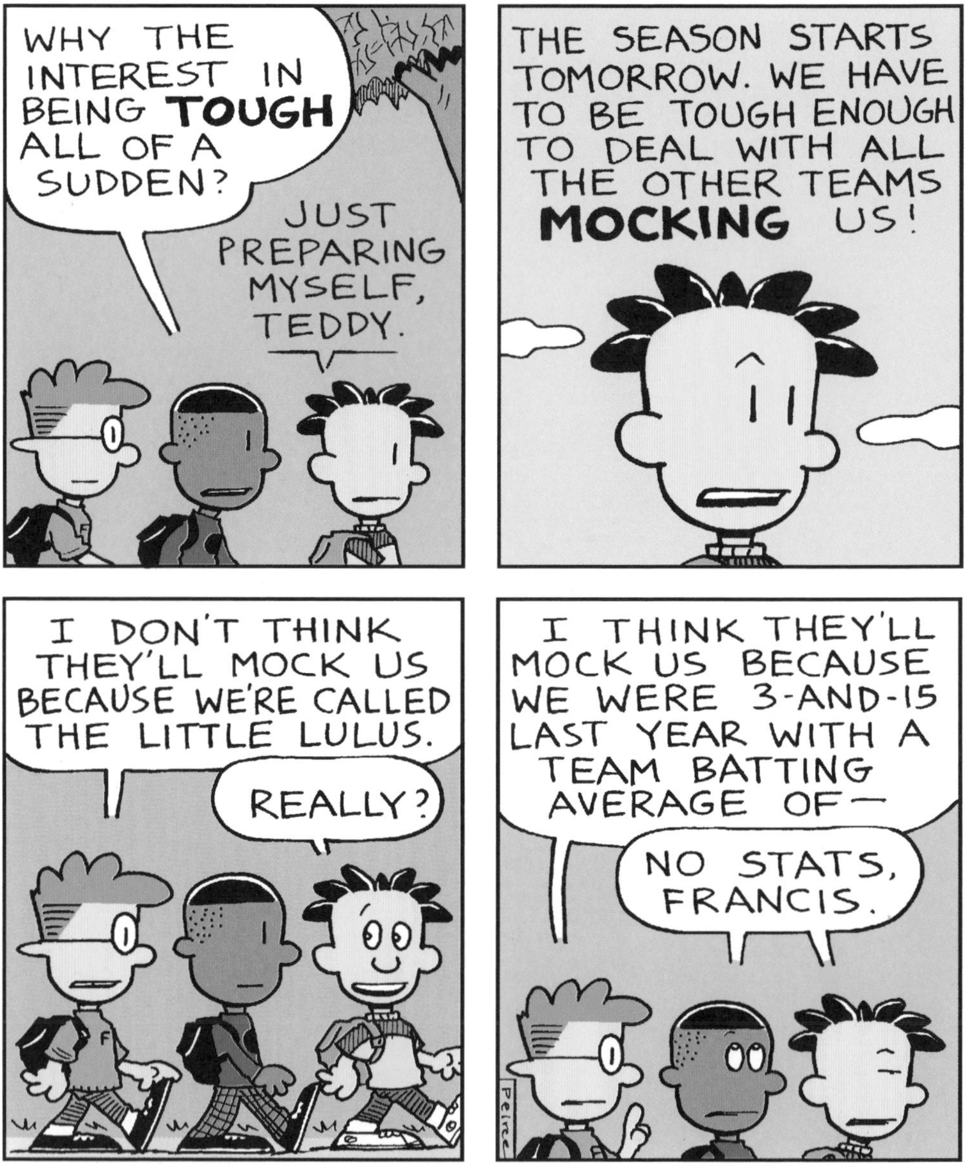
WHY THE INTEREST IN BEING **TOUGH** ALL OF A SUDDEN?
JUST PREPARING MYSELF, TEDDY.
THE SEASON STARTS TOMORROW. WE HAVE TO BE TOUGH ENOUGH TO DEAL WITH ALL THE OTHER TEAMS **MOCKING** US!
I DON'T THINK THEY'LL MOCK US BECAUSE WE'RE CALLED THE LITTLE LULUS.
REALLY?
I THINK THEY'LL MOCK US BECAUSE WE WERE 3-AND-15 LAST YEAR WITH A TEAM BATTING AVERAGE OF—
NO STATS, FRANCIS.
Peirce

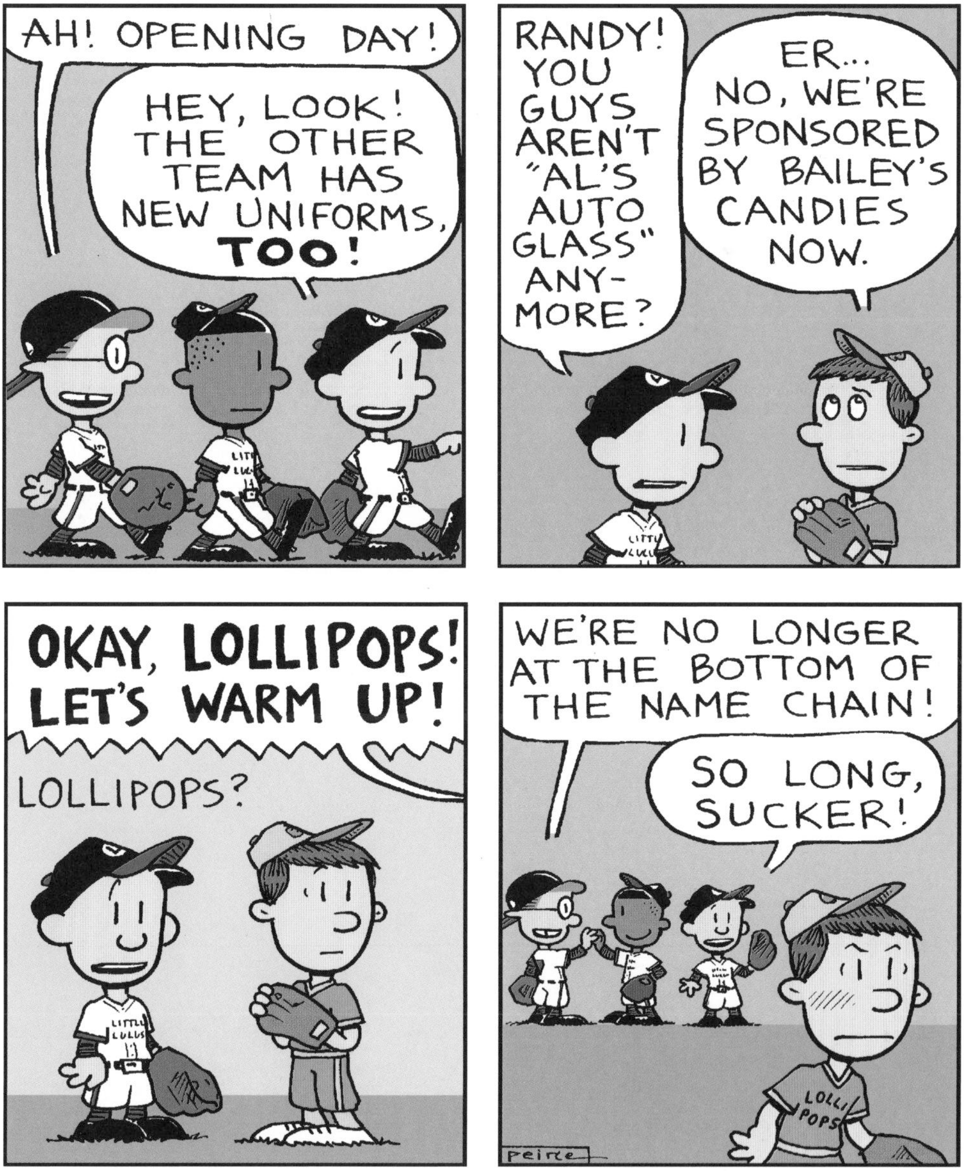
AH! OPENING DAY!
HEY, LOOK! THE OTHER TEAM HAS NEW UNIFORMS, **TOO!**
RANDY! YOU GUYS AREN'T "AL'S AUTO GLASS" ANY- MORE?
ER... NO, WE'RE SPONSORED BY BAILEY'S CANDIES NOW.
OKAY, LOLLIPOPS! LET'S WARM UP!
LOLLIPOPS?
WE'RE NO LONGER AT THE BOTTOM OF THE NAME CHAIN!
SO LONG, SUCKER!
peirce

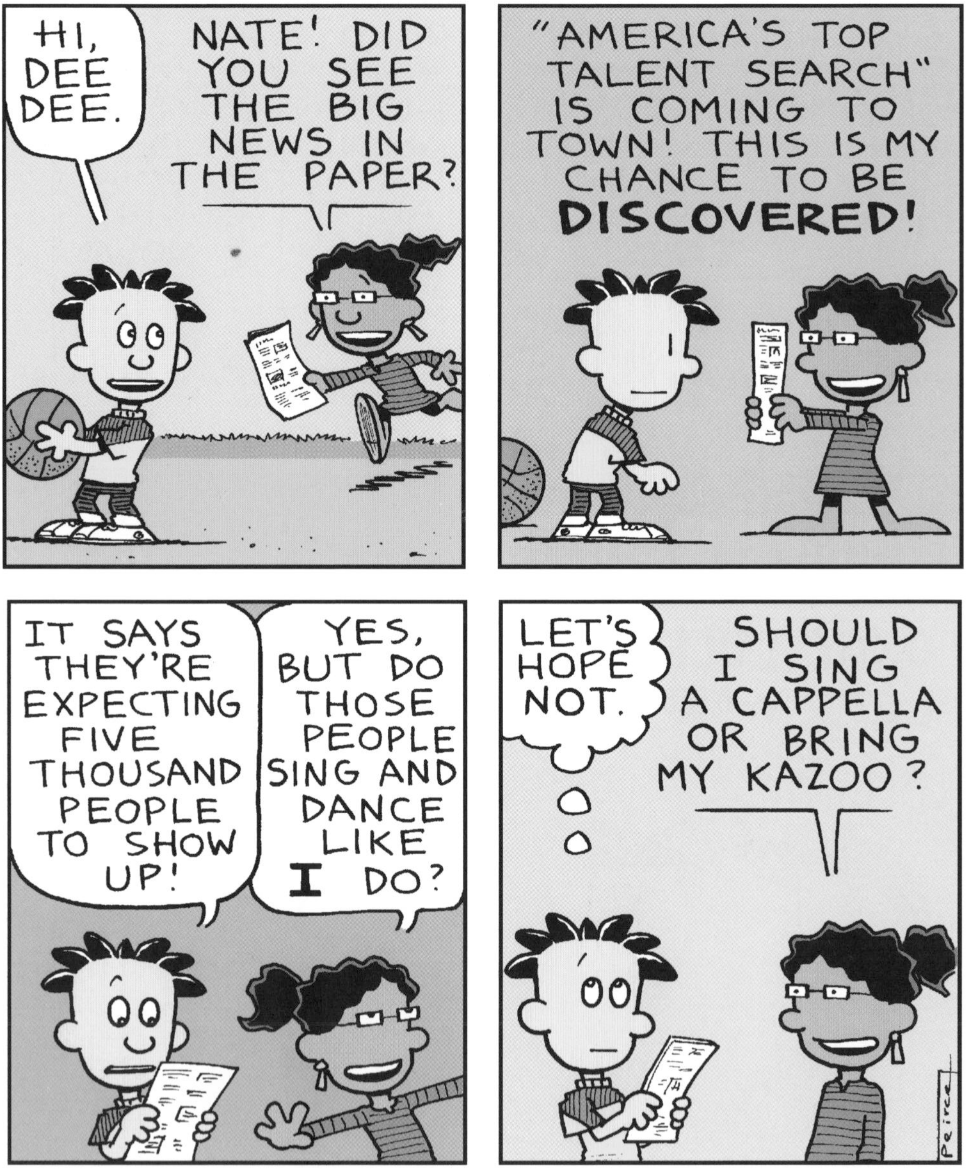
HI, DEE DEE.
NATE! DID YOU SEE THE BIG NEWS IN THE PAPER?
"AMERICA'S TOP TALENT SEARCH" IS COMING TO TOWN! THIS IS MY CHANCE TO BE **DISCOVERED!**
IT SAYS THEY'RE EXPECTING FIVE THOUSAND PEOPLE TO SHOW UP!
YES, BUT DO THOSE PEOPLE SING AND DANCE LIKE **I** DO?
LET'S HOPE NOT.
SHOULD I SING A CAPPELLA OR BRING MY KAZOO?
Peirce

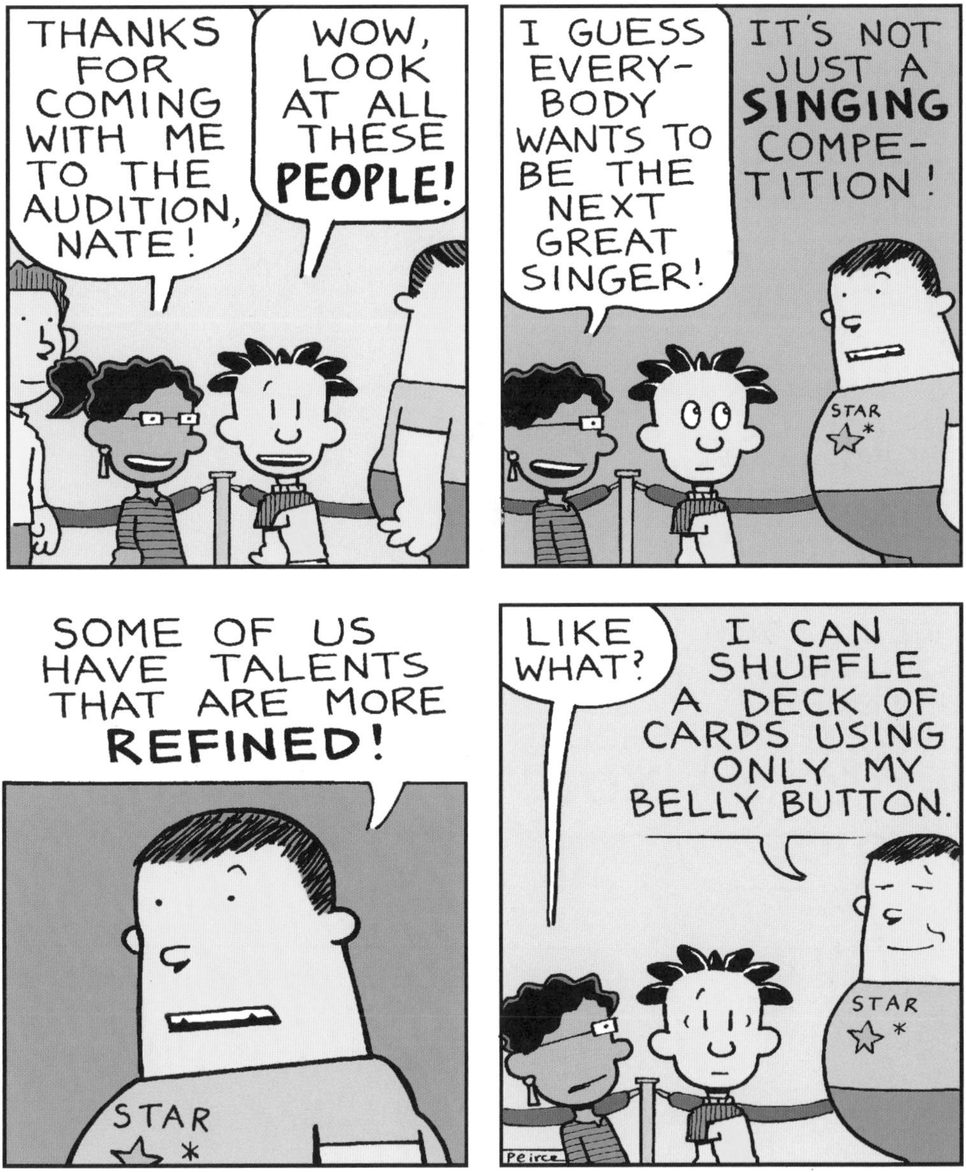
THANKS FOR COMING WITH ME TO THE AUDITION, NATE!
WOW, LOOK AT ALL THESE **PEOPLE!**
I GUESS EVERY-BODY WANTS TO BE THE NEXT GREAT SINGER!
IT'S NOT JUST A **SINGING** COMPE-TITION!
STAR
SOME OF US HAVE TALENTS THAT ARE MORE **REFINED!**
STAR
LIKE WHAT?
I CAN SHUFFLE A DECK OF CARDS USING ONLY MY BELLY BUTTON.
STAR
Peirce

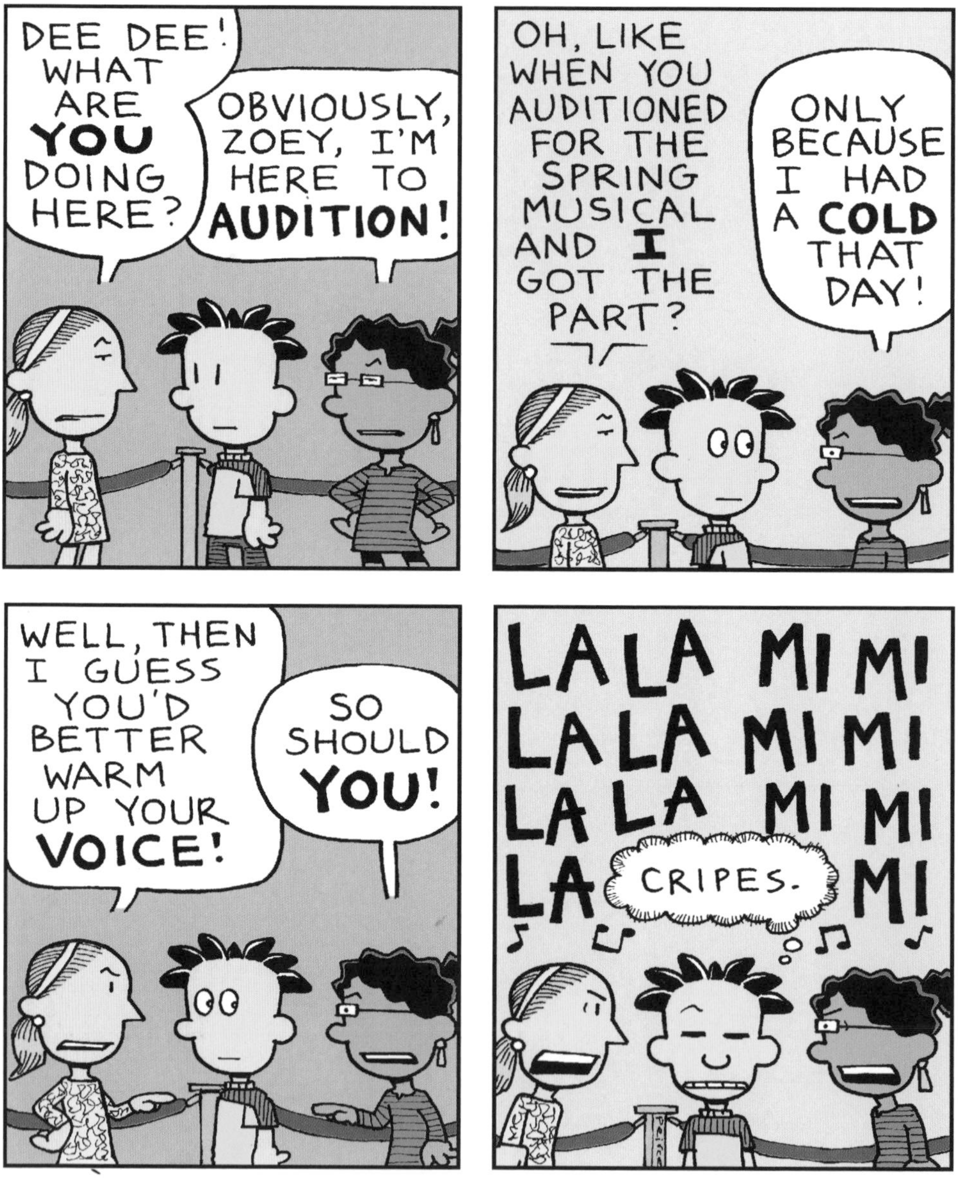
DEE DEE! WHAT ARE **YOU** DOING HERE?
OBVIOUSLY, ZOEY, I'M HERE TO **AUDITION**!
OH, LIKE WHEN YOU AUDITIONED FOR THE SPRING MUSICAL AND **I** GOT THE PART?
ONLY BECAUSE I HAD A **COLD** THAT DAY!
WELL, THEN I GUESS YOU'D BETTER WARM UP YOUR **VOICE**!
SO SHOULD **YOU**!
LA LA MI MI LA LA MI MI LA LA MI MI LA MI
CRIPES.

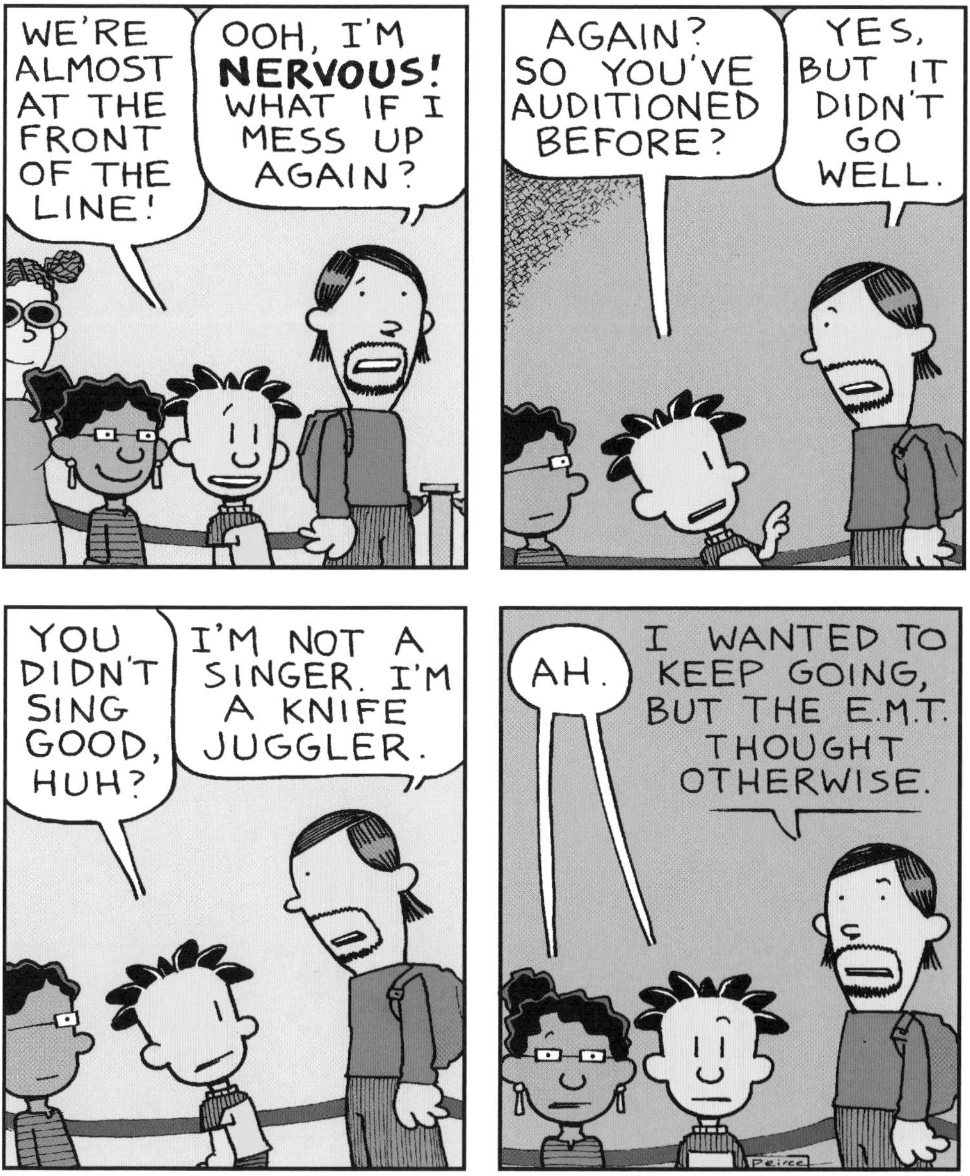
WE'RE ALMOST AT THE FRONT OF THE LINE!
OOH, I'M **NERVOUS!** WHAT IF I MESS UP AGAIN?
AGAIN? SO YOU'VE AUDITIONED BEFORE?
YES, BUT IT DIDN'T GO WELL.
YOU DIDN'T SING GOOD, HUH?
I'M NOT A SINGER. I'M A KNIFE JUGGLER.
AH.
I WANTED TO KEEP GOING, BUT THE E.M.T. THOUGHT OTHERWISE.
Peirce

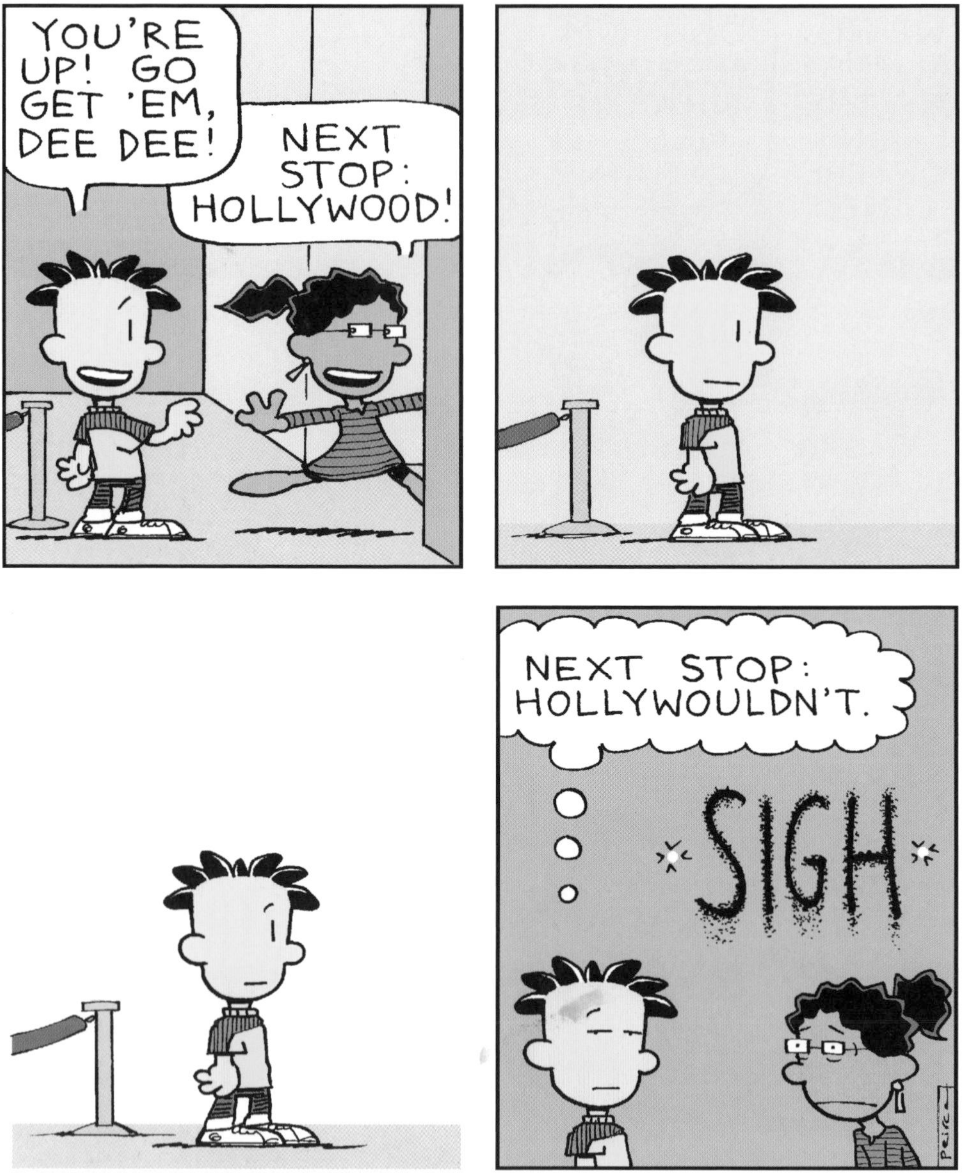
YOU'RE UP! GO GET 'EM, DEE DEE!
NEXT STOP: HOLLYWOOD!
NEXT STOP: HOLLYWOULDN'T.
SIGH
PEIRCE

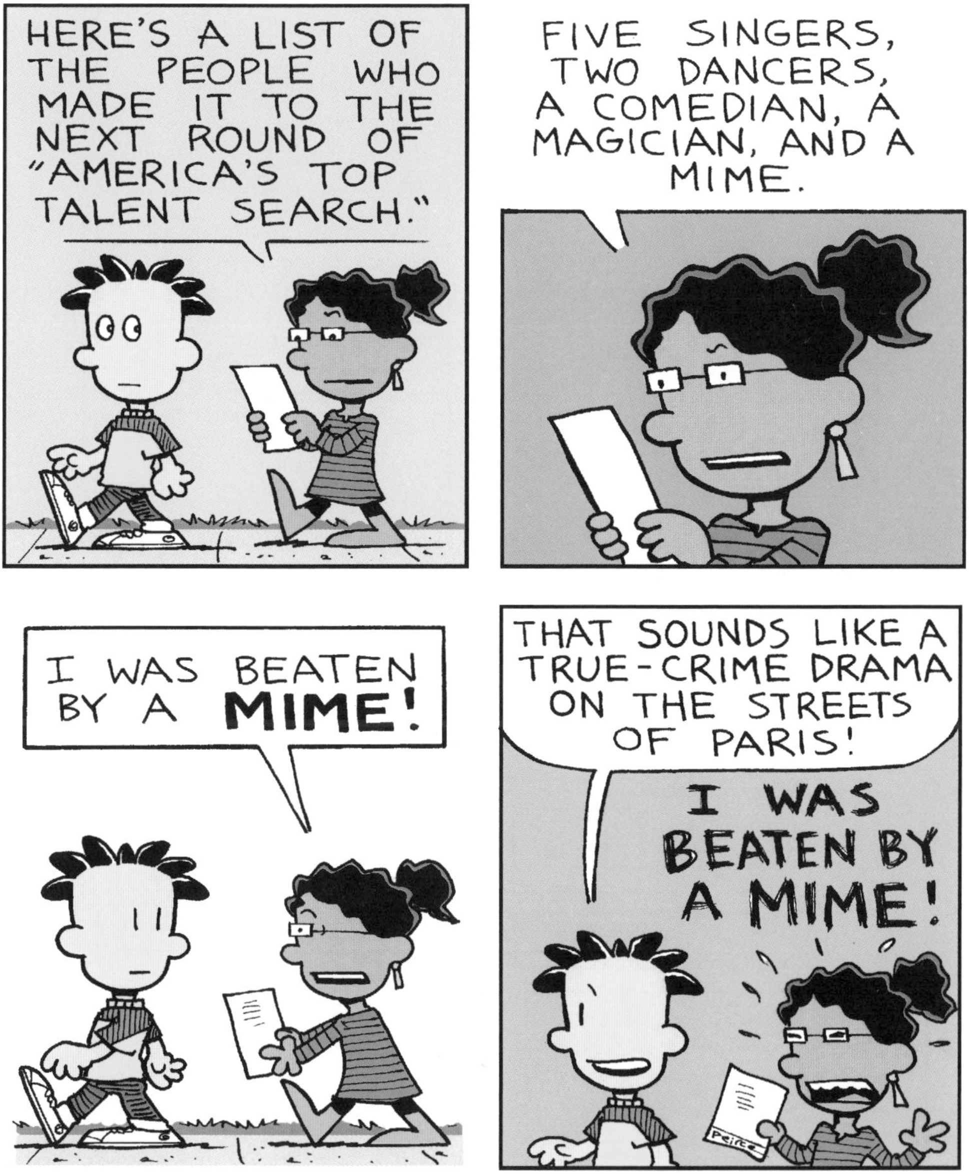
HERE'S A LIST OF THE PEOPLE WHO MADE IT TO THE NEXT ROUND OF "AMERICA'S TOP TALENT SEARCH."
FIVE SINGERS, TWO DANCERS, A COMEDIAN, A MAGICIAN, AND A MIME.
I WAS BEATEN BY A MIME!
THAT SOUNDS LIKE A TRUE-CRIME DRAMA ON THE STREETS OF PARIS!
I WAS BEATEN BY A MIME!
Peirce

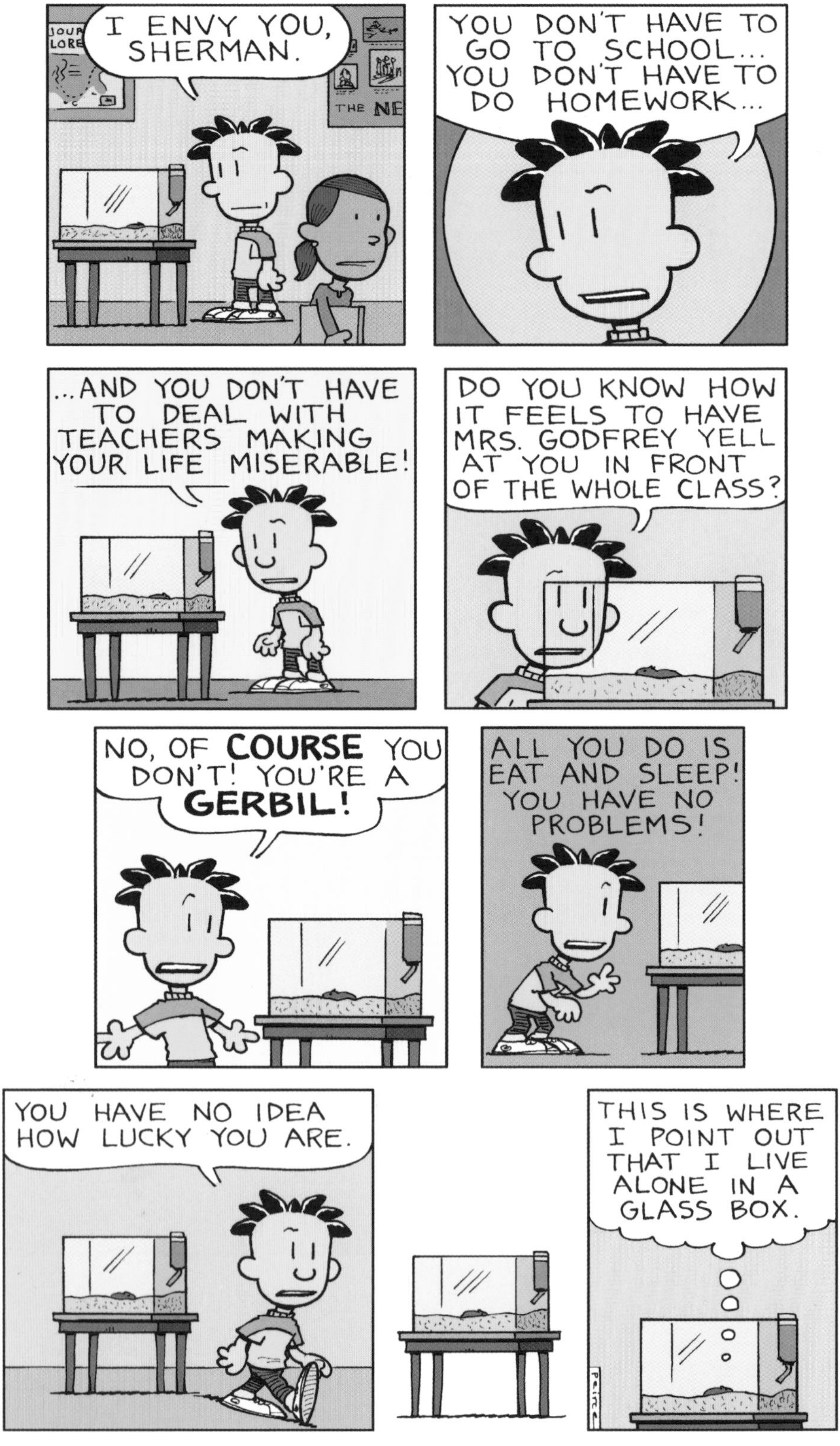
JOUR
LORE
THE NE
I ENVY YOU, SHERMAN.
YOU DON'T HAVE TO GO TO SCHOOL... YOU DON'T HAVE TO DO HOMEWORK...
...AND YOU DON'T HAVE TO DEAL WITH TEACHERS MAKING YOUR LIFE MISERABLE!
DO YOU KNOW HOW IT FEELS TO HAVE MRS. GODFREY YELL AT YOU IN FRONT OF THE WHOLE CLASS?
NO, OF **COURSE** YOU DON'T! YOU'RE A **GERBIL**!
ALL YOU DO IS EAT AND SLEEP! YOU HAVE NO PROBLEMS!
YOU HAVE NO IDEA HOW LUCKY YOU ARE.
THIS IS WHERE I POINT OUT THAT I LIVE ALONE IN A GLASS BOX.
PEIRCE

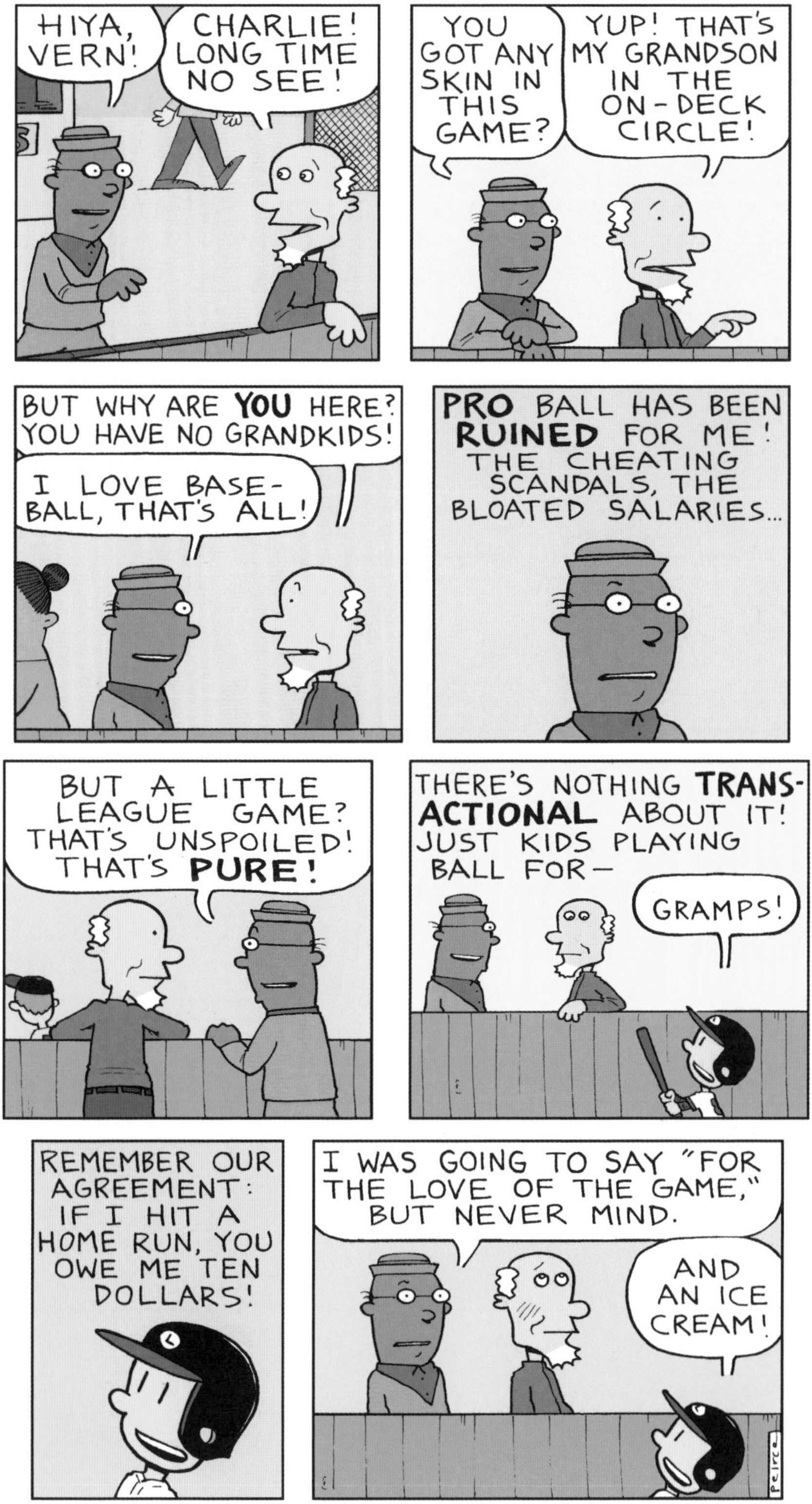
HIYA, VERN!
CHARLIE! LONG TIME NO SEE!
YOU GOT ANY SKIN IN THIS GAME?
YUP! THAT'S MY GRANDSON IN THE ON-DECK CIRCLE!
BUT WHY ARE **YOU** HERE? YOU HAVE NO GRANDKIDS!
I LOVE BASE-BALL, THAT'S ALL!
PRO BALL HAS BEEN **RUINED** FOR ME! THE CHEATING SCANDALS, THE BLOATED SALARIES...
BUT A LITTLE LEAGUE GAME? THAT'S UNSPOILED! THAT'S **PURE**!
THERE'S NOTHING **TRANS-ACTIONAL** ABOUT IT! JUST KIDS PLAYING BALL FOR—
GRAMPS!
REMEMBER OUR AGREEMENT: IF I HIT A HOME RUN, YOU OWE ME TEN DOLLARS!
I WAS GOING TO SAY "FOR THE LOVE OF THE GAME," BUT NEVER MIND.
AND AN ICE CREAM!
Peirce

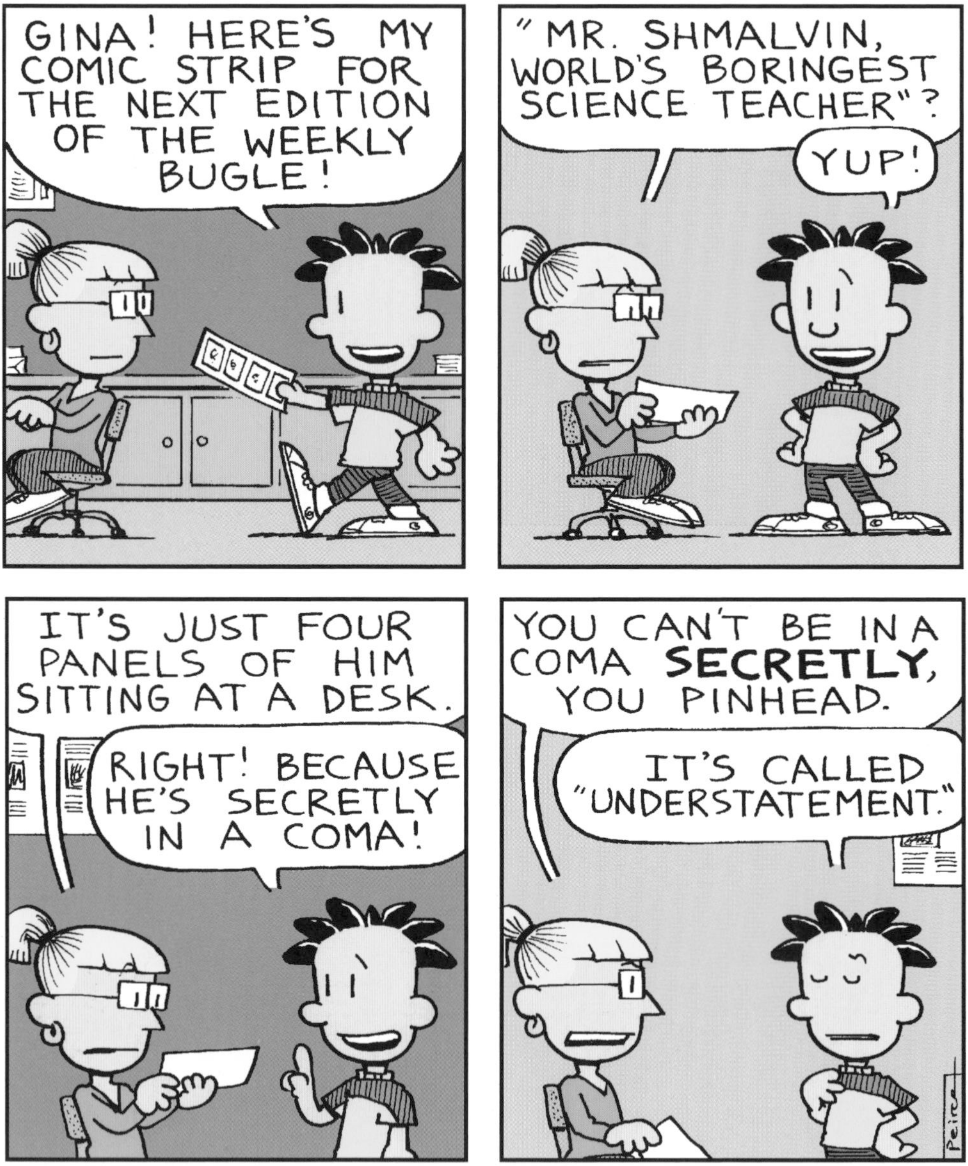
GINA! HERE'S MY COMIC STRIP FOR THE NEXT EDITION OF THE WEEKLY BUGLE!
"MR. SHMALVIN, WORLD'S BORINGEST SCIENCE TEACHER"?
YUP!
IT'S JUST FOUR PANELS OF HIM SITTING AT A DESK.
RIGHT! BECAUSE HE'S SECRETLY IN A COMA!
YOU CAN'T BE IN A COMA **SECRETLY**, YOU PINHEAD.
IT'S CALLED "UNDERSTATEMENT."
Peirce

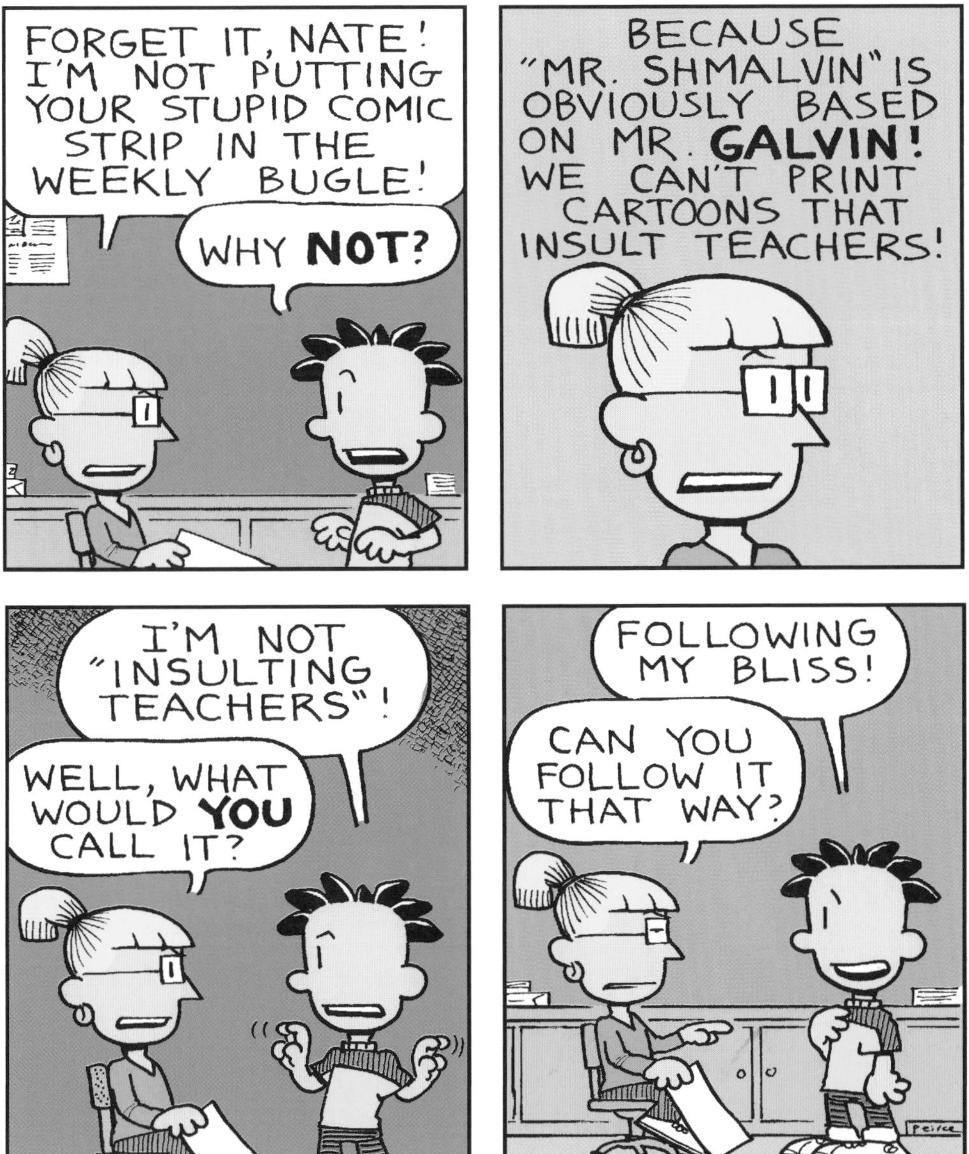
FORGET IT, NATE! I'M NOT PUTTING YOUR STUPID COMIC STRIP IN THE WEEKLY BUGLE!
WHY NOT?
BECAUSE "MR. SHMALVIN" IS OBVIOUSLY BASED ON MR. GALVIN! WE CAN'T PRINT CARTOONS THAT INSULT TEACHERS!
I'M NOT "INSULTING TEACHERS"!
WELL, WHAT WOULD YOU CALL IT?
FOLLOWING MY BLISS!
CAN YOU FOLLOW IT THAT WAY?
PEIRCE

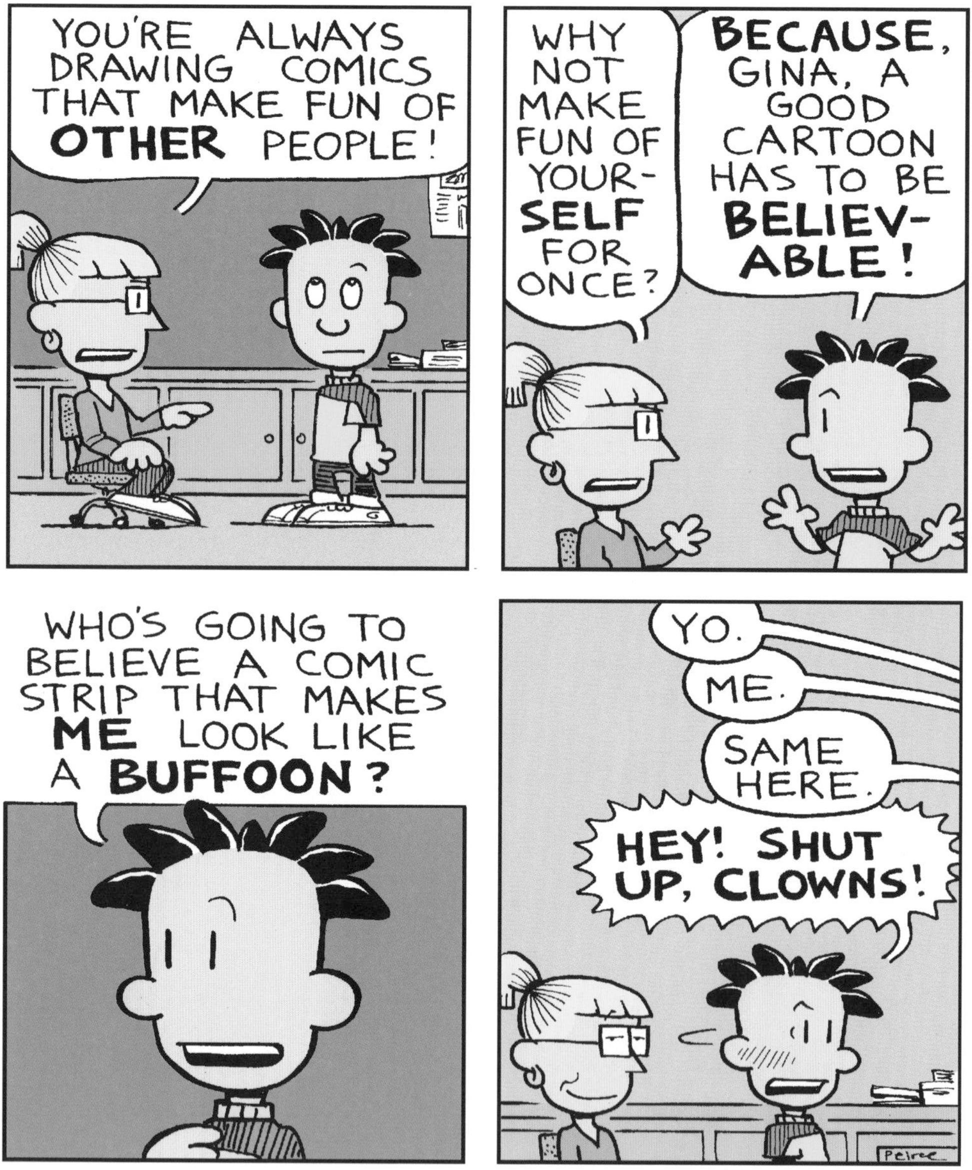
YOU'RE ALWAYS DRAWING COMICS THAT MAKE FUN OF **OTHER** PEOPLE!
WHY NOT MAKE FUN OF YOUR-**SELF** FOR ONCE?
BECAUSE, GINA, A GOOD CARTOON HAS TO BE **BELIEV-ABLE!**
WHO'S GOING TO BELIEVE A COMIC STRIP THAT MAKES **ME** LOOK LIKE A **BUFFOON**?
YO.
ME.
SAME HERE.
HEY! SHUT UP, CLOWNS!
Peirce

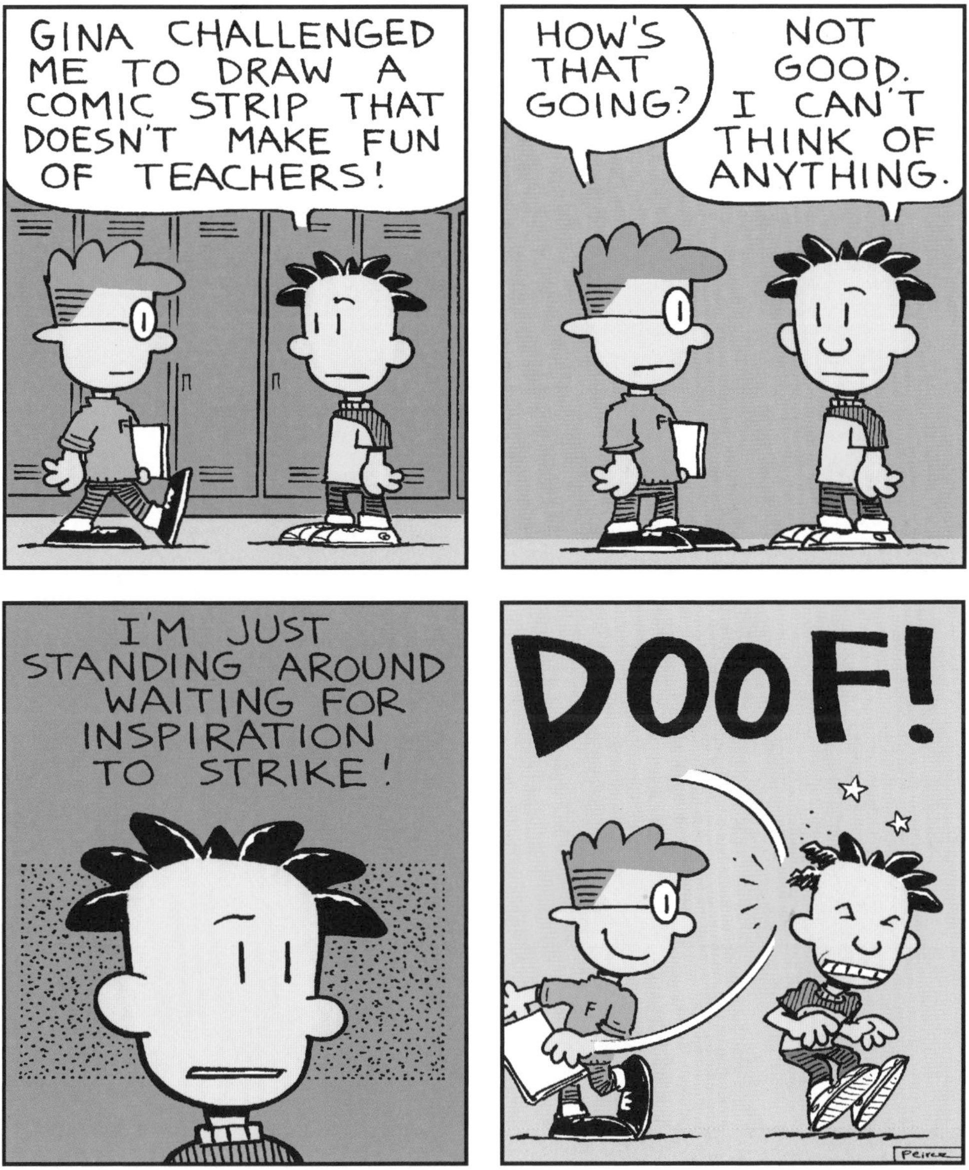
GINA CHALLENGED ME TO DRAW A COMIC STRIP THAT DOESN'T MAKE FUN OF TEACHERS!
HOW'S THAT GOING?
NOT GOOD. I CAN'T THINK OF ANYTHING.
I'M JUST STANDING AROUND WAITING FOR INSPIRATION TO STRIKE!
DOOF!
Peirce

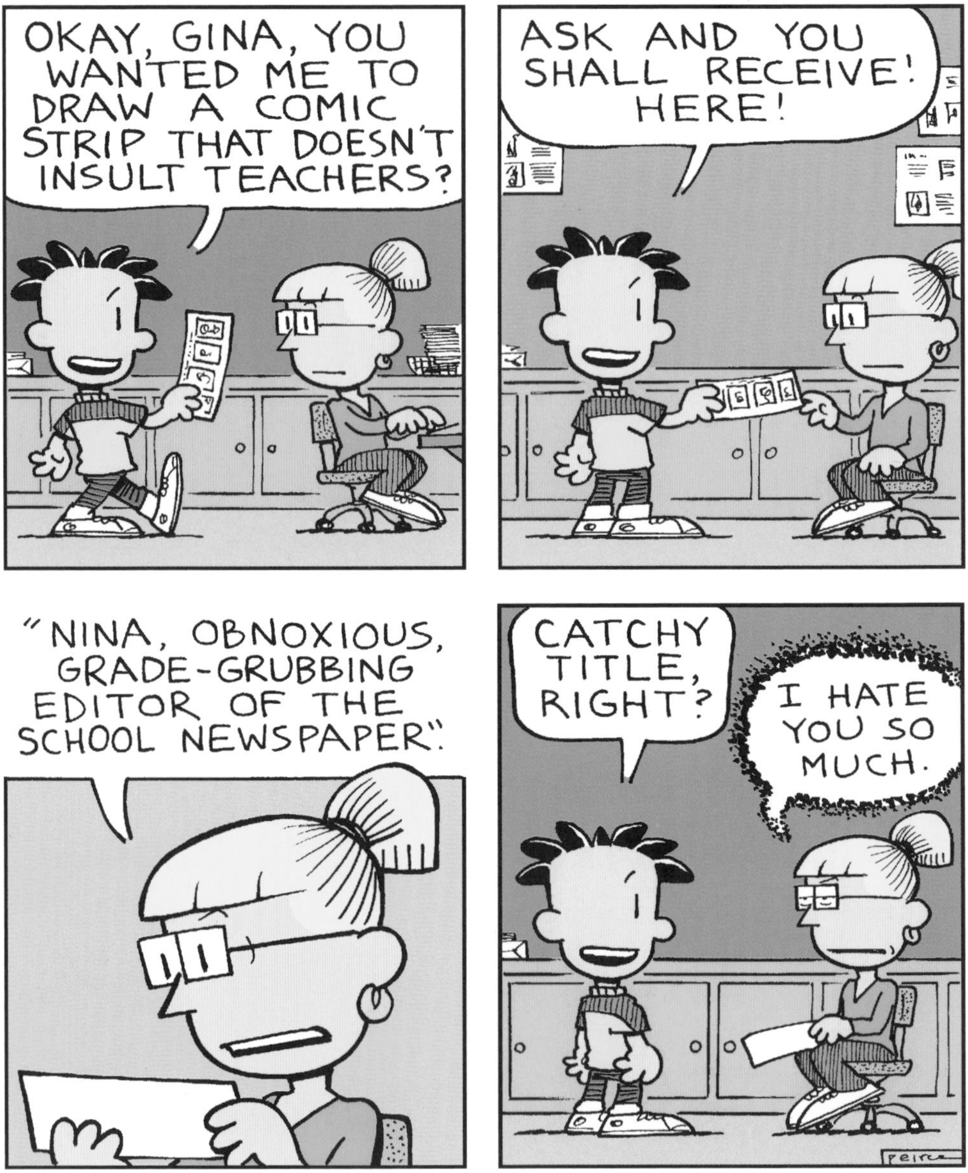
OKAY, GINA, YOU WANTED ME TO DRAW A COMIC STRIP THAT DOESN'T INSULT TEACHERS?
ASK AND YOU SHALL RECEIVE! HERE!
"NINA, OBNOXIOUS, GRADE-GRUBBING EDITOR OF THE SCHOOL NEWSPAPER".
CATCHY TITLE, RIGHT?
I HATE YOU SO MUCH.
peirce

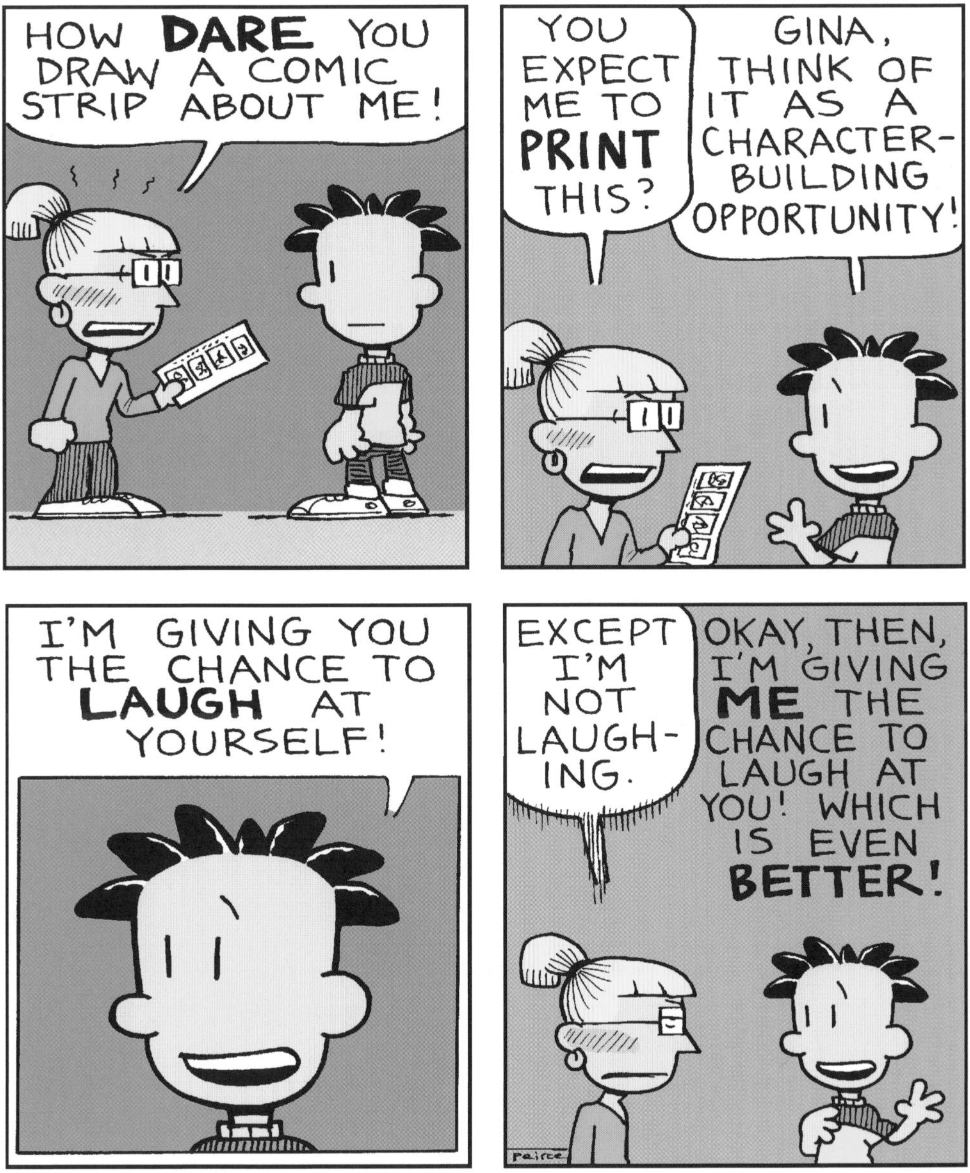
HOW DARE YOU DRAW A COMIC STRIP ABOUT ME!
YOU EXPECT ME TO PRINT THIS?
GINA, THINK OF IT AS A CHARACTER-BUILDING OPPORTUNITY!
I'M GIVING YOU THE CHANCE TO LAUGH AT YOURSELF!
EXCEPT I'M NOT LAUGHING.
OKAY, THEN, I'M GIVING ME THE CHANCE TO LAUGH AT YOU! WHICH IS EVEN BETTER!
Peirce

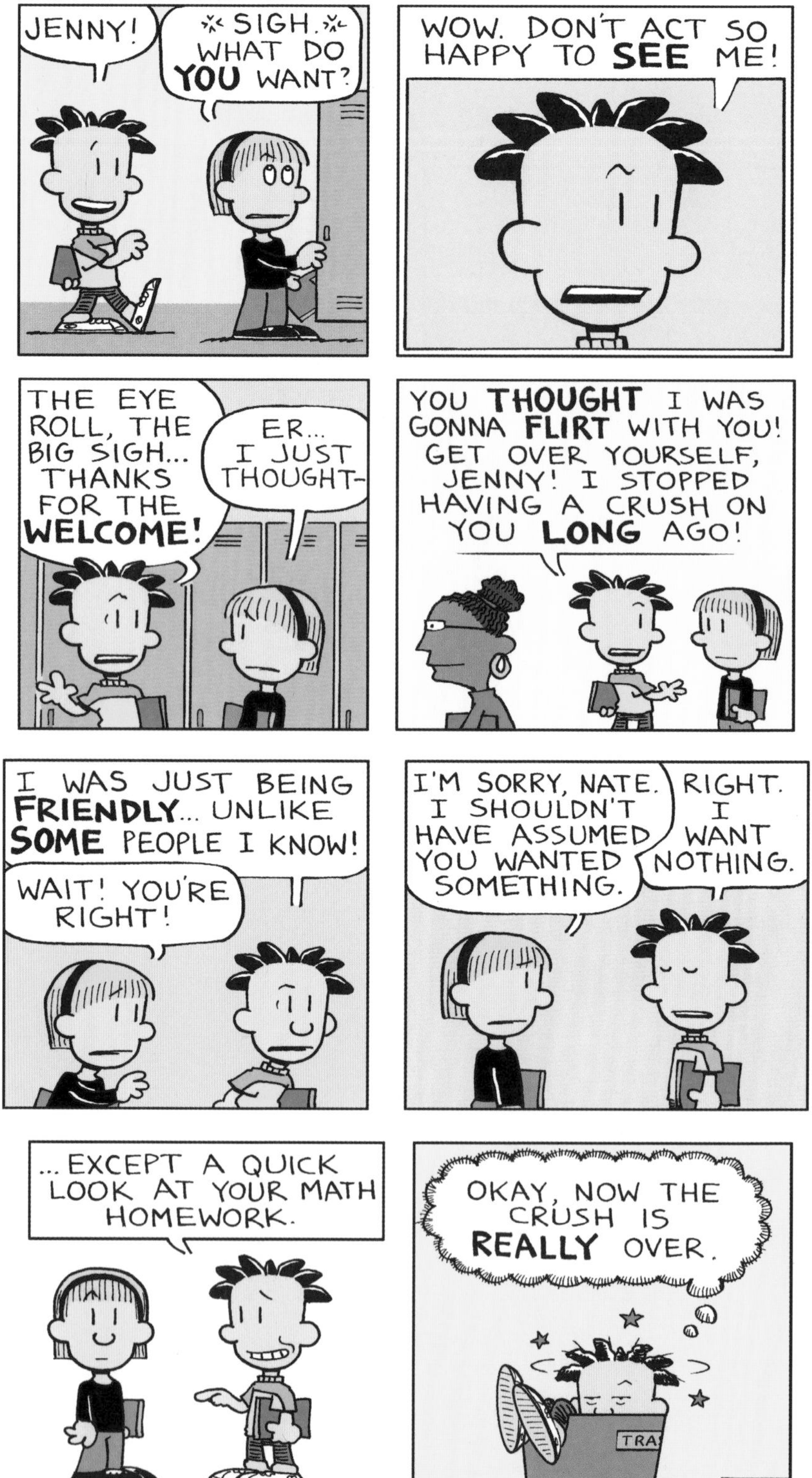
JENNY!
SIGH. WHAT DO YOU WANT?
WOW. DON'T ACT SO HAPPY TO SEE ME!
THE EYE ROLL, THE BIG SIGH... THANKS FOR THE WELCOME!
ER... I JUST THOUGHT-
YOU THOUGHT I WAS GONNA FLIRT WITH YOU! GET OVER YOURSELF, JENNY! I STOPPED HAVING A CRUSH ON YOU LONG AGO!
I WAS JUST BEING FRIENDLY... UNLIKE SOME PEOPLE I KNOW!
WAIT! YOU'RE RIGHT!
I'M SORRY, NATE. I SHOULDN'T HAVE ASSUMED YOU WANTED SOMETHING.
RIGHT. I WANT NOTHING.
... EXCEPT A QUICK LOOK AT YOUR MATH HOMEWORK.
OKAY, NOW THE CRUSH IS REALLY OVER.
TRAS
Peirce

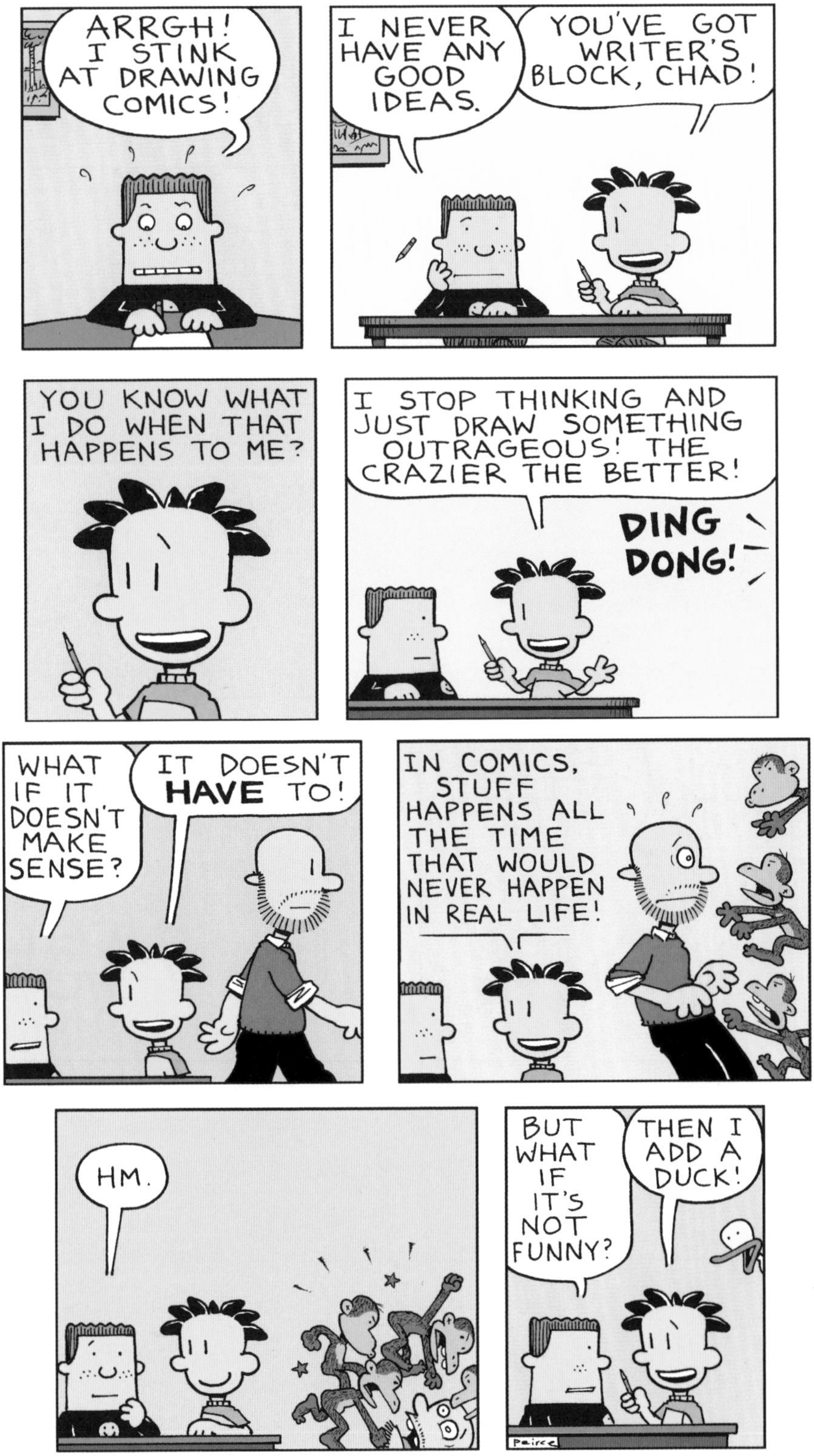
ARRGH! I STINK AT DRAWING COMICS!
I NEVER HAVE ANY GOOD IDEAS.
YOU'VE GOT WRITER'S BLOCK, CHAD!
YOU KNOW WHAT I DO WHEN THAT HAPPENS TO ME?
I STOP THINKING AND JUST DRAW SOMETHING OUTRAGEOUS! THE CRAZIER THE BETTER!
DING DONG!
WHAT IF IT DOESN'T MAKE SENSE?
IT DOESN'T HAVE TO!
IN COMICS, STUFF HAPPENS ALL THE TIME THAT WOULD NEVER HAPPEN IN REAL LIFE!
HM.
BUT WHAT IF IT'S NOT FUNNY?
THEN I ADD A DUCK!
Peirce

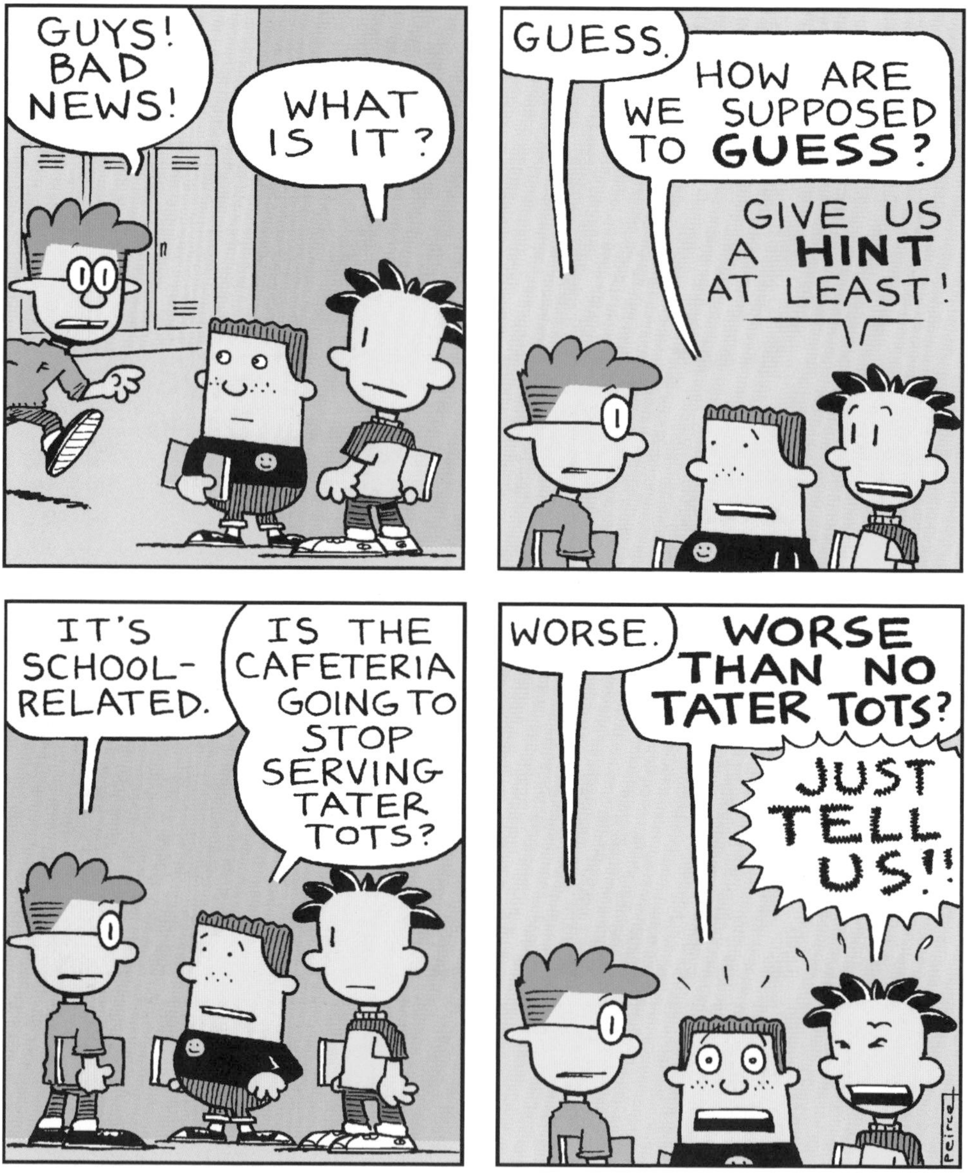
GUYS! BAD NEWS!
WHAT IS IT?
GUESS.
HOW ARE WE SUPPOSED TO **GUESS**?
GIVE US A **HINT** AT LEAST!
IT'S SCHOOL-RELATED.
IS THE CAFETERIA GOING TO STOP SERVING TATER TOTS?
WORSE.
WORSE THAN NO TATER TOTS?
JUST TELL US!!
PEIRCE

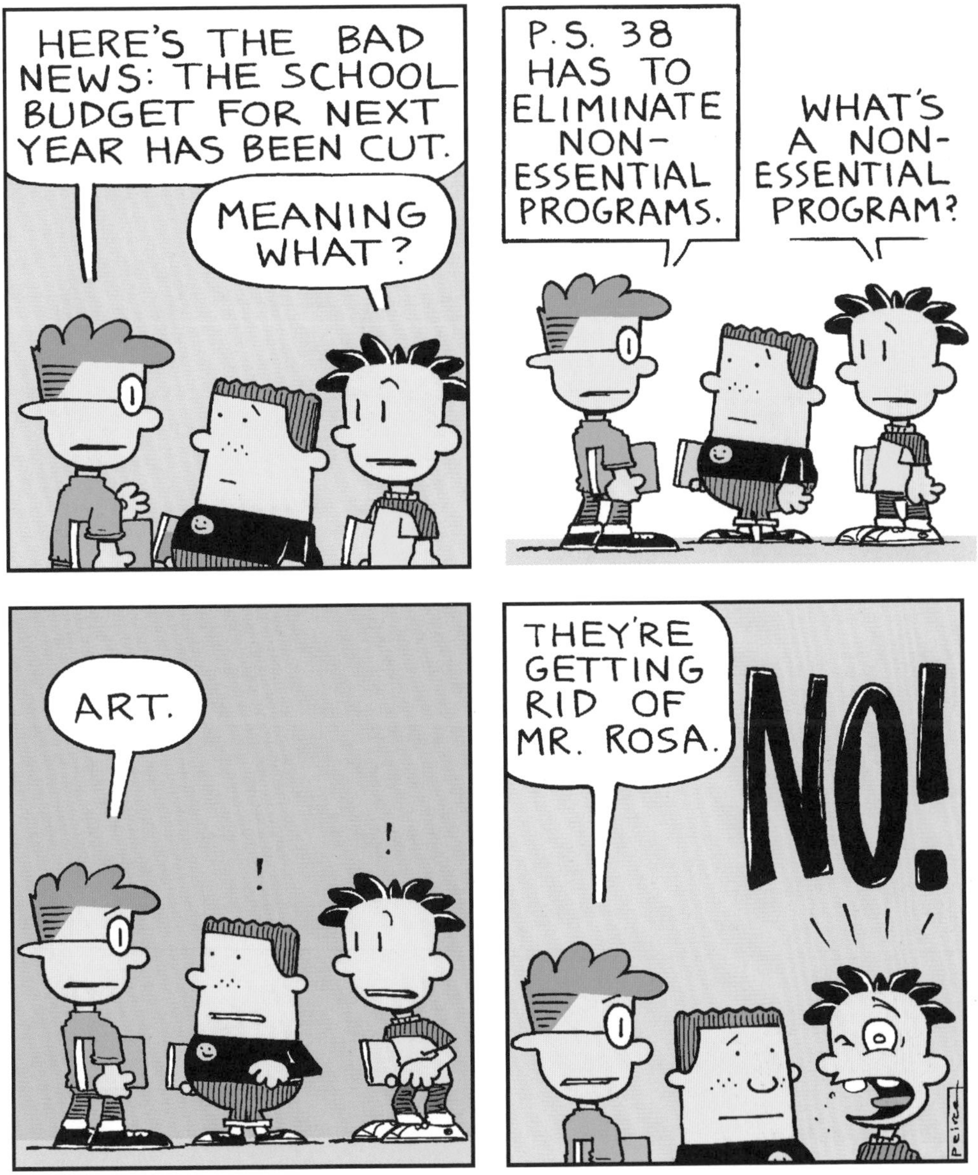
HERE'S THE BAD NEWS: THE SCHOOL BUDGET FOR NEXT YEAR HAS BEEN CUT.
MEANING WHAT?
P.S. 38 HAS TO ELIMINATE NON-ESSENTIAL PROGRAMS.
WHAT'S A NON-ESSENTIAL PROGRAM?
ART.
!
!
THEY'RE GETTING RID OF MR. ROSA.
NO!
peirce

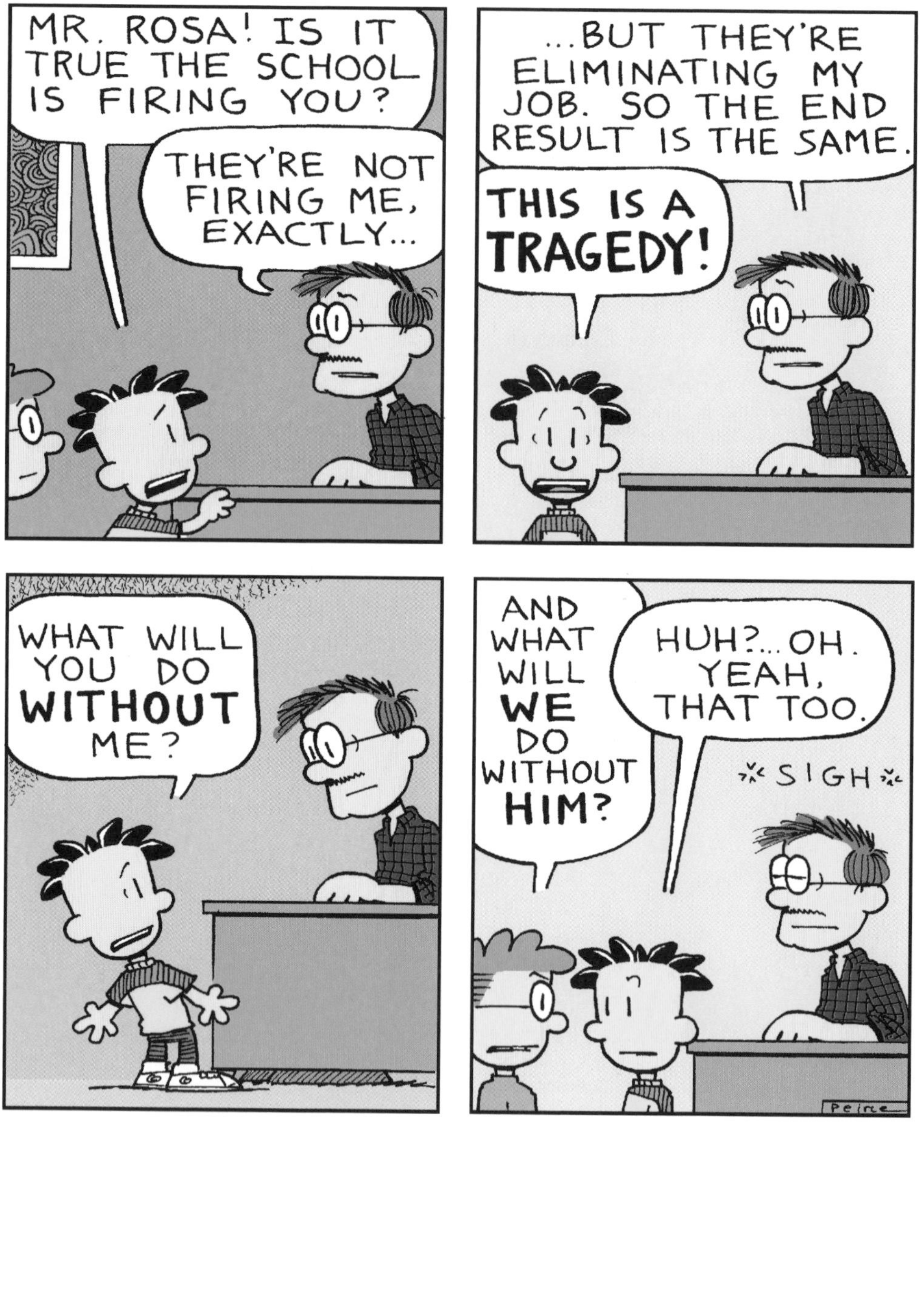
MR. ROSA! IS IT TRUE THE SCHOOL IS FIRING YOU?
THEY'RE NOT FIRING ME, EXACTLY...
...BUT THEY'RE ELIMINATING MY JOB. SO THE END RESULT IS THE SAME.
THIS IS A TRAGEDY!
WHAT WILL YOU DO WITHOUT ME?
AND WHAT WILL WE DO WITHOUT HIM?
HUH?... OH. YEAH, THAT TOO.
SIGH
Peirce

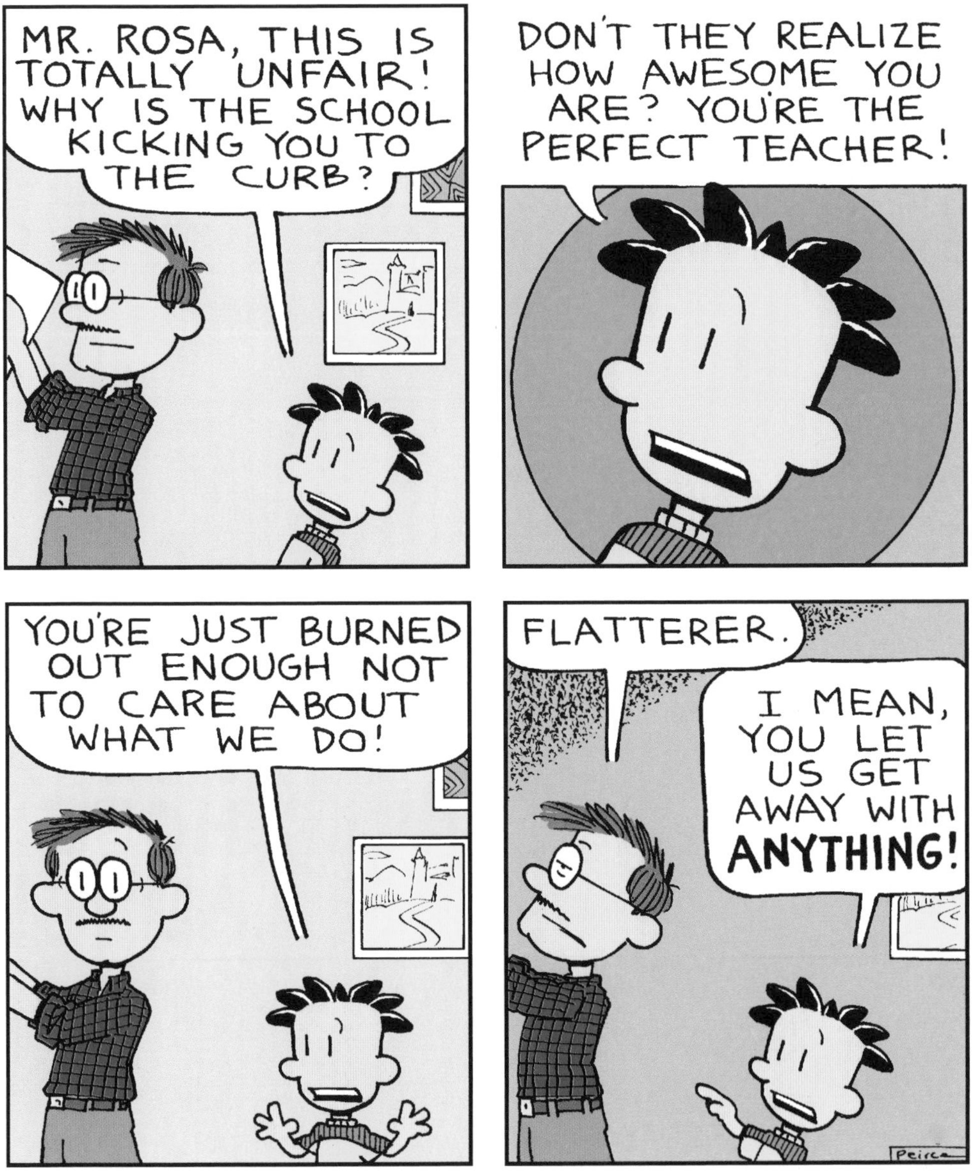
MR. ROSA, THIS IS TOTALLY UNFAIR! WHY IS THE SCHOOL KICKING YOU TO THE CURB?
DON'T THEY REALIZE HOW AWESOME YOU ARE? YOU'RE THE PERFECT TEACHER!
YOU'RE JUST BURNED OUT ENOUGH NOT TO CARE ABOUT WHAT WE DO!
FLATTERER.
I MEAN, YOU LET US GET AWAY WITH **ANYTHING!**
Peirce

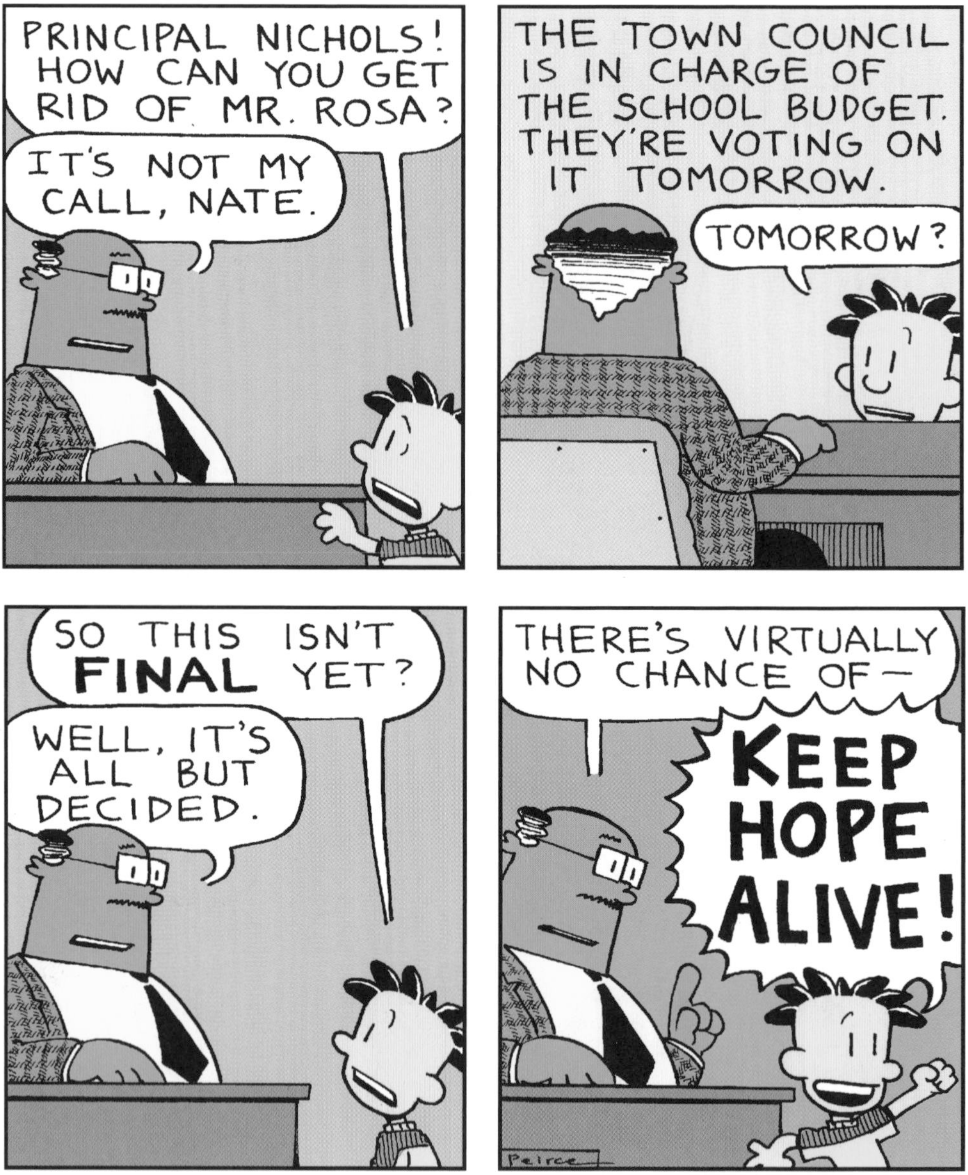
PRINCIPAL NICHOLS! HOW CAN YOU GET RID OF MR. ROSA?
IT'S NOT MY CALL, NATE.
THE TOWN COUNCIL IS IN CHARGE OF THE SCHOOL BUDGET. THEY'RE VOTING ON IT TOMORROW.
TOMORROW?
SO THIS ISN'T **FINAL** YET?
WELL, IT'S ALL BUT DECIDED.
THERE'S VIRTUALLY NO CHANCE OF—
KEEP HOPE ALIVE!
Peirce

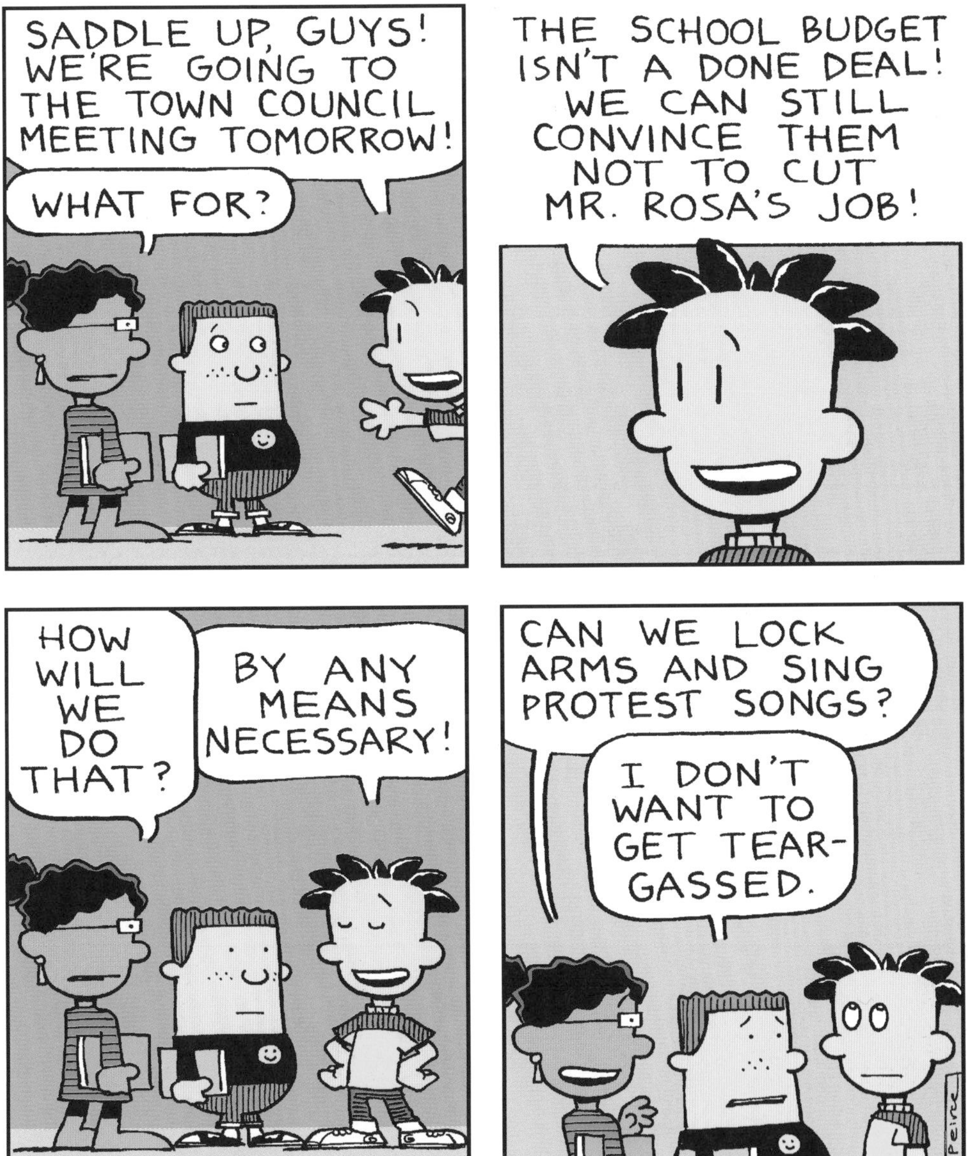
SADDLE UP, GUYS! WE'RE GOING TO THE TOWN COUNCIL MEETING TOMORROW!
WHAT FOR?
THE SCHOOL BUDGET ISN'T A DONE DEAL! WE CAN STILL CONVINCE THEM NOT TO CUT MR. ROSA'S JOB!
HOW WILL WE DO THAT?
BY ANY MEANS NECESSARY!
CAN WE LOCK ARMS AND SING PROTEST SONGS?
I DON'T WANT TO GET TEAR-GASSED.
Peirce

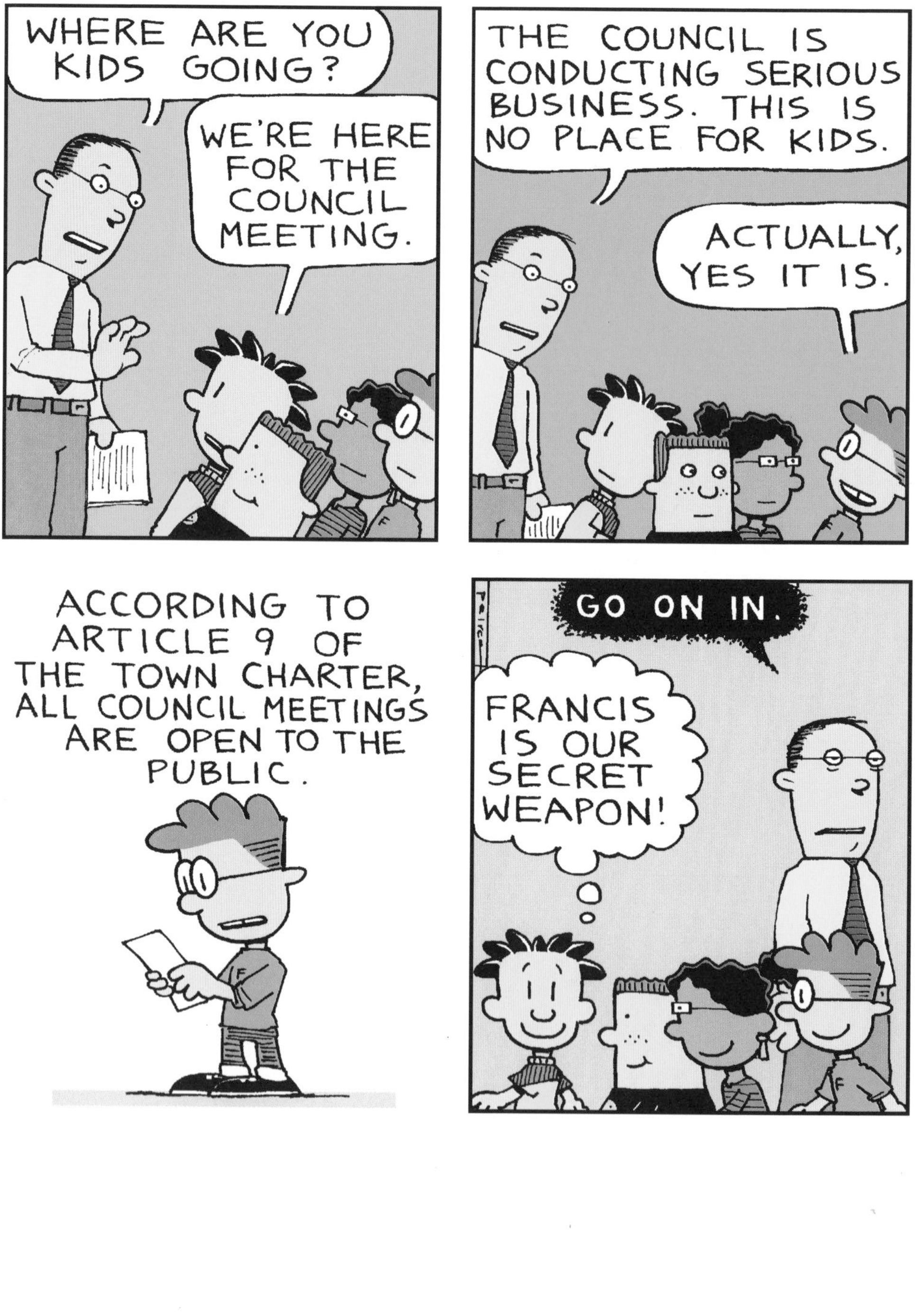
WHERE ARE YOU KIDS GOING?
WE'RE HERE FOR THE COUNCIL MEETING.
THE COUNCIL IS CONDUCTING SERIOUS BUSINESS. THIS IS NO PLACE FOR KIDS.
ACTUALLY, YES IT IS.
ACCORDING TO ARTICLE 9 OF THE TOWN CHARTER, ALL COUNCIL MEETINGS ARE OPEN TO THE PUBLIC.
GO ON IN.
FRANCIS IS OUR SECRET WEAPON!

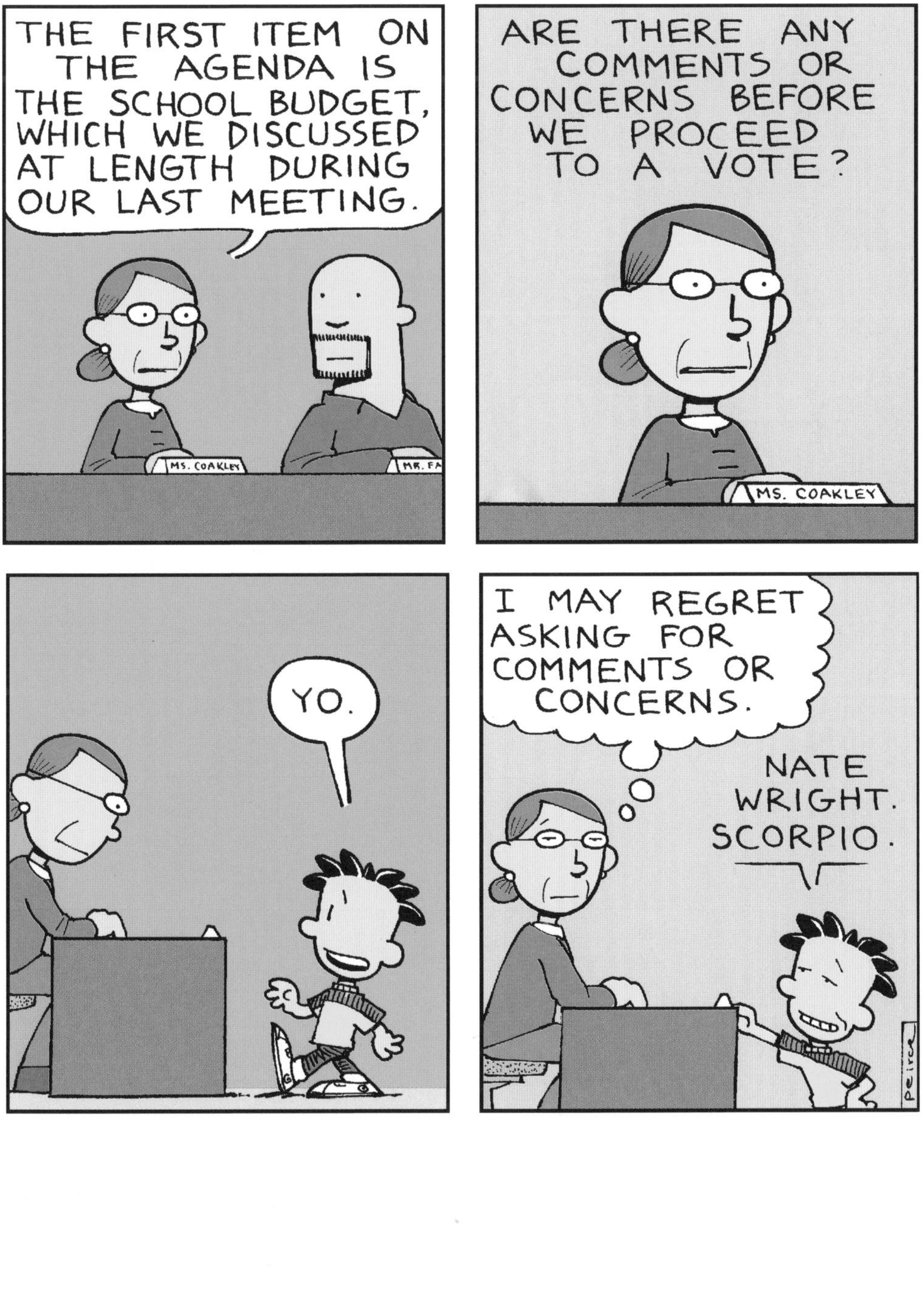
THE FIRST ITEM ON THE AGENDA IS THE SCHOOL BUDGET, WHICH WE DISCUSSED AT LENGTH DURING OUR LAST MEETING.
MS. COAKLEY
MR. FA
ARE THERE ANY COMMENTS OR CONCERNS BEFORE WE PROCEED TO A VOTE?
MS. COAKLEY
YO.
I MAY REGRET ASKING FOR COMMENTS OR CONCERNS.
NATE WRIGHT. SCORPIO.
peirce

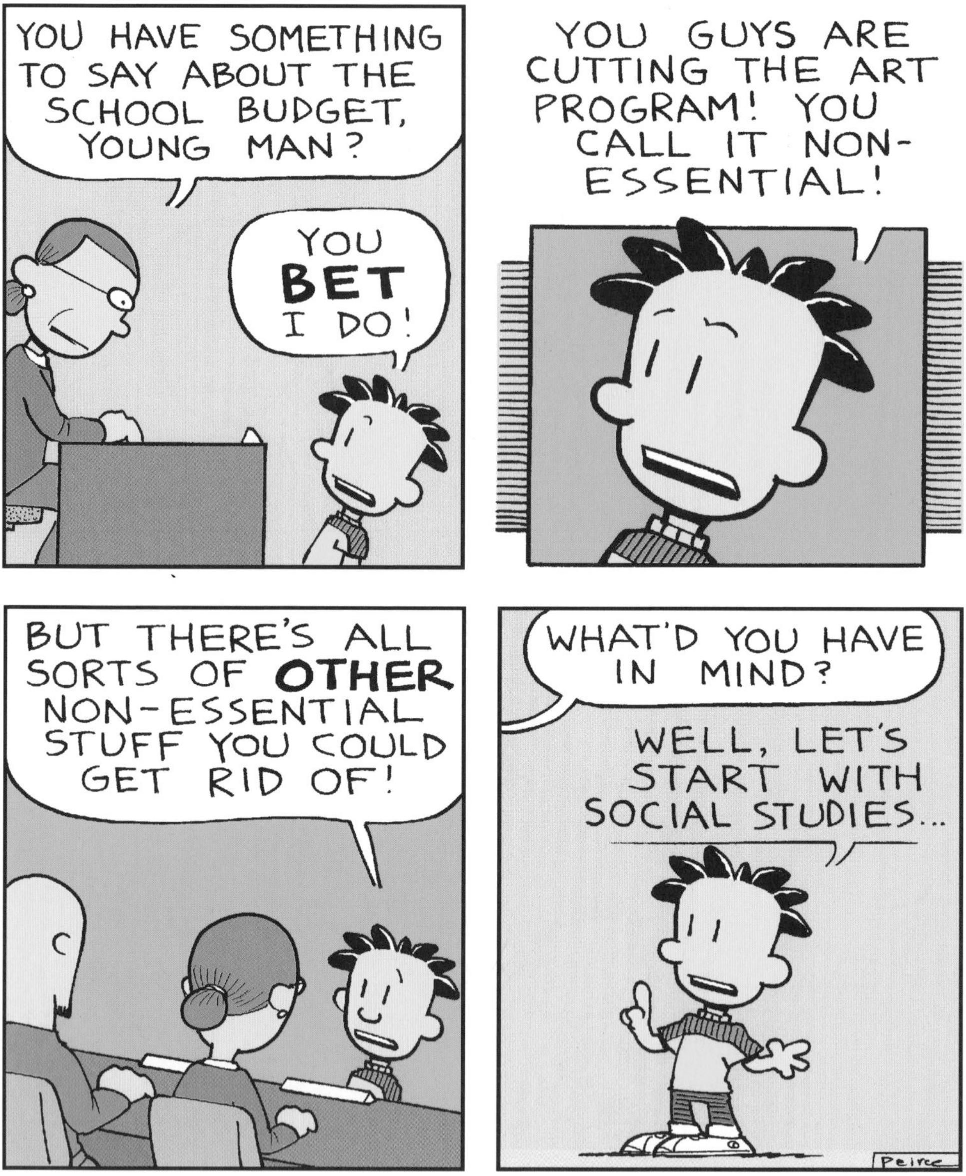
YOU HAVE SOMETHING TO SAY ABOUT THE SCHOOL BUDGET, YOUNG MAN?
YOU **BET** I DO!
YOU GUYS ARE CUTTING THE ART PROGRAM! YOU CALL IT NON-ESSENTIAL!
BUT THERE'S ALL SORTS OF **OTHER** NON-ESSENTIAL STUFF YOU COULD GET RID OF!
WHAT'D YOU HAVE IN MIND?
WELL, LET'S START WITH SOCIAL STUDIES...
Peirce

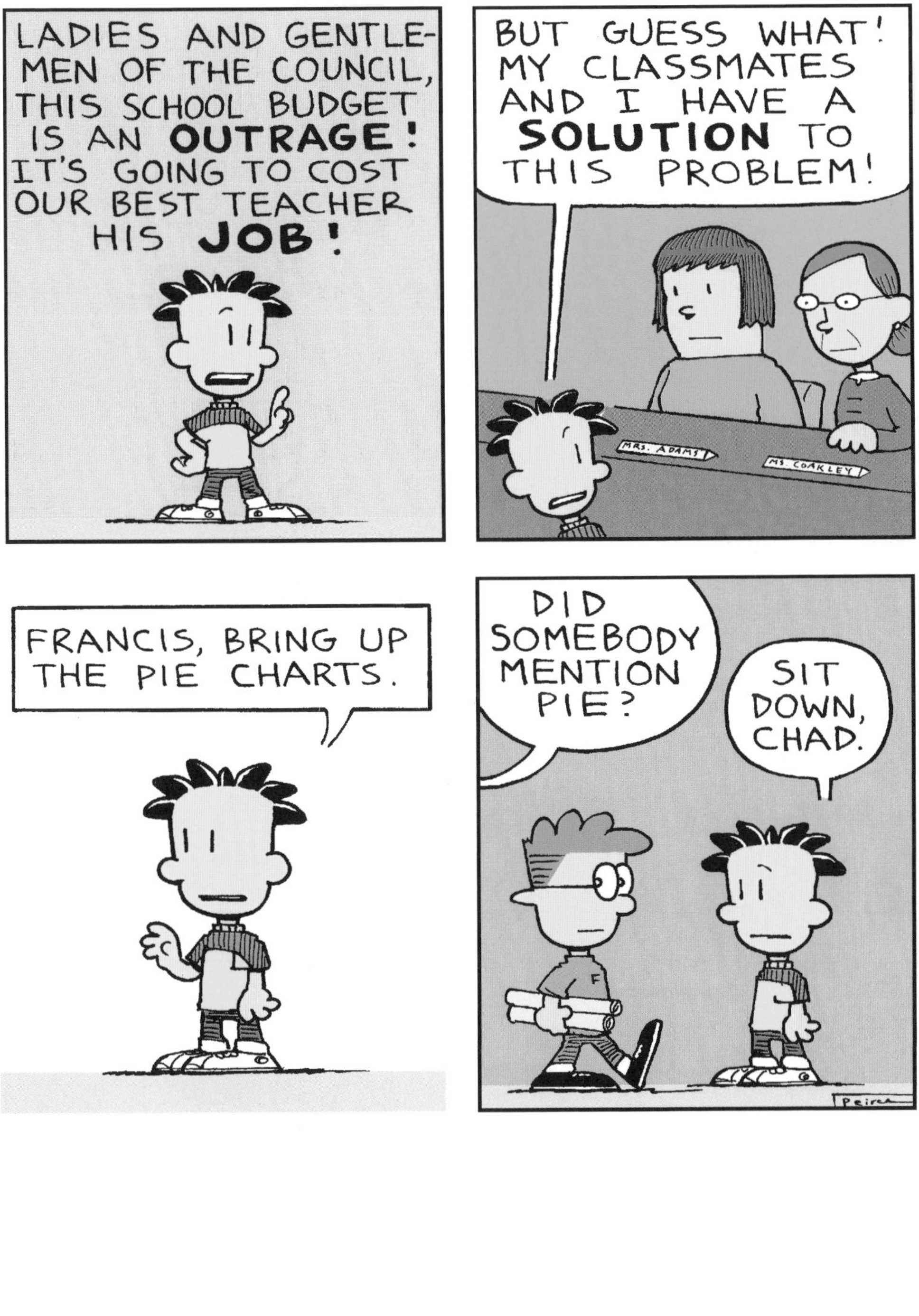
LADIES AND GENTLEMEN OF THE COUNCIL, THIS SCHOOL BUDGET IS AN **OUTRAGE!** IT'S GOING TO COST OUR BEST TEACHER HIS **JOB!**
BUT GUESS WHAT! MY CLASSMATES AND I HAVE A **SOLUTION** TO THIS PROBLEM!
MRS. ADAMS
MS. COAKLEY
FRANCIS, BRING UP THE PIE CHARTS.
DID SOMEBODY MENTION PIE?
SIT DOWN, CHAD.

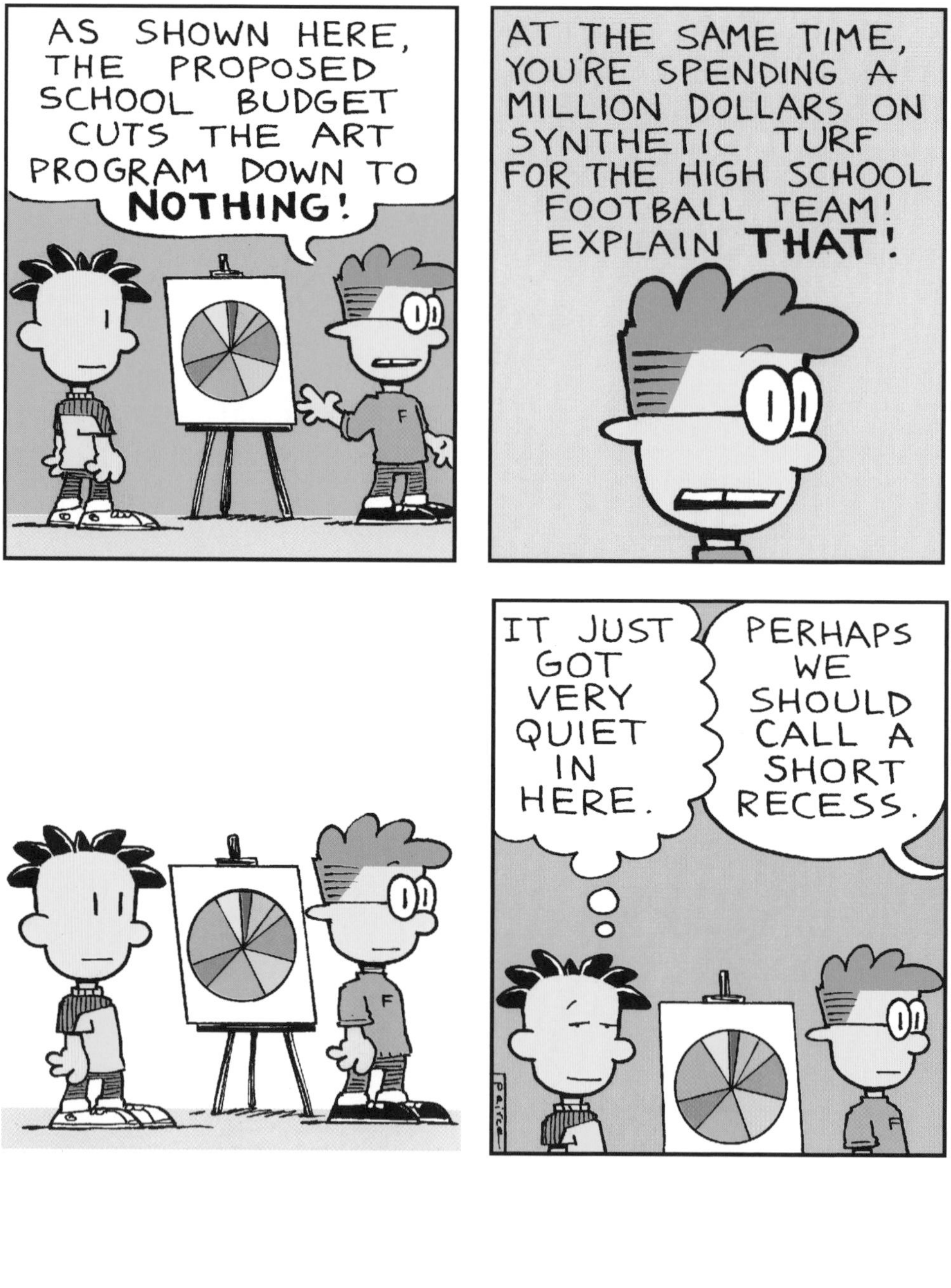

AS SHOWN HERE, THE PROPOSED SCHOOL BUDGET CUTS THE ART PROGRAM DOWN TO **NOTHING**!
AT THE SAME TIME, YOU'RE SPENDING A MILLION DOLLARS ON SYNTHETIC TURF FOR THE HIGH SCHOOL FOOTBALL TEAM! EXPLAIN **THAT**!
IT JUST GOT VERY QUIET IN HERE.
PERHAPS WE SHOULD CALL A SHORT RECESS.

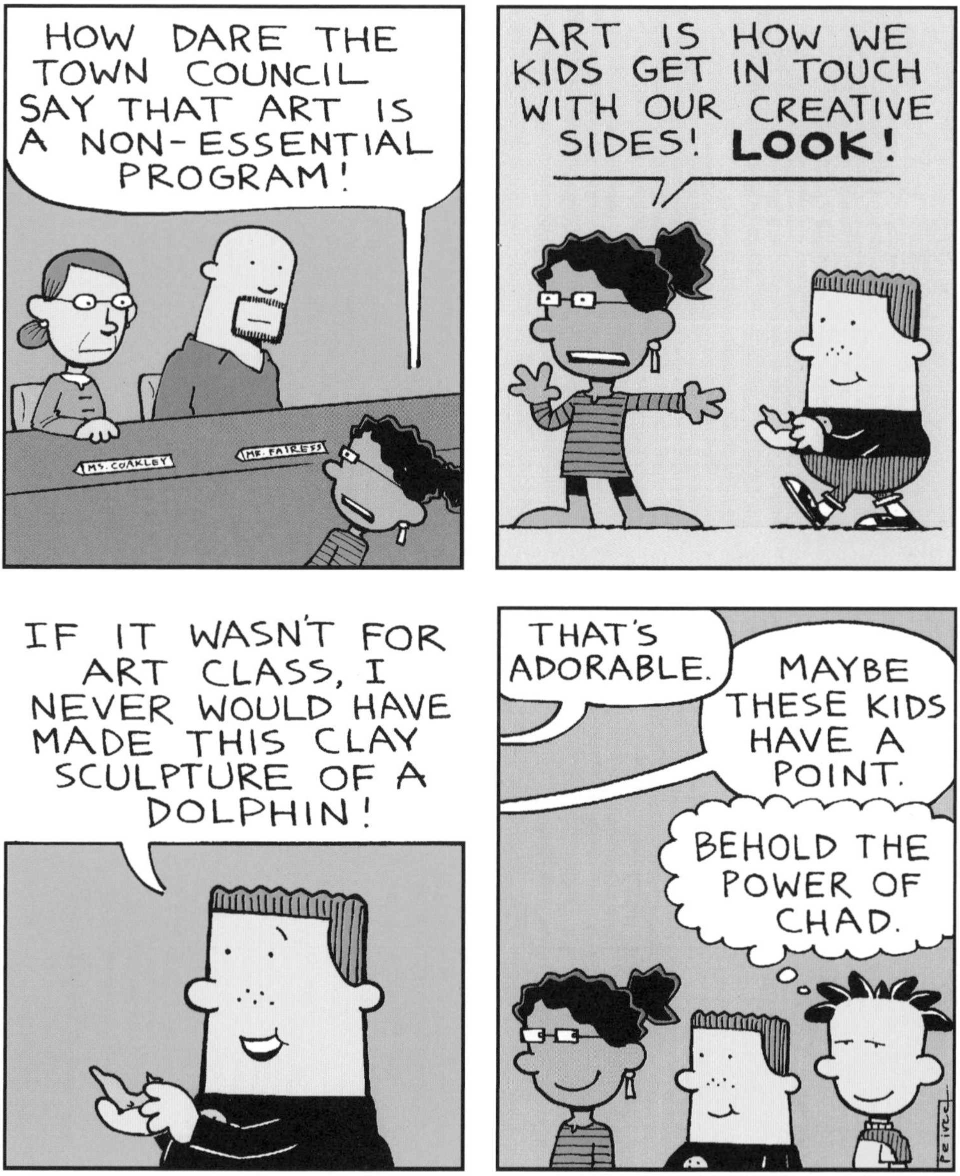
HOW DARE THE TOWN COUNCIL SAY THAT ART IS A NON-ESSENTIAL PROGRAM!
MS. COAKLEY
MR. FAIRESS
ART IS HOW WE KIDS GET IN TOUCH WITH OUR CREATIVE SIDES! LOOK!
IF IT WASN'T FOR ART CLASS, I NEVER WOULD HAVE MADE THIS CLAY SCULPTURE OF A DOLPHIN!
THAT'S ADORABLE.
MAYBE THESE KIDS HAVE A POINT.
BEHOLD THE POWER OF CHAD.

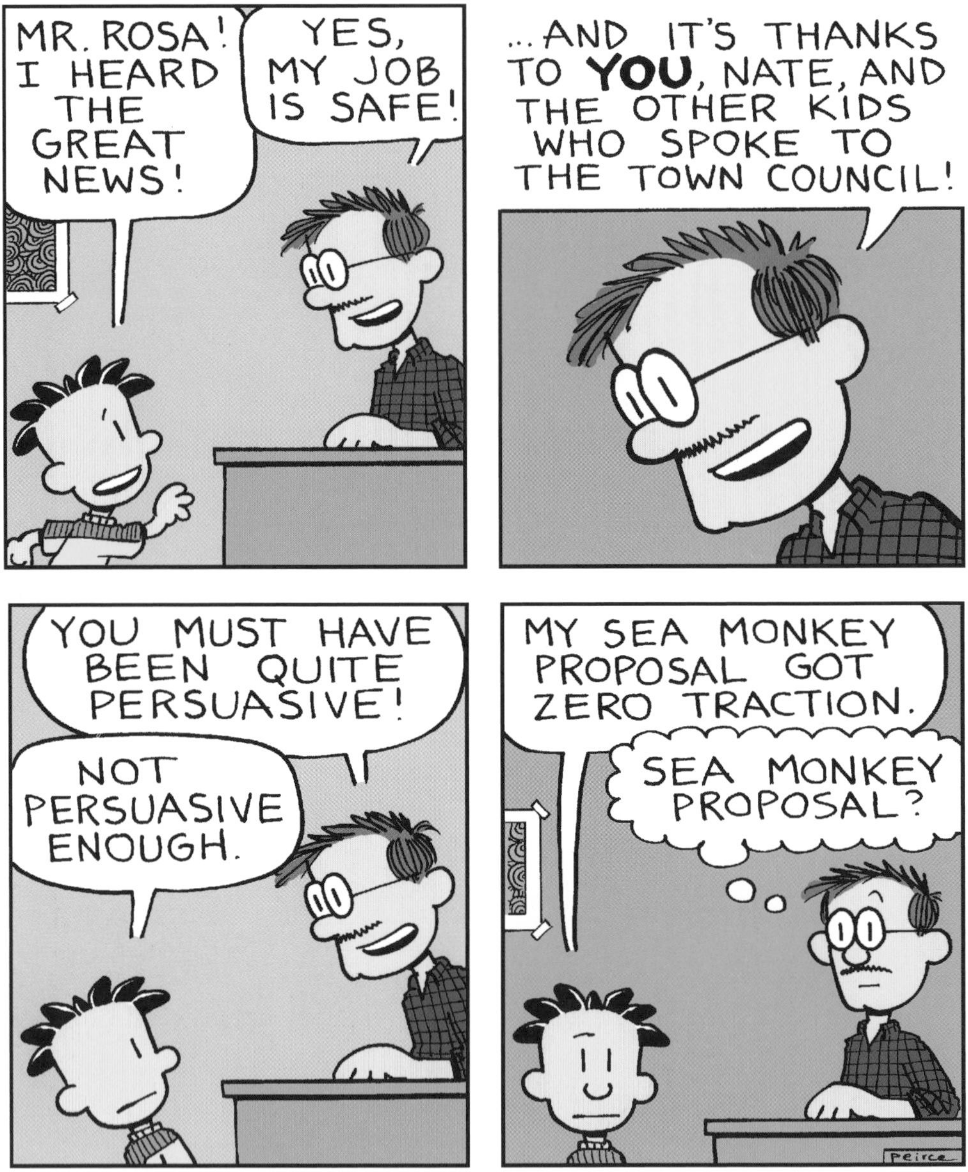
MR. ROSA! I HEARD THE GREAT NEWS!
YES, MY JOB IS SAFE!
...AND IT'S THANKS TO **YOU**, NATE, AND THE OTHER KIDS WHO SPOKE TO THE TOWN COUNCIL!
YOU MUST HAVE BEEN QUITE PERSUASIVE!
NOT PERSUASIVE ENOUGH.
MY SEA MONKEY PROPOSAL GOT ZERO TRACTION.
SEA MONKEY PROPOSAL?
PEIRCE

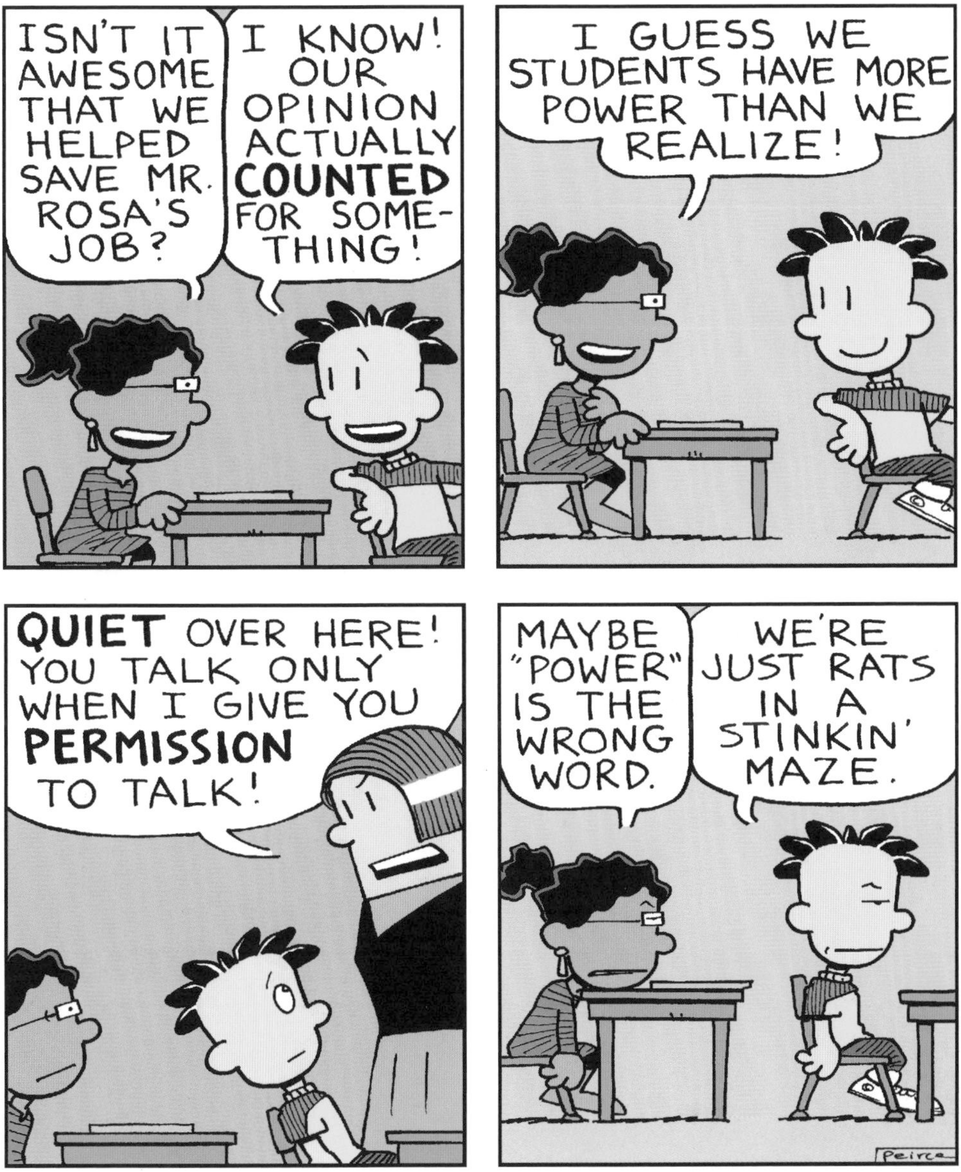
ISN'T IT AWESOME THAT WE HELPED SAVE MR. ROSA'S JOB?
I KNOW! OUR OPINION ACTUALLY **COUNTED** FOR SOME-THING!
I GUESS WE STUDENTS HAVE MORE POWER THAN WE REALIZE!
QUIET OVER HERE! YOU TALK ONLY WHEN I GIVE YOU **PERMISSION** TO TALK!
MAYBE "POWER" IS THE WRONG WORD.
WE'RE JUST RATS IN A STINKIN' MAZE.
Peirce

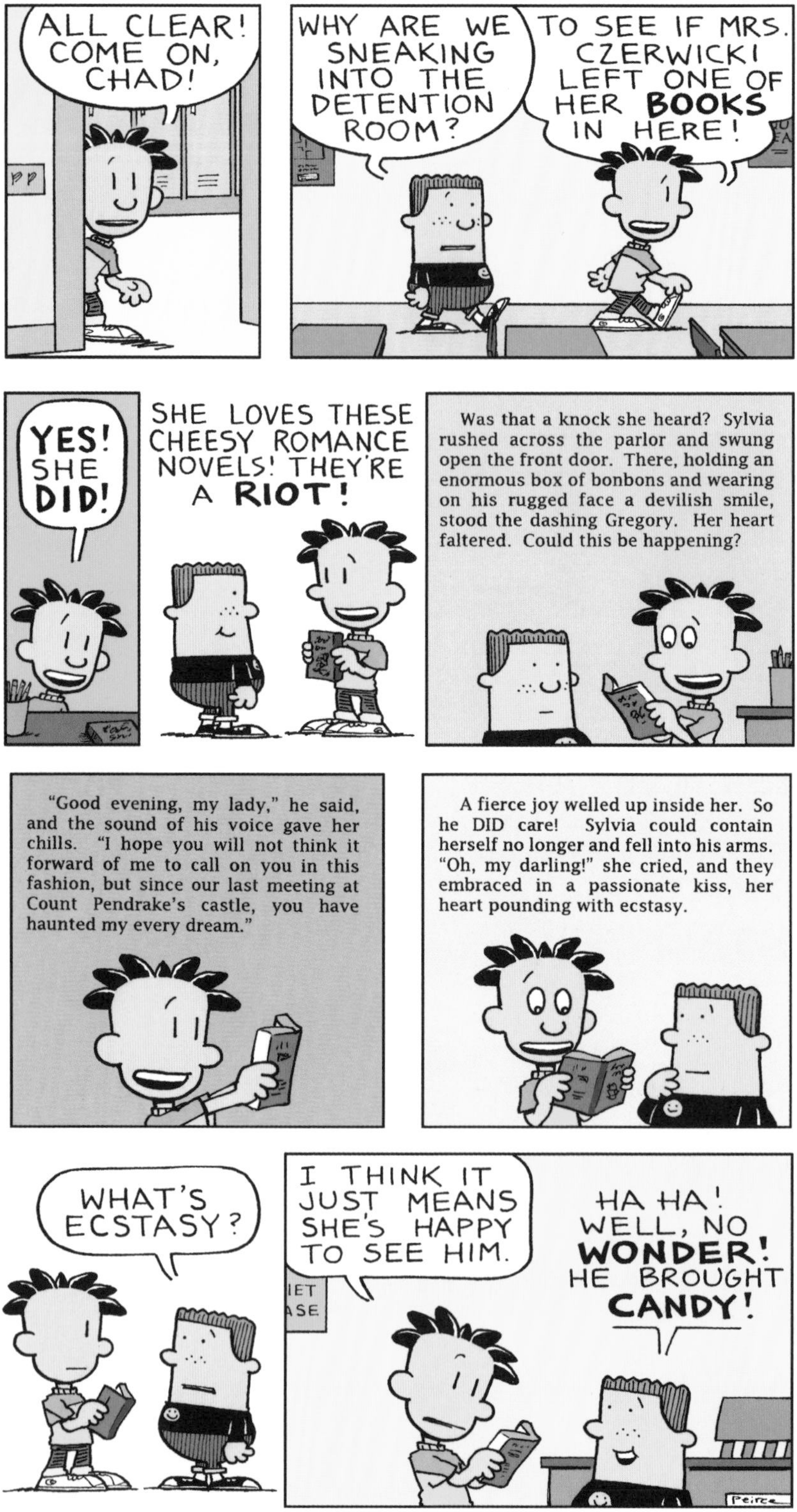
ALL CLEAR! COME ON, CHAD!
WHY ARE WE SNEAKING INTO THE DETENTION ROOM?
TO SEE IF MRS. CZERWICKI LEFT ONE OF HER BOOKS IN HERE!
YES! SHE DID!
SHE LOVES THESE CHEESY ROMANCE NOVELS! THEY'RE A RIOT!
Was that a knock she heard? Sylvia rushed across the parlor and swung open the front door. There, holding an enormous box of bonbons and wearing on his rugged face a devilish smile, stood the dashing Gregory. Her heart faltered. Could this be happening?
"Good evening, my lady," he said, and the sound of his voice gave her chills. "I hope you will not think it forward of me to call on you in this fashion, but since our last meeting at Count Pendrake's castle, you have haunted my every dream."
A fierce joy welled up inside her. So he DID care! Sylvia could contain herself no longer and fell into his arms. "Oh, my darling!" she cried, and they embraced in a passionate kiss, her heart pounding with ecstasy.
WHAT'S ECSTASY?
I THINK IT JUST MEANS SHE'S HAPPY TO SEE HIM.
HA HA! WELL, NO WONDER! HE BROUGHT CANDY!
Peirce

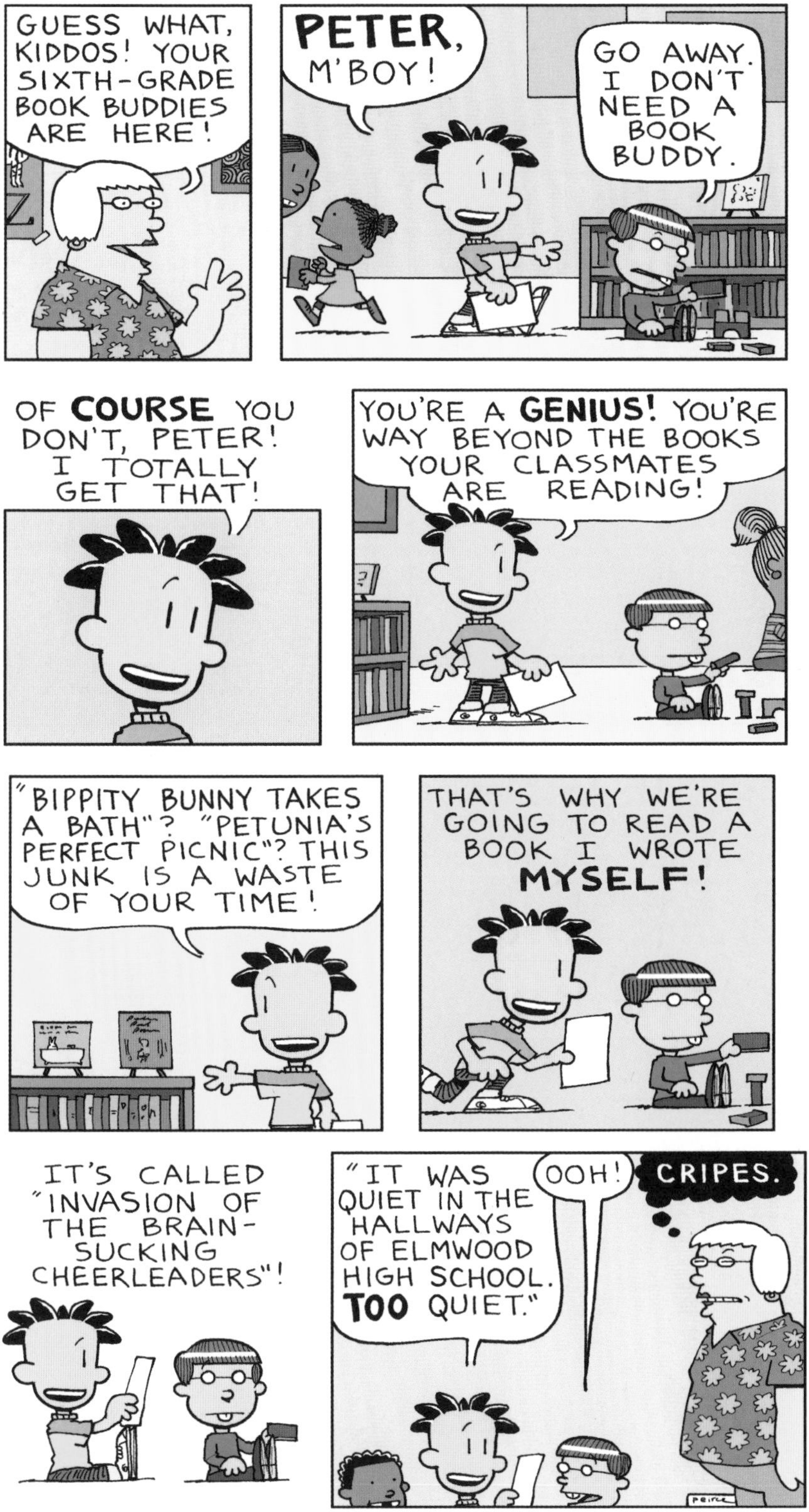
GUESS WHAT, KIDDOS! YOUR SIXTH-GRADE BOOK BUDDIES ARE HERE!
PETER, M'BOY!
GO AWAY. I DON'T NEED A BOOK BUDDY.
OF COURSE YOU DON'T, PETER! I TOTALLY GET THAT!
YOU'RE A GENIUS! YOU'RE WAY BEYOND THE BOOKS YOUR CLASSMATES ARE READING!
"BIPPITY BUNNY TAKES A BATH"? "PETUNIA'S PERFECT PICNIC"? THIS JUNK IS A WASTE OF YOUR TIME!
THAT'S WHY WE'RE GOING TO READ A BOOK I WROTE MYSELF!
IT'S CALLED "INVASION OF THE BRAIN-SUCKING CHEERLEADERS"!
"IT WAS QUIET IN THE HALLWAYS OF ELMWOOD HIGH SCHOOL. TOO QUIET."
OOH!
CRIPES.
PEIRCE

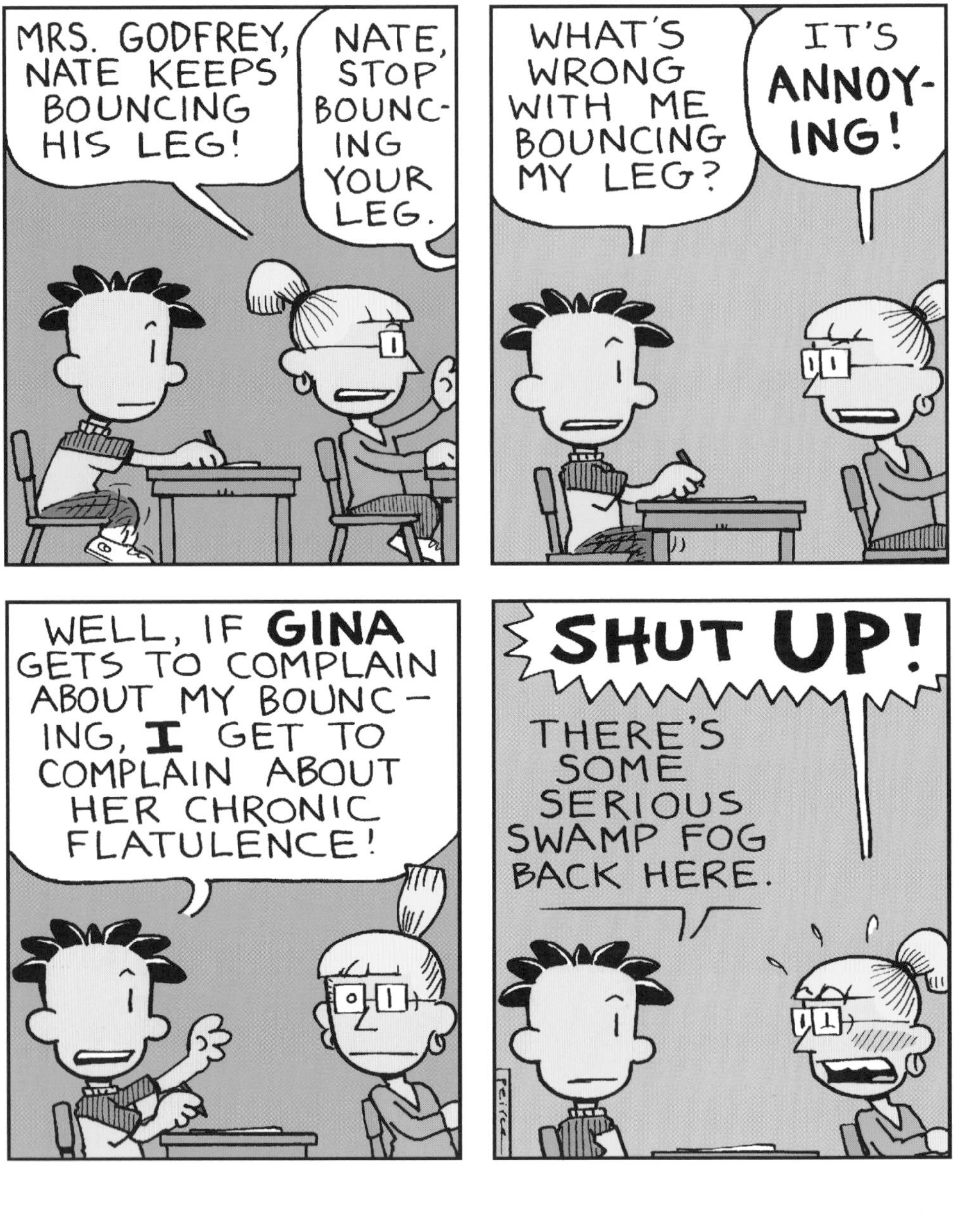
MRS. GODFREY, NATE KEEPS BOUNCING HIS LEG!
NATE, STOP BOUNCING YOUR LEG.
WHAT'S WRONG WITH ME BOUNCING MY LEG?
IT'S **ANNOYING!**
WELL, IF **GINA** GETS TO COMPLAIN ABOUT MY BOUNCING, **I** GET TO COMPLAIN ABOUT HER CHRONIC FLATULENCE!
SHUT UP!
THERE'S SOME SERIOUS SWAMP FOG BACK HERE.
PEIRCE

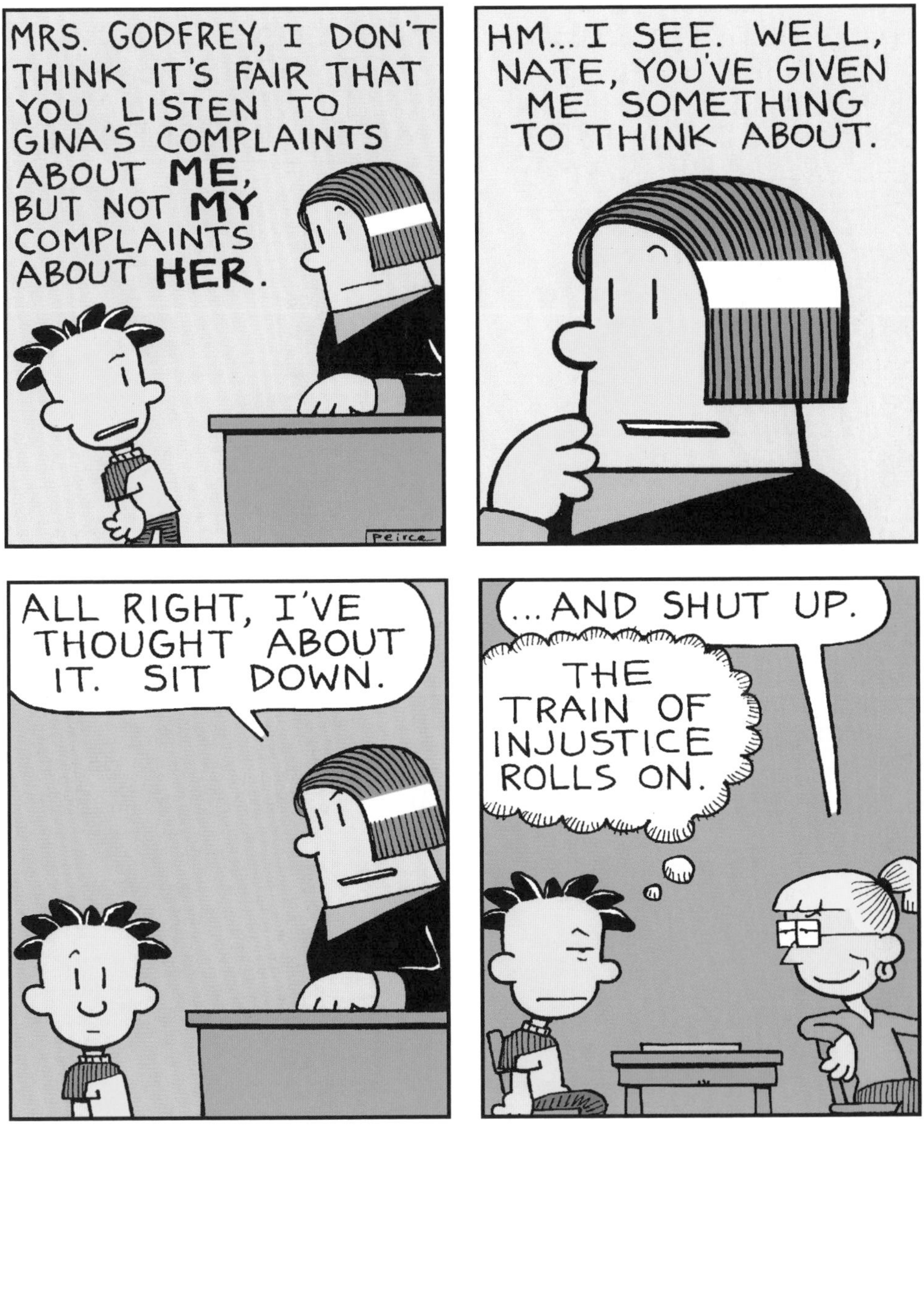
MRS. GODFREY, I DON'T THINK IT'S FAIR THAT YOU LISTEN TO GINA'S COMPLAINTS ABOUT **ME**, BUT NOT **MY** COMPLAINTS ABOUT **HER**.
peirce
HM... I SEE. WELL, NATE, YOU'VE GIVEN ME SOMETHING TO THINK ABOUT.
ALL RIGHT, I'VE THOUGHT ABOUT IT. SIT DOWN.
...AND SHUT UP.
THE TRAIN OF INJUSTICE ROLLS ON.

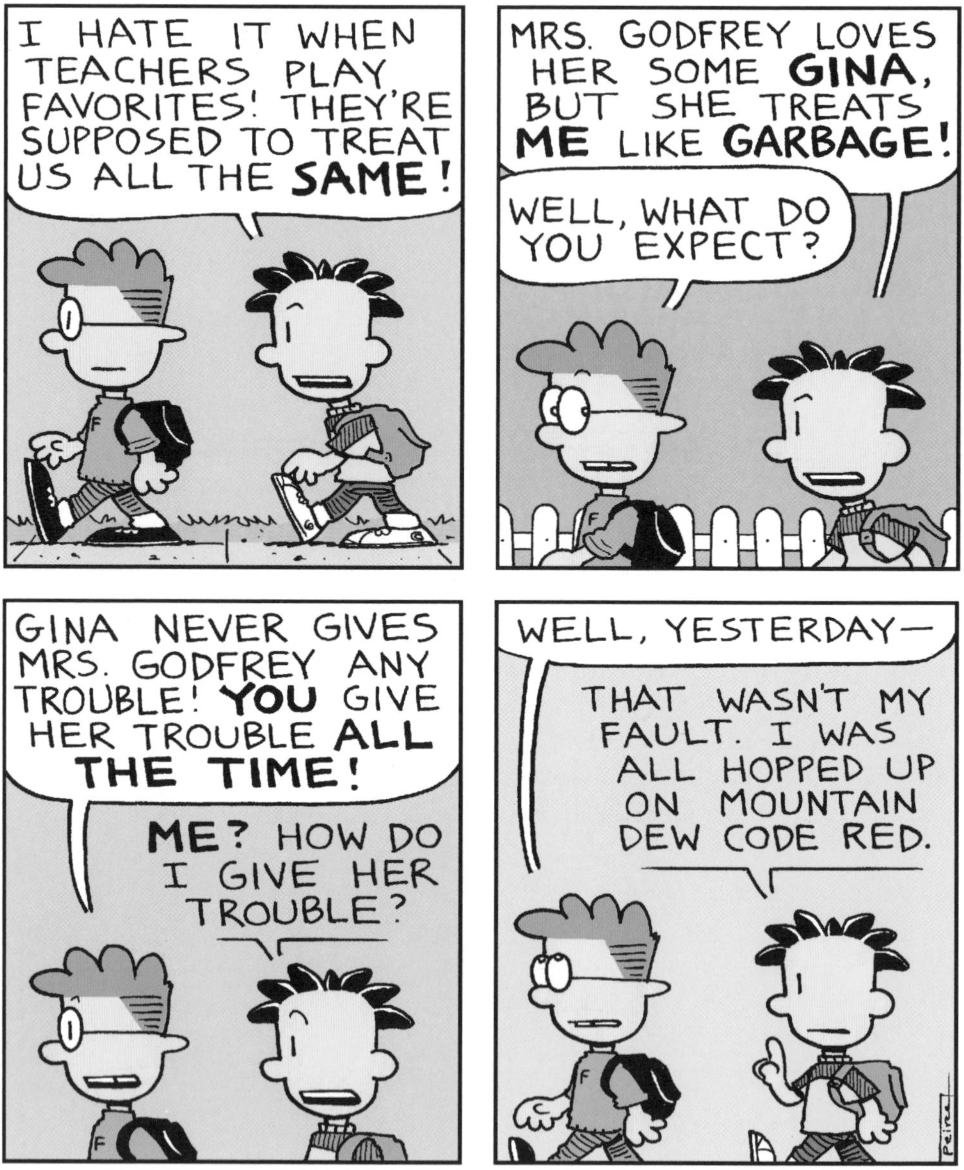
I HATE IT WHEN TEACHERS PLAY FAVORITES! THEY'RE SUPPOSED TO TREAT US ALL THE SAME!
MRS. GODFREY LOVES HER SOME GINA, BUT SHE TREATS ME LIKE GARBAGE!
WELL, WHAT DO YOU EXPECT?
GINA NEVER GIVES MRS. GODFREY ANY TROUBLE! YOU GIVE HER TROUBLE ALL THE TIME!
ME? HOW DO I GIVE HER TROUBLE?
WELL, YESTERDAY—
THAT WASN'T MY FAULT. I WAS ALL HOPPED UP ON MOUNTAIN DEW CODE RED.
Peirce

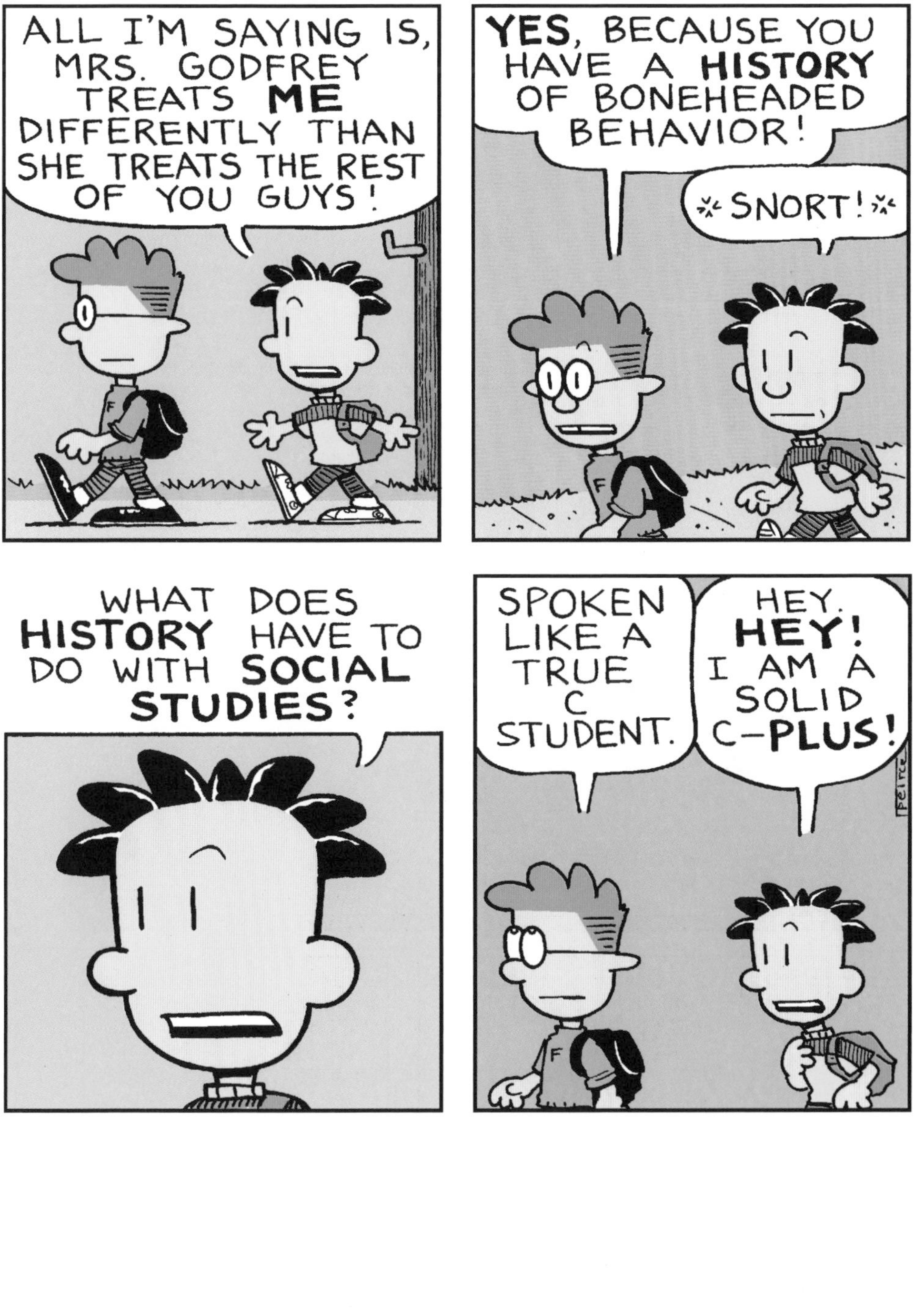
ALL I'M SAYING IS, MRS. GODFREY TREATS ME DIFFERENTLY THAN SHE TREATS THE REST OF YOU GUYS!
YES, BECAUSE YOU HAVE A HISTORY OF BONEHEADED BEHAVIOR!
SNORT!
WHAT DOES HISTORY HAVE TO DO WITH SOCIAL STUDIES?
SPOKEN LIKE A TRUE C STUDENT.
HEY. HEY! I AM A SOLID C-PLUS!
PEIRCE

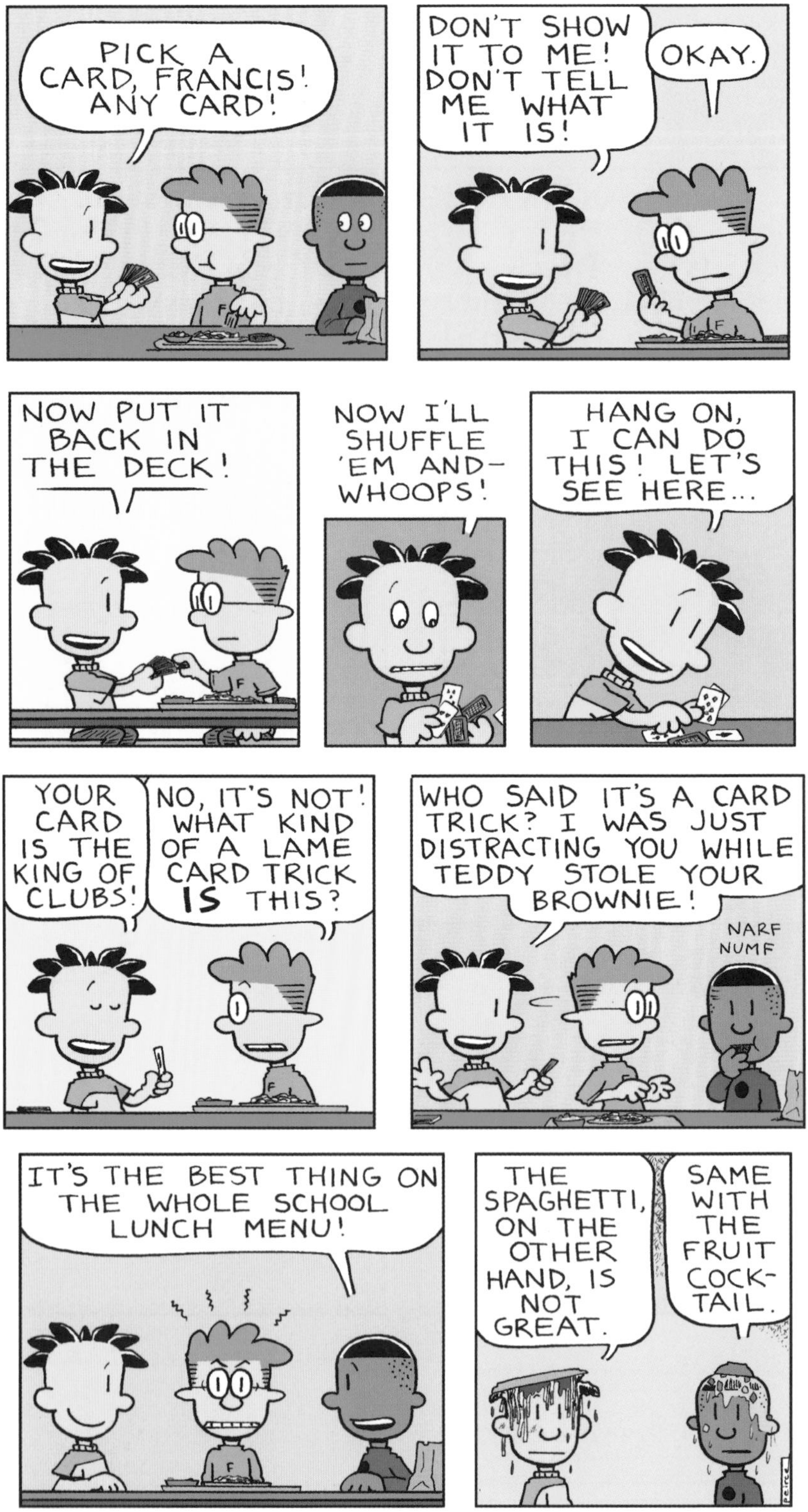
PICK A CARD, FRANCIS! ANY CARD!
DON'T SHOW IT TO ME! DON'T TELL ME WHAT IT IS!
OKAY.
NOW PUT IT BACK IN THE DECK!
NOW I'LL SHUFFLE 'EM AND- WHOOPS!
HANG ON, I CAN DO THIS! LET'S SEE HERE...
YOUR CARD IS THE KING OF CLUBS!
NO, IT'S NOT! WHAT KIND OF A LAME CARD TRICK **IS** THIS?
WHO SAID IT'S A CARD TRICK? I WAS JUST DISTRACTING YOU WHILE TEDDY STOLE YOUR BROWNIE!
NARF NUMF
IT'S THE BEST THING ON THE WHOLE SCHOOL LUNCH MENU!
THE SPAGHETTI, ON THE OTHER HAND, IS NOT GREAT.
SAME WITH THE FRUIT COCK-TAIL.

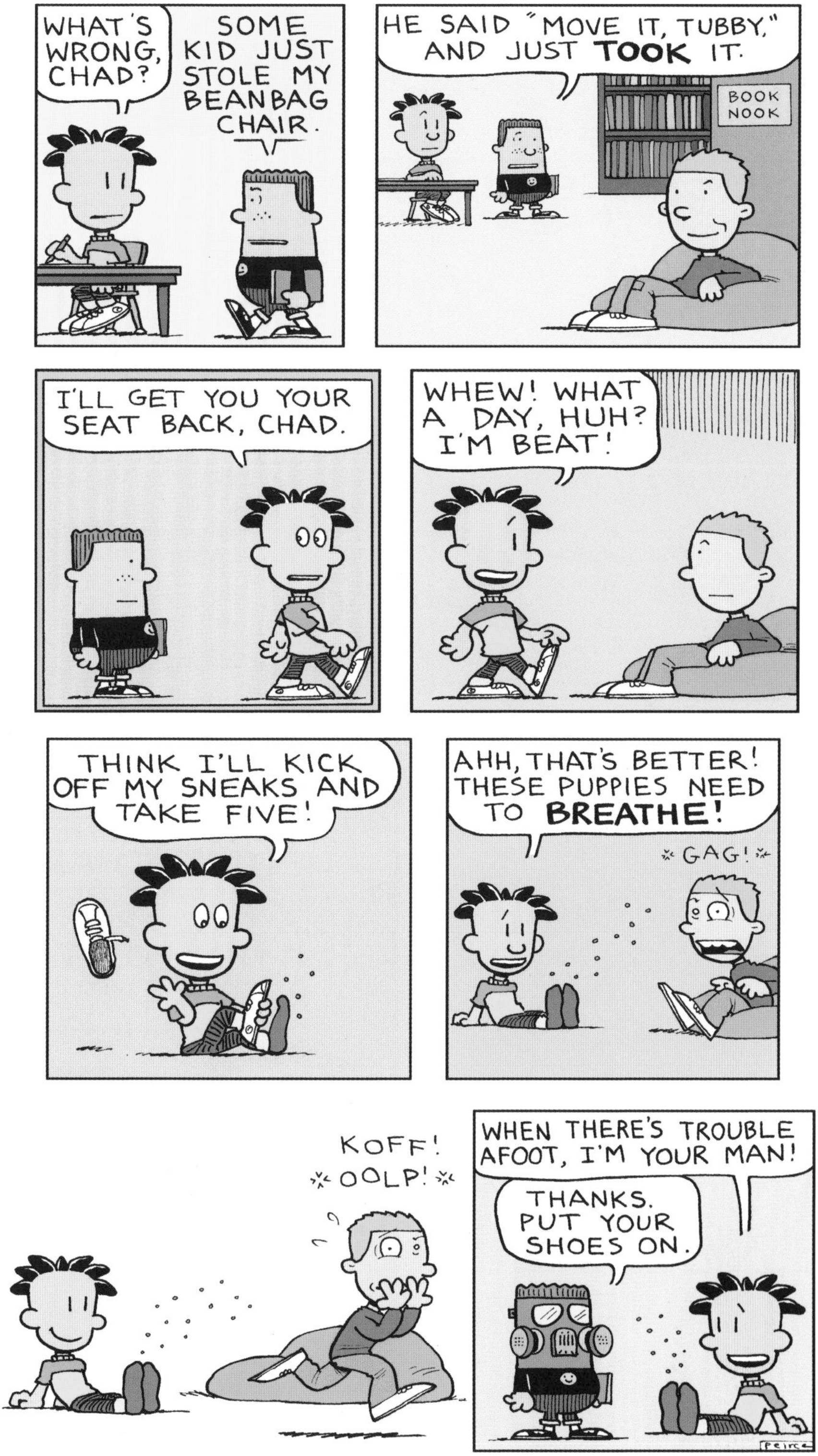
WHAT'S WRONG, CHAD?
SOME KID JUST STOLE MY BEANBAG CHAIR.
HE SAID "MOVE IT, TUBBY," AND JUST **TOOK** IT.
BOOK NOOK
I'LL GET YOU YOUR SEAT BACK, CHAD.
WHEW! WHAT A DAY, HUH? I'M BEAT!
THINK I'LL KICK OFF MY SNEAKS AND TAKE FIVE!
AHH, THAT'S BETTER! THESE PUPPIES NEED TO **BREATHE**!
GAG!
KOFF!
OOLP!
WHEN THERE'S TROUBLE AFOOT, I'M YOUR MAN!
THANKS. PUT YOUR SHOES ON.
Peirce

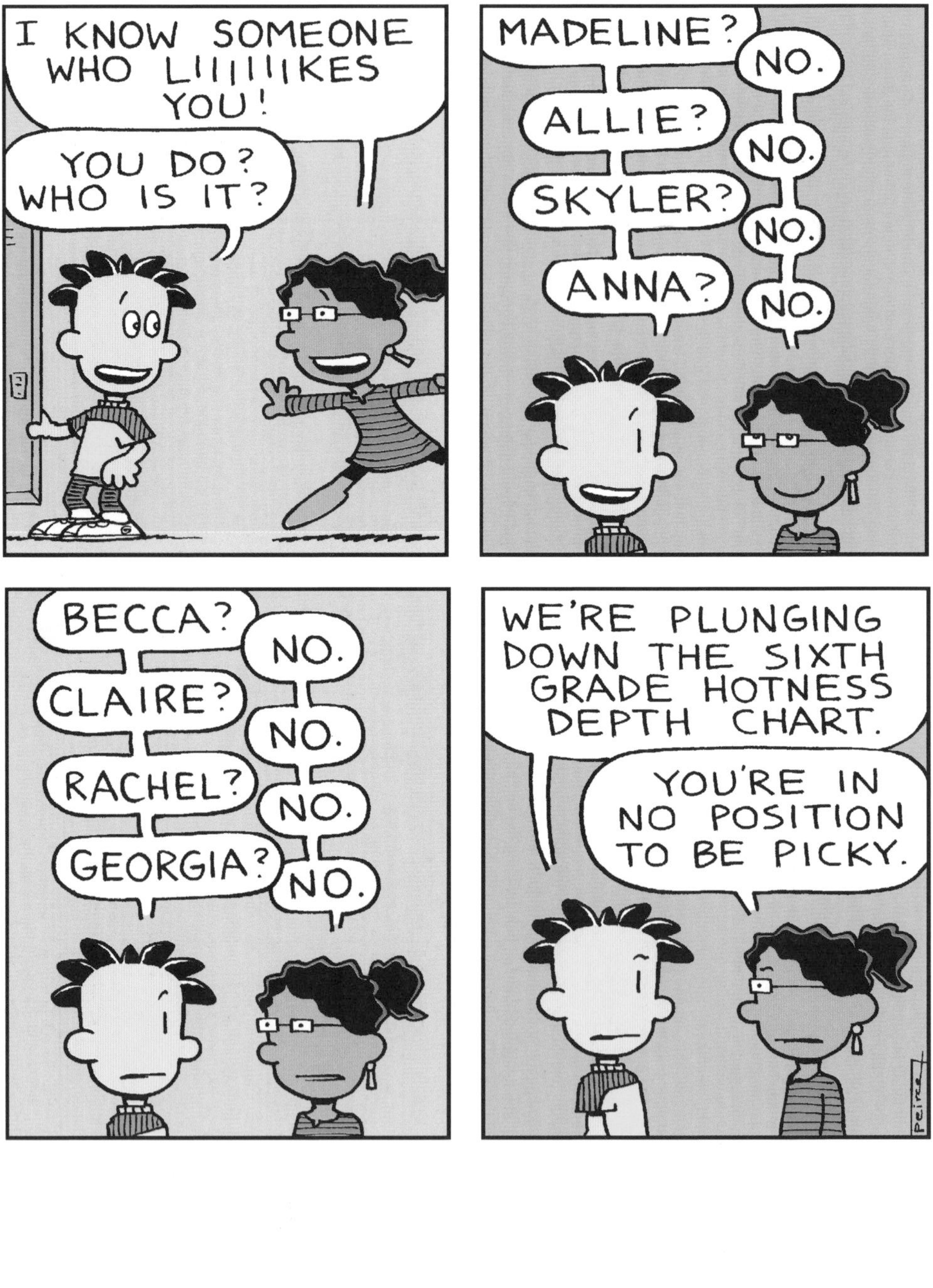
I KNOW SOMEONE WHO LIIIIIIKES YOU!
YOU DO? WHO IS IT?
MADELINE?
NO.
ALLIE?
NO.
SKYLER?
NO.
ANNA?
NO.
BECCA?
NO.
CLAIRE?
NO.
RACHEL?
NO.
GEORGIA?
NO.
WE'RE PLUNGING DOWN THE SIXTH GRADE HOTNESS DEPTH CHART.
YOU'RE IN NO POSITION TO BE PICKY.
Peirce

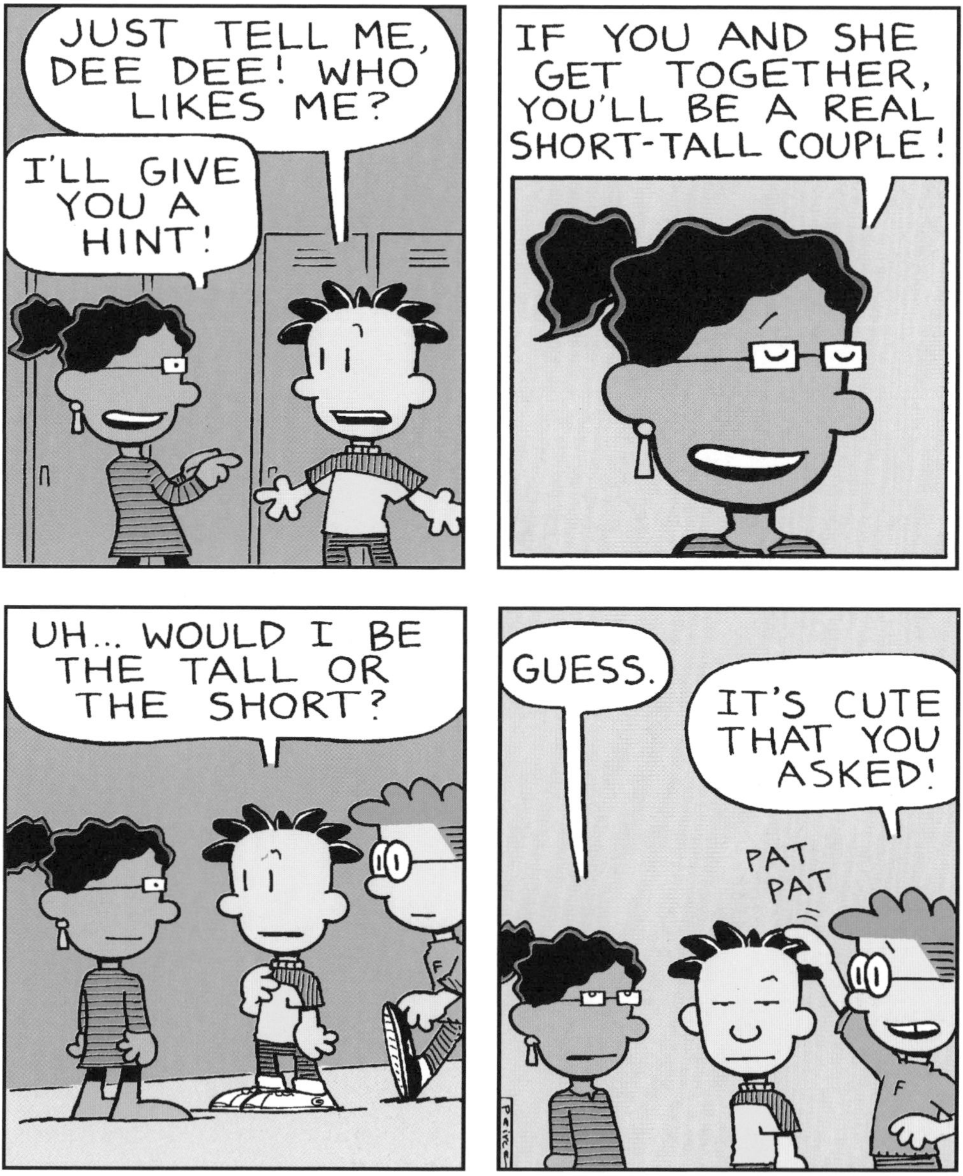
JUST TELL ME, DEE DEE! WHO LIKES ME?
I'LL GIVE YOU A HINT!
IF YOU AND SHE GET TOGETHER, YOU'LL BE A REAL SHORT-TALL COUPLE!
UH... WOULD I BE THE TALL OR THE SHORT?
GUESS.
IT'S CUTE THAT YOU ASKED!
PAT PAT

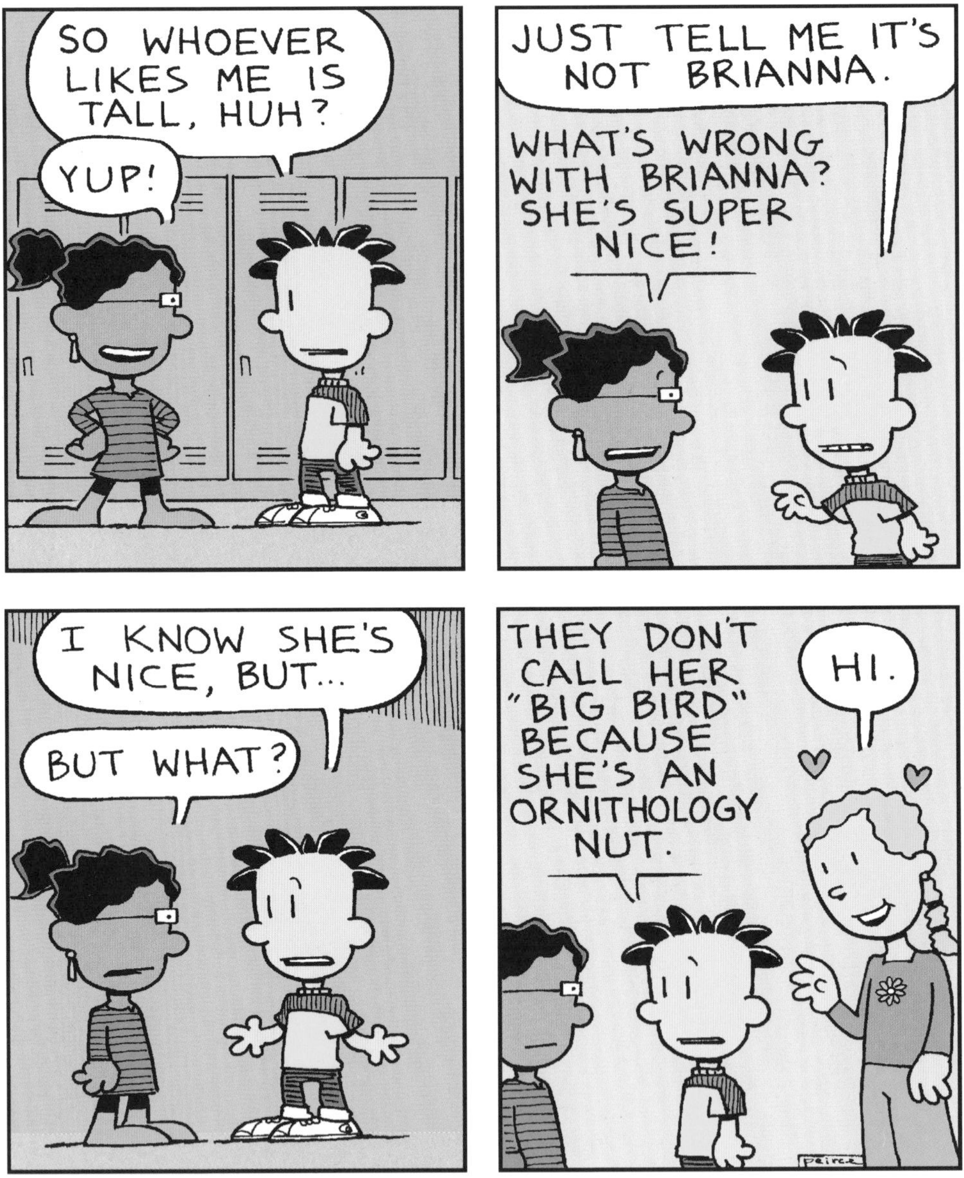
SO WHOEVER LIKES ME IS TALL, HUH?
YUP!
JUST TELL ME IT'S NOT BRIANNA.
WHAT'S WRONG WITH BRIANNA? SHE'S SUPER NICE!
I KNOW SHE'S NICE, BUT...
BUT WHAT?
THEY DON'T CALL HER "BIG BIRD" BECAUSE SHE'S AN ORNITHOLOGY NUT.
HI.
peirce

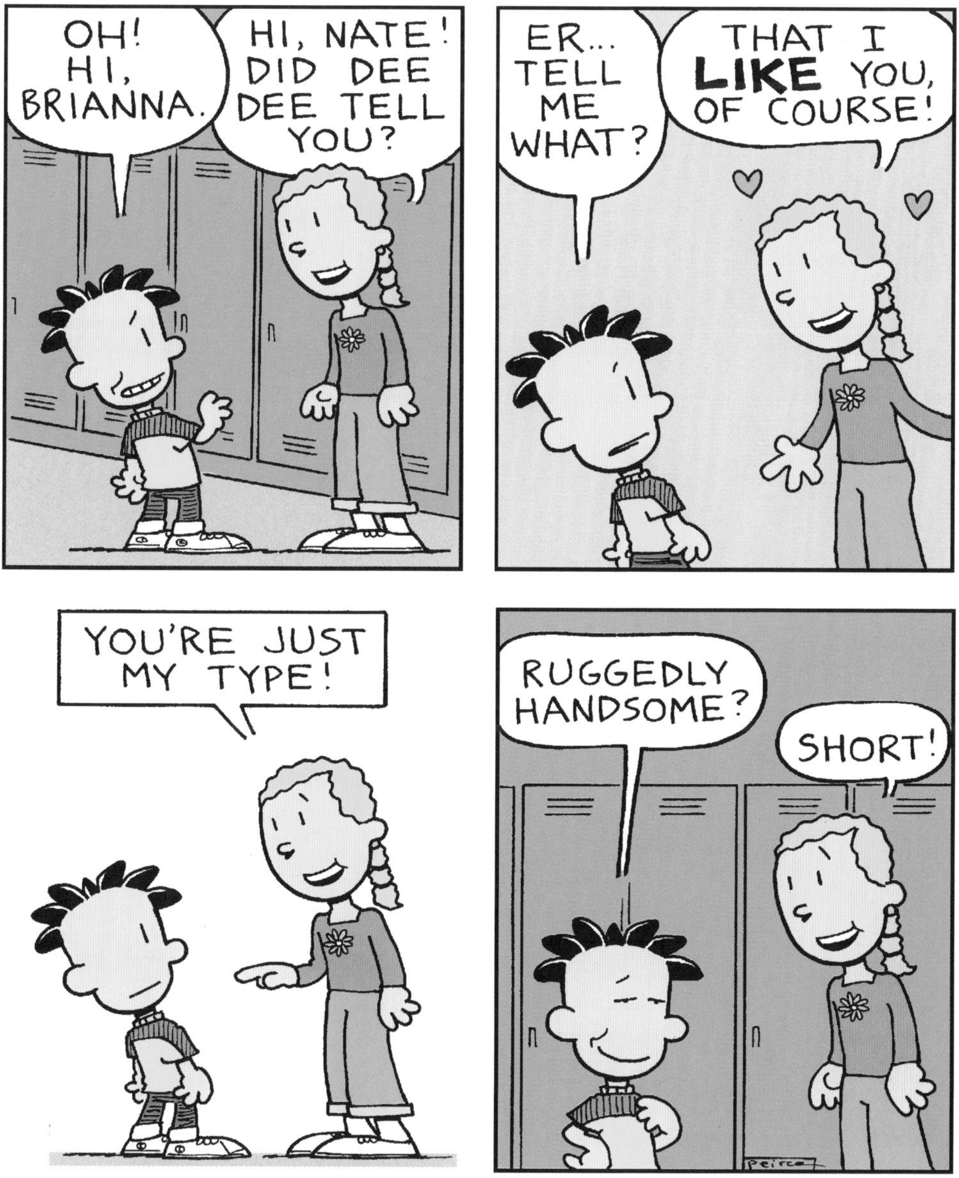
OH! HI, BRIANNA.
HI, NATE! DID DEE DEE TELL YOU?
ER... TELL ME WHAT?
THAT I **LIKE** YOU, OF COURSE!
YOU'RE JUST MY TYPE!
RUGGEDLY HANDSOME?
SHORT!
peirce

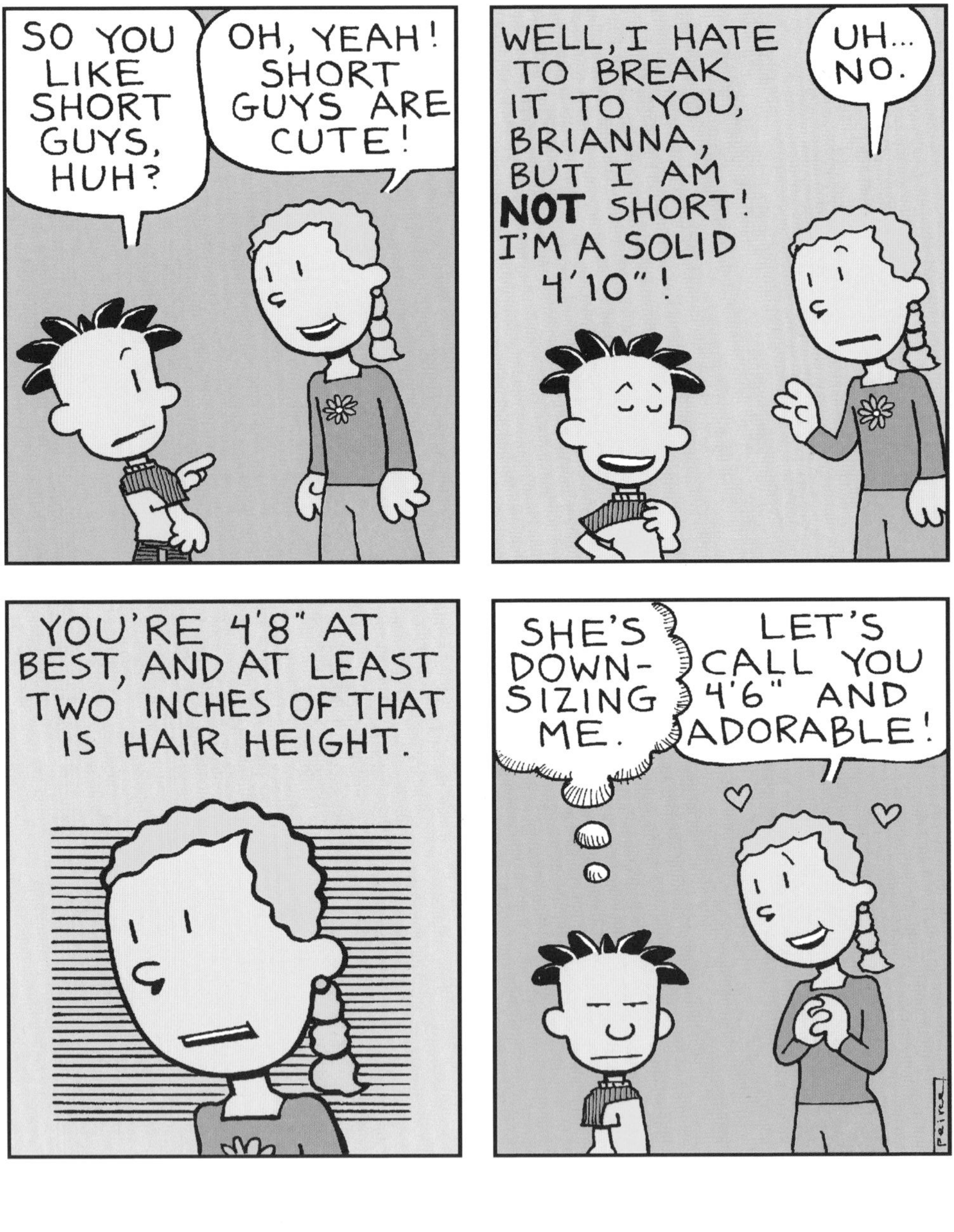
SO YOU LIKE SHORT GUYS, HUH?
OH, YEAH! SHORT GUYS ARE CUTE!
WELL, I HATE TO BREAK IT TO YOU, BRIANNA, BUT I AM **NOT** SHORT! I'M A SOLID 4'10"!
UH... NO.
YOU'RE 4'8" AT BEST, AND AT LEAST TWO INCHES OF THAT IS HAIR HEIGHT.
SHE'S DOWN-SIZING ME.
LET'S CALL YOU 4'6" AND ADORABLE!
peirce

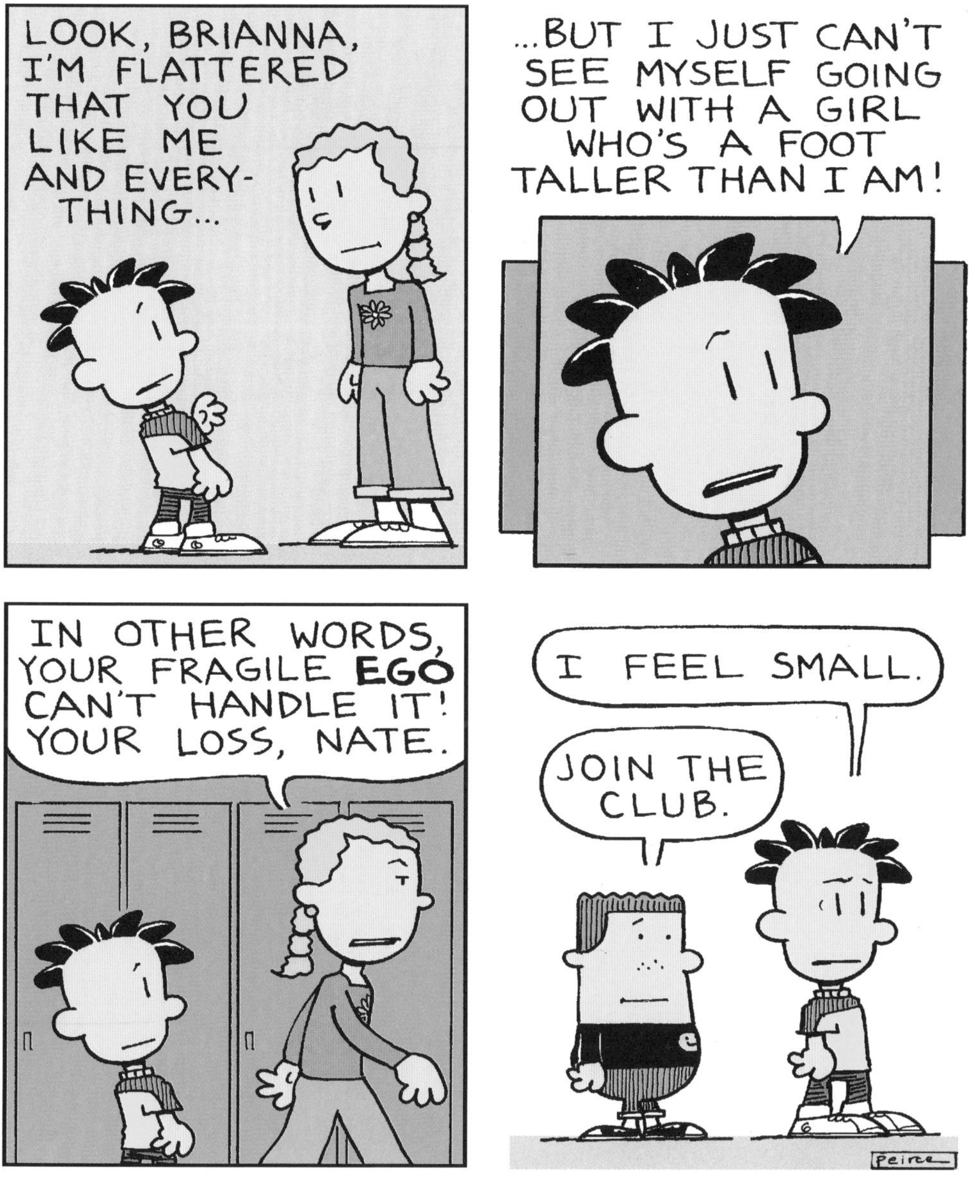
LOOK, BRIANNA, I'M FLATTERED THAT YOU LIKE ME AND EVERY-THING...
...BUT I JUST CAN'T SEE MYSELF GOING OUT WITH A GIRL WHO'S A FOOT TALLER THAN I AM!
IN OTHER WORDS, YOUR FRAGILE **EGO** CAN'T HANDLE IT! YOUR LOSS, NATE.
I FEEL SMALL.
JOIN THE CLUB.
Peirce

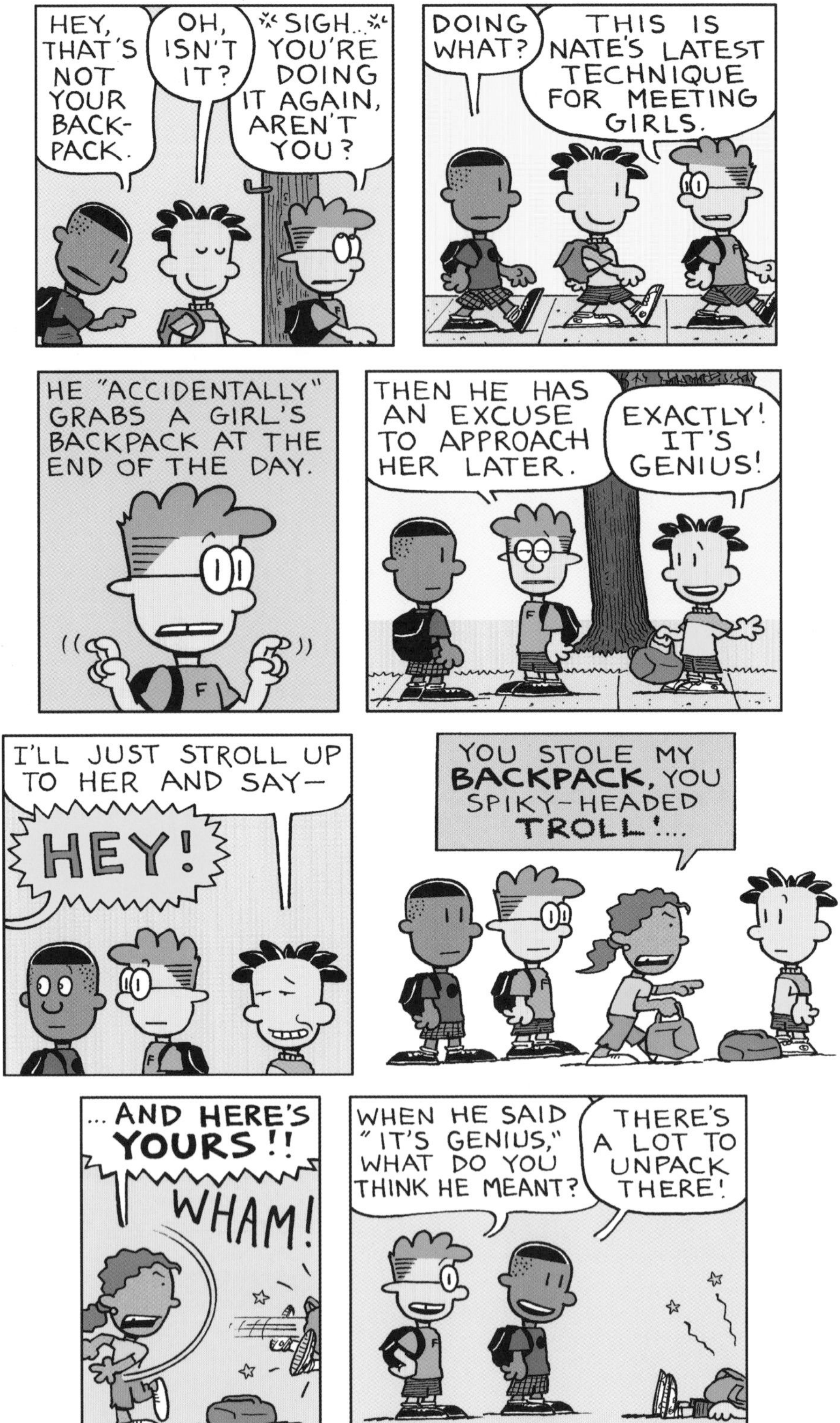
HEY, THAT'S NOT YOUR BACK-PACK.
OH, ISN'T IT?
SIGH... YOU'RE DOING IT AGAIN, AREN'T YOU?
DOING WHAT?
THIS IS NATE'S LATEST TECHNIQUE FOR MEETING GIRLS.
HE "ACCIDENTALLY" GRABS A GIRL'S BACKPACK AT THE END OF THE DAY.
THEN HE HAS AN EXCUSE TO APPROACH HER LATER.
EXACTLY! IT'S GENIUS!
I'LL JUST STROLL UP TO HER AND SAY—
HEY!
YOU STOLE MY BACKPACK, YOU SPIKY-HEADED TROLL!...
...AND HERE'S YOURS!!
WHAM!
WHEN HE SAID "IT'S GENIUS," WHAT DO YOU THINK HE MEANT?
THERE'S A LOT TO UNPACK THERE!
peirce

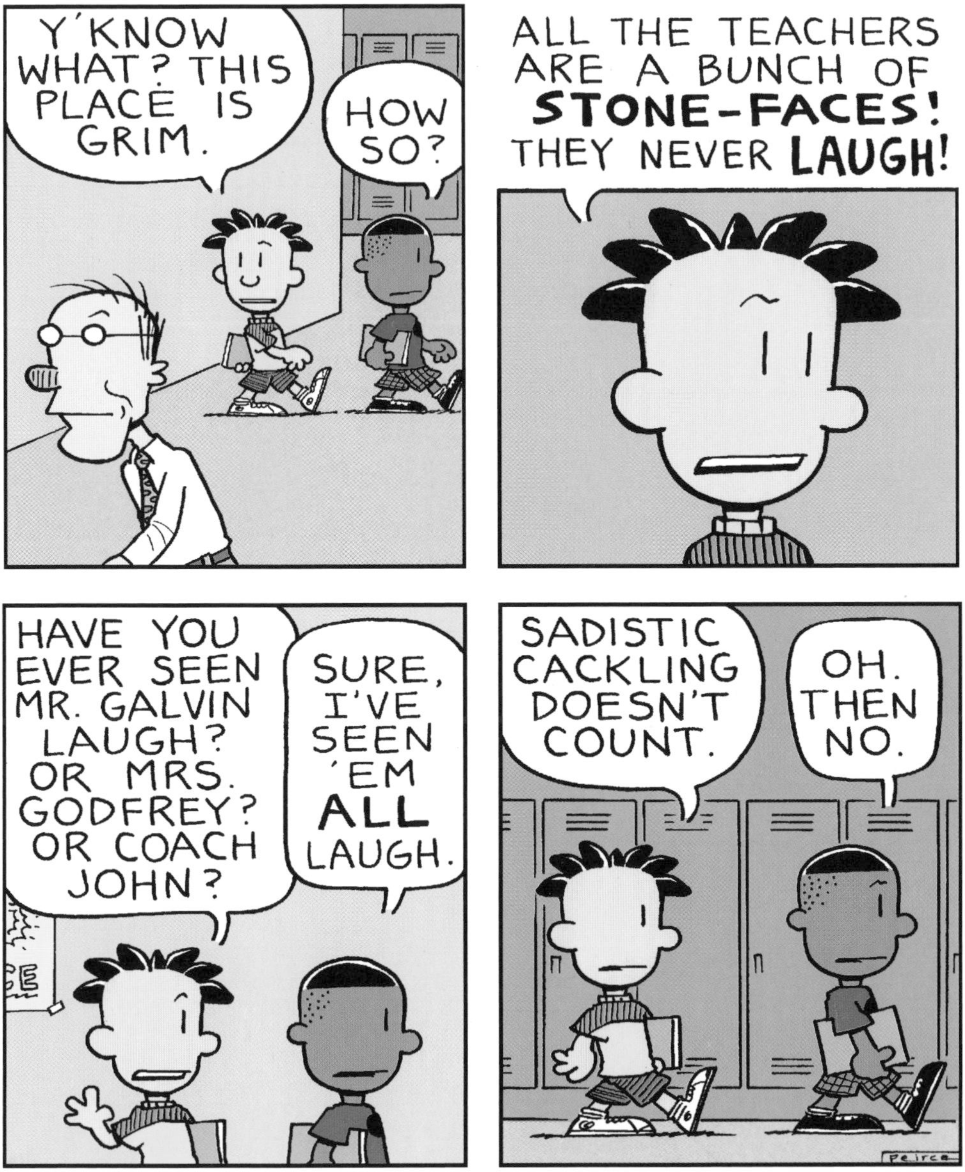
Y'KNOW WHAT? THIS PLACE IS GRIM.
HOW SO?
ALL THE TEACHERS ARE A BUNCH OF **STONE-FACES!** THEY NEVER **LAUGH!**
HAVE YOU EVER SEEN MR. GALVIN LAUGH? OR MRS. GODFREY? OR COACH JOHN?
SURE, I'VE SEEN 'EM **ALL** LAUGH.
SADISTIC CACKLING DOESN'T COUNT.
OH. THEN NO.
Peirce

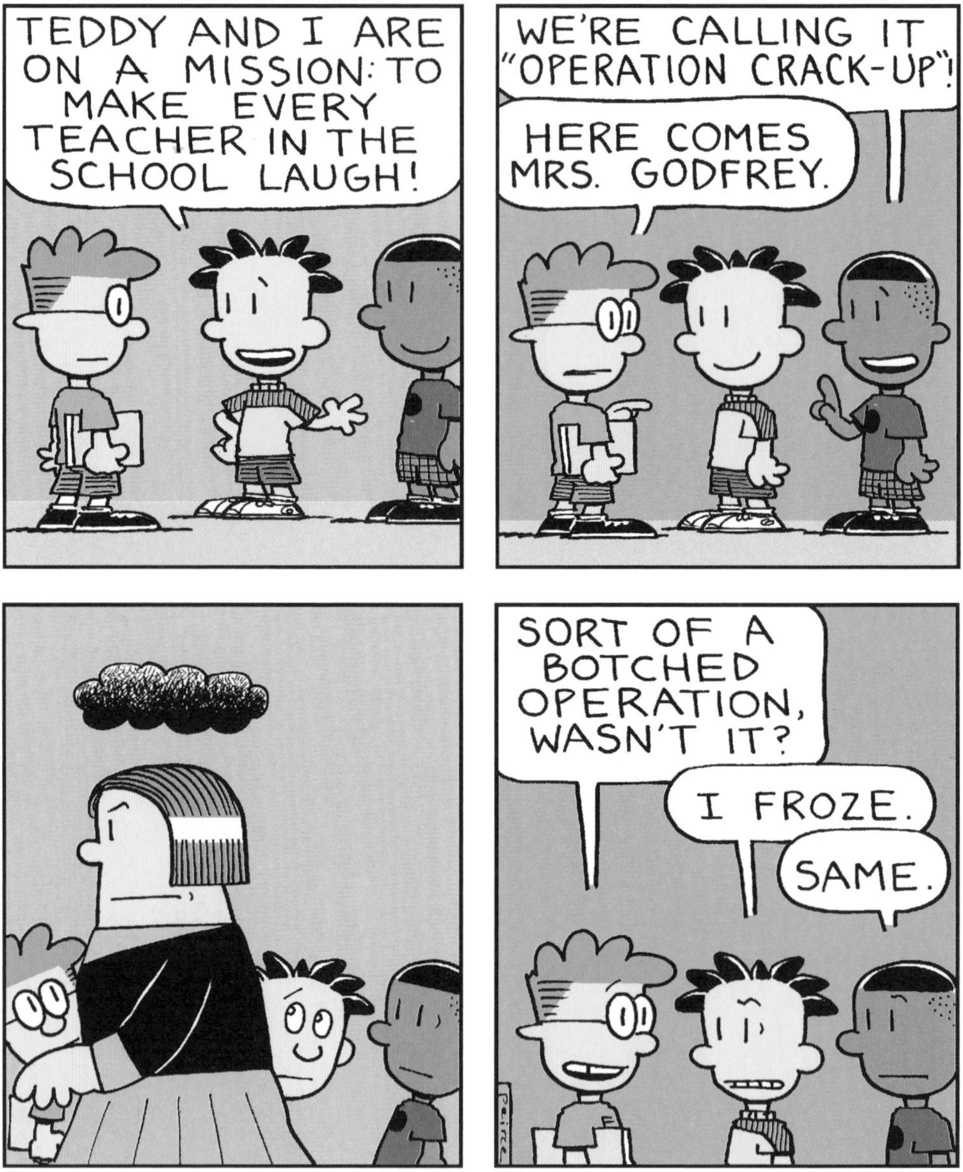
TEDDY AND I ARE ON A MISSION: TO MAKE EVERY TEACHER IN THE SCHOOL LAUGH!
WE'RE CALLING IT "OPERATION CRACK-UP"!
HERE COMES MRS. GODFREY.
SORT OF A BOTCHED OPERATION, WASN'T IT?
I FROZE.
SAME.
Peirce

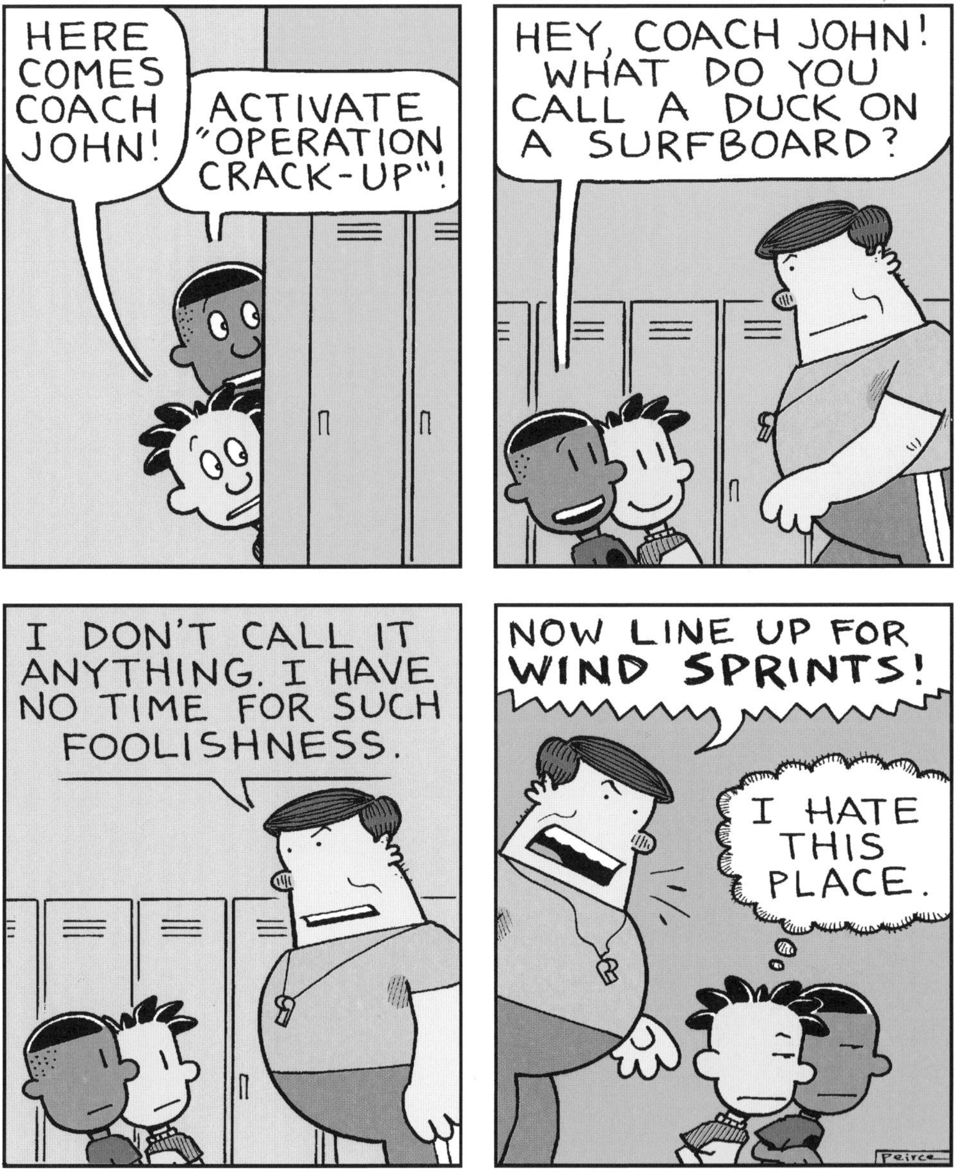
HERE COMES COACH JOHN!
ACTIVATE "OPERATION CRACK-UP"!
HEY, COACH JOHN! WHAT DO YOU CALL A DUCK ON A SURFBOARD?
I DON'T CALL IT ANYTHING. I HAVE NO TIME FOR SUCH FOOLISHNESS.
NOW LINE UP FOR WIND SPRINTS!
I HATE THIS PLACE.
Peirce

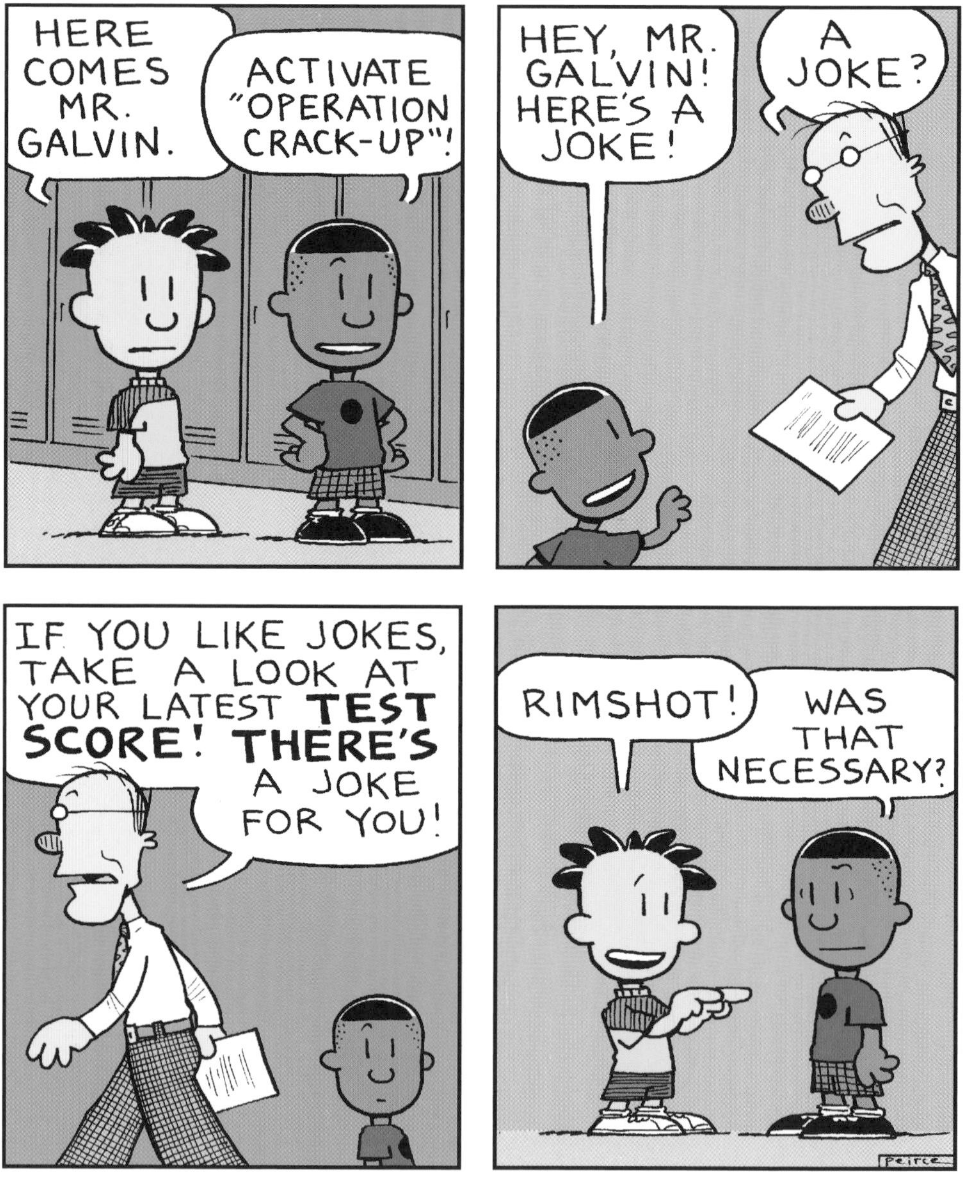
HERE COMES MR. GALVIN.
ACTIVATE "OPERATION CRACK-UP"!
HEY, MR. GALVIN! HERE'S A JOKE!
A JOKE?
IF YOU LIKE JOKES, TAKE A LOOK AT YOUR LATEST **TEST SCORE! THERE'S** A JOKE FOR YOU!
RIMSHOT!
WAS THAT NECESSARY?
PEIRCE

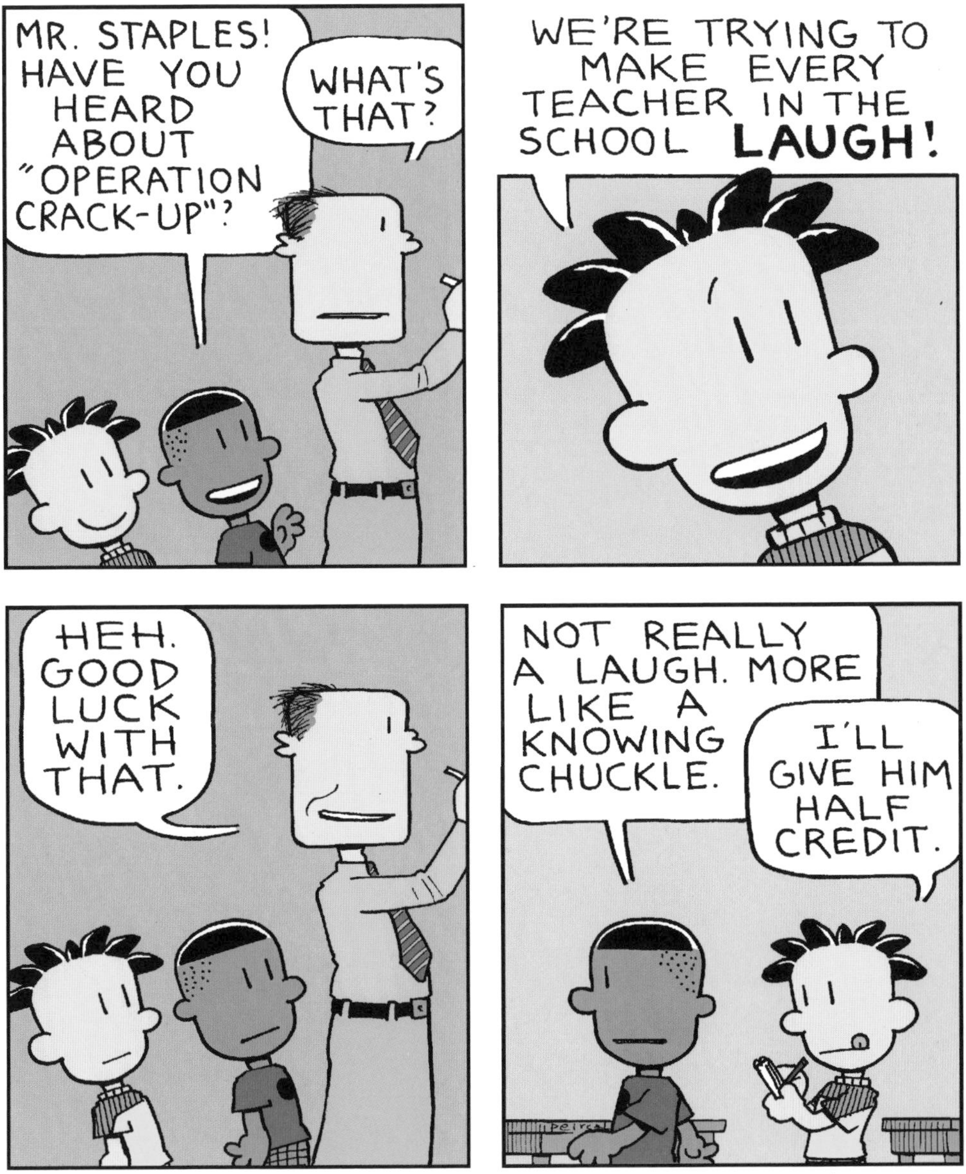
MR. STAPLES! HAVE YOU HEARD ABOUT "OPERATION CRACK-UP"?
WHAT'S THAT?
WE'RE TRYING TO MAKE EVERY TEACHER IN THE SCHOOL **LAUGH!**
HEH. GOOD LUCK WITH THAT.
NOT REALLY A LAUGH. MORE LIKE A KNOWING CHUCKLE.
I'LL GIVE HIM HALF CREDIT.
peirce

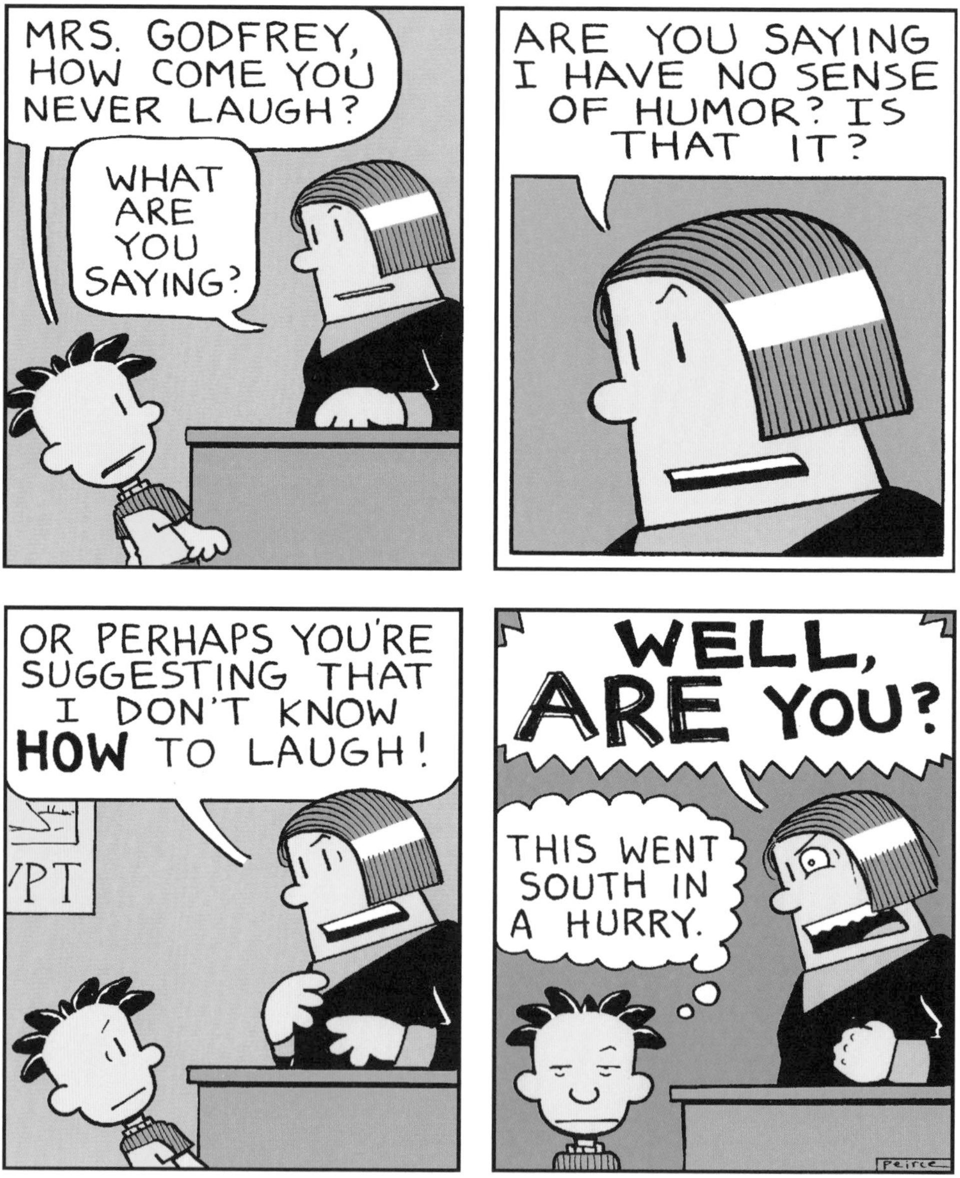
MRS. GODFREY, HOW COME YOU NEVER LAUGH?
WHAT ARE YOU SAYING?
ARE YOU SAYING I HAVE NO SENSE OF HUMOR? IS THAT IT?
OR PERHAPS YOU'RE SUGGESTING THAT I DON'T KNOW **HOW** TO LAUGH!
WELL, ARE YOU?
THIS WENT SOUTH IN A HURRY.
peirce

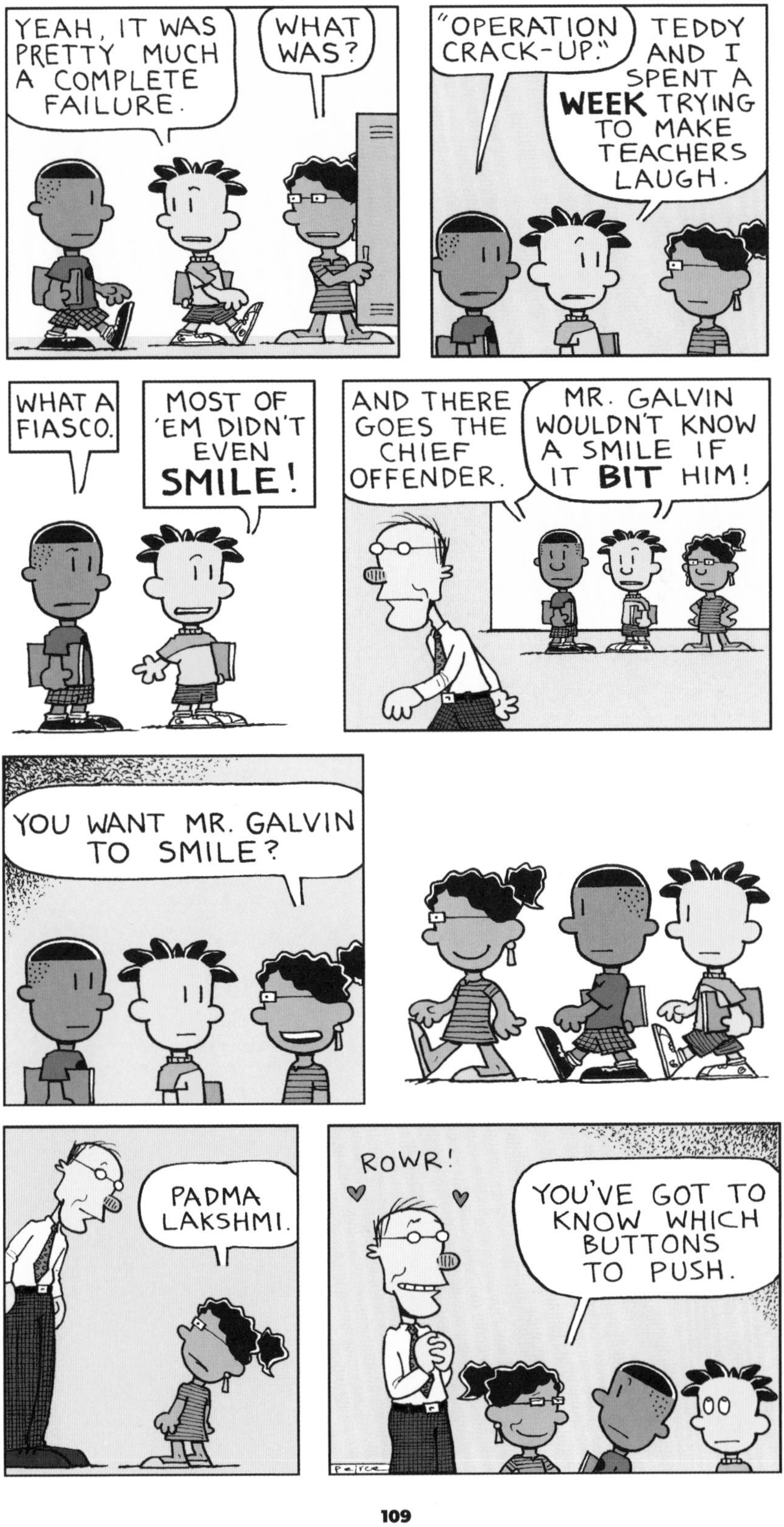
YEAH, IT WAS PRETTY MUCH A COMPLETE FAILURE.
WHAT WAS?
"OPERATION CRACK-UP."
TEDDY AND I SPENT A **WEEK** TRYING TO MAKE TEACHERS LAUGH.
WHAT A FIASCO.
MOST OF 'EM DIDN'T EVEN **SMILE**!
AND THERE GOES THE CHIEF OFFENDER.
MR. GALVIN WOULDN'T KNOW A SMILE IF IT **BIT** HIM!
YOU WANT MR. GALVIN TO SMILE?
PADMA LAKSHMI.
ROWR!
YOU'VE GOT TO KNOW WHICH BUTTONS TO PUSH.
peirce

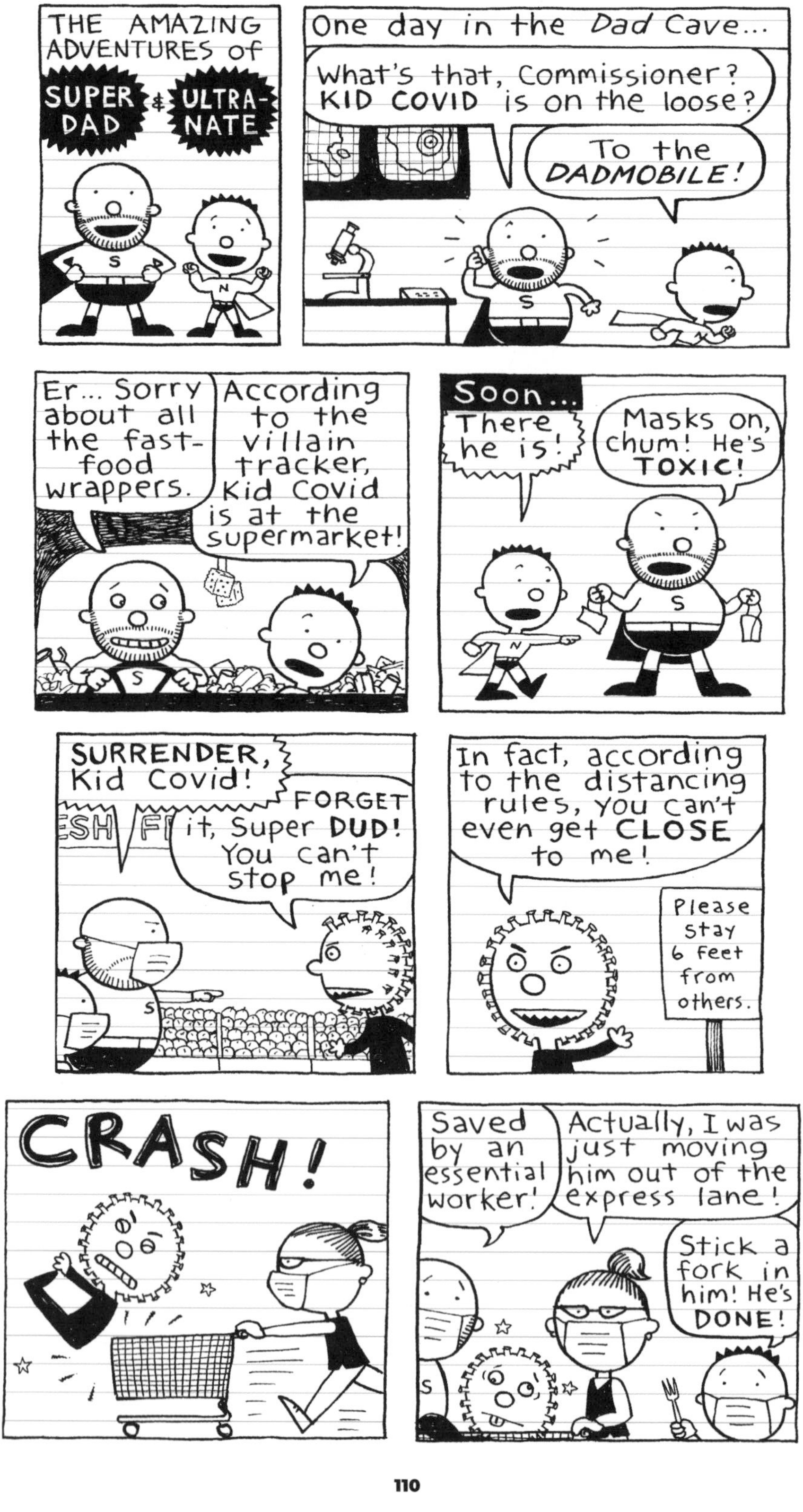
THE AMAZING ADVENTURES of
SUPER DAD & ULTRA-NATE
One day in the Dad Cave...
What's that, Commissioner? KID COVID is on the loose?
To the DADMOBILE!
Er... Sorry about all the fast-food wrappers.
According to the villain tracker, Kid Covid is at the supermarket!
Soon...
There he is!
Masks on, chum! He's TOXIC!
SURRENDER, Kid Covid!
FORGET it, Super DUD! You can't stop me!
In fact, according to the distancing rules, you can't even get CLOSE to me!
Please stay 6 feet from others.
CRASH!
Saved by an essential worker!
Actually, I was just moving him out of the express lane!
Stick a fork in him! He's DONE!

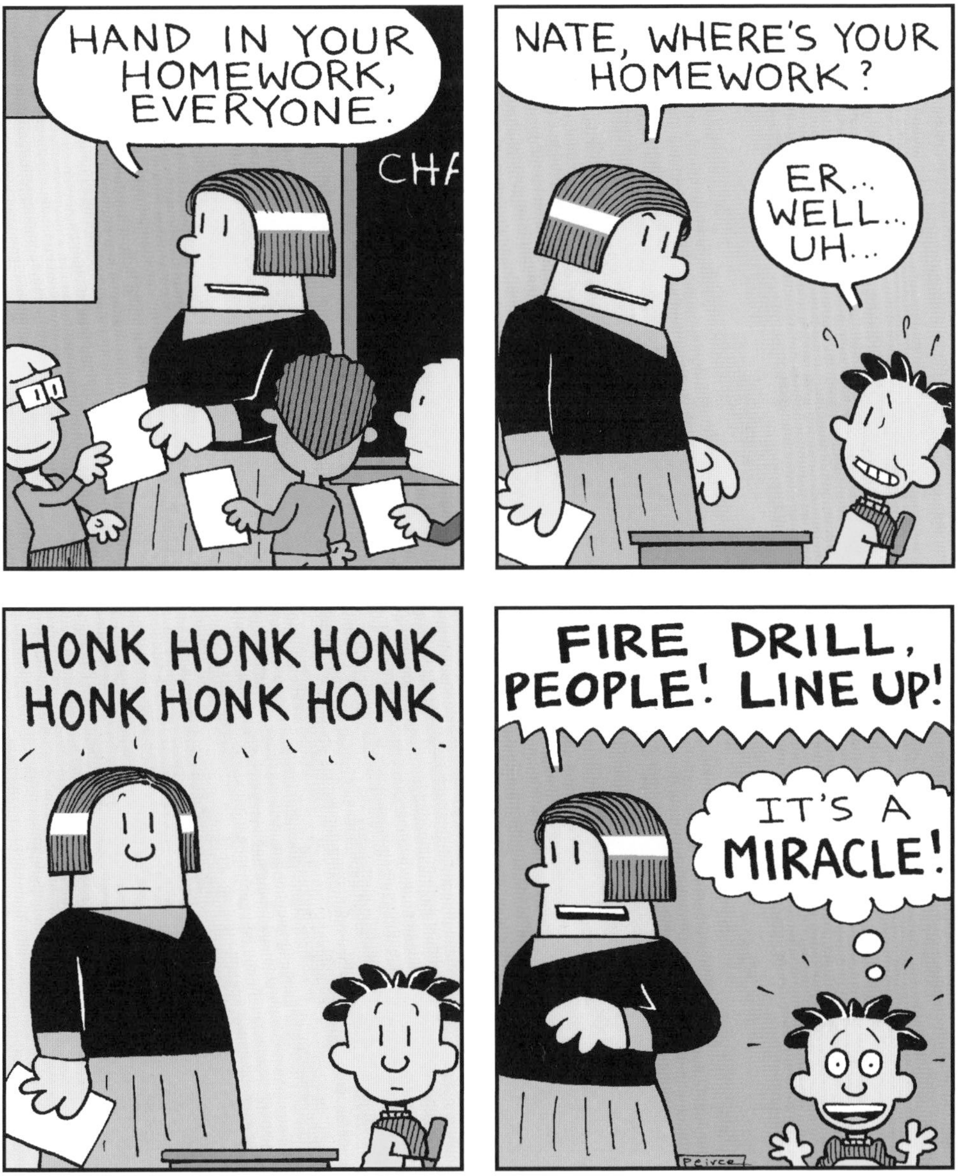
HAND IN YOUR HOMEWORK, EVERYONE.
CHA
NATE, WHERE'S YOUR HOMEWORK?
ER... WELL... UH...
HONK HONK HONK HONK HONK HONK
FIRE DRILL, PEOPLE! LINE UP!
IT'S A MIRACLE!
Peirce

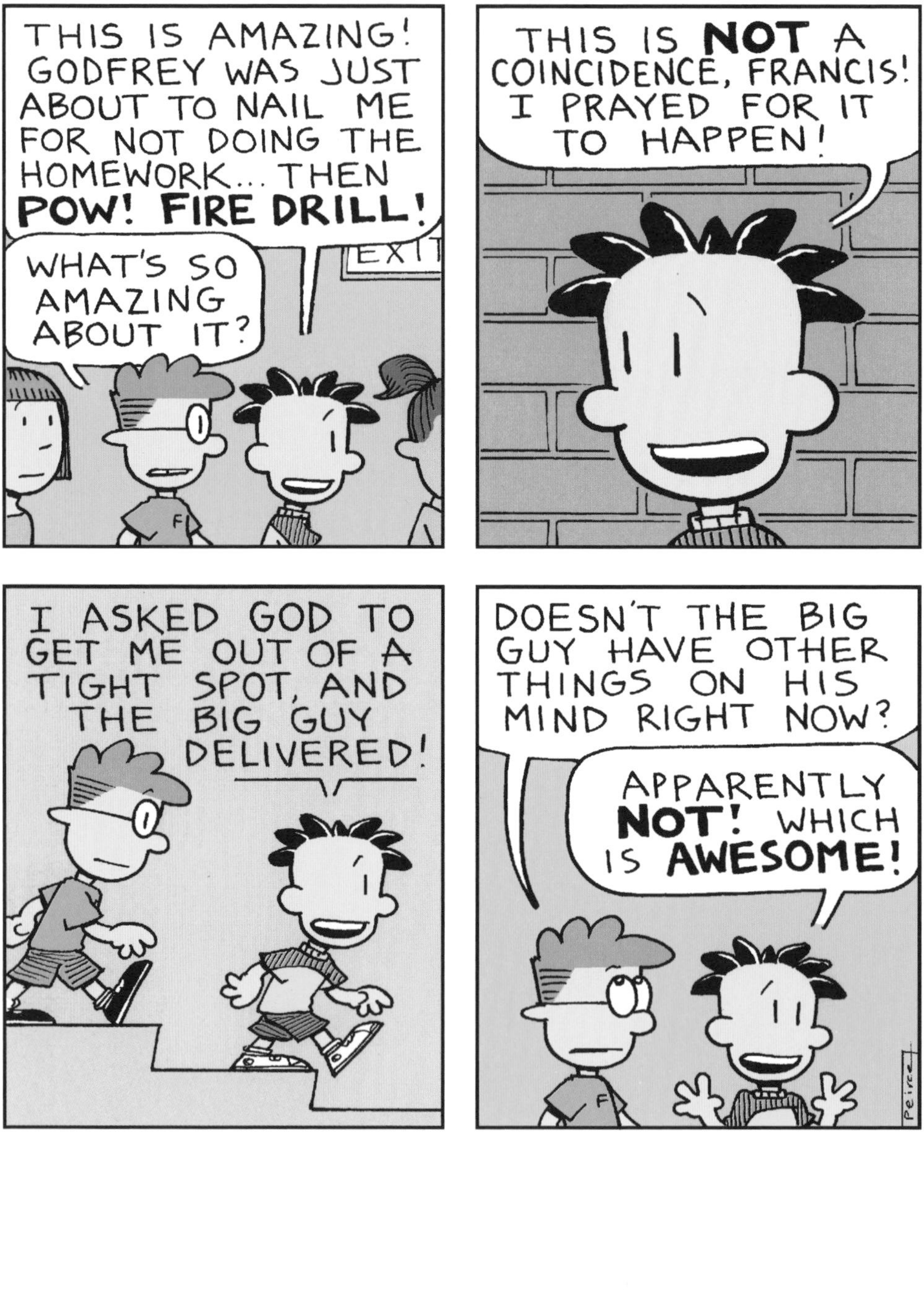
THIS IS AMAZING! GODFREY WAS JUST ABOUT TO NAIL ME FOR NOT DOING THE HOMEWORK... THEN **POW! FIRE DRILL!**
WHAT'S SO AMAZING ABOUT IT?
EXIT
THIS IS **NOT** A COINCIDENCE, FRANCIS! I PRAYED FOR IT TO HAPPEN!
I ASKED GOD TO GET ME OUT OF A TIGHT SPOT, AND THE BIG GUY DELIVERED!
DOESN'T THE BIG GUY HAVE OTHER THINGS ON HIS MIND RIGHT NOW?
APPARENTLY **NOT!** WHICH IS **AWESOME!**

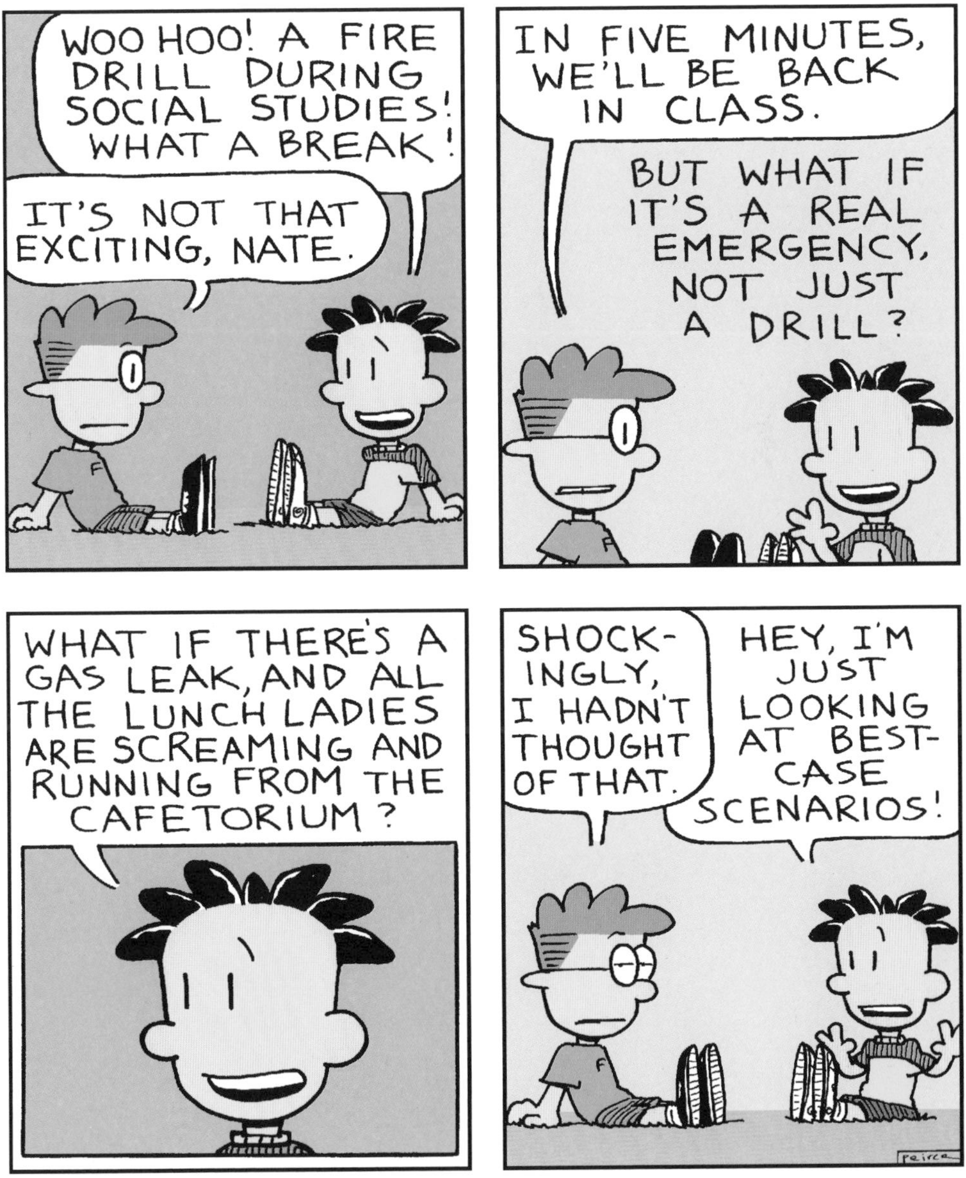
WOO HOO! A FIRE DRILL DURING SOCIAL STUDIES! WHAT A BREAK!
IT'S NOT THAT EXCITING, NATE.
IN FIVE MINUTES, WE'LL BE BACK IN CLASS.
BUT WHAT IF IT'S A REAL EMERGENCY, NOT JUST A DRILL?
WHAT IF THERE'S A GAS LEAK, AND ALL THE LUNCH LADIES ARE SCREAMING AND RUNNING FROM THE CAFETORIUM?
SHOCKINGLY, I HADN'T THOUGHT OF THAT.
HEY, I'M JUST LOOKING AT BEST-CASE SCENARIOS!
peirce

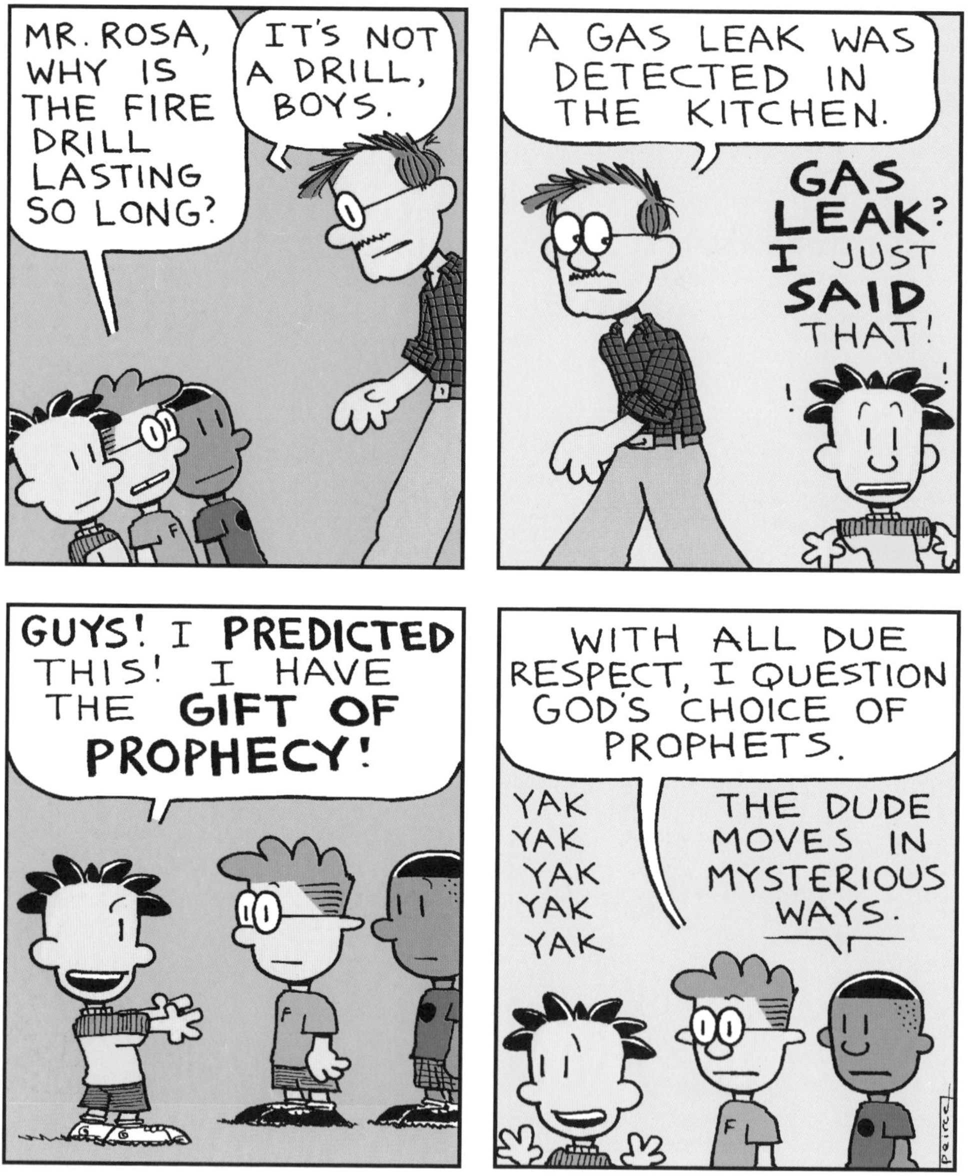
MR. ROSA, WHY IS THE FIRE DRILL LASTING SO LONG?
IT'S NOT A DRILL, BOYS.
A GAS LEAK WAS DETECTED IN THE KITCHEN.
GAS LEAK? I JUST SAID THAT!
GUYS! I PREDICTED THIS! I HAVE THE GIFT OF PROPHECY!
WITH ALL DUE RESPECT, I QUESTION GOD'S CHOICE OF PROPHETS.
YAK YAK YAK YAK YAK
THE DUDE MOVES IN MYSTERIOUS WAYS.

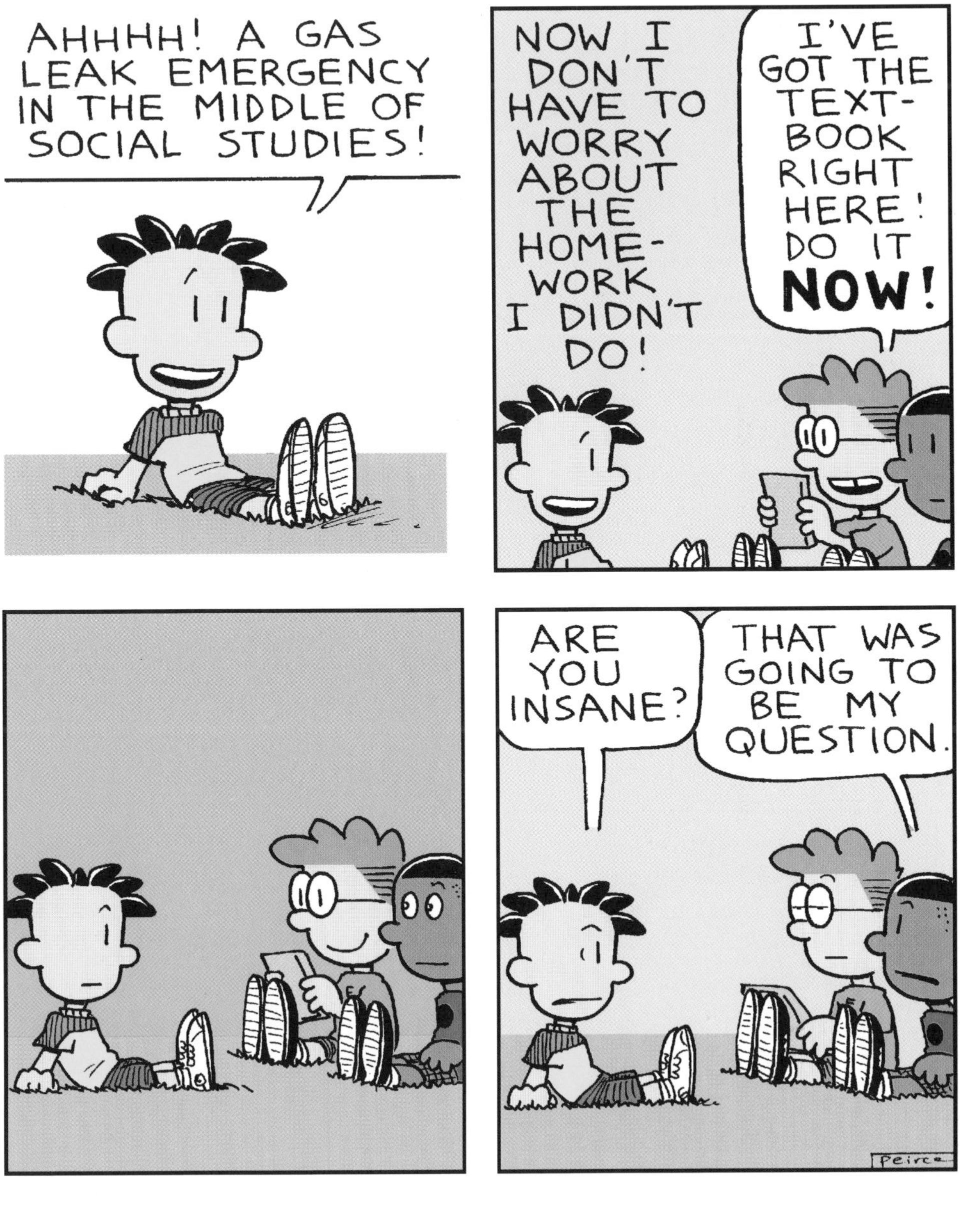
AHHHH! A GAS LEAK EMERGENCY IN THE MIDDLE OF SOCIAL STUDIES!
NOW I DON'T HAVE TO WORRY ABOUT THE HOME-WORK I DIDN'T DO!
I'VE GOT THE TEXT-BOOK RIGHT HERE! DO IT NOW!
ARE YOU INSANE?
THAT WAS GOING TO BE MY QUESTION.
Peirce

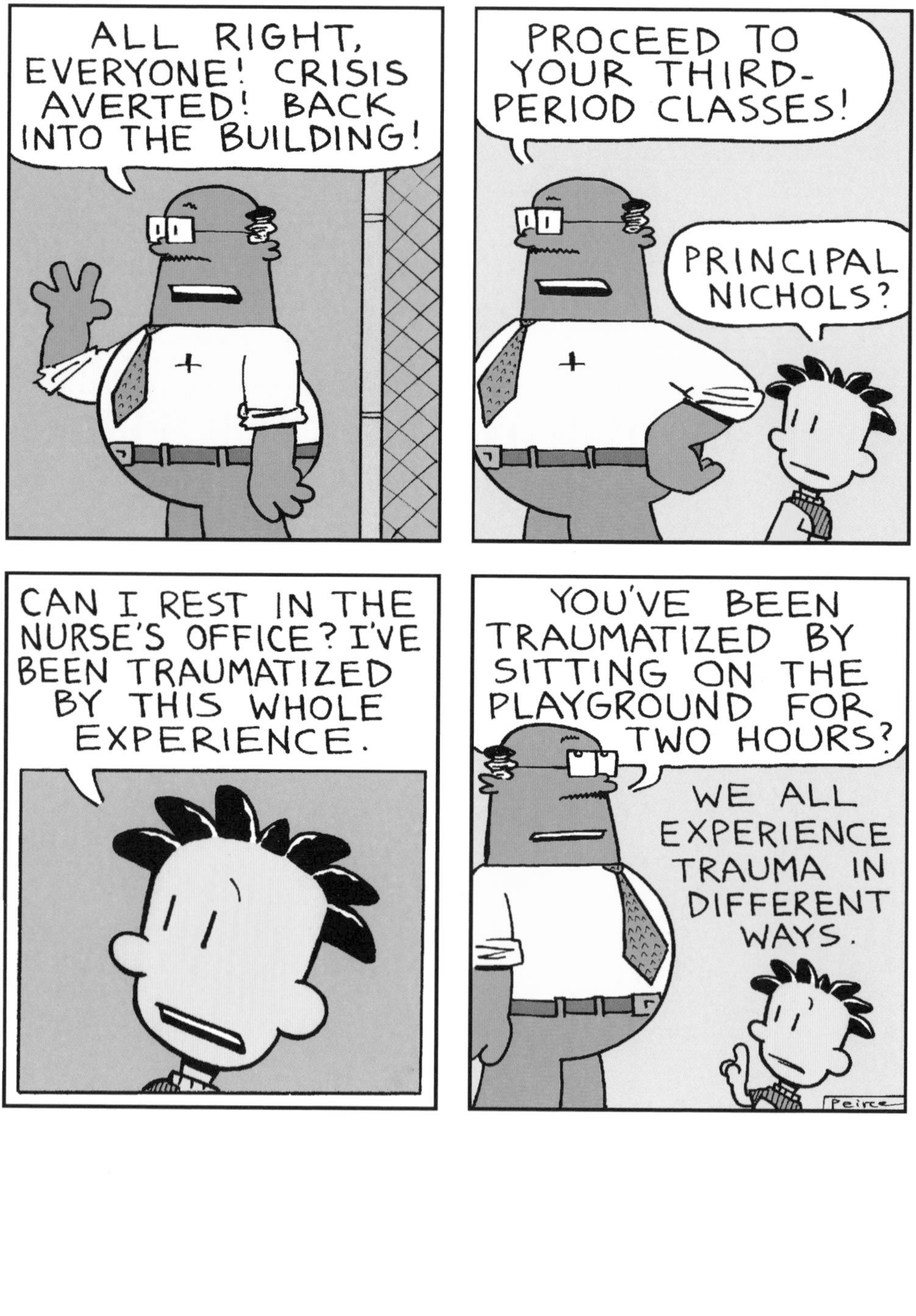
ALL RIGHT, EVERYONE! CRISIS AVERTED! BACK INTO THE BUILDING!
PROCEED TO YOUR THIRD-PERIOD CLASSES!
PRINCIPAL NICHOLS?
CAN I REST IN THE NURSE'S OFFICE? I'VE BEEN TRAUMATIZED BY THIS WHOLE EXPERIENCE.
YOU'VE BEEN TRAUMATIZED BY SITTING ON THE PLAYGROUND FOR TWO HOURS?
WE ALL EXPERIENCE TRAUMA IN DIFFERENT WAYS.
Peirce

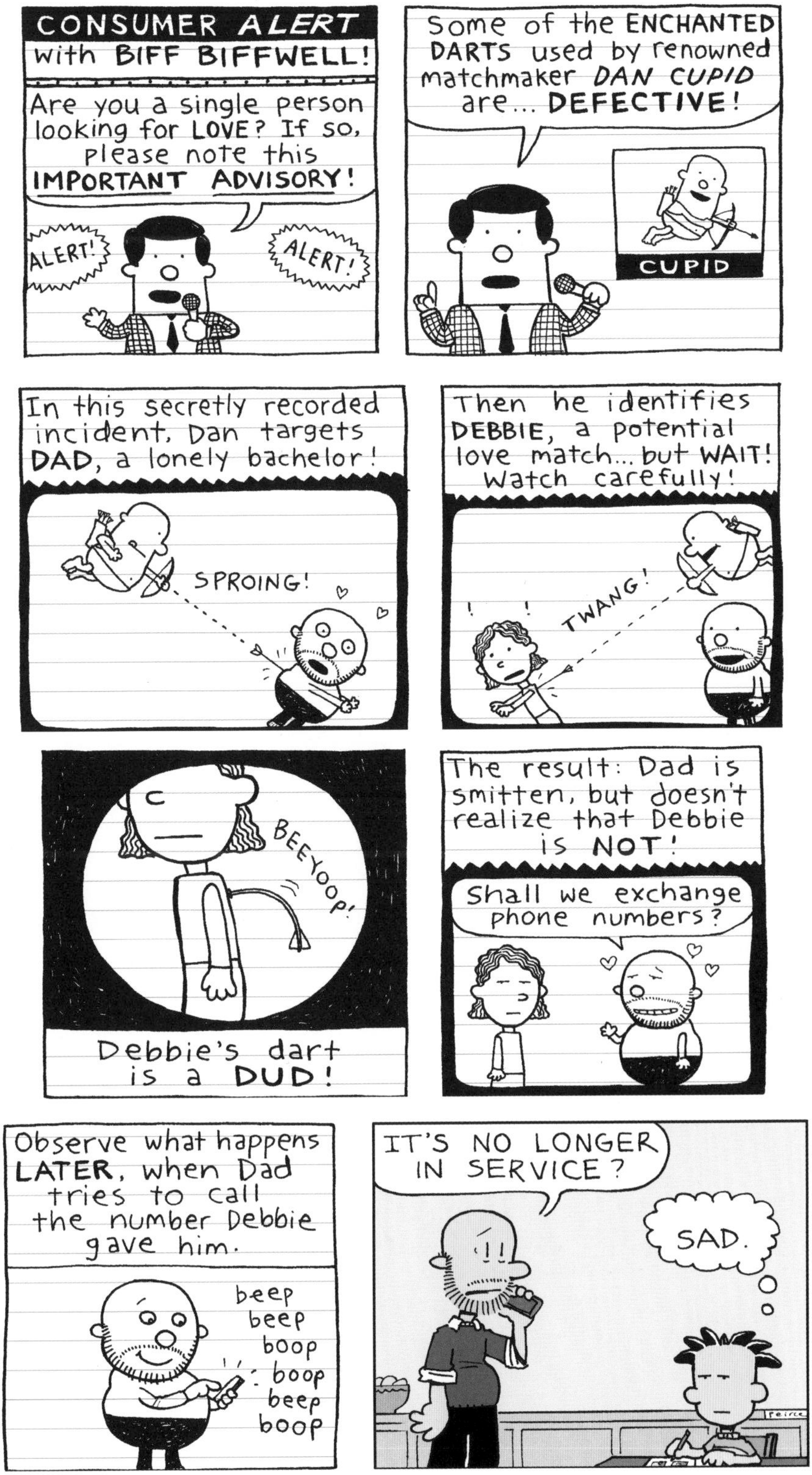
CONSUMER ALERT
with BIFF BIFFWELL!
Are you a single person looking for LOVE? If so, please note this IMPORTANT ADVISORY!
ALERT!
ALERT!
Some of the ENCHANTED DARTS used by renowned matchmaker DAN CUPID are... DEFECTIVE!
CUPID
In this secretly recorded incident, Dan targets DAD, a lonely bachelor!
SPROING!
Then he identifies DEBBIE, a potential love match... but WAIT! Watch carefully!
TWANG!
BEEYOOP!
Debbie's dart is a DUD!
The result: Dad is smitten, but doesn't realize that Debbie is NOT!
Shall we exchange phone numbers?
Observe what happens LATER, when Dad tries to call the number Debbie gave him.
beep
beep
boop
boop
beep
boop
IT'S NO LONGER IN SERVICE?
SAD.
Peirce

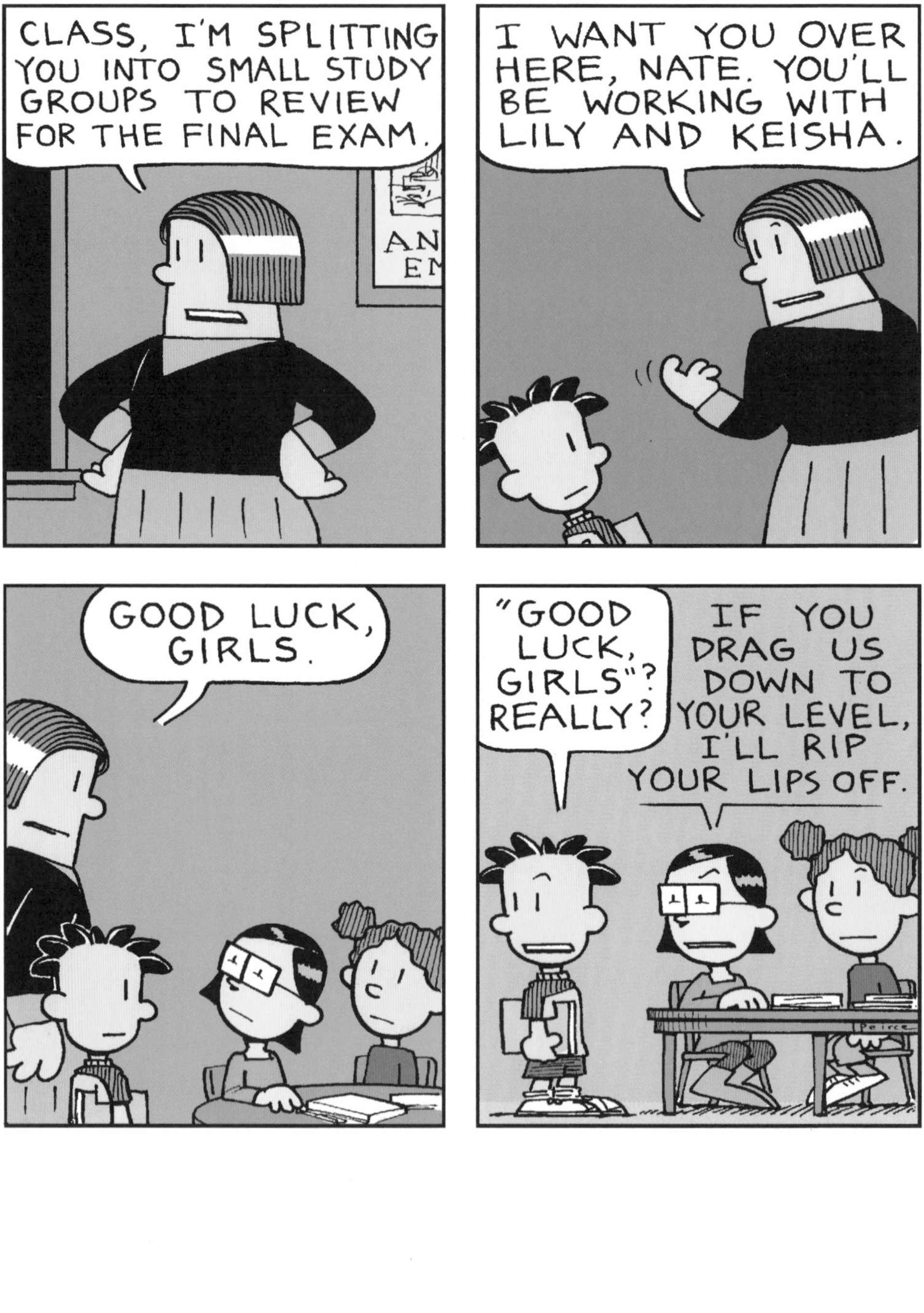
CLASS, I'M SPLITTING YOU INTO SMALL STUDY GROUPS TO REVIEW FOR THE FINAL EXAM.
I WANT YOU OVER HERE, NATE. YOU'LL BE WORKING WITH LILY AND KEISHA.
GOOD LUCK, GIRLS.
"GOOD LUCK, GIRLS"? REALLY?
IF YOU DRAG US DOWN TO YOUR LEVEL, I'LL RIP YOUR LIPS OFF.

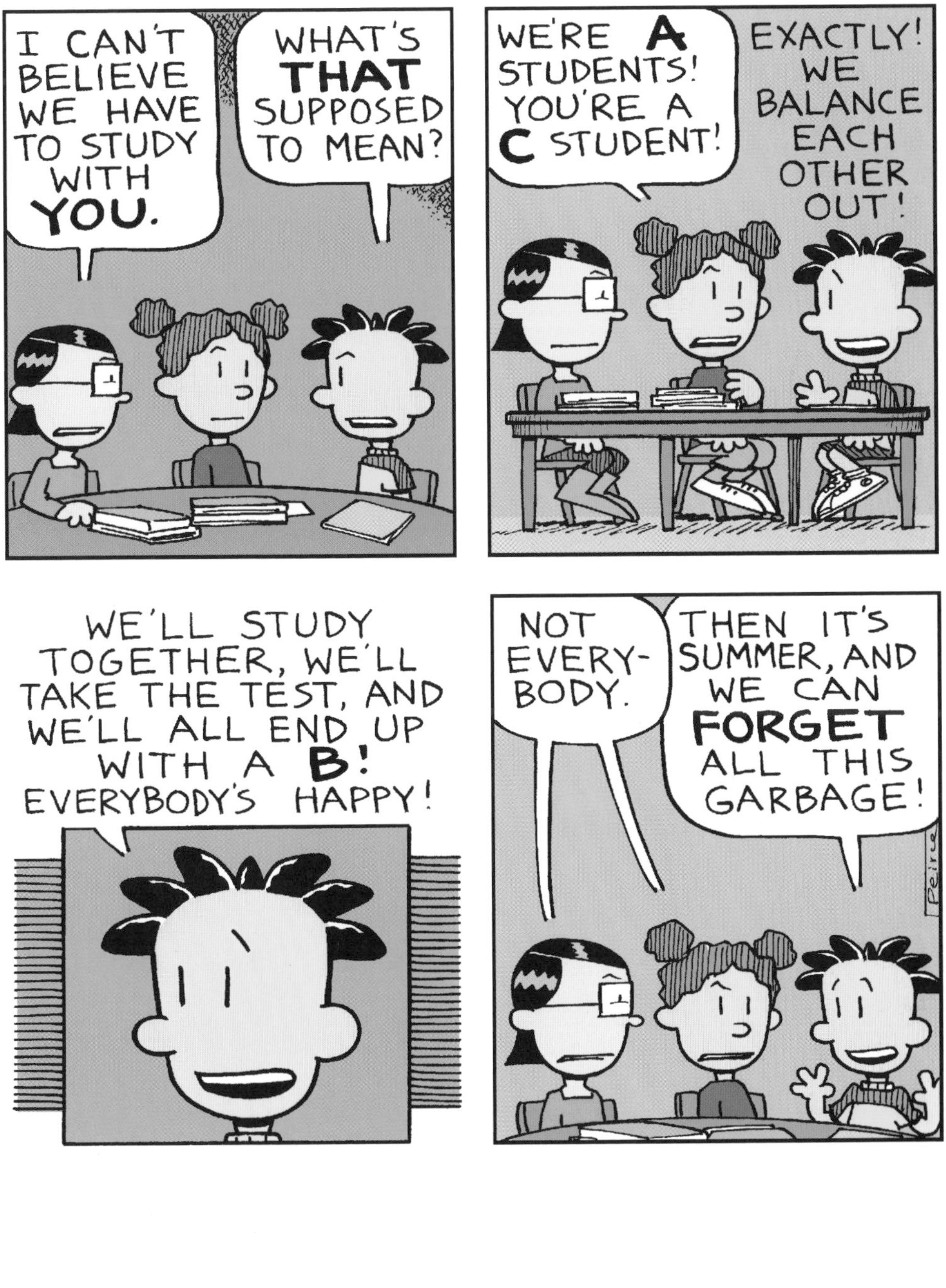
I CAN'T BELIEVE WE HAVE TO STUDY WITH **YOU**.
WHAT'S **THAT** SUPPOSED TO MEAN?
WE'RE **A** STUDENTS! YOU'RE A **C** STUDENT!
EXACTLY! WE BALANCE EACH OTHER OUT!
WE'LL STUDY TOGETHER, WE'LL TAKE THE TEST, AND WE'LL ALL END UP WITH A **B**! EVERYBODY'S HAPPY!
NOT EVERY-BODY.
THEN IT'S SUMMER, AND WE CAN **FORGET** ALL THIS GARBAGE!
Peirce

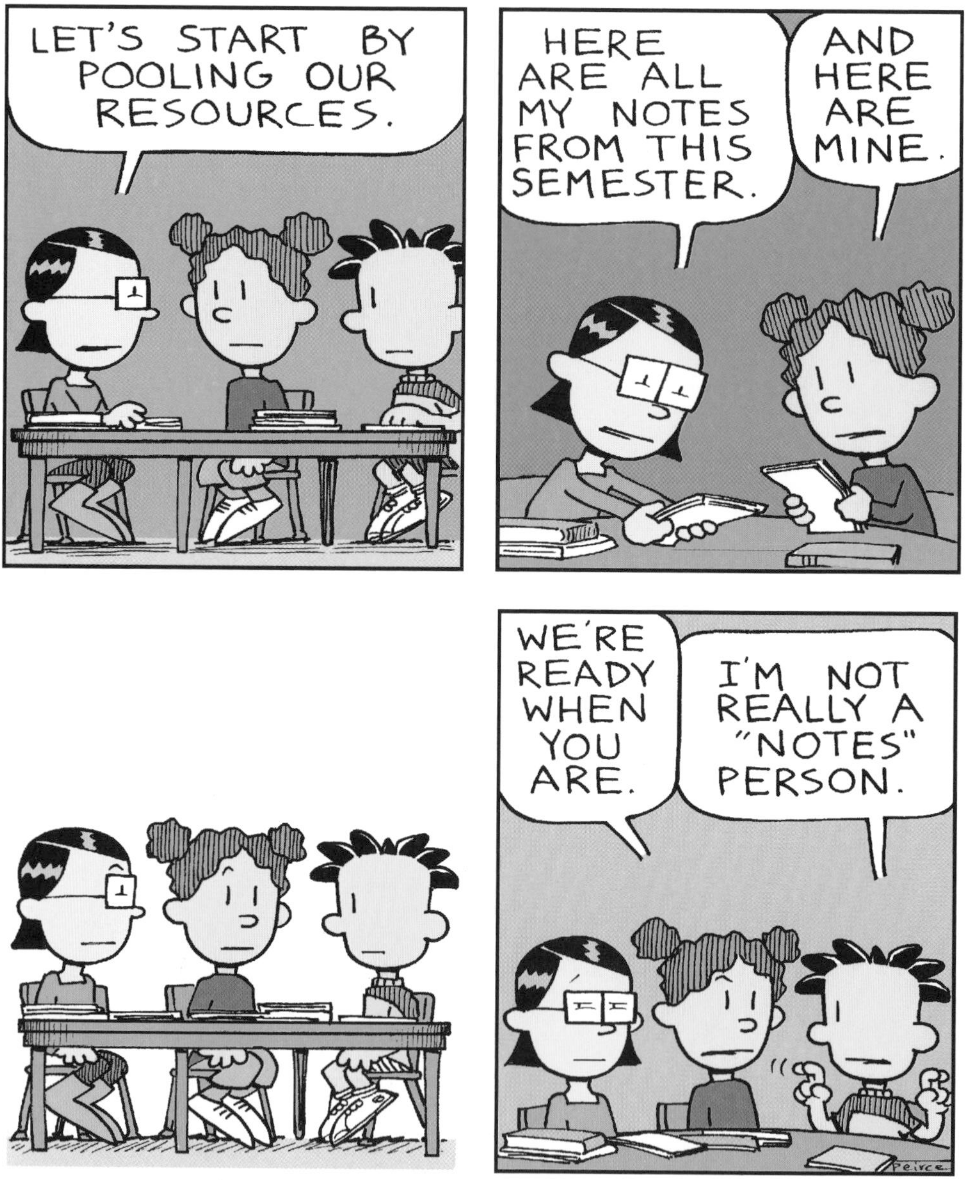
LET'S START BY POOLING OUR RESOURCES.
HERE ARE ALL MY NOTES FROM THIS SEMESTER.
AND HERE ARE MINE.
WE'RE READY WHEN YOU ARE.
I'M NOT REALLY A "NOTES" PERSON.
Peirce

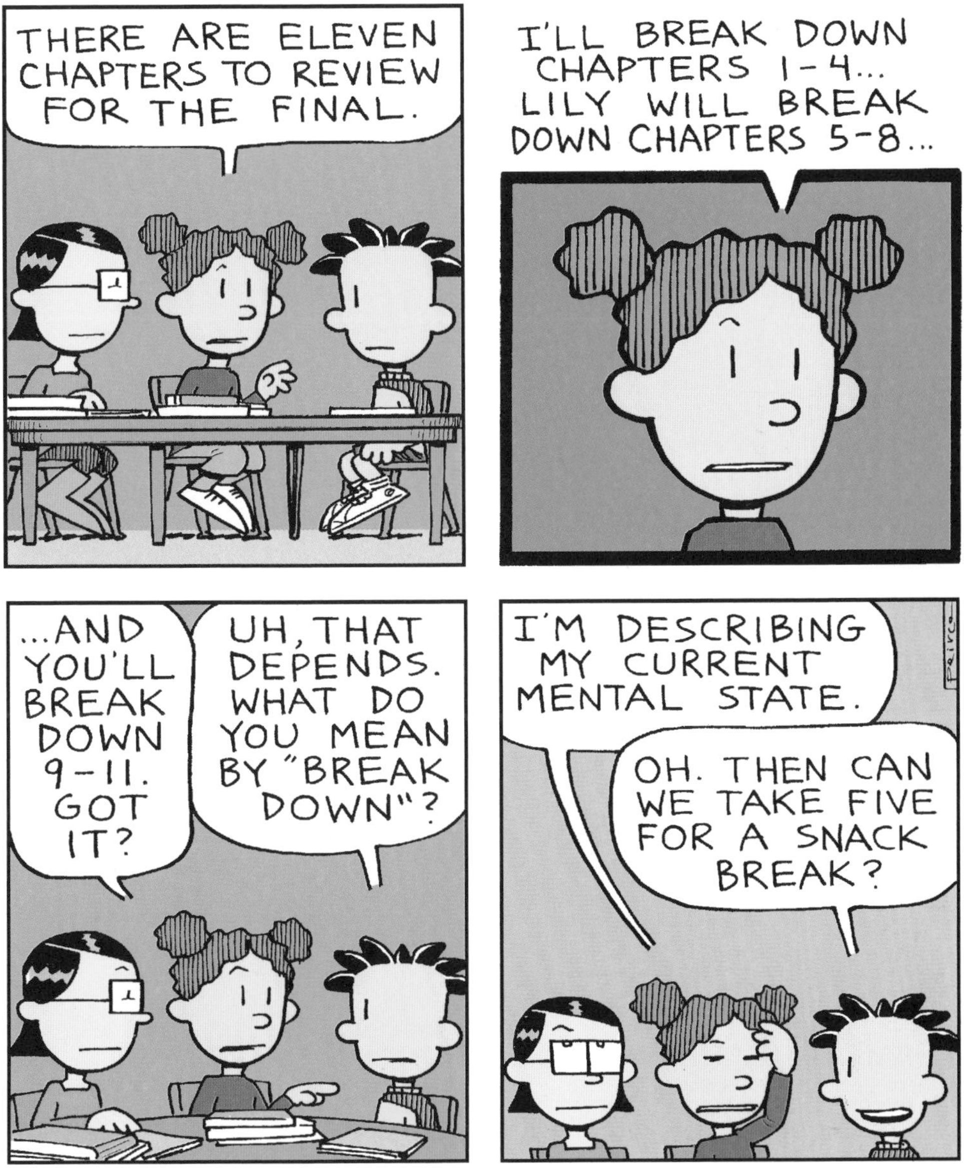
THERE ARE ELEVEN CHAPTERS TO REVIEW FOR THE FINAL.
I'LL BREAK DOWN CHAPTERS 1-4... LILY WILL BREAK DOWN CHAPTERS 5-8...
...AND YOU'LL BREAK DOWN 9-11. GOT IT?
UH, THAT DEPENDS. WHAT DO YOU MEAN BY "BREAK DOWN"?
I'M DESCRIBING MY CURRENT MENTAL STATE.
OH. THEN CAN WE TAKE FIVE FOR A SNACK BREAK?

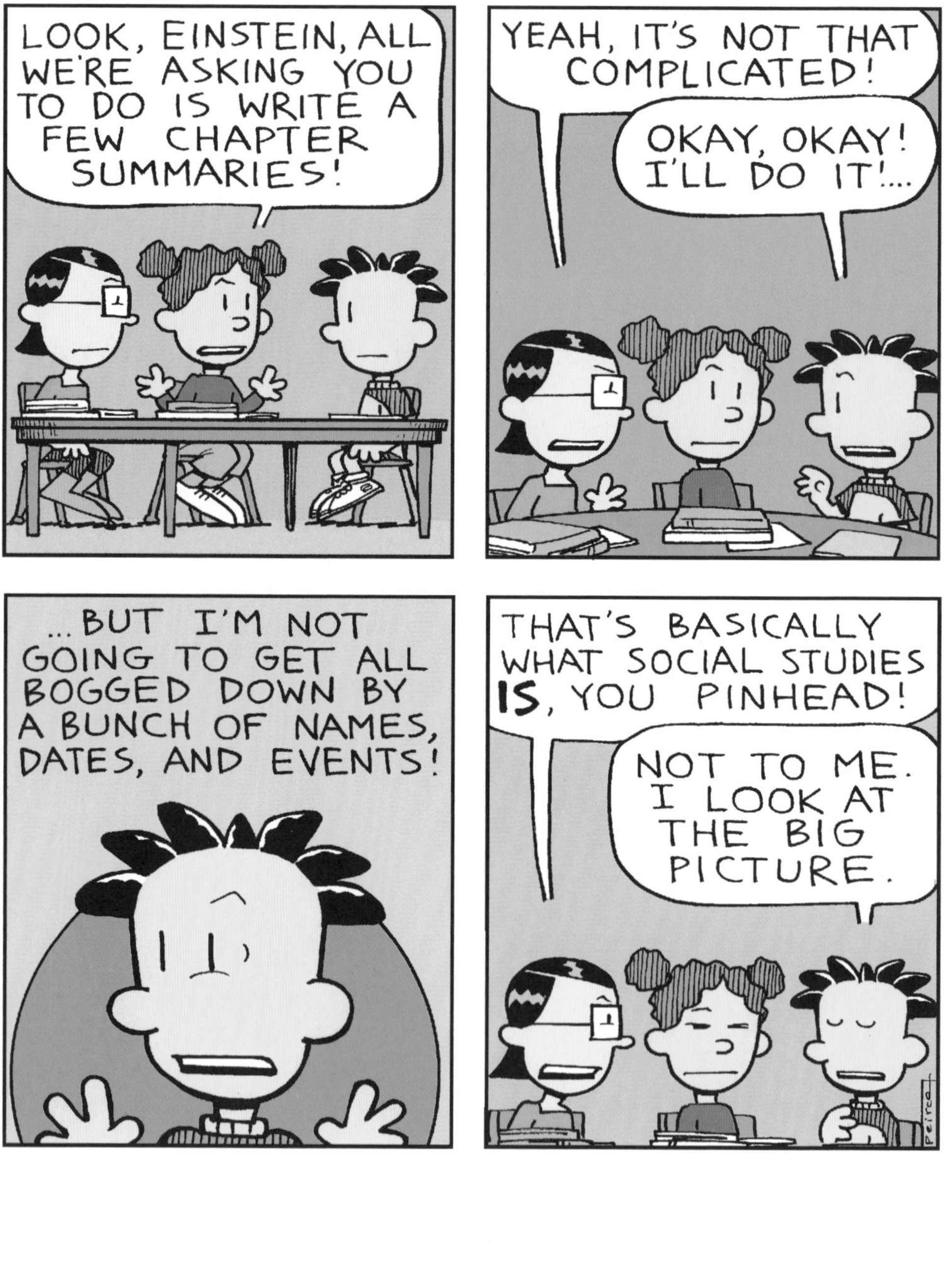
LOOK, EINSTEIN, ALL WE'RE ASKING YOU TO DO IS WRITE A FEW CHAPTER SUMMARIES!
YEAH, IT'S NOT THAT COMPLICATED!
OKAY, OKAY! I'LL DO IT!...
...BUT I'M NOT GOING TO GET ALL BOGGED DOWN BY A BUNCH OF NAMES, DATES, AND EVENTS!
THAT'S BASICALLY WHAT SOCIAL STUDIES IS, YOU PINHEAD!
NOT TO ME. I LOOK AT THE BIG PICTURE.
Peirce

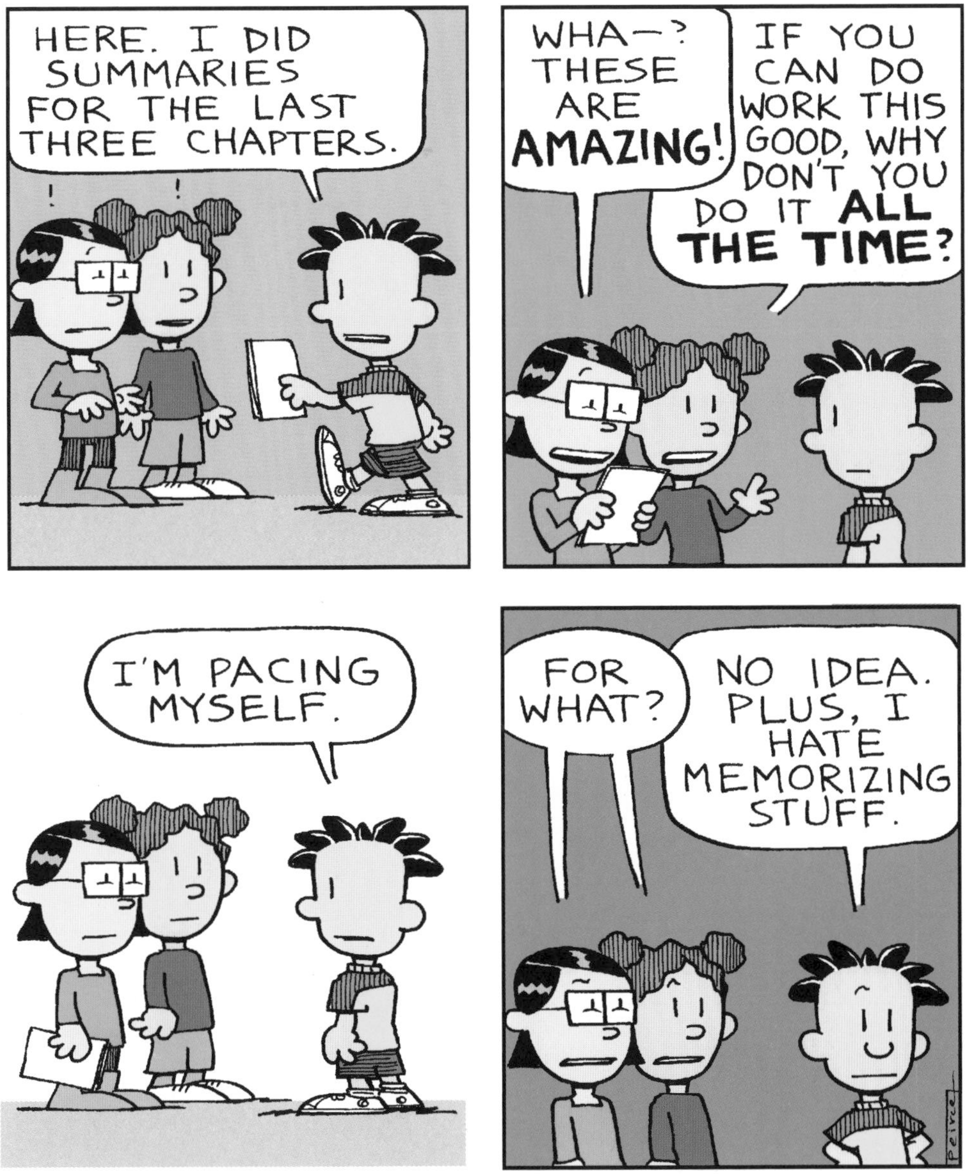
HERE. I DID SUMMARIES FOR THE LAST THREE CHAPTERS.
WHA—? THESE ARE **AMAZING**!
IF YOU CAN DO WORK THIS GOOD, WHY DON'T YOU DO IT **ALL THE TIME**?
I'M PACING MYSELF.
FOR WHAT?
NO IDEA. PLUS, I HATE MEMORIZING STUFF.
peirce

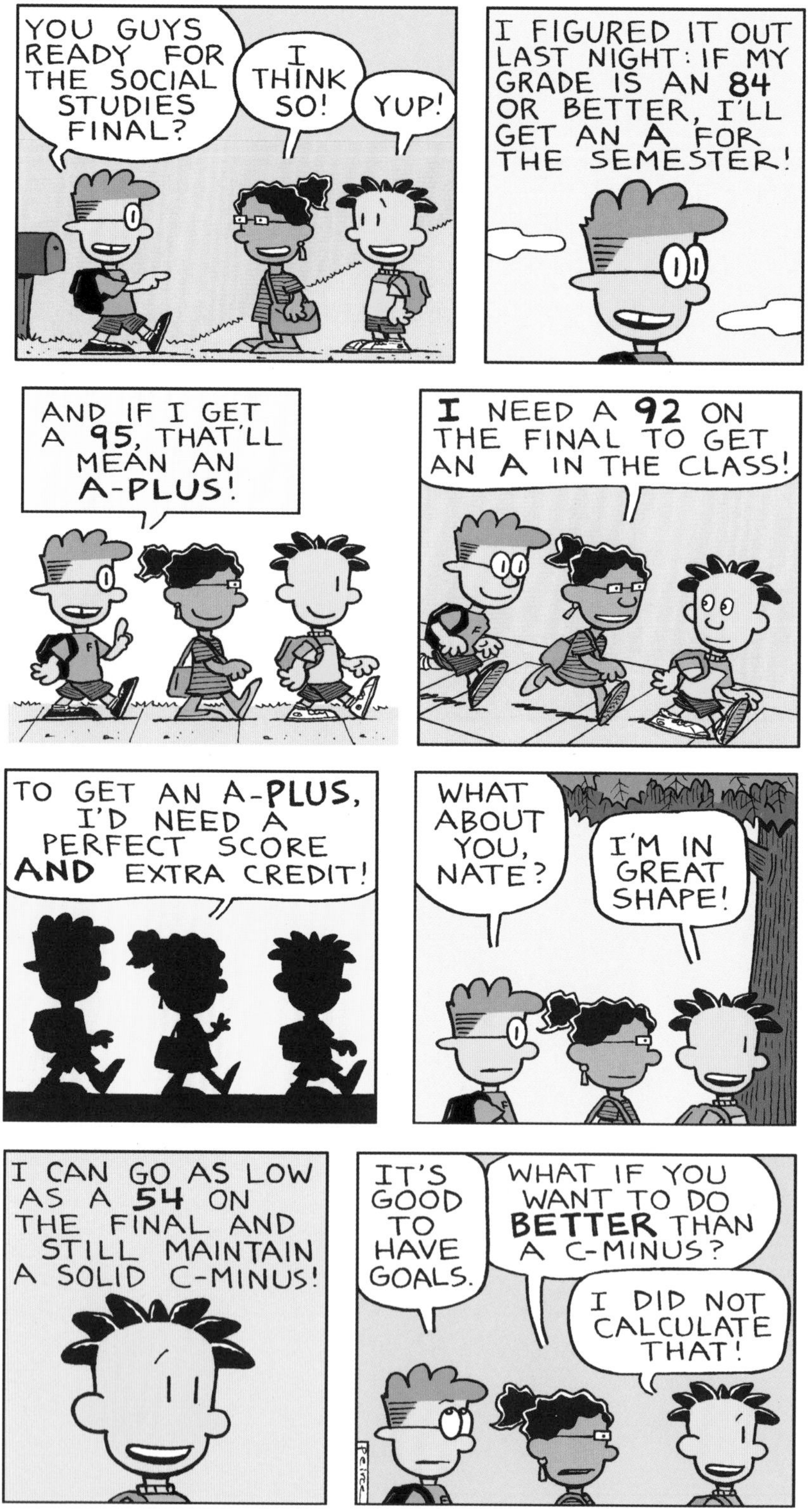
YOU GUYS READY FOR THE SOCIAL STUDIES FINAL?
I THINK SO!
YUP!
I FIGURED IT OUT LAST NIGHT: IF MY GRADE IS AN 84 OR BETTER, I'LL GET AN A FOR THE SEMESTER!
AND IF I GET A 95, THAT'LL MEAN AN A-PLUS!
I NEED A 92 ON THE FINAL TO GET AN A IN THE CLASS!
TO GET AN A-PLUS, I'D NEED A PERFECT SCORE AND EXTRA CREDIT!
WHAT ABOUT YOU, NATE?
I'M IN GREAT SHAPE!
I CAN GO AS LOW AS A 54 ON THE FINAL AND STILL MAINTAIN A SOLID C-MINUS!
IT'S GOOD TO HAVE GOALS.
WHAT IF YOU WANT TO DO BETTER THAN A C-MINUS?
I DID NOT CALCULATE THAT!

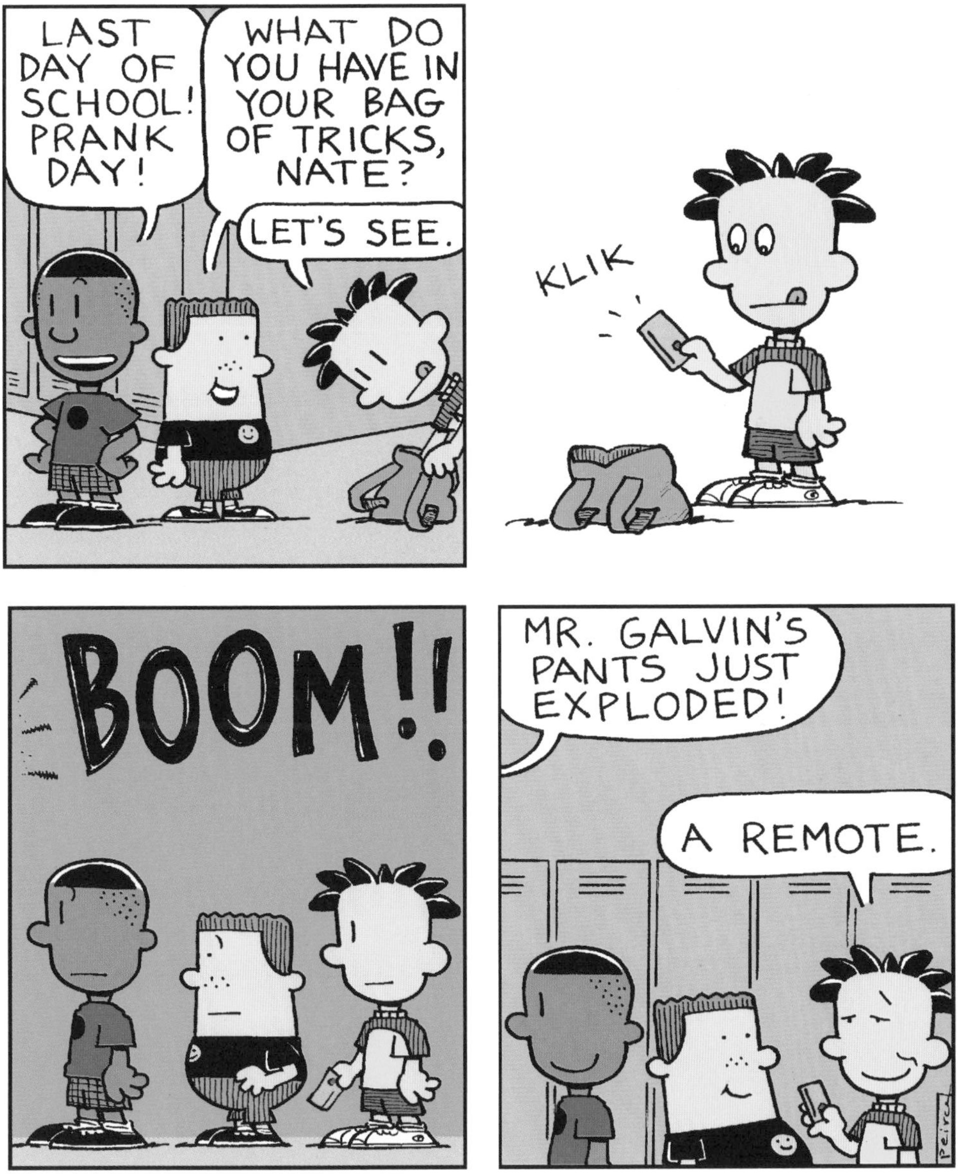
LAST DAY OF SCHOOL! PRANK DAY!
WHAT DO YOU HAVE IN YOUR BAG OF TRICKS, NATE?
LET'S SEE.
KLIK
BOOM!!
MR. GALVIN'S PANTS JUST EXPLODED!
A REMOTE.
Peirce

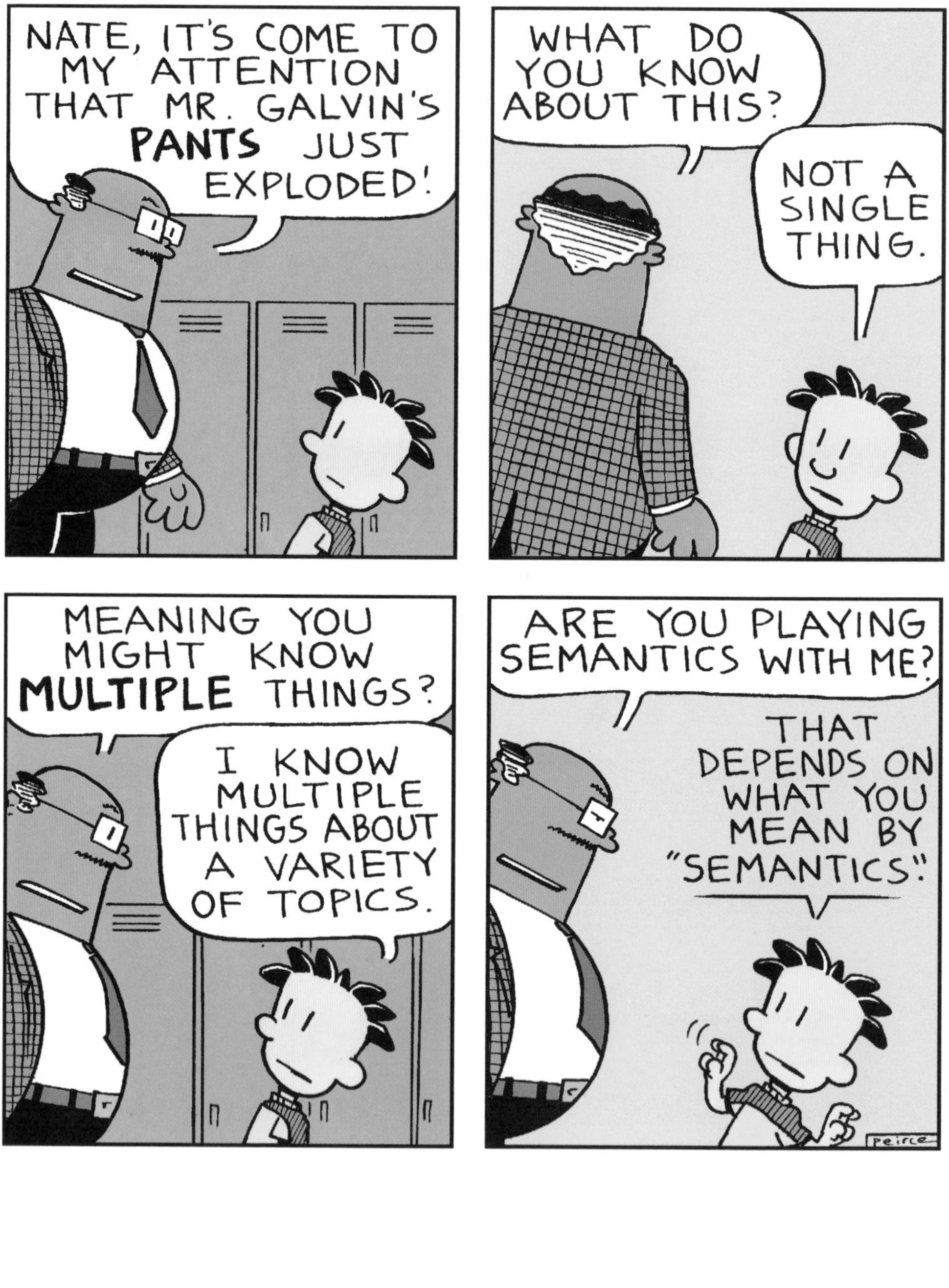
NATE, IT'S COME TO MY ATTENTION THAT MR. GALVIN'S **PANTS** JUST EXPLODED!
WHAT DO YOU KNOW ABOUT THIS?
NOT A SINGLE THING.
MEANING YOU MIGHT KNOW **MULTIPLE** THINGS?
I KNOW MULTIPLE THINGS ABOUT A VARIETY OF TOPICS.
ARE YOU PLAYING SEMANTICS WITH ME?
THAT DEPENDS ON WHAT YOU MEAN BY "SEMANTICS."
peirce

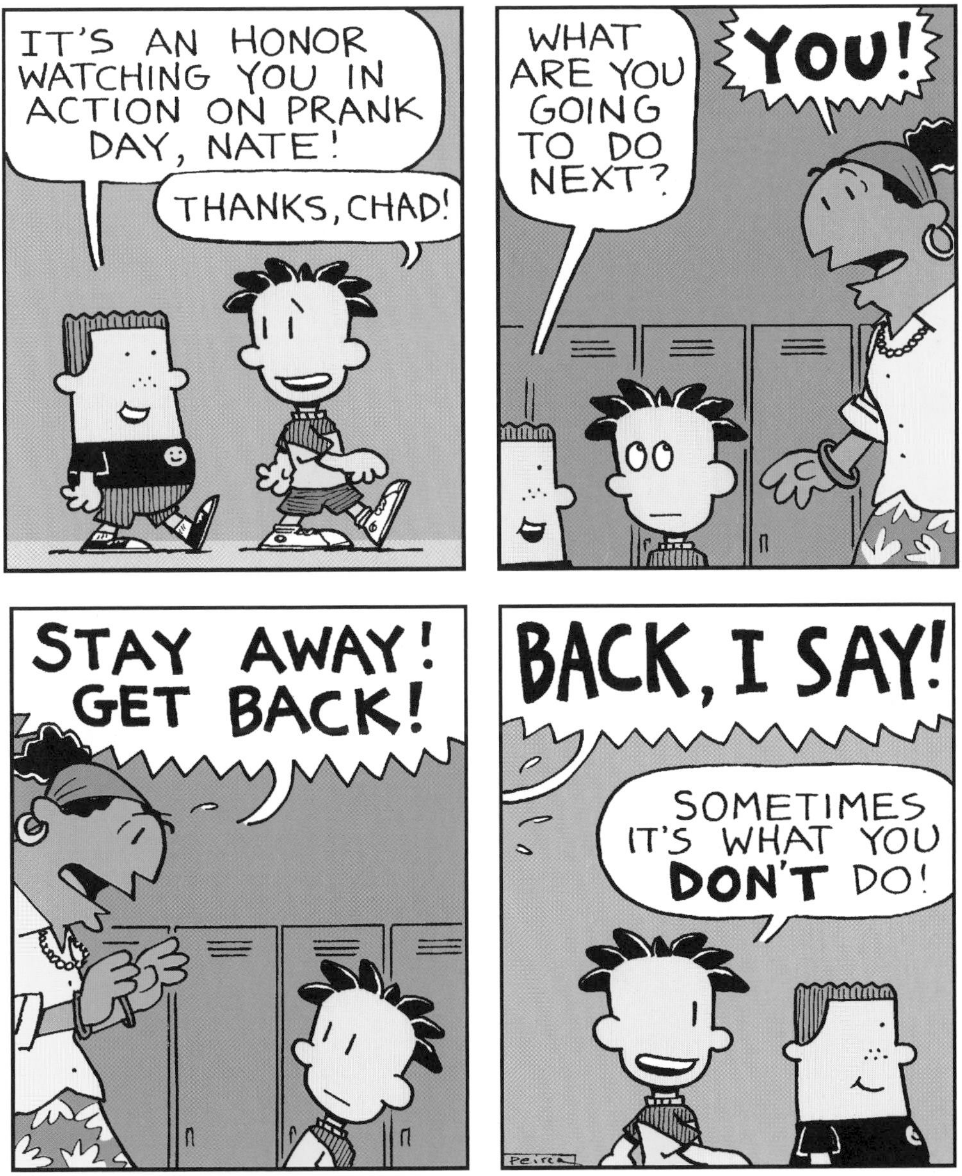
IT'S AN HONOR WATCHING YOU IN ACTION ON PRANK DAY, NATE!
THANKS, CHAD!
WHAT ARE YOU GOING TO DO NEXT?
YOU!
STAY AWAY! GET BACK!
BACK, I SAY!
SOMETIMES IT'S WHAT YOU **DON'T** DO!

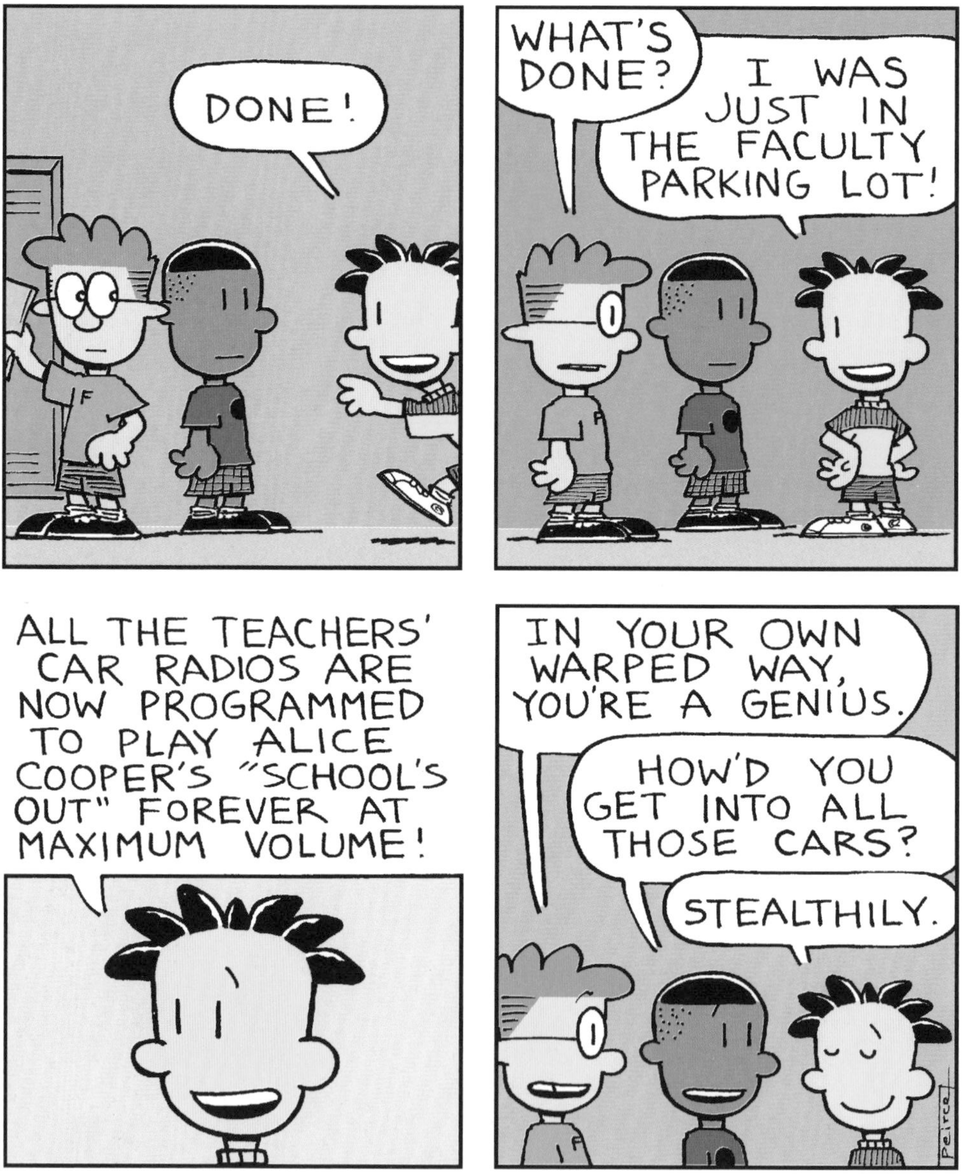
DONE!
WHAT'S DONE?
I WAS JUST IN THE FACULTY PARKING LOT!
ALL THE TEACHERS' CAR RADIOS ARE NOW PROGRAMMED TO PLAY ALICE COOPER'S "SCHOOL'S OUT" FOREVER AT MAXIMUM VOLUME!
IN YOUR OWN WARPED WAY, YOU'RE A GENIUS.
HOW'D YOU GET INTO ALL THOSE CARS?
STEALTHILY.
peirce

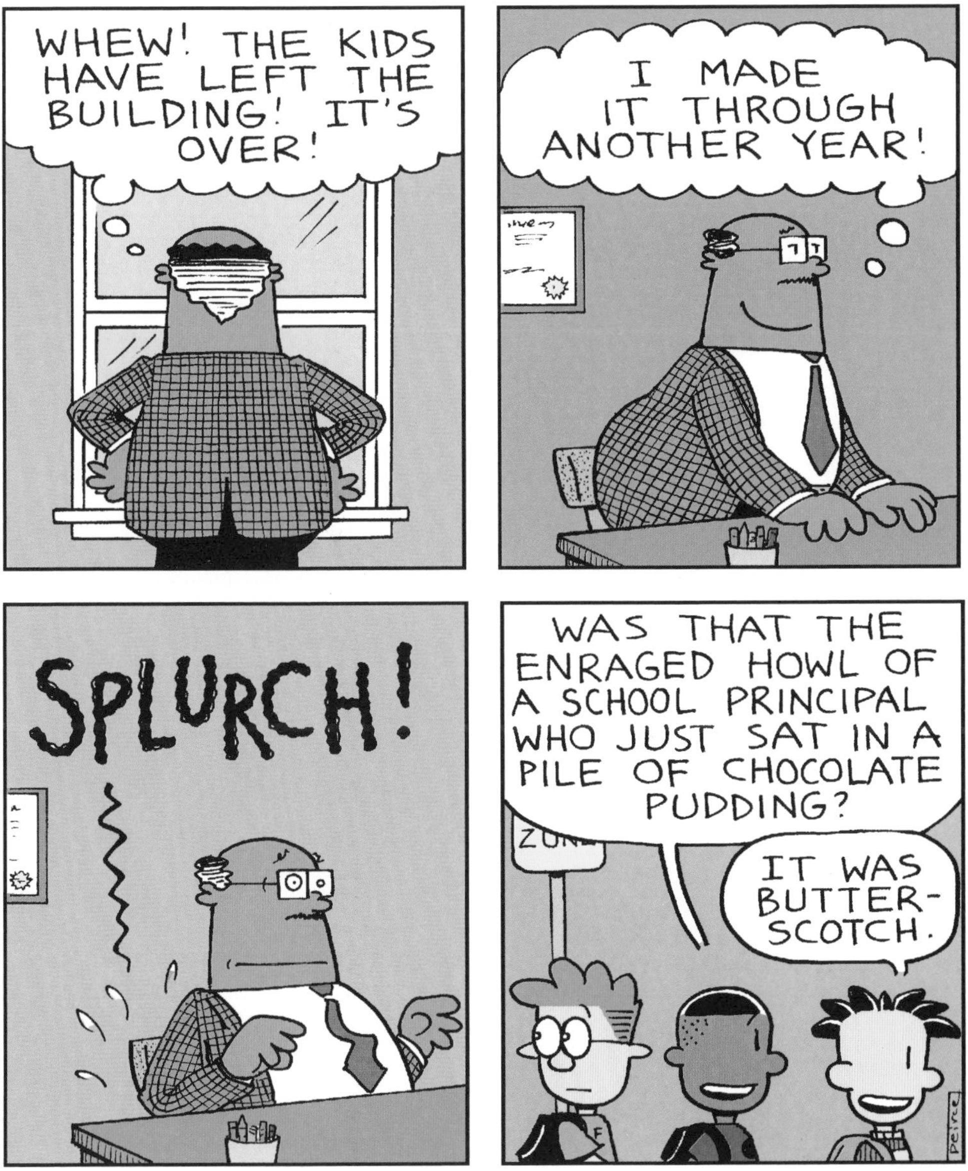
WHEW! THE KIDS HAVE LEFT THE BUILDING! IT'S OVER!
I MADE IT THROUGH ANOTHER YEAR!
SPLURCH!
WAS THAT THE ENRAGED HOWL OF A SCHOOL PRINCIPAL WHO JUST SAT IN A PILE OF CHOCOLATE PUDDING?
IT WAS BUTTER-SCOTCH.

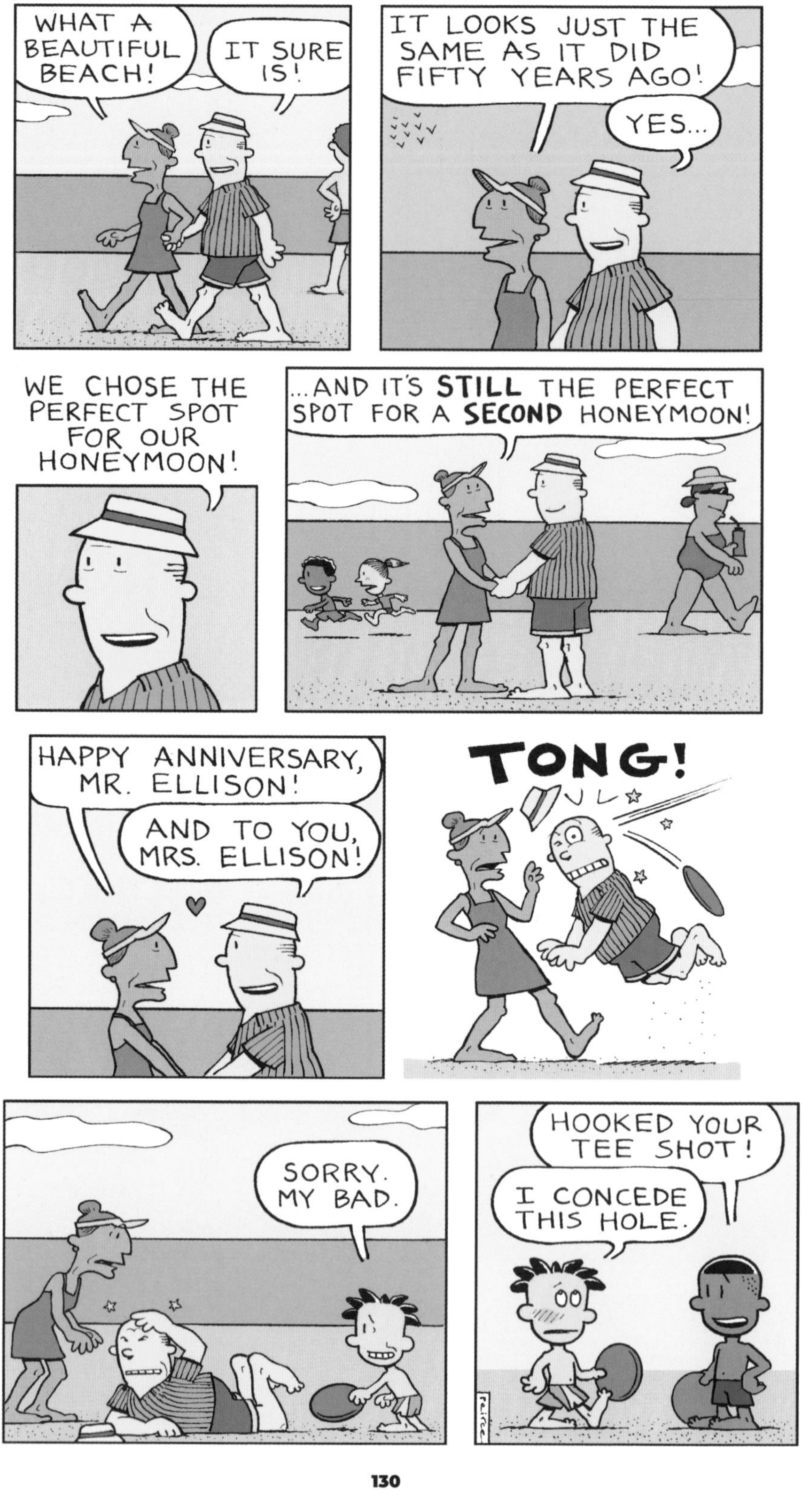
WHAT A BEAUTIFUL BEACH!
IT SURE IS!
IT LOOKS JUST THE SAME AS IT DID FIFTY YEARS AGO!
YES...
WE CHOSE THE PERFECT SPOT FOR OUR HONEYMOON!
...AND IT'S **STILL** THE PERFECT SPOT FOR A **SECOND** HONEYMOON!
HAPPY ANNIVERSARY, MR. ELLISON!
AND TO YOU, MRS. ELLISON!
TONG!
SORRY. MY BAD.
HOOKED YOUR TEE SHOT!
I CONCEDE THIS HOLE.
peirce

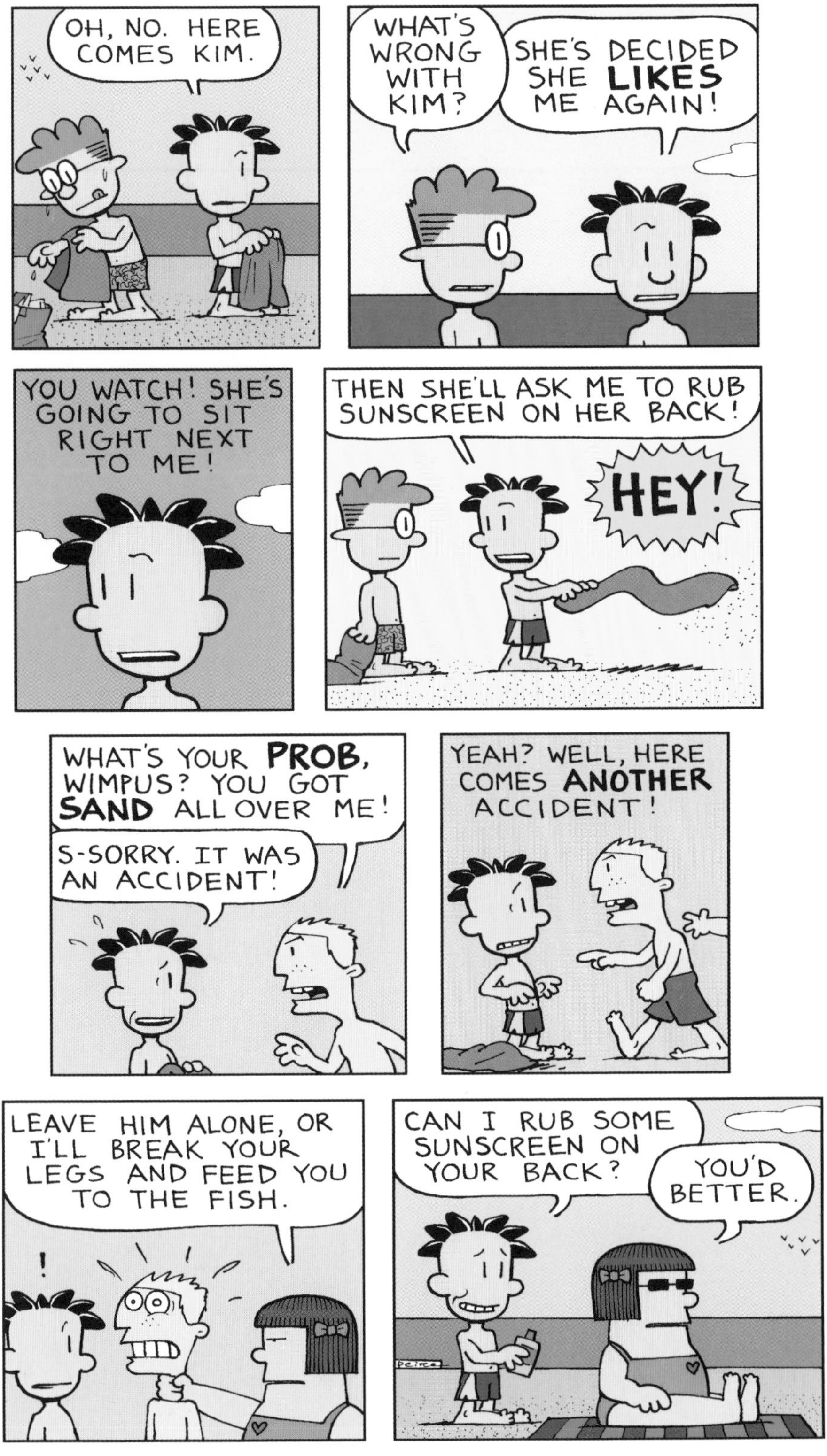
OH, NO. HERE COMES KIM.
WHAT'S WRONG WITH KIM?
SHE'S DECIDED SHE **LIKES** ME AGAIN!
YOU WATCH! SHE'S GOING TO SIT RIGHT NEXT TO ME!
THEN SHE'LL ASK ME TO RUB SUNSCREEN ON HER BACK!
HEY!
WHAT'S YOUR **PROB**, WIMPUS? YOU GOT **SAND** ALL OVER ME!
S-SORRY. IT WAS AN ACCIDENT!
YEAH? WELL, HERE COMES **ANOTHER** ACCIDENT!
LEAVE HIM ALONE, OR I'LL BREAK YOUR LEGS AND FEED YOU TO THE FISH.
!
CAN I RUB SOME SUNSCREEN ON YOUR BACK?
YOU'D BETTER.
peirce

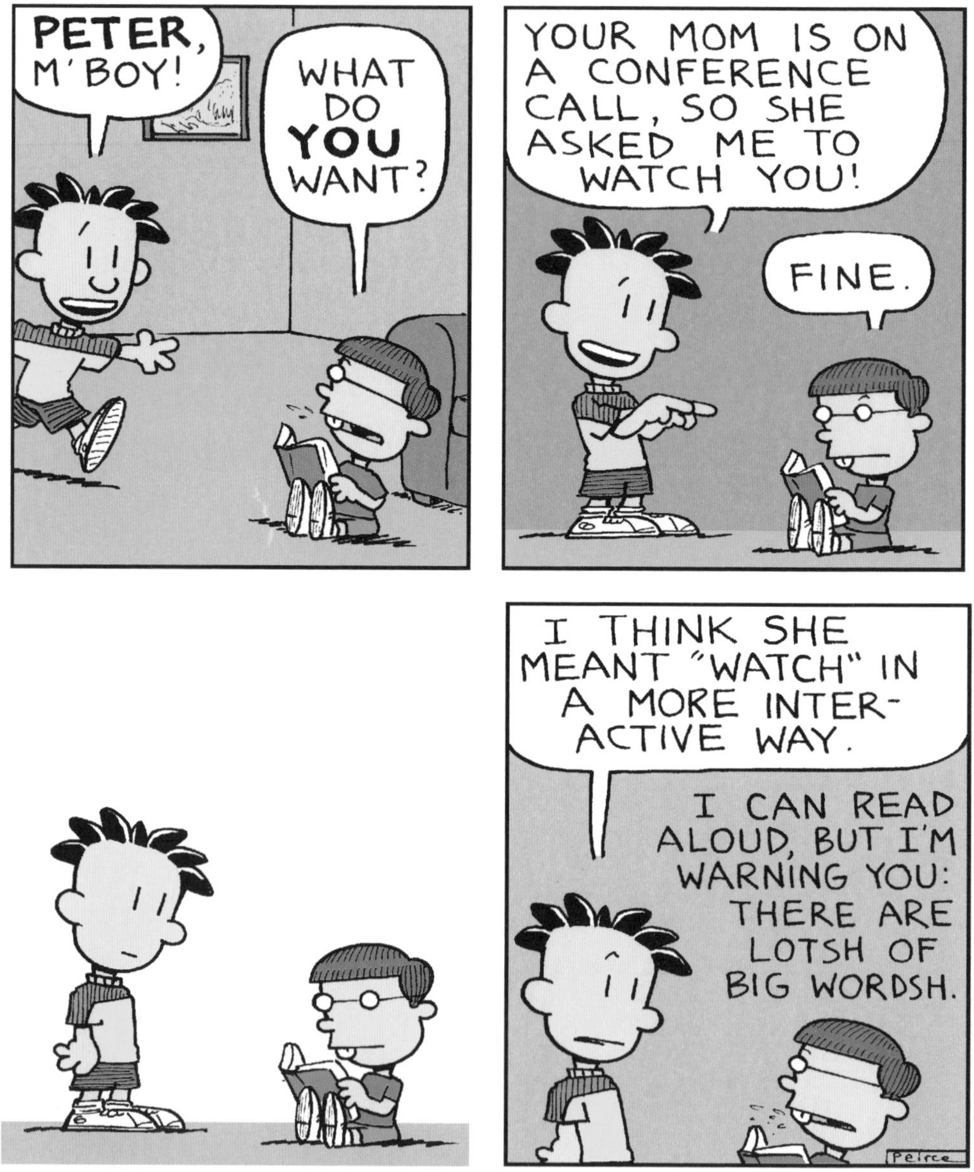
PETER, M'BOY!
WHAT DO YOU WANT?
YOUR MOM IS ON A CONFERENCE CALL, SO SHE ASKED ME TO WATCH YOU!
FINE.
I THINK SHE MEANT "WATCH" IN A MORE INTER-ACTIVE WAY.
I CAN READ ALOUD, BUT I'M WARNING YOU: THERE ARE LOTSH OF BIG WORDSH.
Peirce

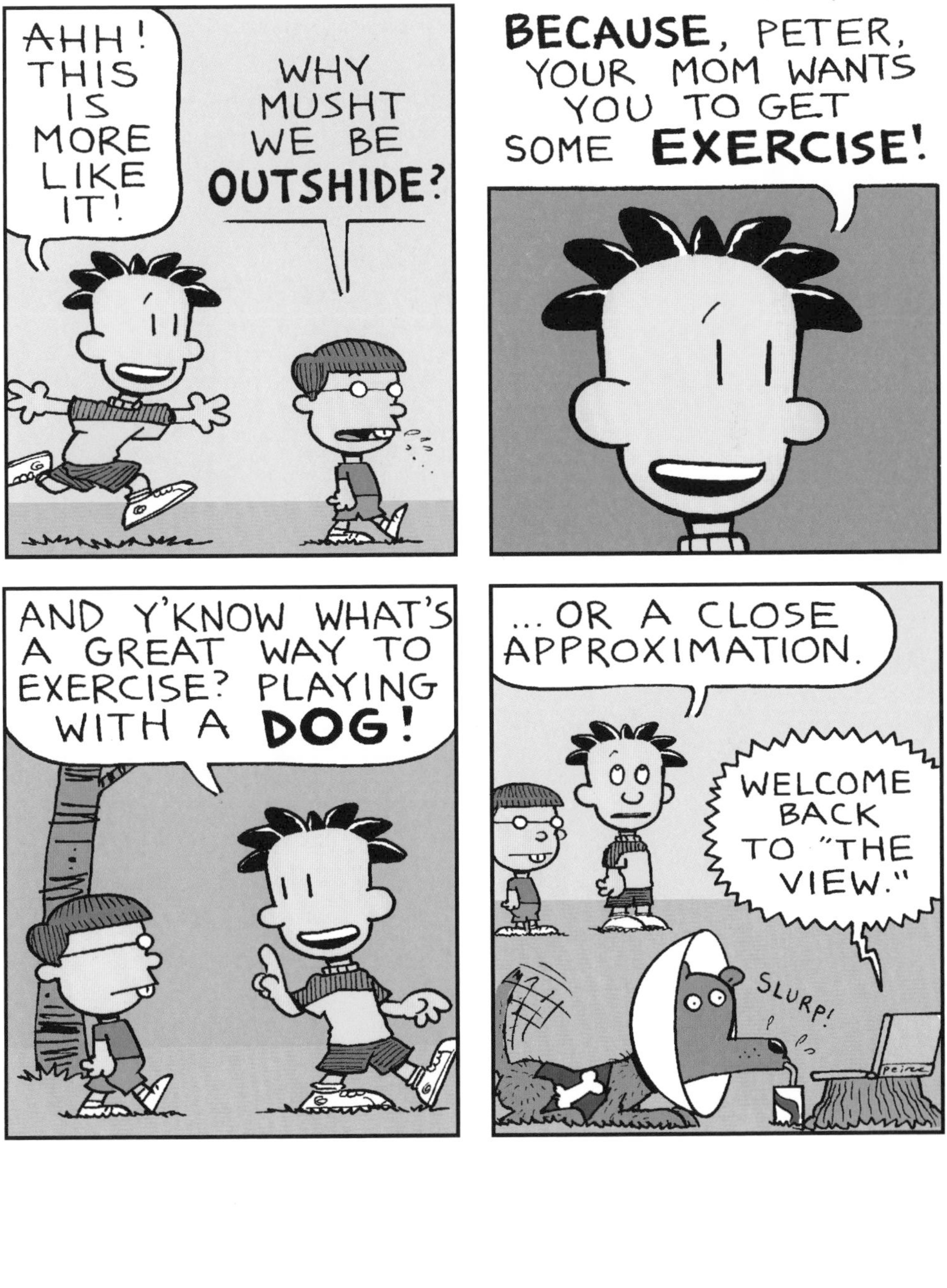

AHH! THIS IS MORE LIKE IT!
WHY MUSHT WE BE OUTSHIDE?
BECAUSE, PETER, YOUR MOM WANTS YOU TO GET SOME EXERCISE!
AND Y'KNOW WHAT'S A GREAT WAY TO EXERCISE? PLAYING WITH A DOG!
...OR A CLOSE APPROXIMATION.
WELCOME BACK TO "THE VIEW."
SLURP!

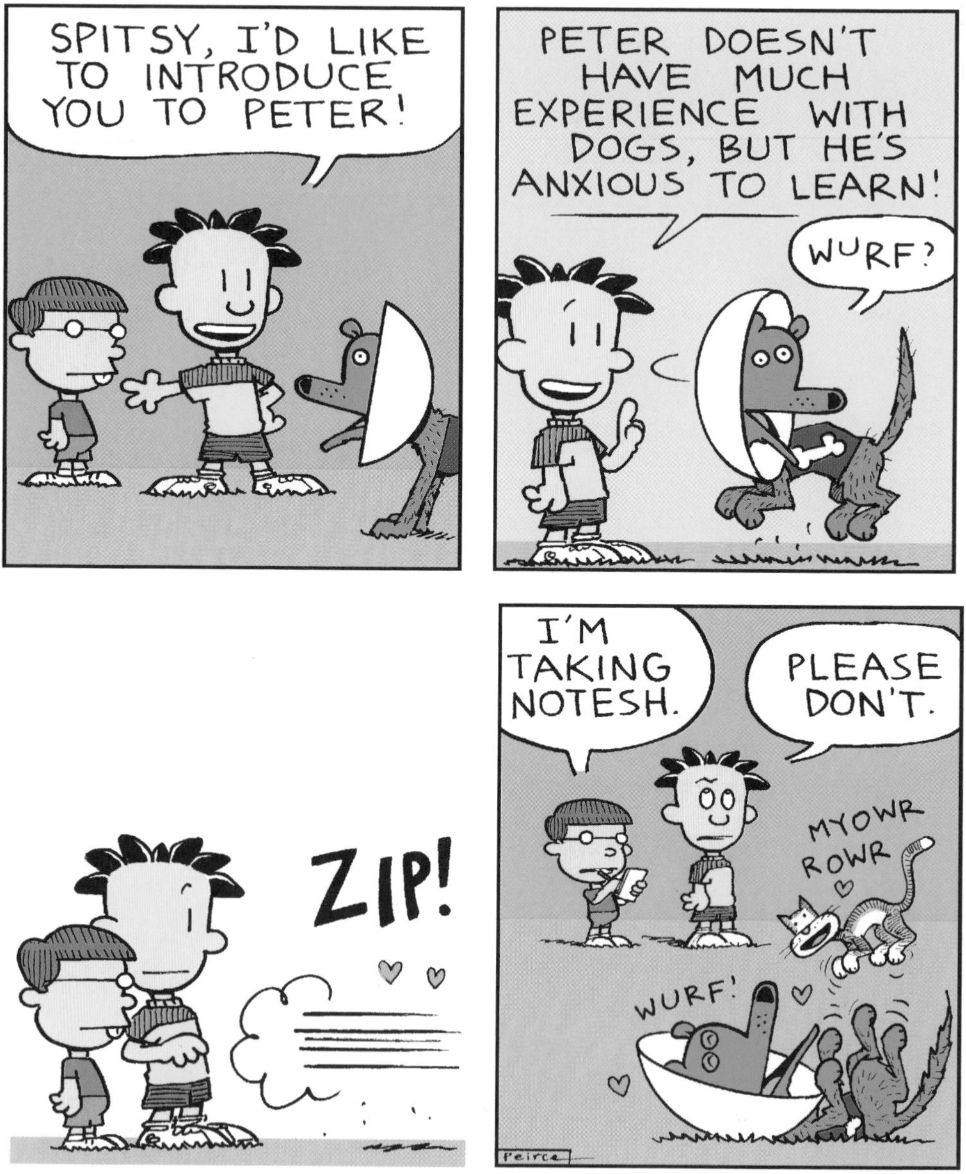
SPITSY, I'D LIKE TO INTRODUCE YOU TO PETER!
PETER DOESN'T HAVE MUCH EXPERIENCE WITH DOGS, BUT HE'S ANXIOUS TO LEARN!
WURF?
ZIP!
I'M TAKING NOTESH.
PLEASE DON'T.
MYOWR ROWR
WURF!
Peirce

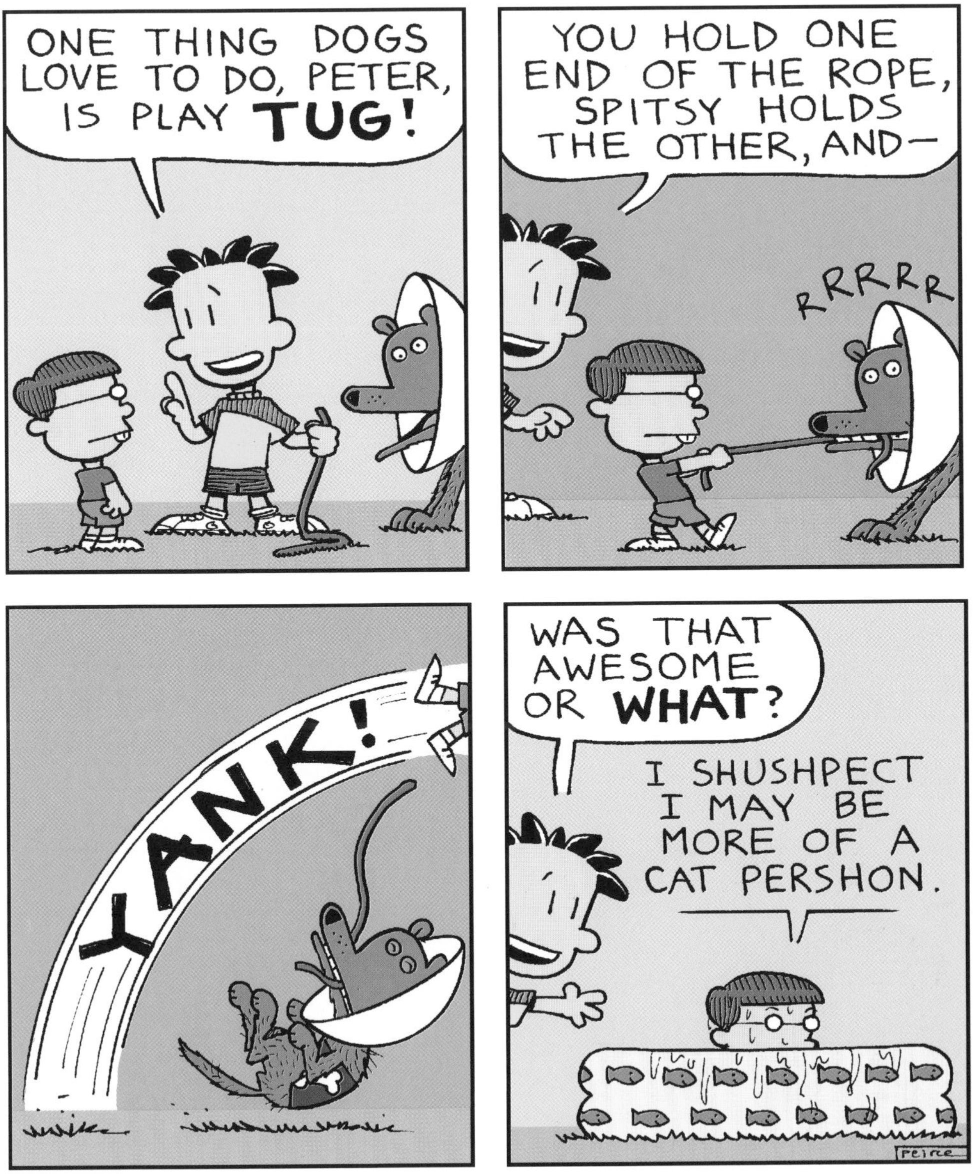
ONE THING DOGS LOVE TO DO, PETER, IS PLAY **TUG**!
YOU HOLD ONE END OF THE ROPE, SPITSY HOLDS THE OTHER, AND—
RRRRR
YANK!
WAS THAT AWESOME OR **WHAT**?
I SHUSHPECT I MAY BE MORE OF A CAT PERSHON.
peirce

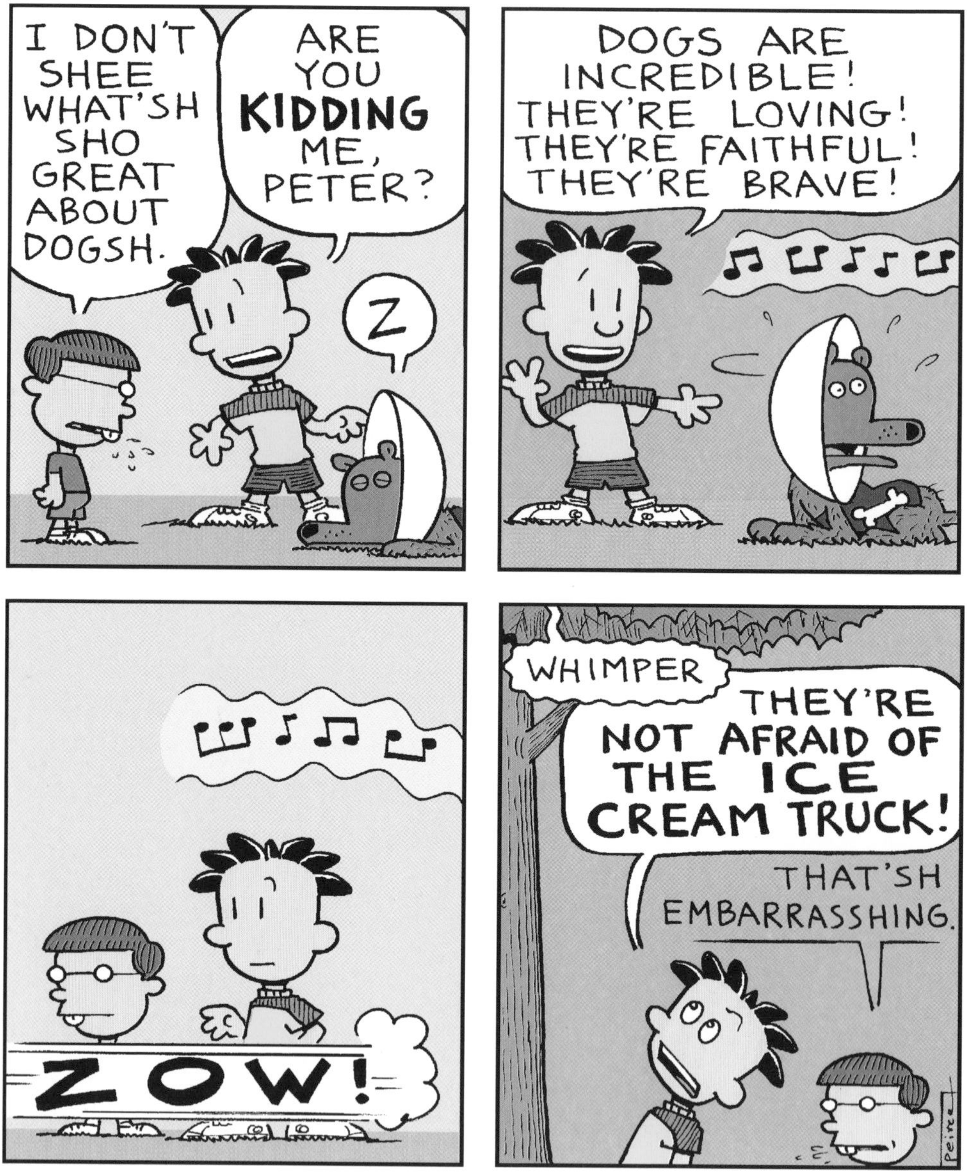
I DON'T SHEE WHAT'SH SHO GREAT ABOUT DOGSH.
ARE YOU **KIDDING** ME, PETER?
Z
DOGS ARE INCREDIBLE! THEY'RE LOVING! THEY'RE FAITHFUL! THEY'RE BRAVE!
ZOW!
WHIMPER
THEY'RE **NOT AFRAID OF THE ICE CREAM TRUCK!**
THAT'SH EMBARRASSHING.
Peirce

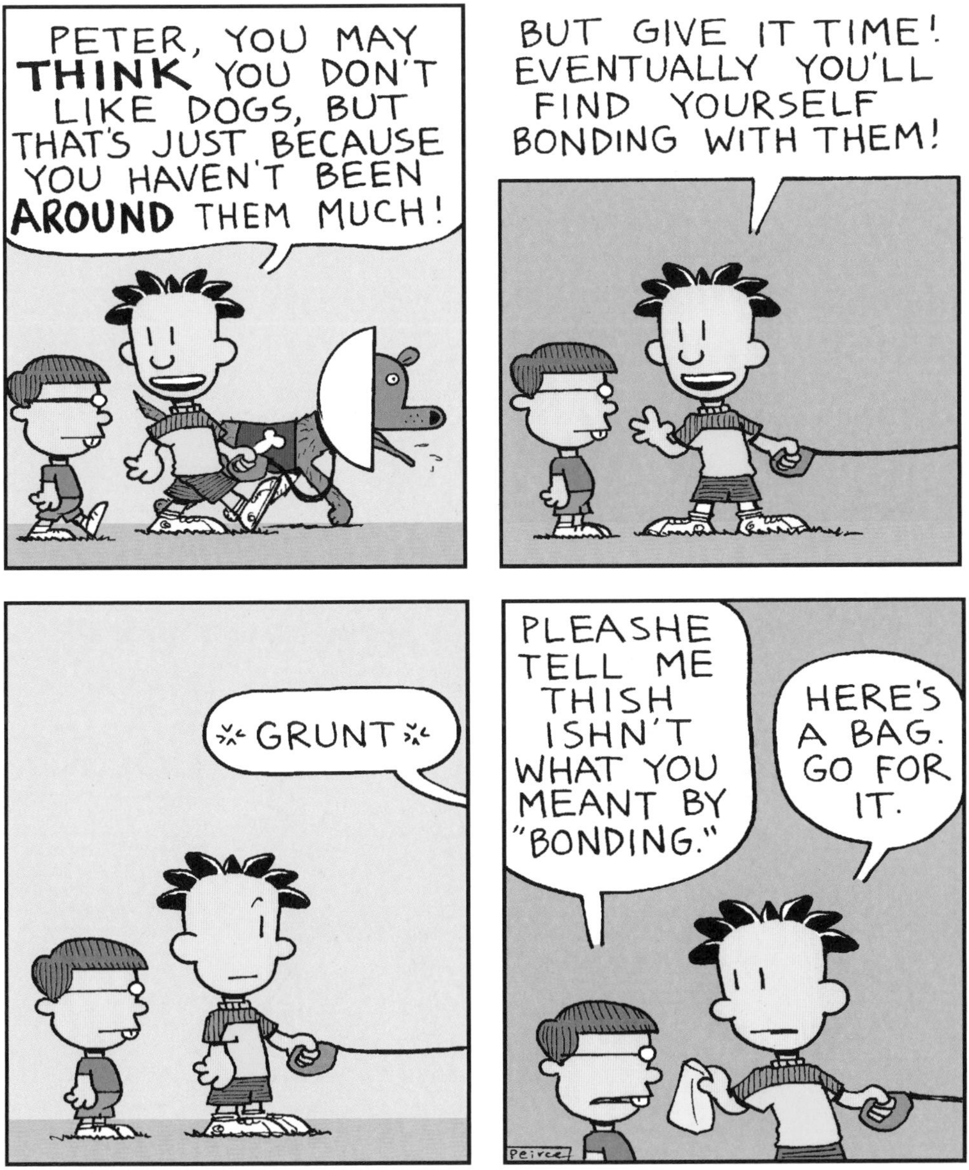
PETER, YOU MAY **THINK** YOU DON'T LIKE DOGS, BUT THAT'S JUST BECAUSE YOU HAVEN'T BEEN **AROUND** THEM MUCH!
BUT GIVE IT TIME! EVENTUALLY YOU'LL FIND YOURSELF BONDING WITH THEM!
GRUNT
PLEASHE TELL ME THISH ISHN'T WHAT YOU MEANT BY "BONDING."
HERE'S A BAG. GO FOR IT.
Peirce

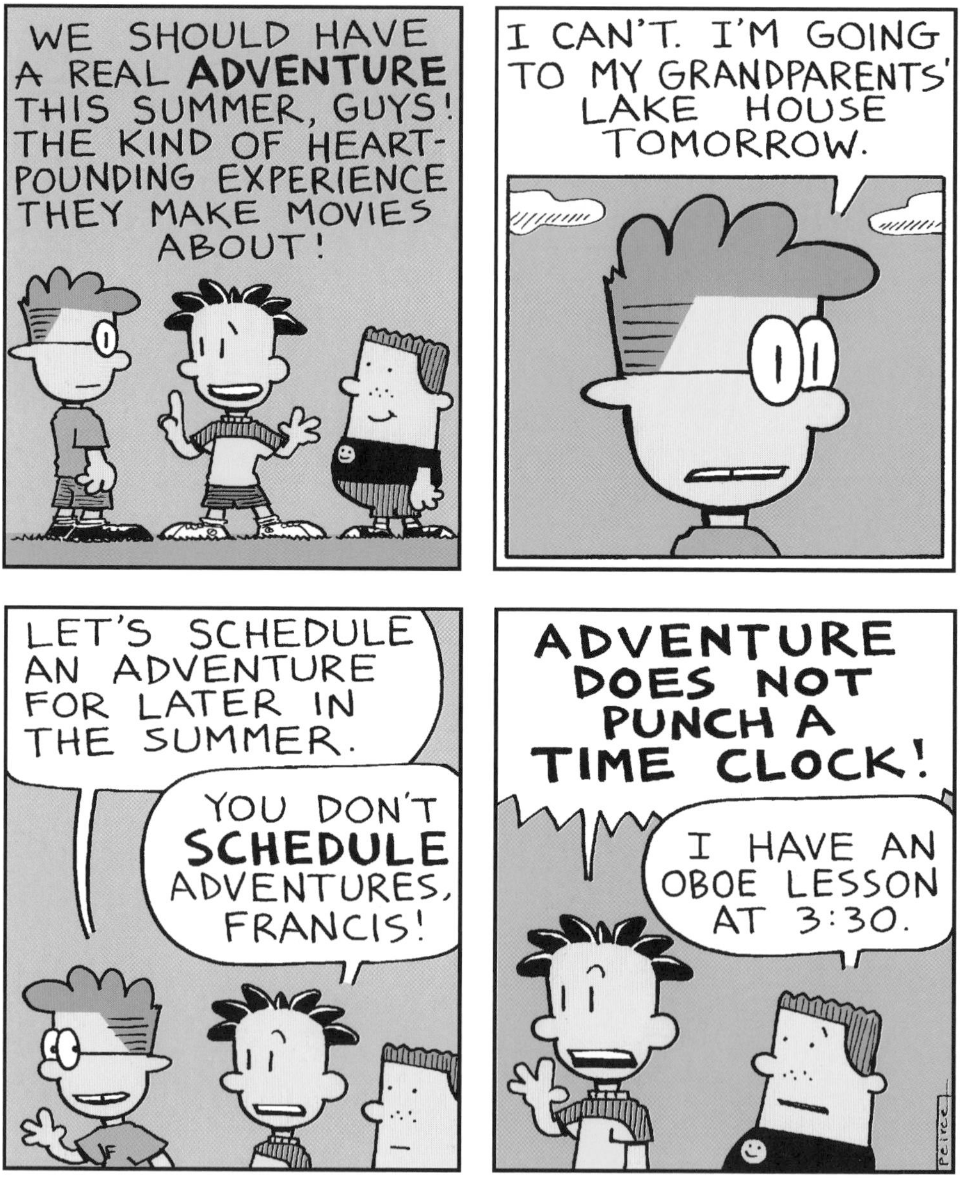
WE SHOULD HAVE A REAL ADVENTURE THIS SUMMER, GUYS! THE KIND OF HEART-POUNDING EXPERIENCE THEY MAKE MOVIES ABOUT!
I CAN'T. I'M GOING TO MY GRANDPARENTS' LAKE HOUSE TOMORROW.
LET'S SCHEDULE AN ADVENTURE FOR LATER IN THE SUMMER.
YOU DON'T SCHEDULE ADVENTURES, FRANCIS!
ADVENTURE DOES NOT PUNCH A TIME CLOCK!
I HAVE AN OBOE LESSON AT 3:30.
peirce

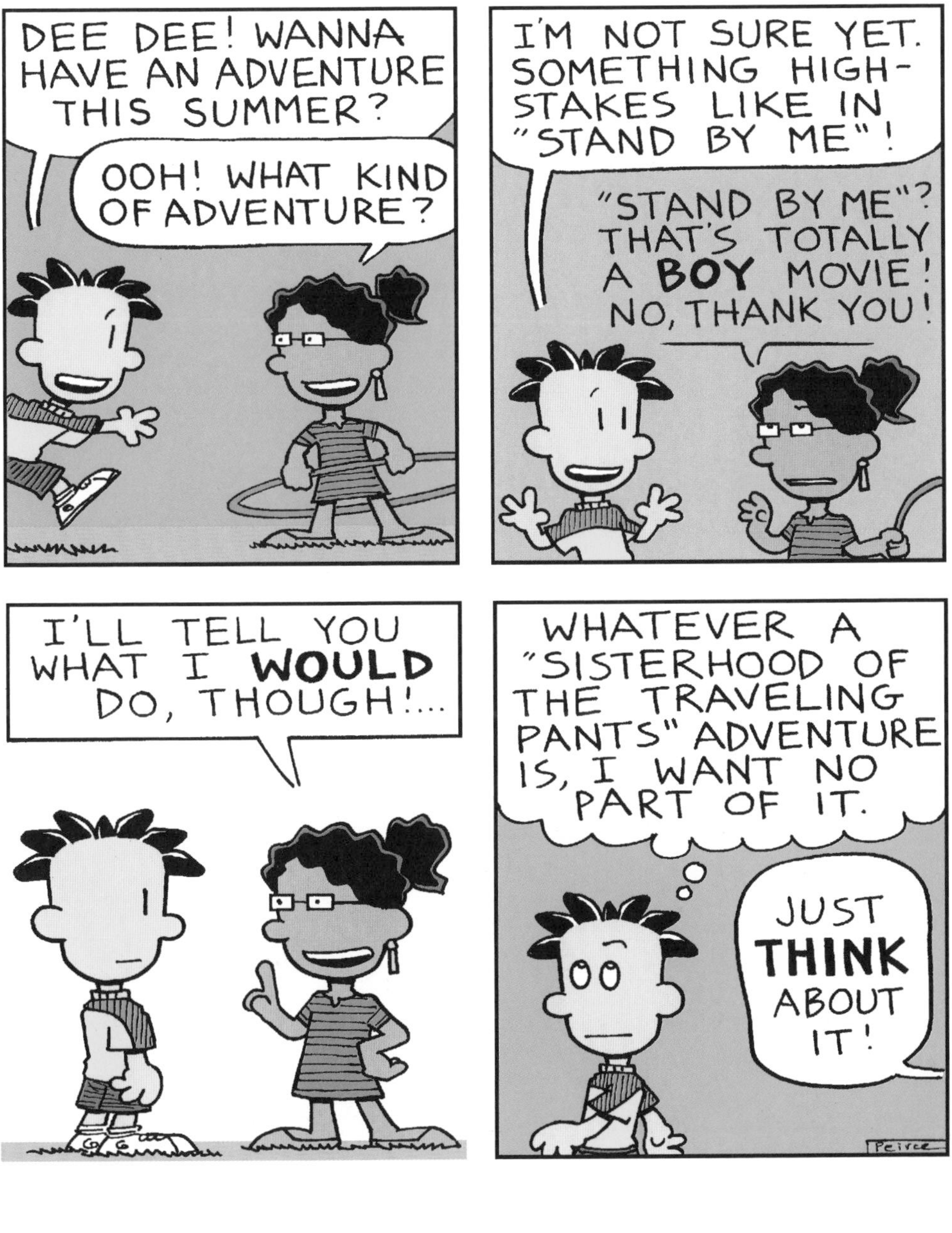
DEE DEE! WANNA HAVE AN ADVENTURE THIS SUMMER?
OOH! WHAT KIND OF ADVENTURE?
I'M NOT SURE YET. SOMETHING HIGH-STAKES LIKE IN "STAND BY ME"!
"STAND BY ME"? THAT'S TOTALLY A **BOY** MOVIE! NO, THANK YOU!
I'LL TELL YOU WHAT I **WOULD** DO, THOUGH!...
WHATEVER A "SISTERHOOD OF THE TRAVELING PANTS" ADVENTURE IS, I WANT NO PART OF IT.
JUST **THINK** ABOUT IT!
Peirce

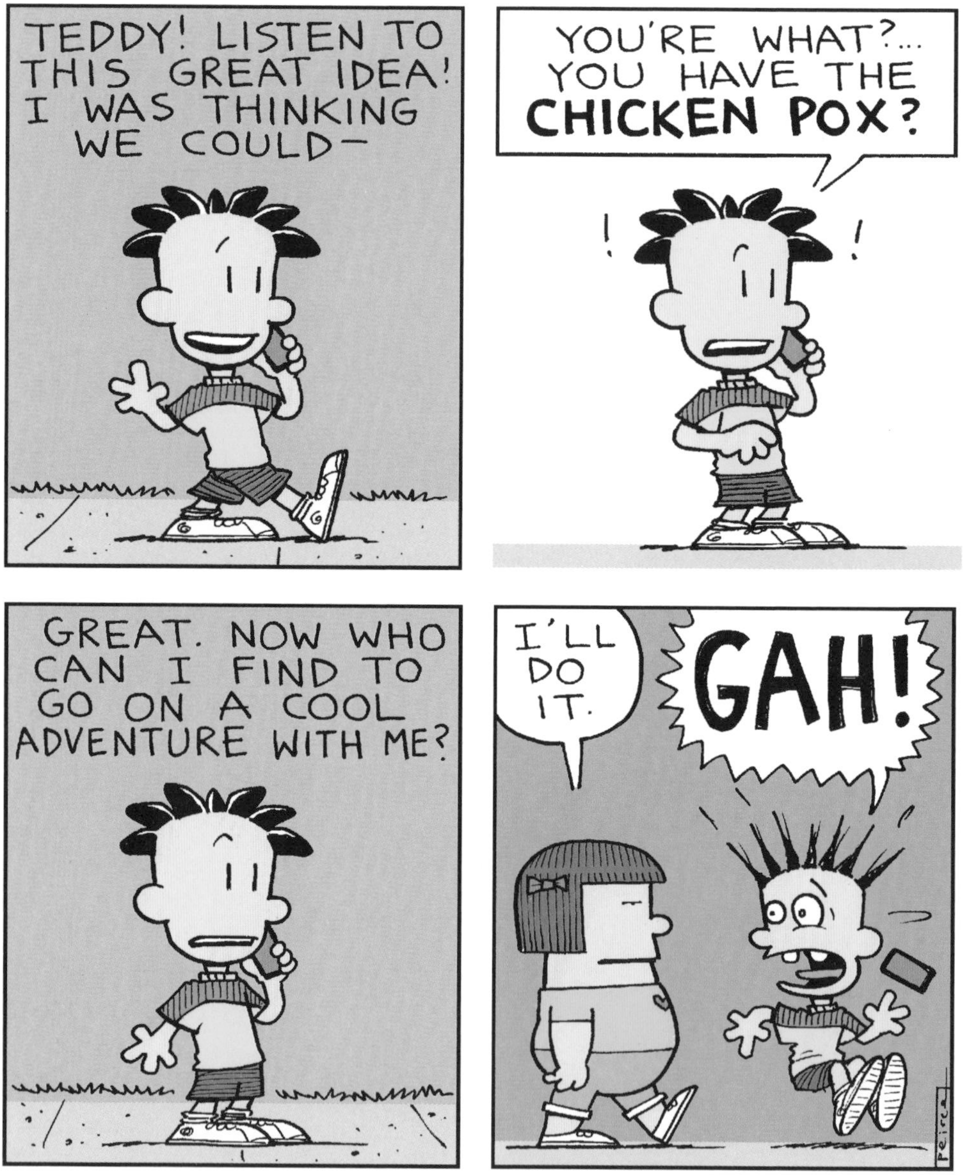
TEDDY! LISTEN TO THIS GREAT IDEA! I WAS THINKING WE COULD-
YOU'RE WHAT?... YOU HAVE THE **CHICKEN POX**?
GREAT. NOW WHO CAN I FIND TO GO ON A COOL ADVENTURE WITH ME?
I'LL DO IT.
GAH!
Peirce

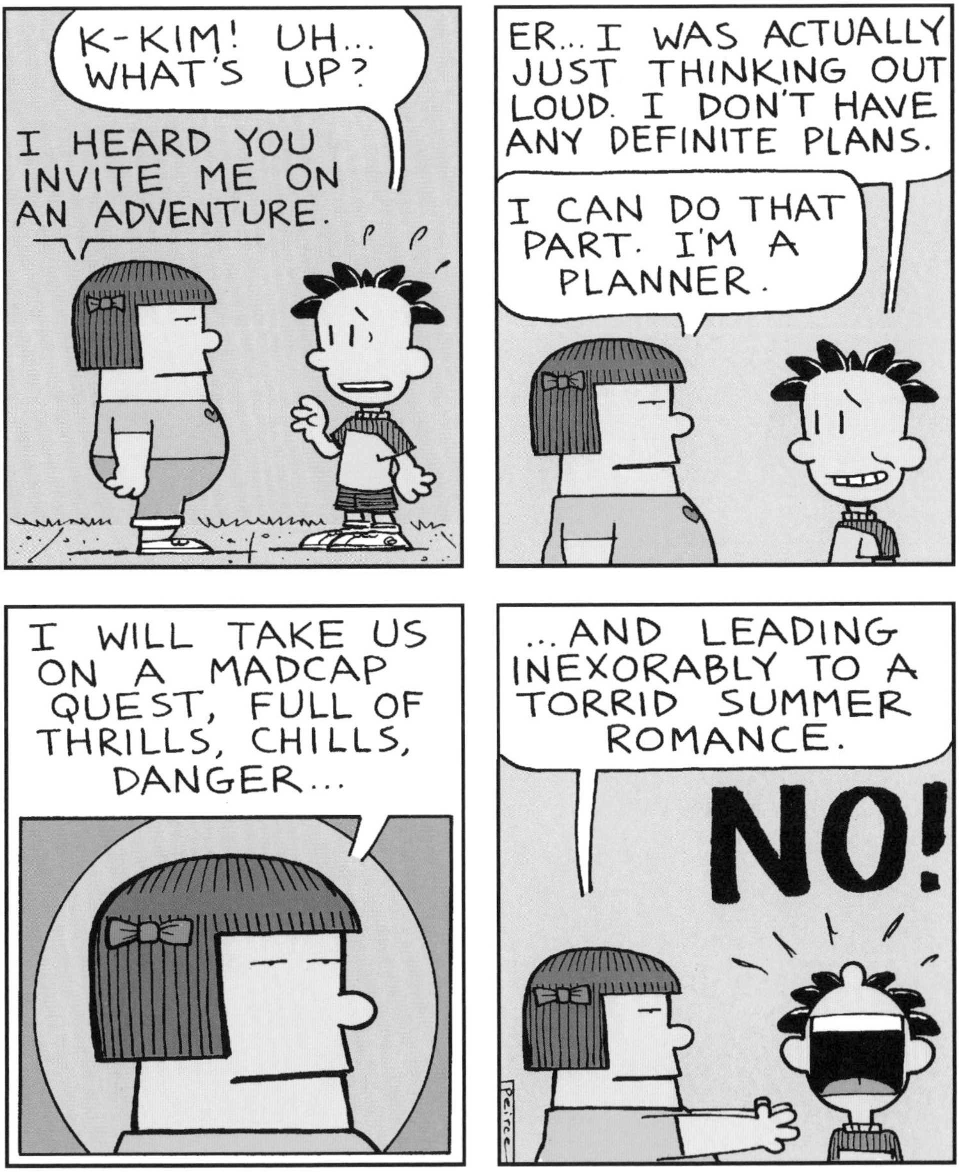
K-KIM! UH... WHAT'S UP?
I HEARD YOU INVITE ME ON AN ADVENTURE.
ER... I WAS ACTUALLY JUST THINKING OUT LOUD. I DON'T HAVE ANY DEFINITE PLANS.
I CAN DO THAT PART. I'M A PLANNER.
I WILL TAKE US ON A MADCAP QUEST, FULL OF THRILLS, CHILLS, DANGER...
...AND LEADING INEXORABLY TO A TORRID SUMMER ROMANCE.
NO!
Peirce

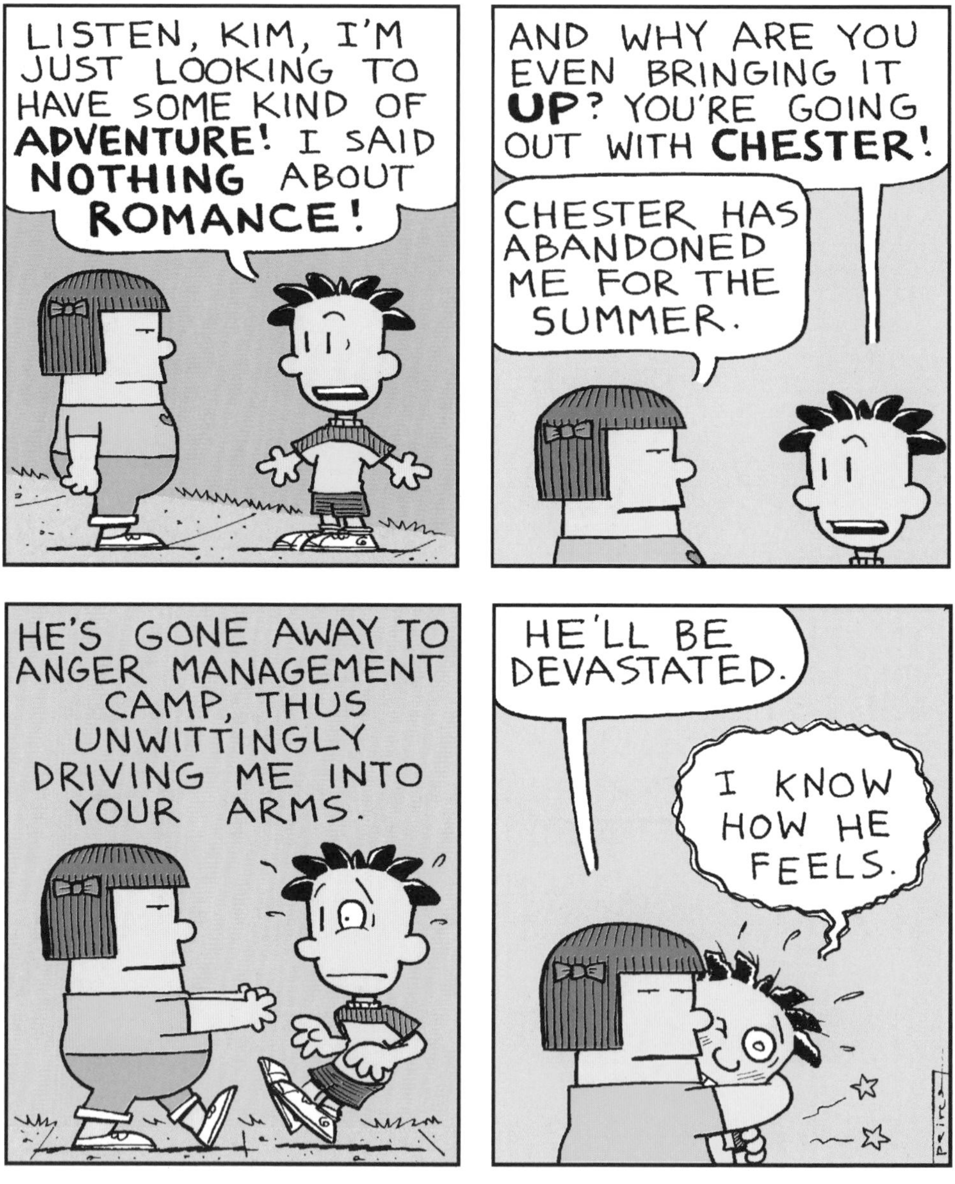
LISTEN, KIM, I'M JUST LOOKING TO HAVE SOME KIND OF **ADVENTURE!** I SAID **NOTHING** ABOUT **ROMANCE!**
AND WHY ARE YOU EVEN BRINGING IT **UP**? YOU'RE GOING OUT WITH **CHESTER**!
CHESTER HAS ABANDONED ME FOR THE SUMMER.
HE'S GONE AWAY TO ANGER MANAGEMENT CAMP, THUS UNWITTINGLY DRIVING ME INTO YOUR ARMS.
HE'LL BE DEVASTATED.
I KNOW HOW HE FEELS.
PEIRCE

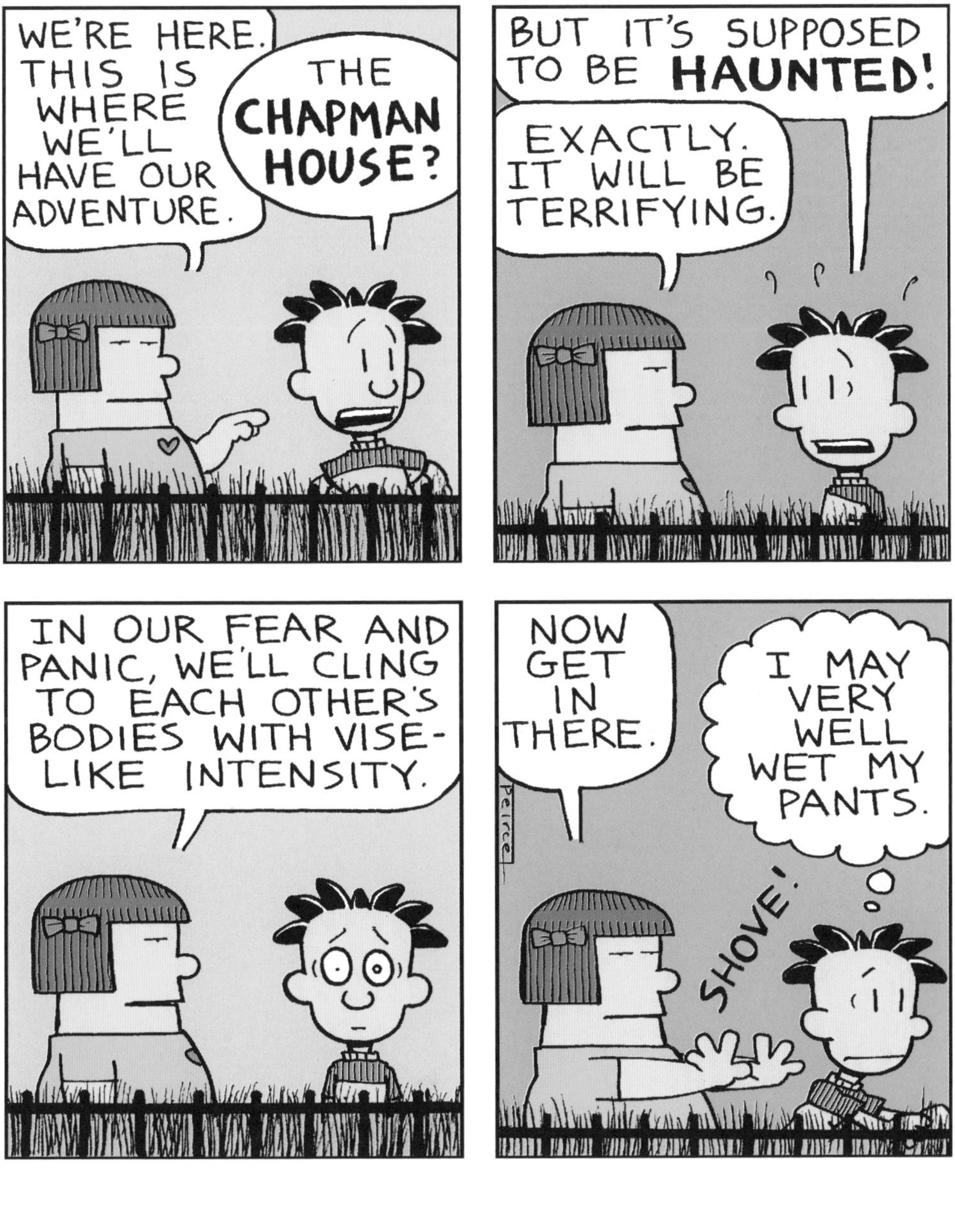
WE'RE HERE. THIS IS WHERE WE'LL HAVE OUR ADVENTURE.
THE **CHAPMAN HOUSE**?
BUT IT'S SUPPOSED TO BE **HAUNTED**!
EXACTLY. IT WILL BE TERRIFYING.
IN OUR FEAR AND PANIC, WE'LL CLING TO EACH OTHER'S BODIES WITH VISE-LIKE INTENSITY.
NOW GET IN THERE.
I MAY VERY WELL WET MY PANTS.
SHOVE!
peirce

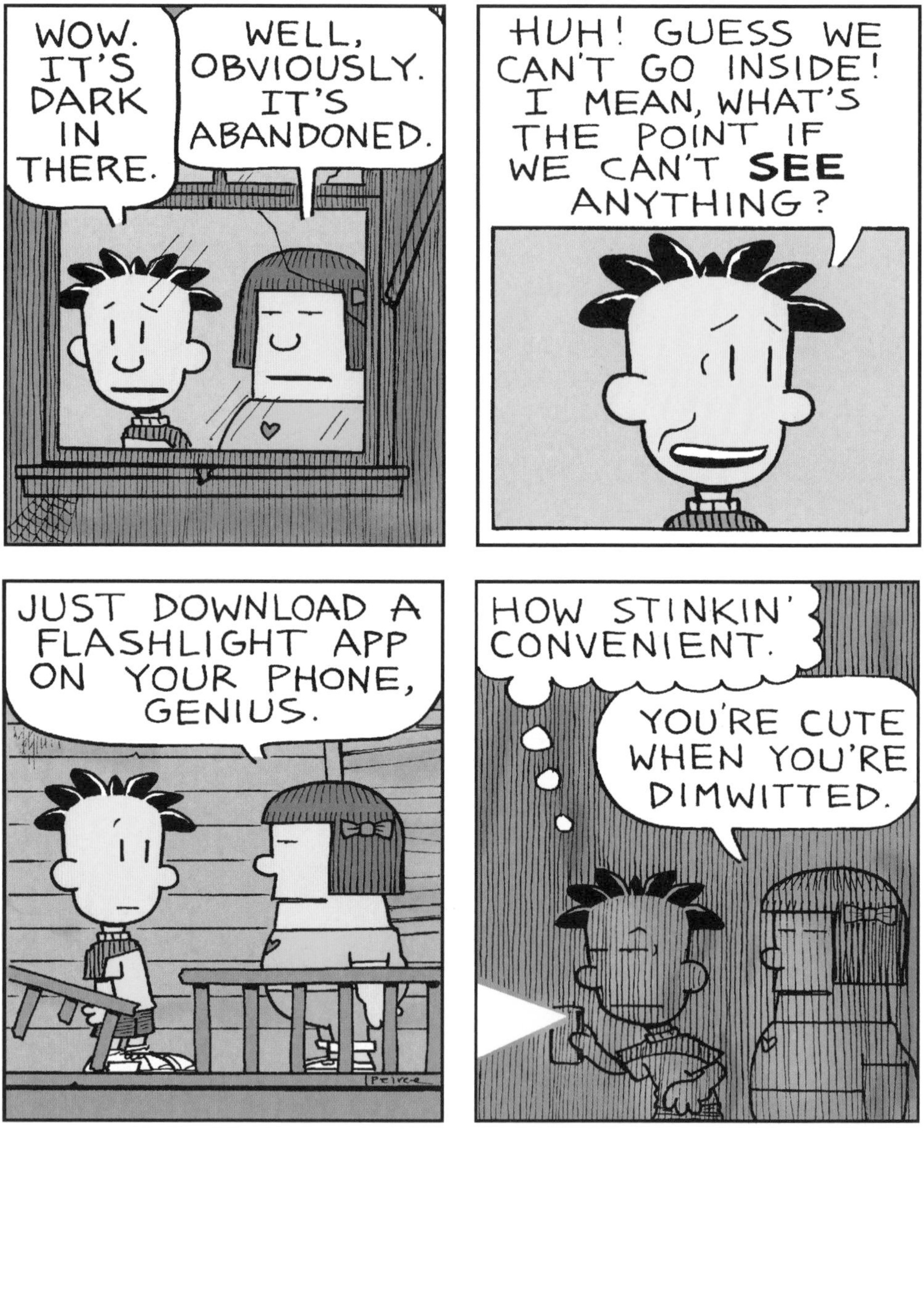
WOW. IT'S DARK IN THERE.
WELL, OBVIOUSLY. IT'S ABANDONED.
HUH! GUESS WE CAN'T GO INSIDE! I MEAN, WHAT'S THE POINT IF WE CAN'T **SEE** ANYTHING?
JUST DOWNLOAD A FLASHLIGHT APP ON YOUR PHONE, GENIUS.
Peirce
HOW STINKIN' CONVENIENT.
YOU'RE CUTE WHEN YOU'RE DIMWITTED.

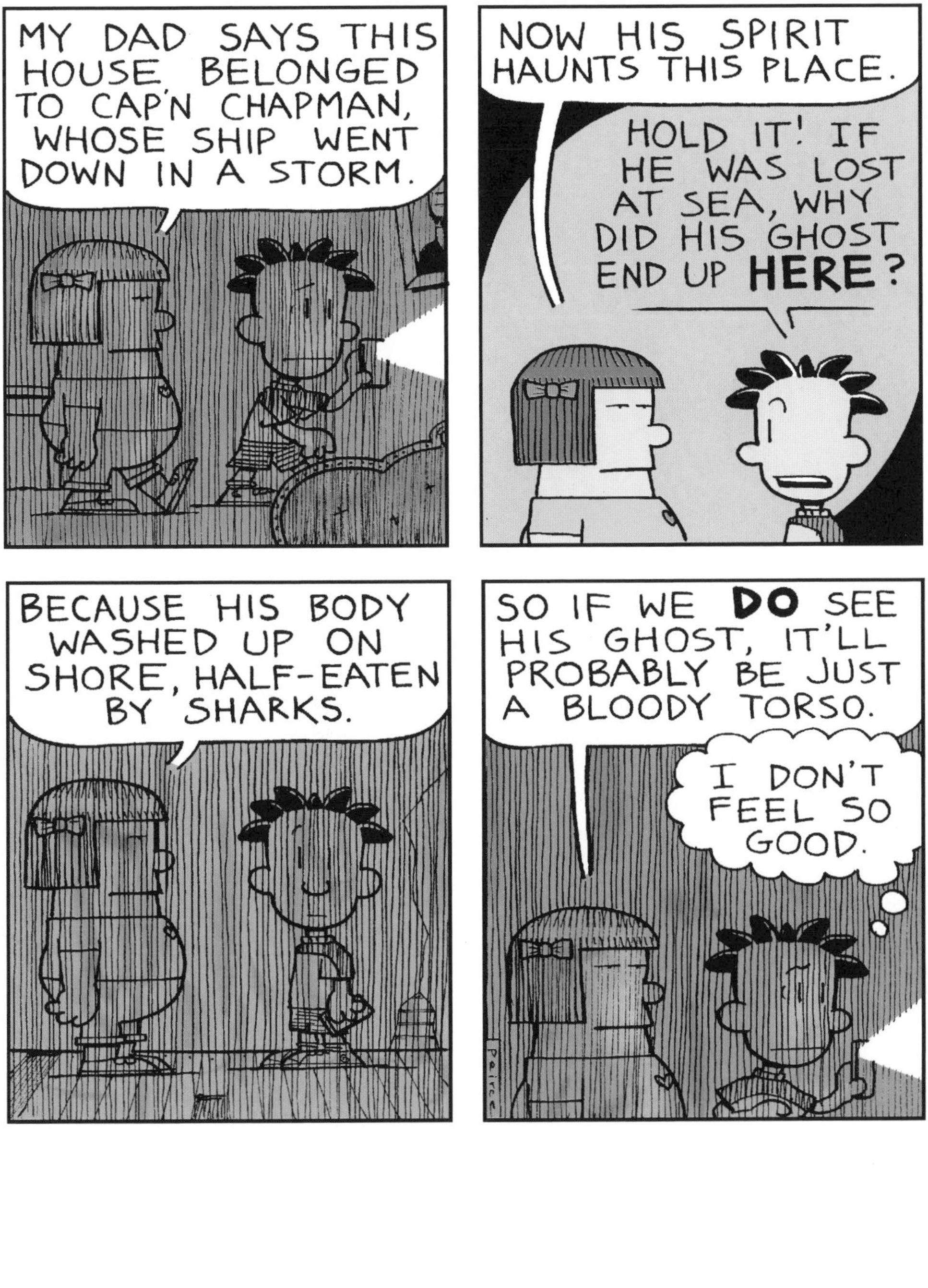
MY DAD SAYS THIS HOUSE BELONGED TO CAP'N CHAPMAN, WHOSE SHIP WENT DOWN IN A STORM.
NOW HIS SPIRIT HAUNTS THIS PLACE.
HOLD IT! IF HE WAS LOST AT SEA, WHY DID HIS GHOST END UP **HERE**?
BECAUSE HIS BODY WASHED UP ON SHORE, HALF-EATEN BY SHARKS.
SO IF WE **DO** SEE HIS GHOST, IT'LL PROBABLY BE JUST A BLOODY TORSO.
I DON'T FEEL SO GOOD.
Peirce

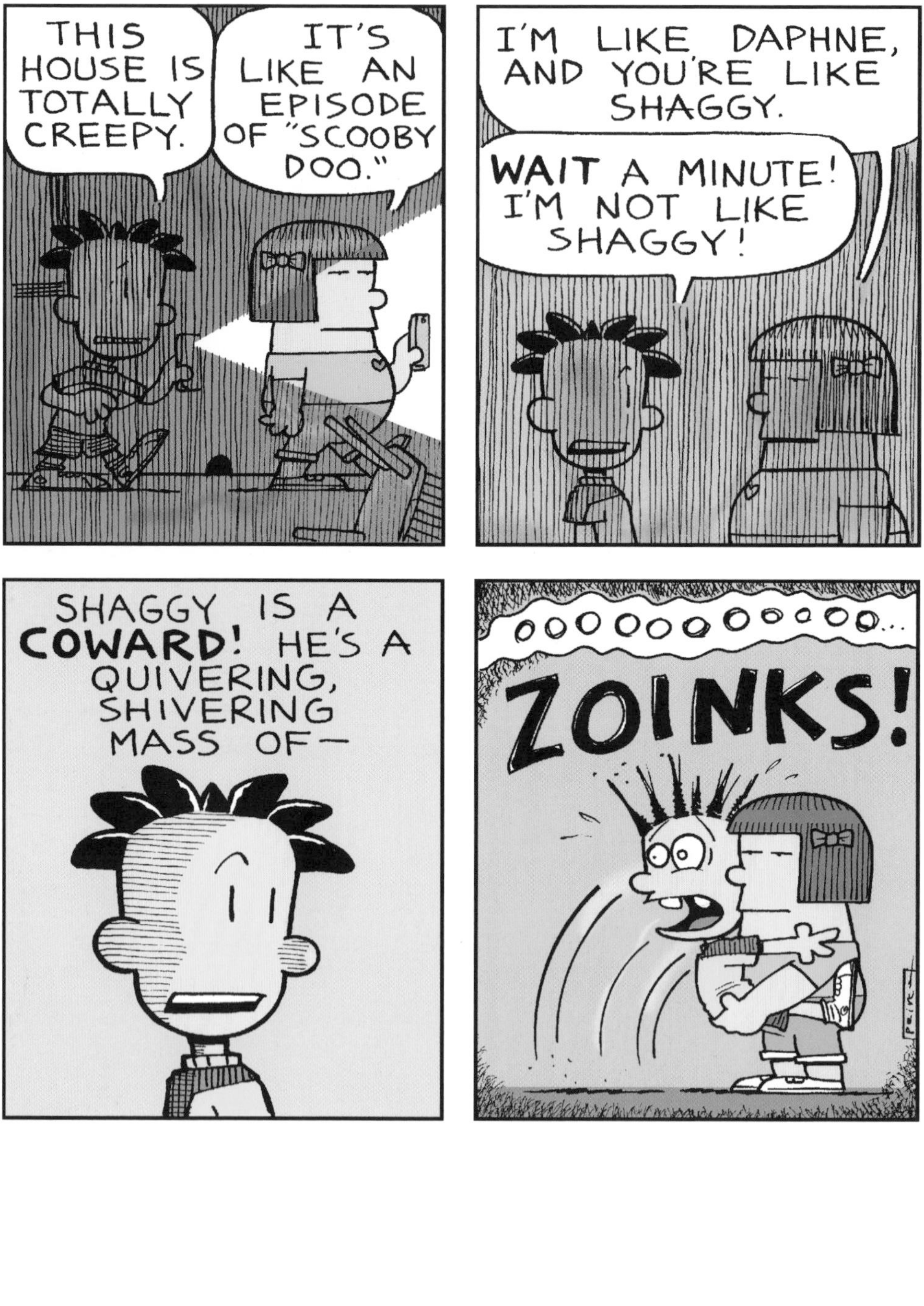
THIS HOUSE IS TOTALLY CREEPY.
IT'S LIKE AN EPISODE OF "SCOOBY DOO."
I'M LIKE DAPHNE, AND YOU'RE LIKE SHAGGY.
WAIT A MINUTE! I'M NOT LIKE SHAGGY!
SHAGGY IS A COWARD! HE'S A QUIVERING, SHIVERING MASS OF—
OOOOOOOOOOOO...
ZOINKS!

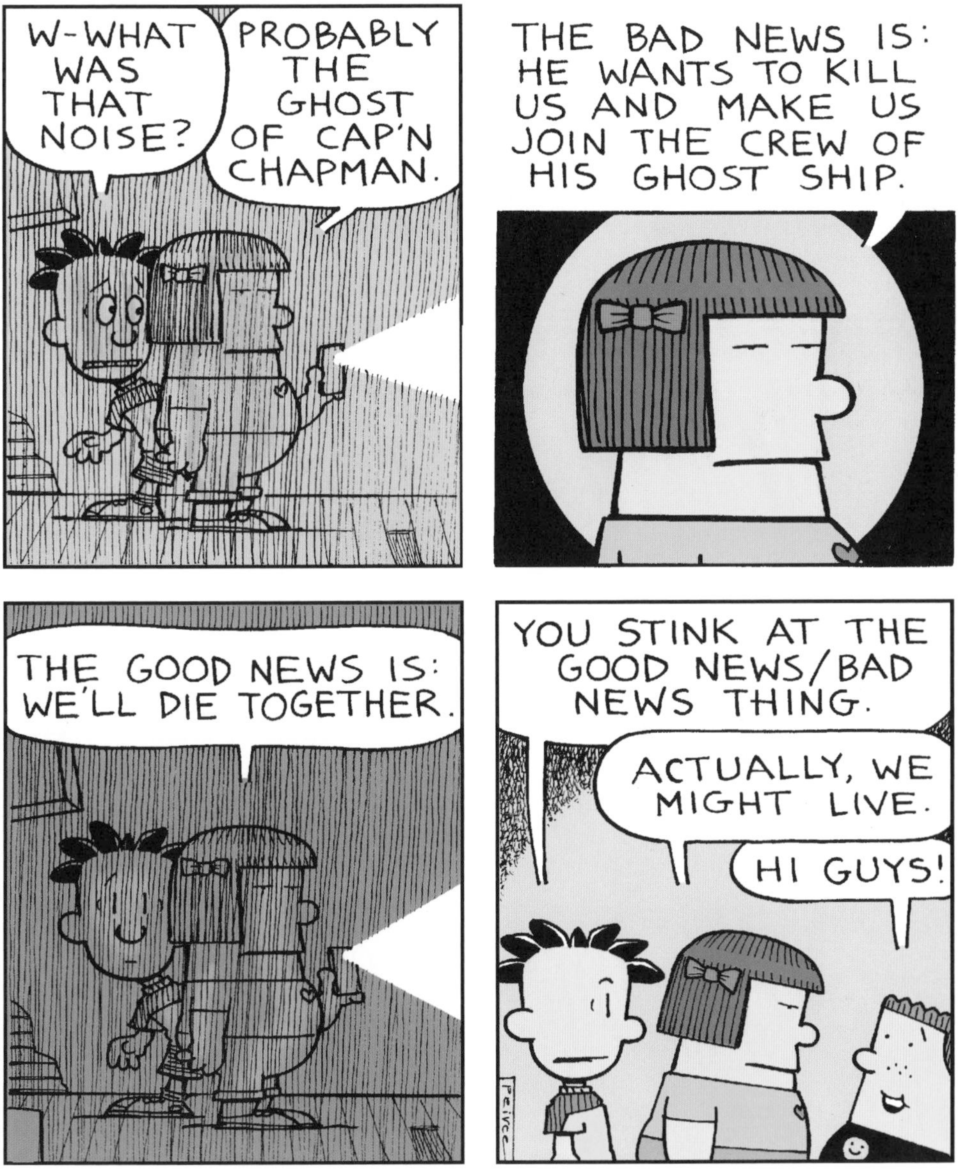
W-WHAT WAS THAT NOISE?
PROBABLY THE GHOST OF CAP'N CHAPMAN.
THE BAD NEWS IS: HE WANTS TO KILL US AND MAKE US JOIN THE CREW OF HIS GHOST SHIP.
THE GOOD NEWS IS: WE'LL DIE TOGETHER.
YOU STINK AT THE GOOD NEWS/BAD NEWS THING.
ACTUALLY, WE MIGHT LIVE.
HI GUYS!
peirce

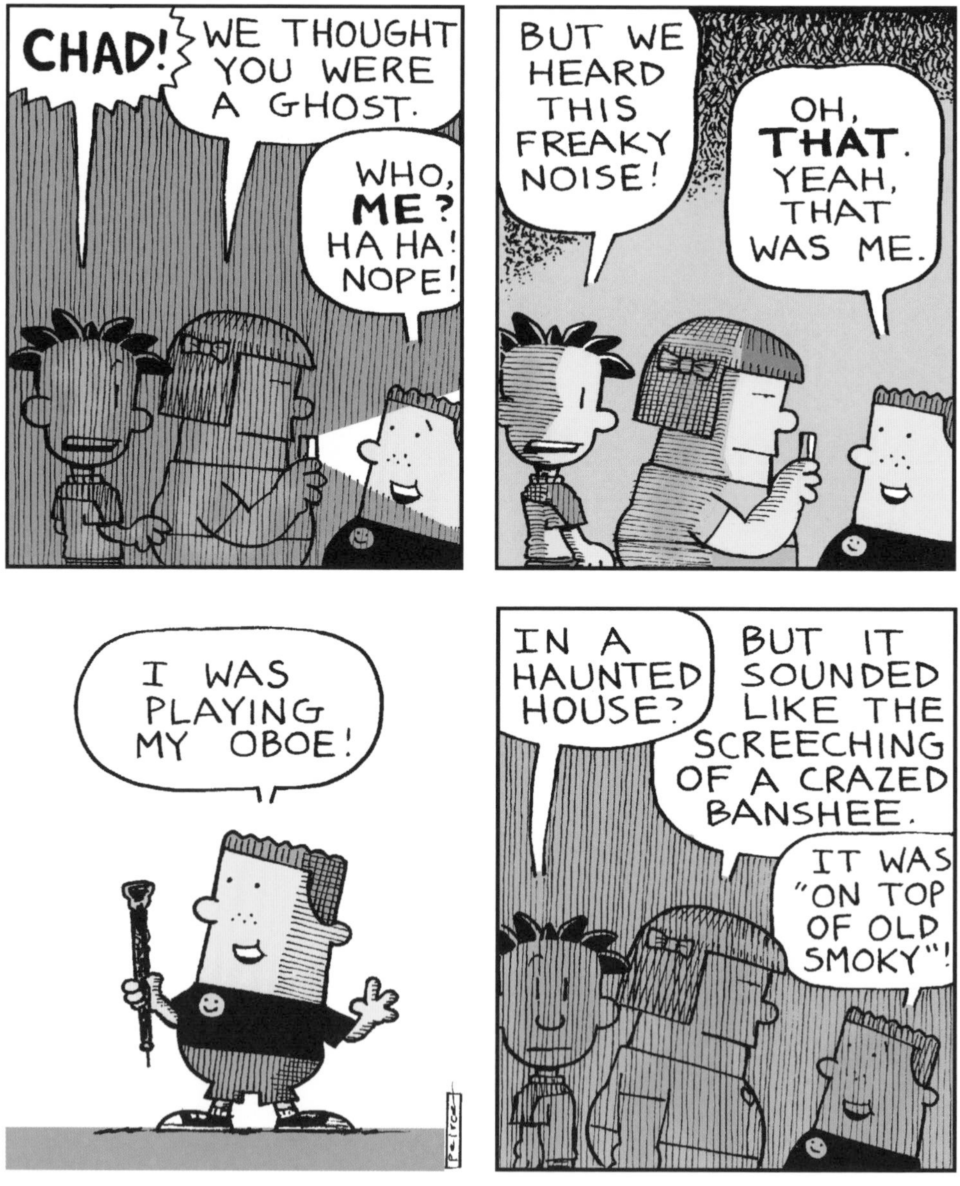
CHAD!
WE THOUGHT YOU WERE A GHOST.
WHO, **ME**? HA HA! NOPE!
BUT WE HEARD THIS FREAKY NOISE!
OH, **THAT**. YEAH, THAT WAS ME.
I WAS PLAYING MY OBOE!
IN A HAUNTED HOUSE?
BUT IT SOUNDED LIKE THE SCREECHING OF A CRAZED BANSHEE.
IT WAS "ON TOP OF OLD SMOKY"!

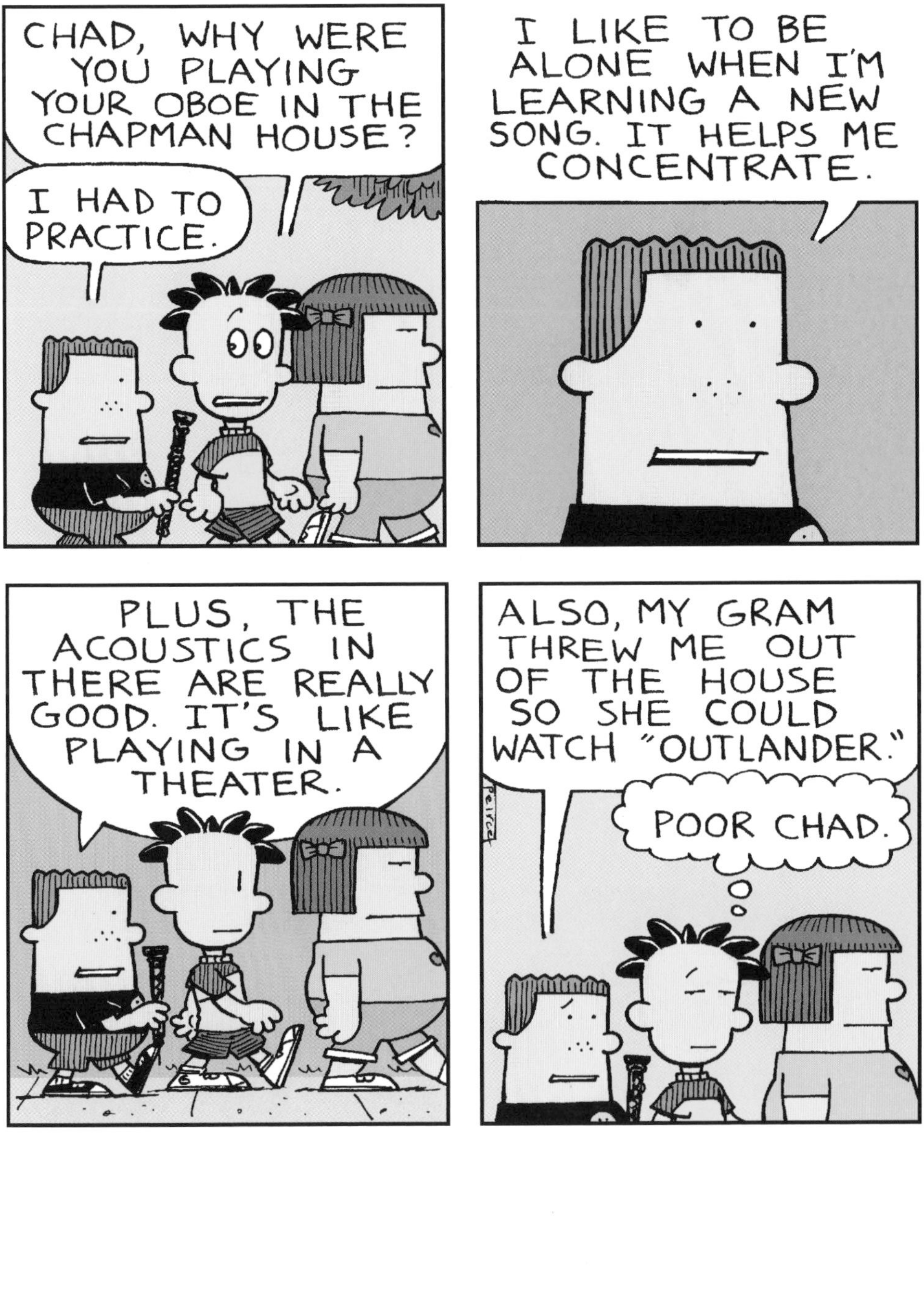
CHAD, WHY WERE YOU PLAYING YOUR OBOE IN THE CHAPMAN HOUSE?
I HAD TO PRACTICE.
I LIKE TO BE ALONE WHEN I'M LEARNING A NEW SONG. IT HELPS ME CONCENTRATE.
PLUS, THE ACOUSTICS IN THERE ARE REALLY GOOD. IT'S LIKE PLAYING IN A THEATER.
ALSO, MY GRAM THREW ME OUT OF THE HOUSE SO SHE COULD WATCH "OUTLANDER."
POOR CHAD.
peirce

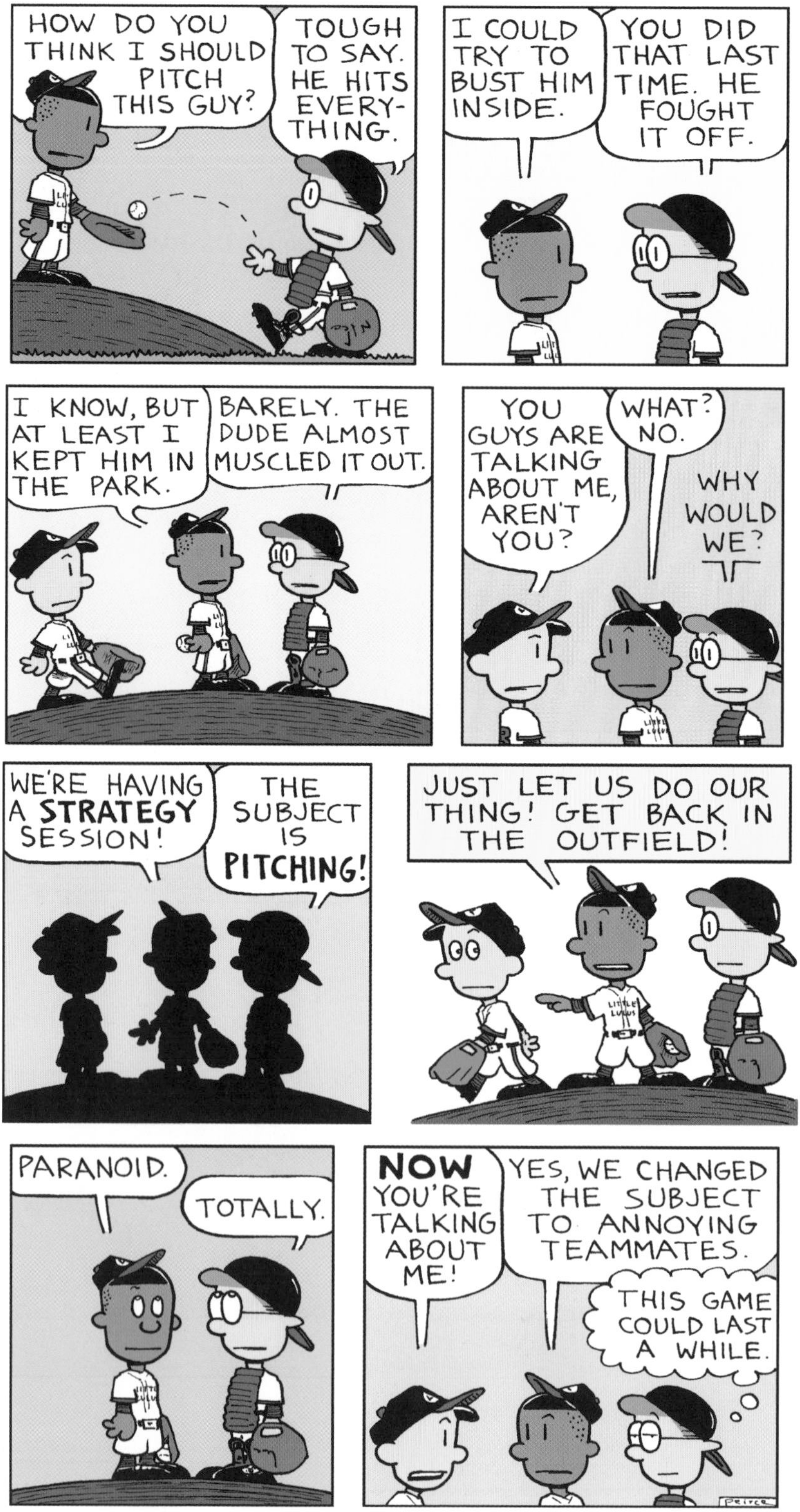
HOW DO YOU THINK I SHOULD PITCH THIS GUY?
TOUGH TO SAY. HE HITS EVERY-THING.
I COULD TRY TO BUST HIM INSIDE.
YOU DID THAT LAST TIME. HE FOUGHT IT OFF.
I KNOW, BUT AT LEAST I KEPT HIM IN THE PARK.
BARELY. THE DUDE ALMOST MUSCLED IT OUT.
YOU GUYS ARE TALKING ABOUT ME, AREN'T YOU?
WHAT? NO.
WHY WOULD WE?
WE'RE HAVING A **STRATEGY** SESSION!
THE SUBJECT IS **PITCHING!**
JUST LET US DO OUR THING! GET BACK IN THE OUTFIELD!
PARANOID.
TOTALLY.
NOW YOU'RE TALKING ABOUT ME!
YES, WE CHANGED THE SUBJECT TO ANNOYING TEAMMATES.
THIS GAME COULD LAST A WHILE.

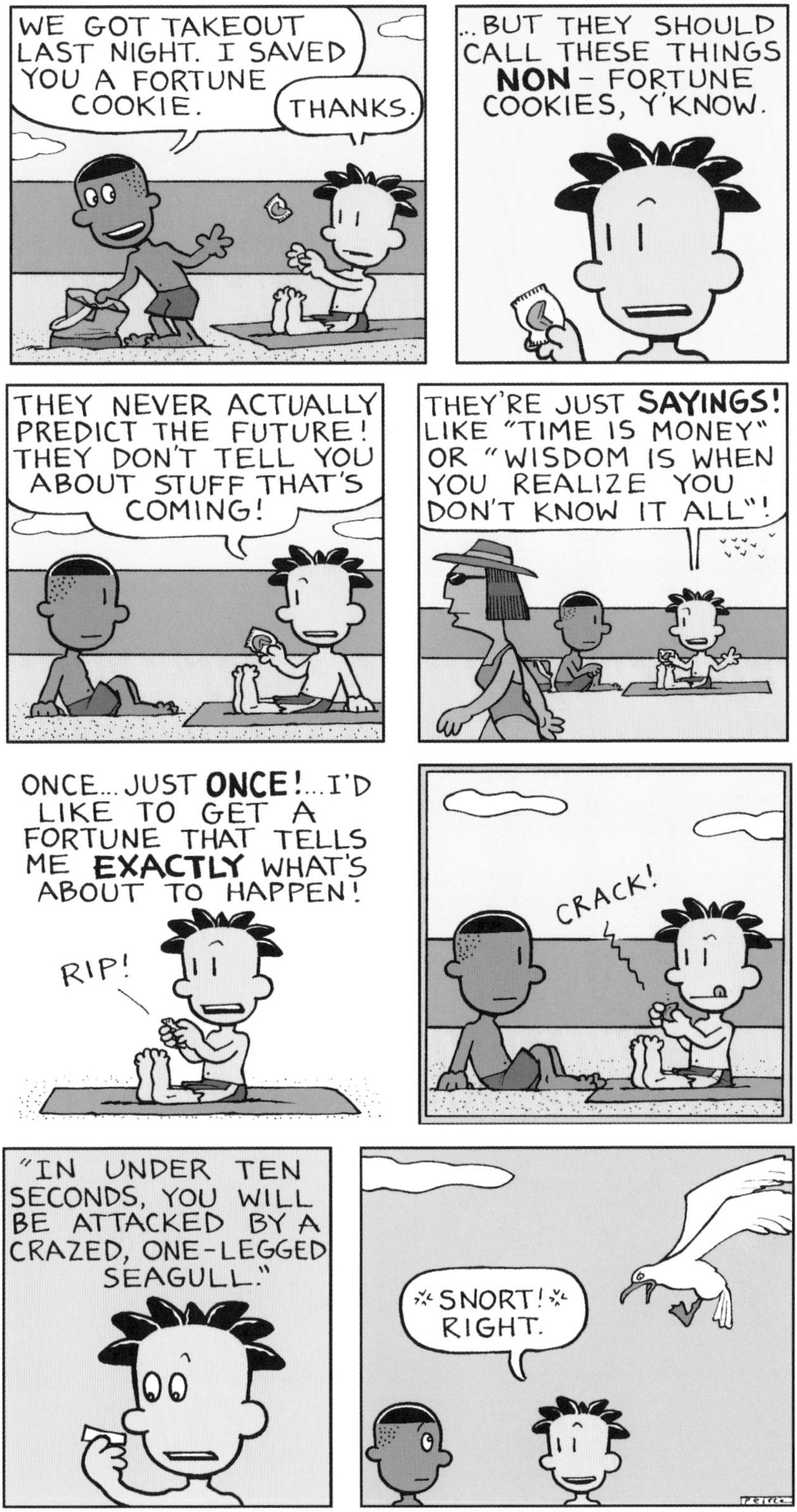
WE GOT TAKEOUT LAST NIGHT. I SAVED YOU A FORTUNE COOKIE.
THANKS.
...BUT THEY SHOULD CALL THESE THINGS NON-FORTUNE COOKIES, Y'KNOW.
THEY NEVER ACTUALLY PREDICT THE FUTURE! THEY DON'T TELL YOU ABOUT STUFF THAT'S COMING!
THEY'RE JUST SAYINGS! LIKE "TIME IS MONEY" OR "WISDOM IS WHEN YOU REALIZE YOU DON'T KNOW IT ALL"!
ONCE... JUST ONCE!... I'D LIKE TO GET A FORTUNE THAT TELLS ME EXACTLY WHAT'S ABOUT TO HAPPEN!
RIP!
CRACK!
"IN UNDER TEN SECONDS, YOU WILL BE ATTACKED BY A CRAZED, ONE-LEGGED SEAGULL."
SNORT! RIGHT.

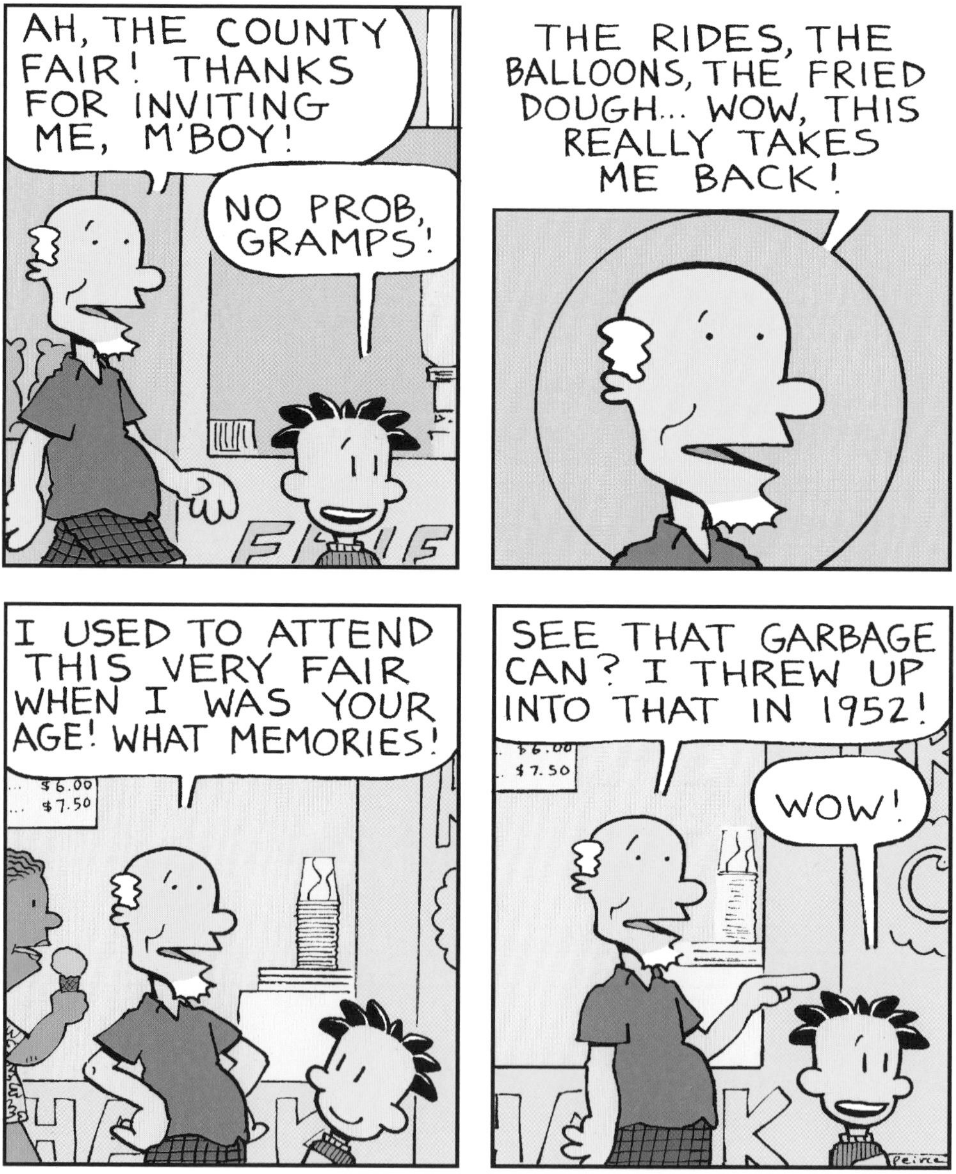
AH, THE COUNTY FAIR! THANKS FOR INVITING ME, M'BOY!
NO PROB, GRAMPS!
THE RIDES, THE BALLOONS, THE FRIED DOUGH... WOW, THIS REALLY TAKES ME BACK!
I USED TO ATTEND THIS VERY FAIR WHEN I WAS YOUR AGE! WHAT MEMORIES!
$6.00
$7.50
SEE THAT GARBAGE CAN? I THREW UP INTO THAT IN 1952!
WOW!
Peirce

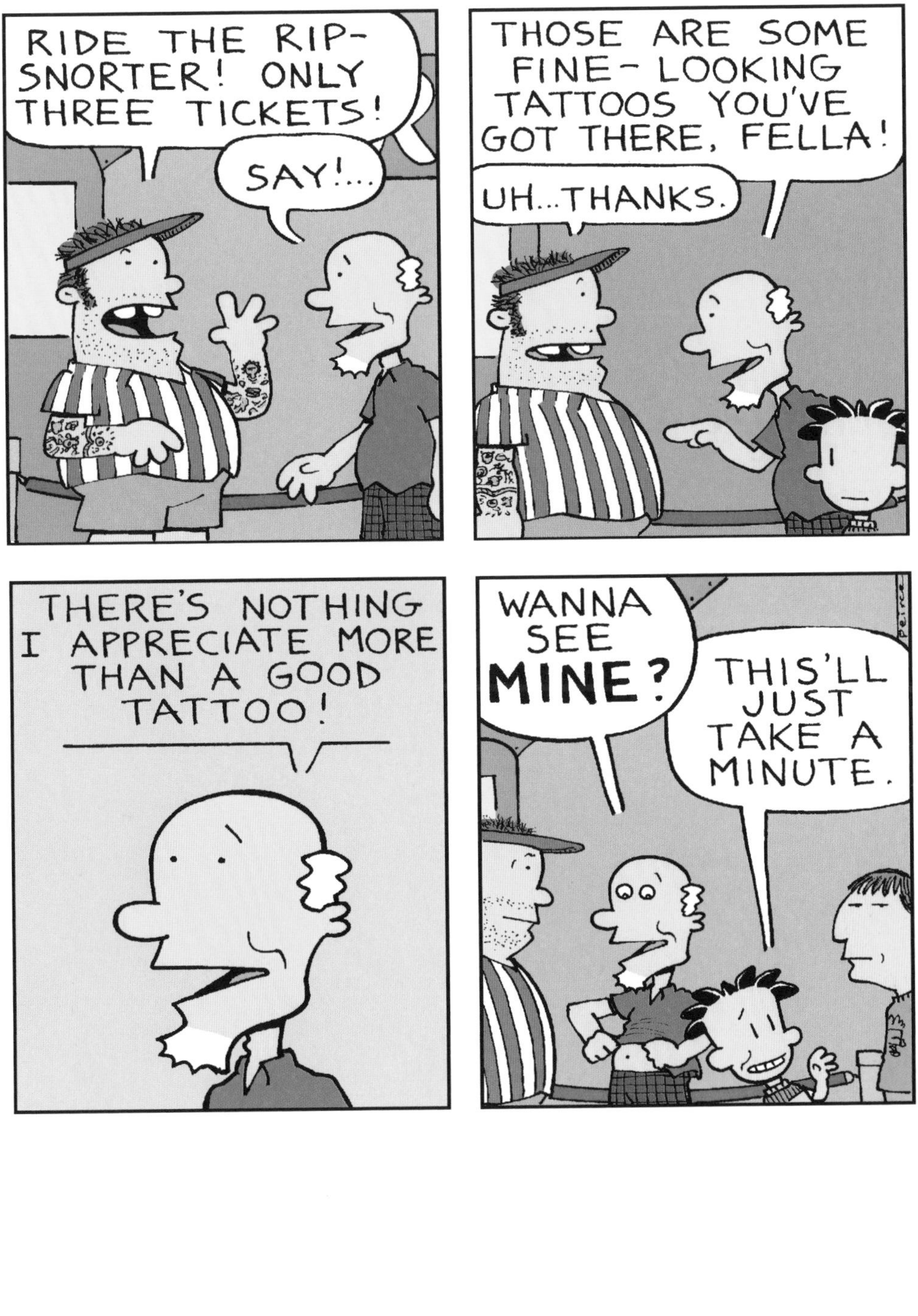
RIDE THE RIP-SNORTER! ONLY THREE TICKETS!
SAY!...
THOSE ARE SOME FINE-LOOKING TATTOOS YOU'VE GOT THERE, FELLA!
UH...THANKS.
THERE'S NOTHING I APPRECIATE MORE THAN A GOOD TATTOO!
WANNA SEE **MINE**?
THIS'LL JUST TAKE A MINUTE.
PEIRCE

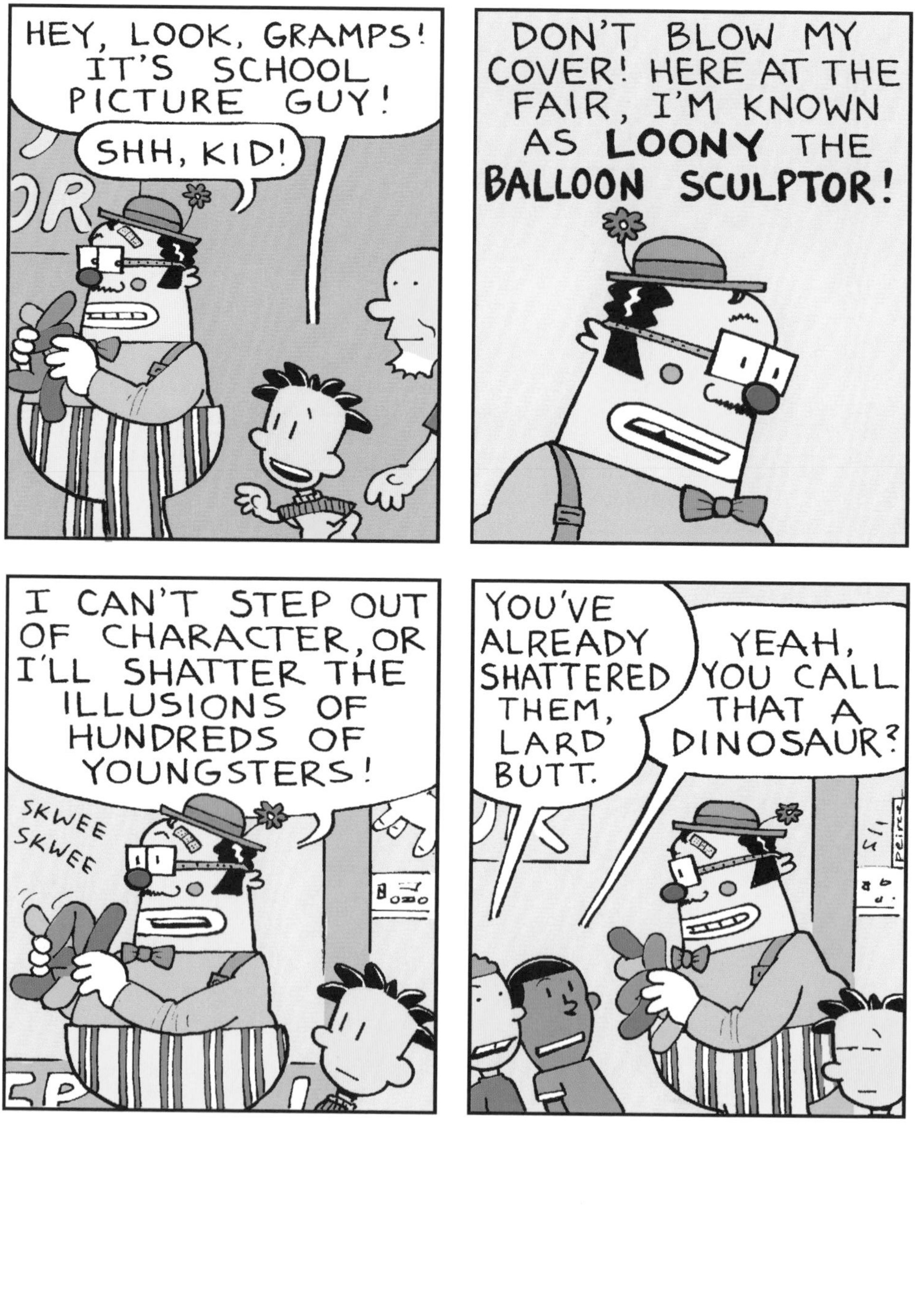
HEY, LOOK, GRAMPS! IT'S SCHOOL PICTURE GUY!
SHH, KID!
DON'T BLOW MY COVER! HERE AT THE FAIR, I'M KNOWN AS **LOONY** THE **BALLOON SCULPTOR!**
I CAN'T STEP OUT OF CHARACTER, OR I'LL SHATTER THE ILLUSIONS OF HUNDREDS OF YOUNGSTERS!
SKWEE SKWEE
YOU'VE ALREADY SHATTERED THEM, LARD BUTT.
YEAH, YOU CALL THAT A DINOSAUR?
peirce

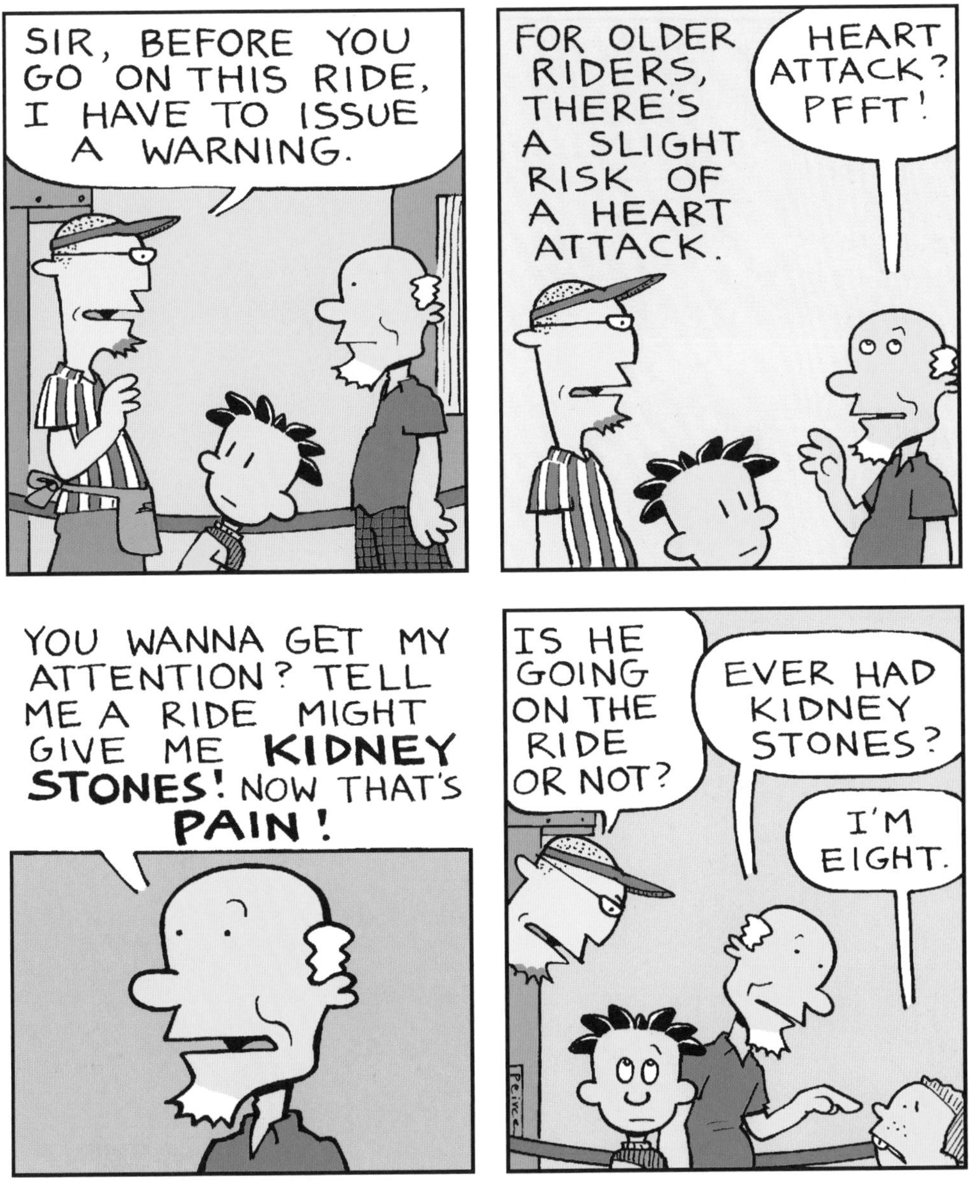
SIR, BEFORE YOU GO ON THIS RIDE, I HAVE TO ISSUE A WARNING.
FOR OLDER RIDERS, THERE'S A SLIGHT RISK OF A HEART ATTACK.
HEART ATTACK? PFFT!
YOU WANNA GET MY ATTENTION? TELL ME A RIDE MIGHT GIVE ME **KIDNEY STONES!** NOW THAT'S **PAIN!**
IS HE GOING ON THE RIDE OR NOT?
EVER HAD KIDNEY STONES?
I'M EIGHT.
PEIRCE

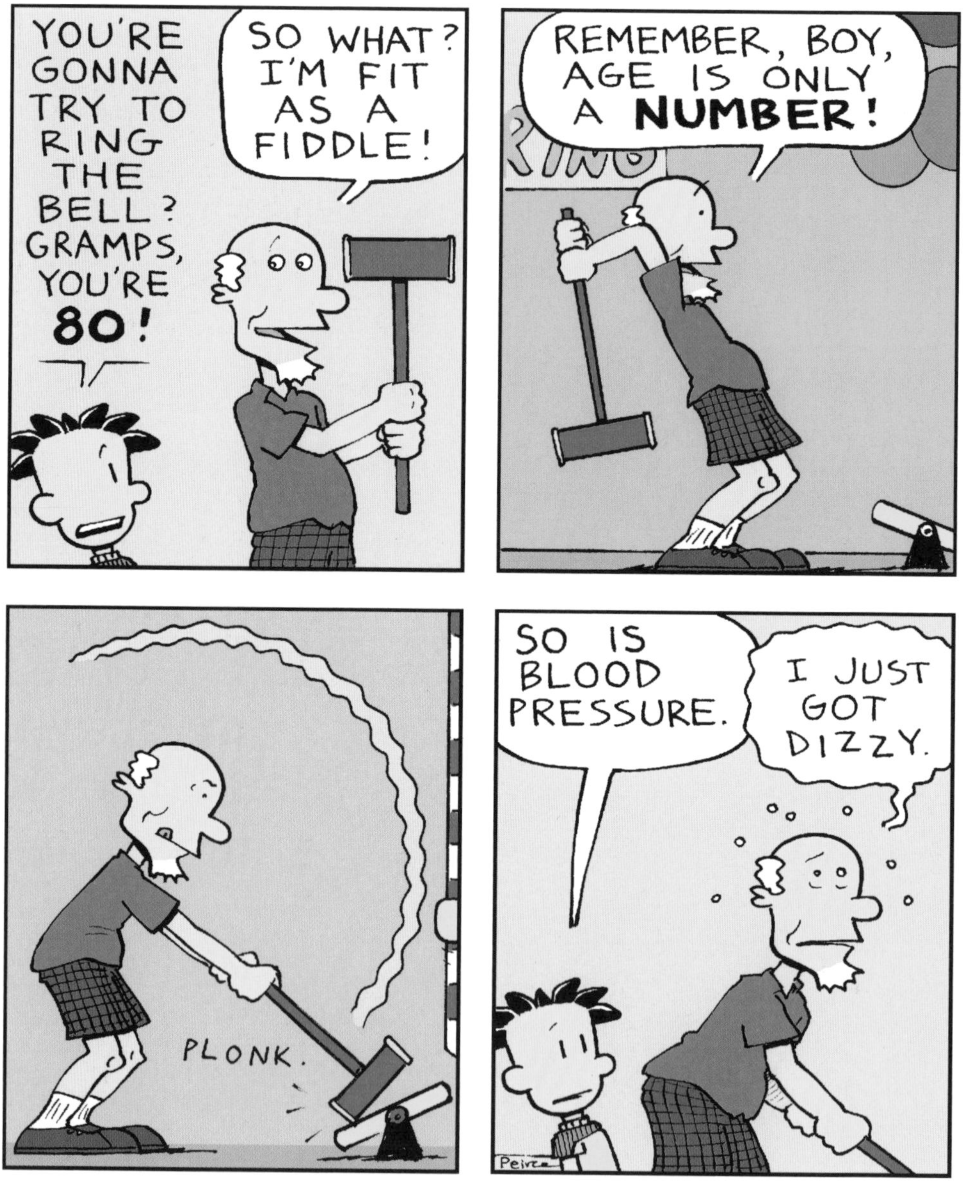
YOU'RE GONNA TRY TO RING THE BELL? GRAMPS, YOU'RE **80**!
SO WHAT? I'M FIT AS A FIDDLE!
REMEMBER, BOY, AGE IS ONLY A **NUMBER**!
PLONK.
SO IS BLOOD PRESSURE.
I JUST GOT DIZZY.
Peirce

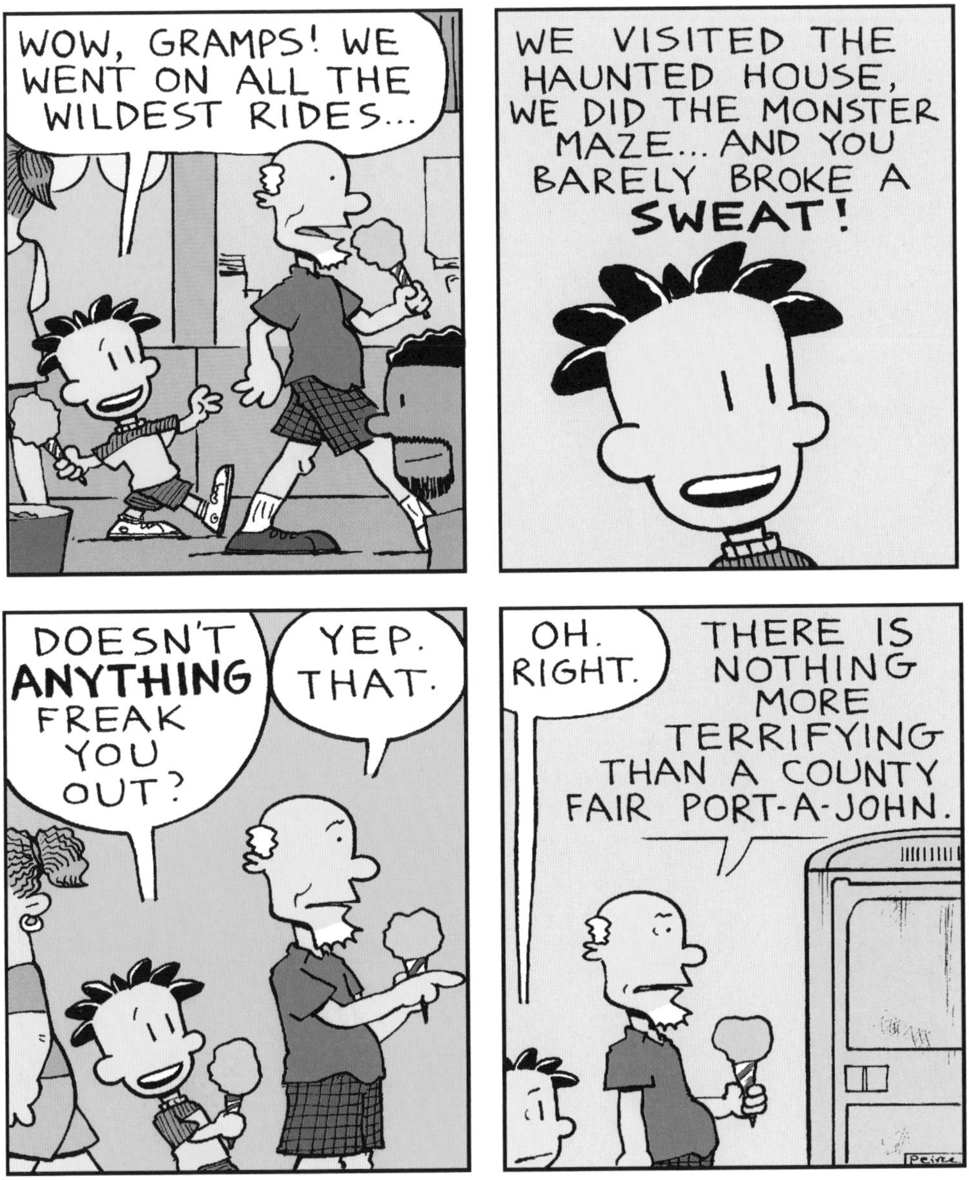
WOW, GRAMPS! WE WENT ON ALL THE WILDEST RIDES...
WE VISITED THE HAUNTED HOUSE, WE DID THE MONSTER MAZE... AND YOU BARELY BROKE A SWEAT!
DOESN'T ANYTHING FREAK YOU OUT?
YEP. THAT.
OH. RIGHT.
THERE IS NOTHING MORE TERRIFYING THAN A COUNTY FAIR PORT-A-JOHN.
Peirce

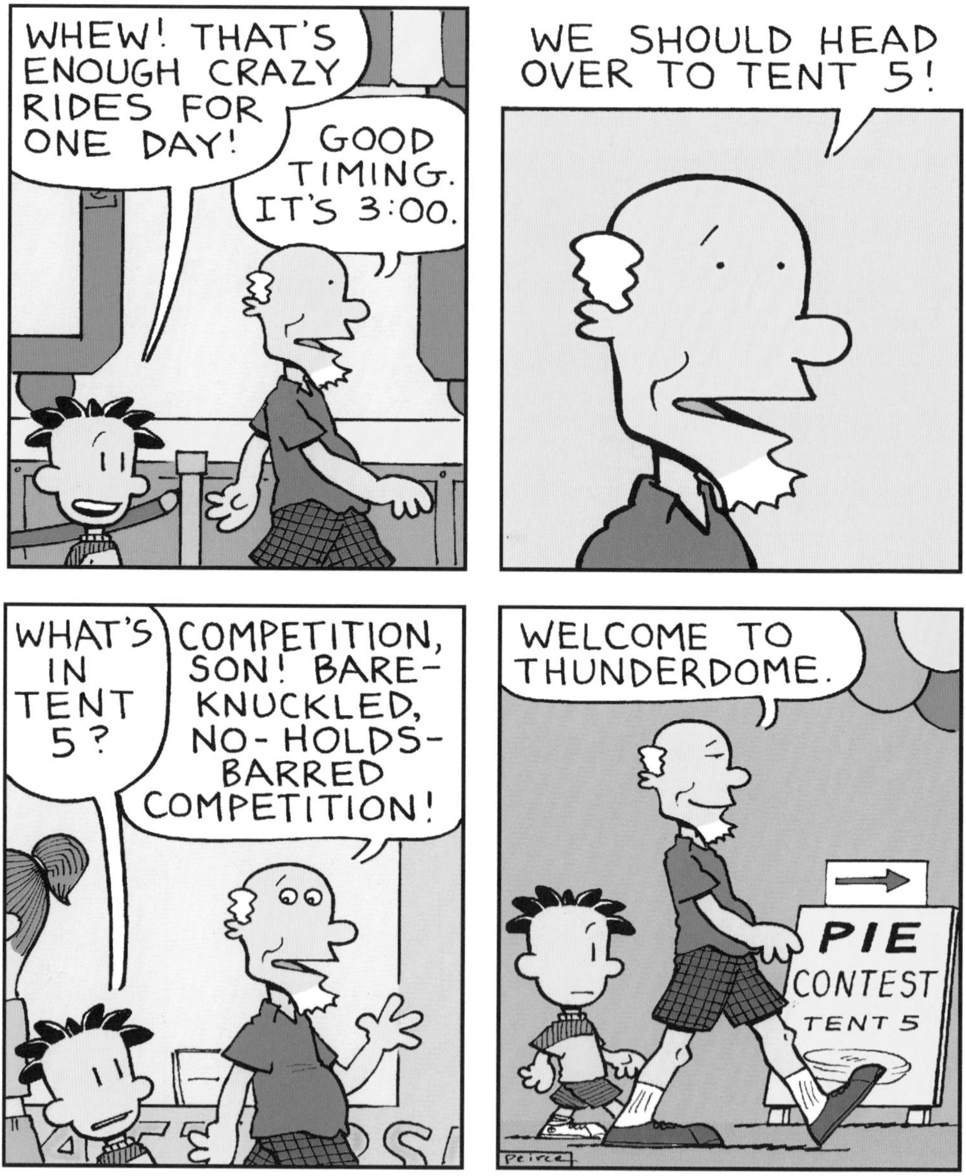
WHEW! THAT'S ENOUGH CRAZY RIDES FOR ONE DAY!
GOOD TIMING. IT'S 3:00.
WE SHOULD HEAD OVER TO TENT 5!
WHAT'S IN TENT 5?
COMPETITION, SON! BARE-KNUCKLED, NO-HOLDS-BARRED COMPETITION!
WELCOME TO THUNDERDOME.
PIE CONTEST TENT 5
PEIRCE

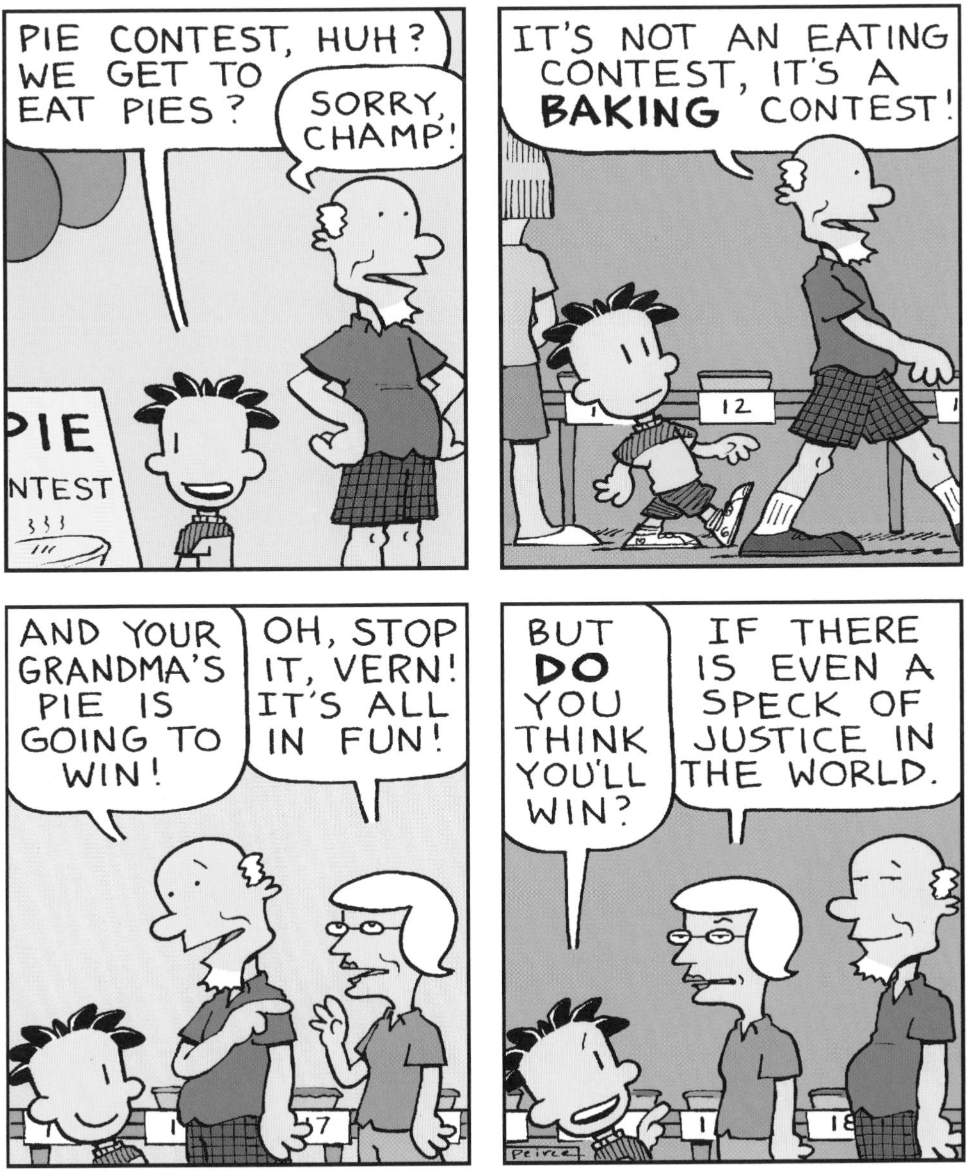
PIE CONTEST, HUH? WE GET TO EAT PIES?
SORRY, CHAMP!
PIE
NTEST
IT'S NOT AN EATING CONTEST, IT'S A **BAKING** CONTEST!
12
AND YOUR GRANDMA'S PIE IS GOING TO WIN!
OH, STOP IT, VERN! IT'S ALL IN FUN!
BUT **DO** YOU THINK YOU'LL WIN?
IF THERE IS EVEN A SPECK OF JUSTICE IN THE WORLD.
PEIRCE

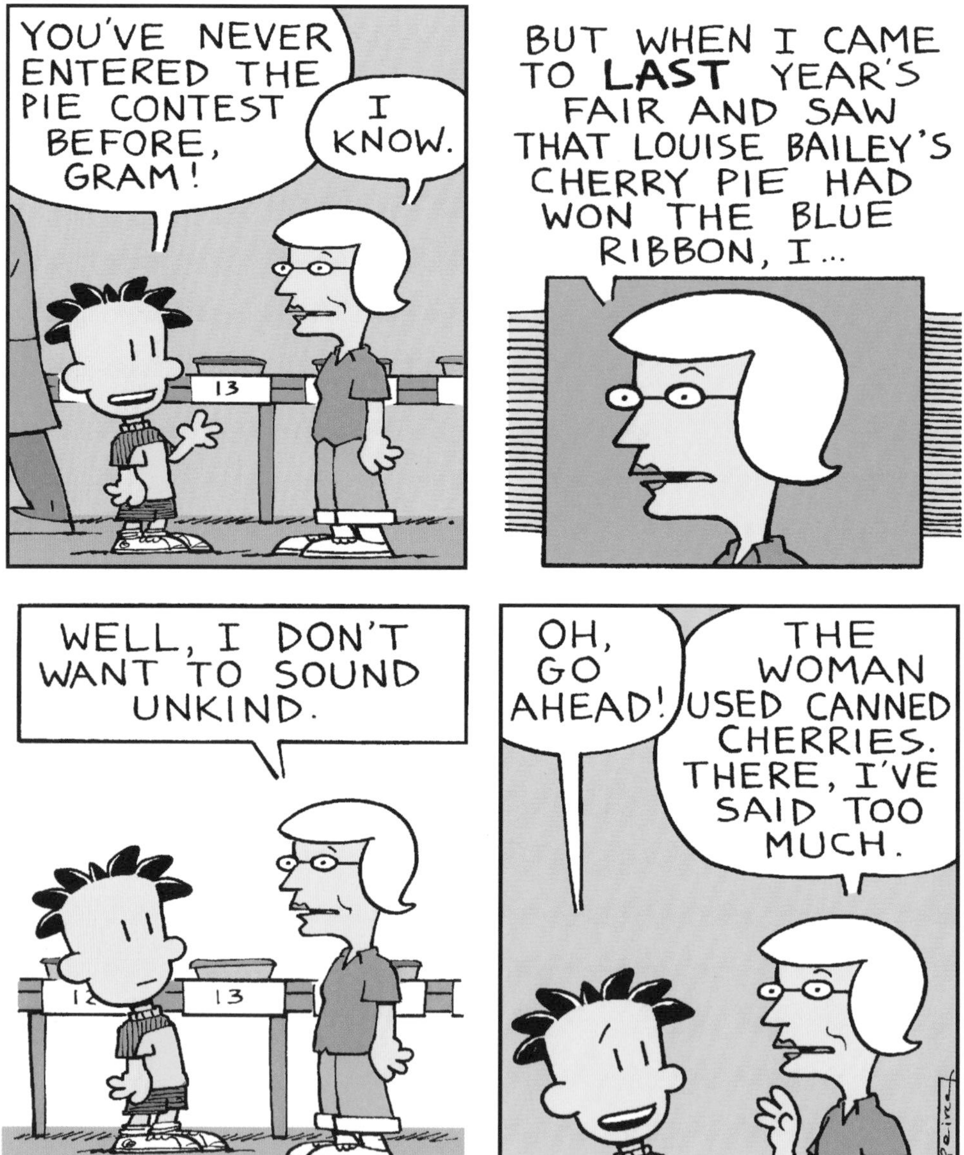
YOU'VE NEVER ENTERED THE PIE CONTEST BEFORE, GRAM!
I KNOW.
13
BUT WHEN I CAME TO **LAST** YEAR'S FAIR AND SAW THAT LOUISE BAILEY'S CHERRY PIE HAD WON THE BLUE RIBBON, I...
WELL, I DON'T WANT TO SOUND UNKIND.
12
13
OH, GO AHEAD!
THE WOMAN USED CANNED CHERRIES. THERE, I'VE SAID TOO MUCH.
Peirce

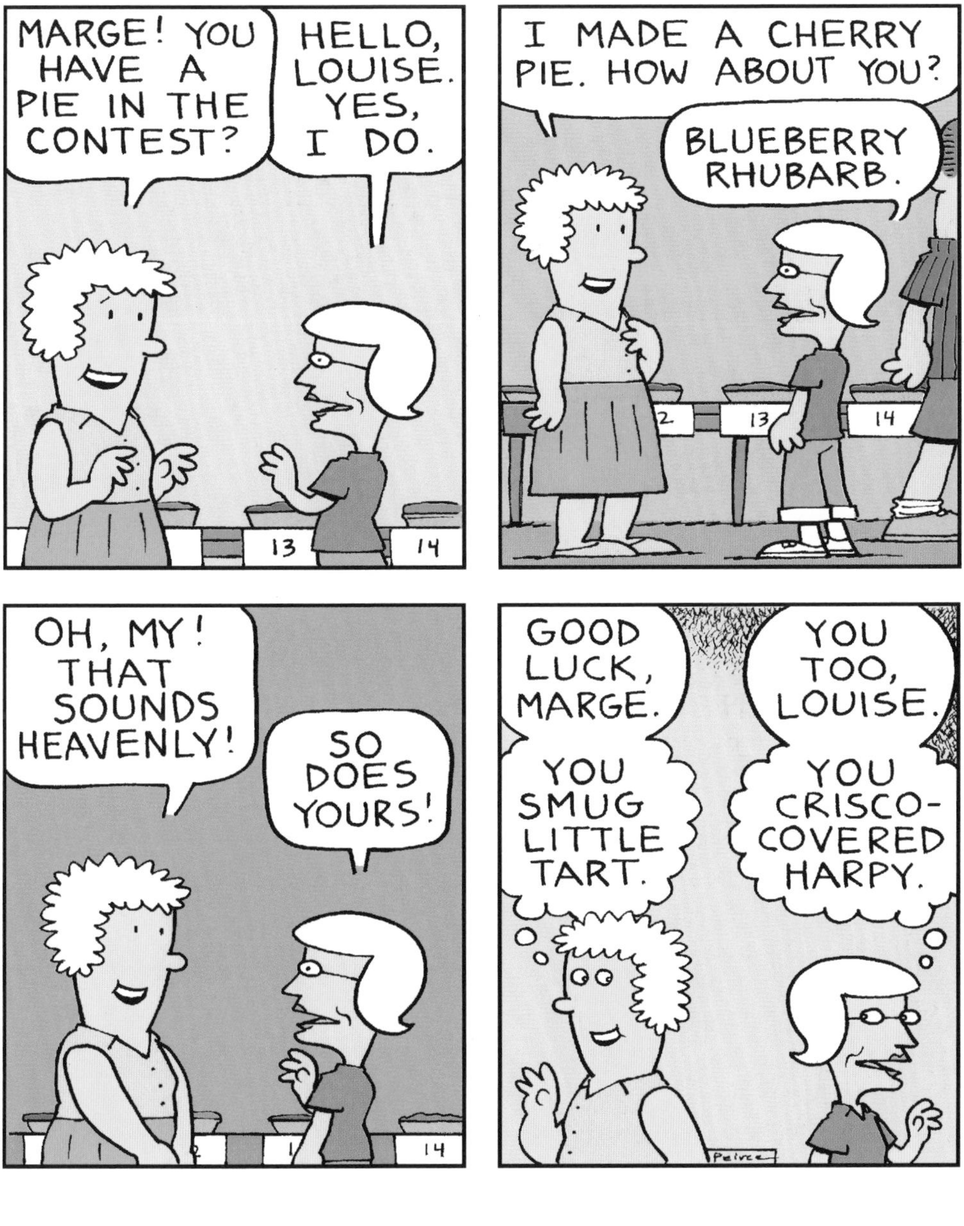
MARGE! YOU HAVE A PIE IN THE CONTEST?
HELLO, LOUISE. YES, I DO.
13
14
I MADE A CHERRY PIE. HOW ABOUT YOU?
BLUEBERRY RHUBARB.
13
14
OH, MY! THAT SOUNDS HEAVENLY!
SO DOES YOURS!
14
GOOD LUCK, MARGE.
YOU SMUG LITTLE TART.
YOU TOO, LOUISE.
YOU CRISCO-COVERED HARPY.
Peirce

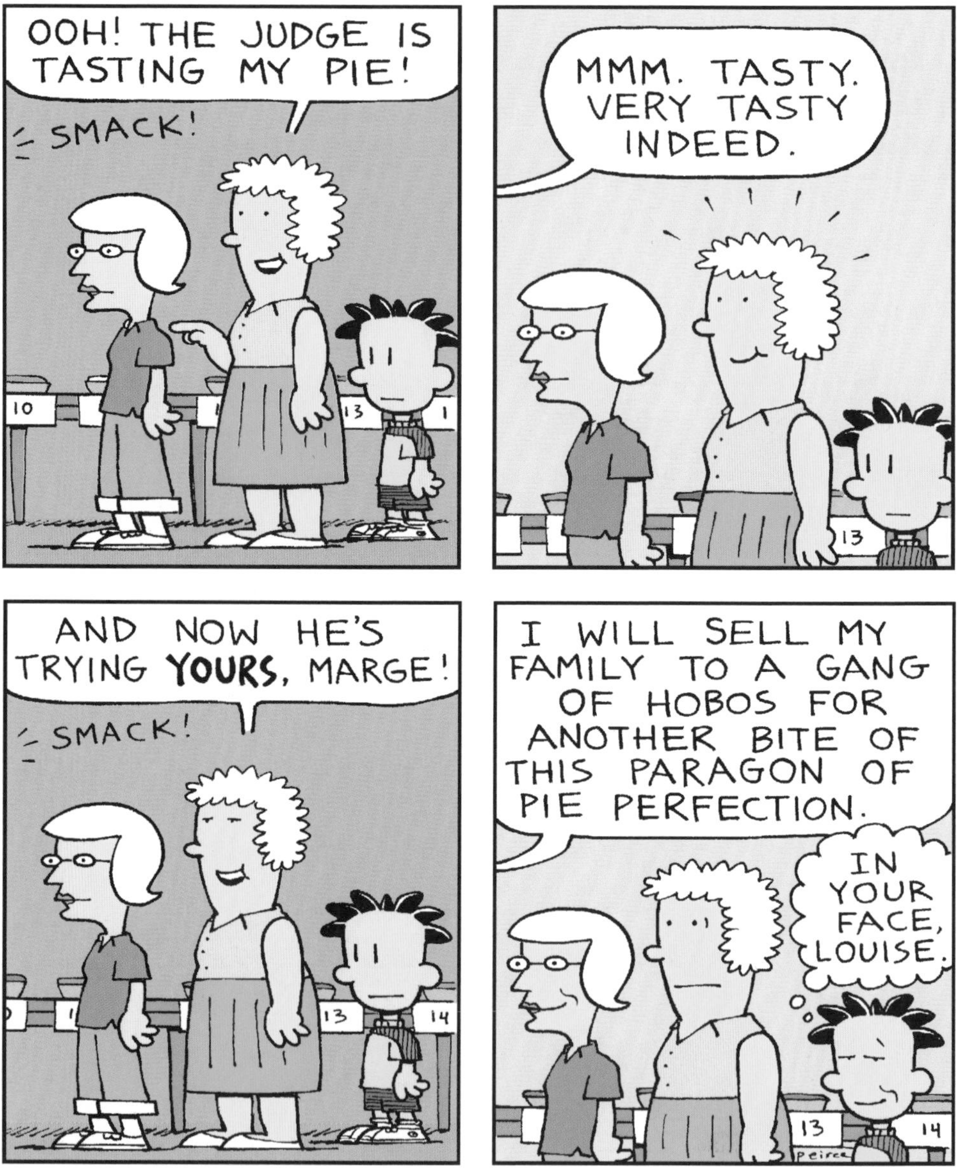
OOH! THE JUDGE IS TASTING MY PIE!
SMACK!
10
13
MMM. TASTY. VERY TASTY INDEED.
13
AND NOW HE'S TRYING **YOURS**, MARGE!
SMACK!
13
14
I WILL SELL MY FAMILY TO A GANG OF HOBOS FOR ANOTHER BITE OF THIS PARAGON OF PIE PERFECTION.
IN YOUR FACE, LOUISE.
13
14
peirce

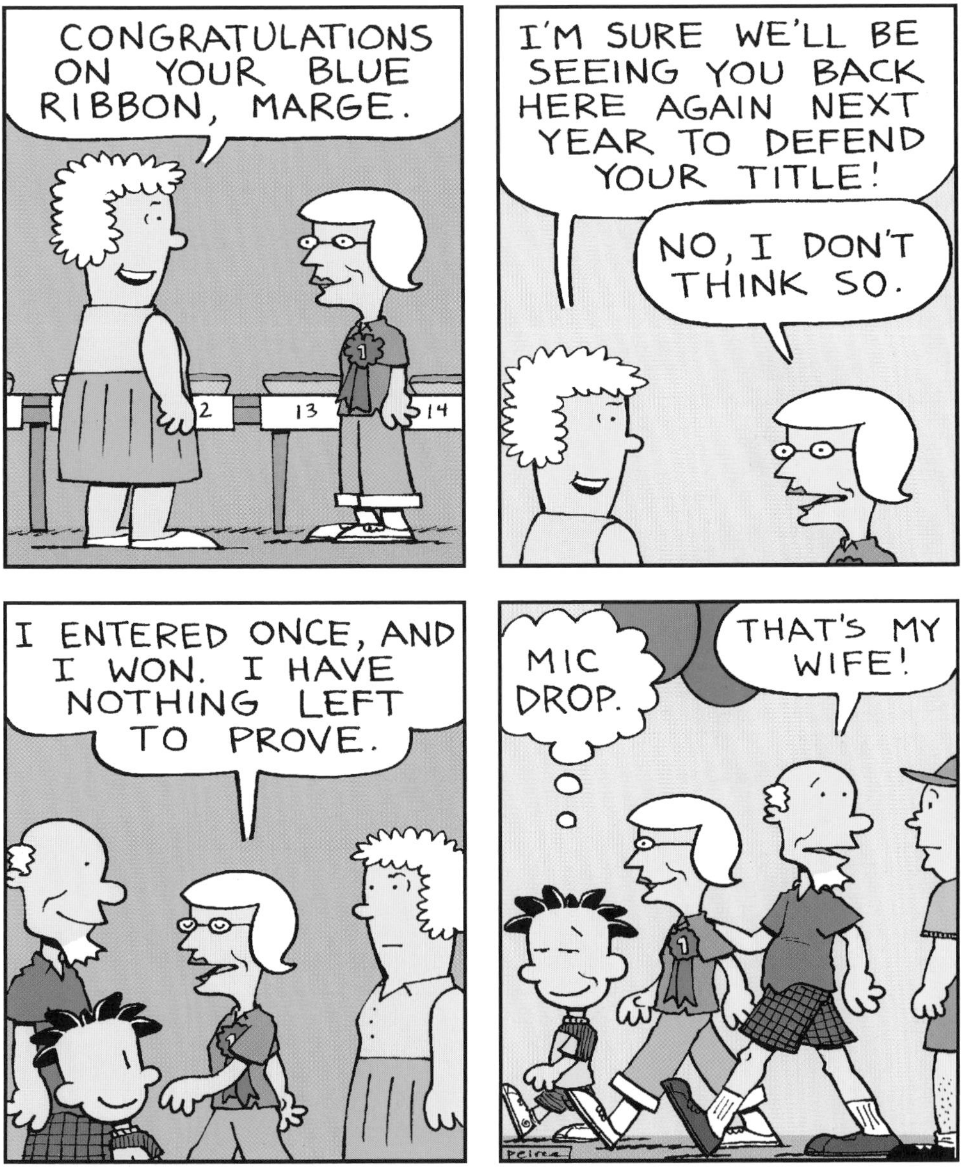
CONGRATULATIONS ON YOUR BLUE RIBBON, MARGE.
I'M SURE WE'LL BE SEEING YOU BACK HERE AGAIN NEXT YEAR TO DEFEND YOUR TITLE!
NO, I DON'T THINK SO.
I ENTERED ONCE, AND I WON. I HAVE NOTHING LEFT TO PROVE.
MIC DROP.
THAT'S MY WIFE!
PEIRCE

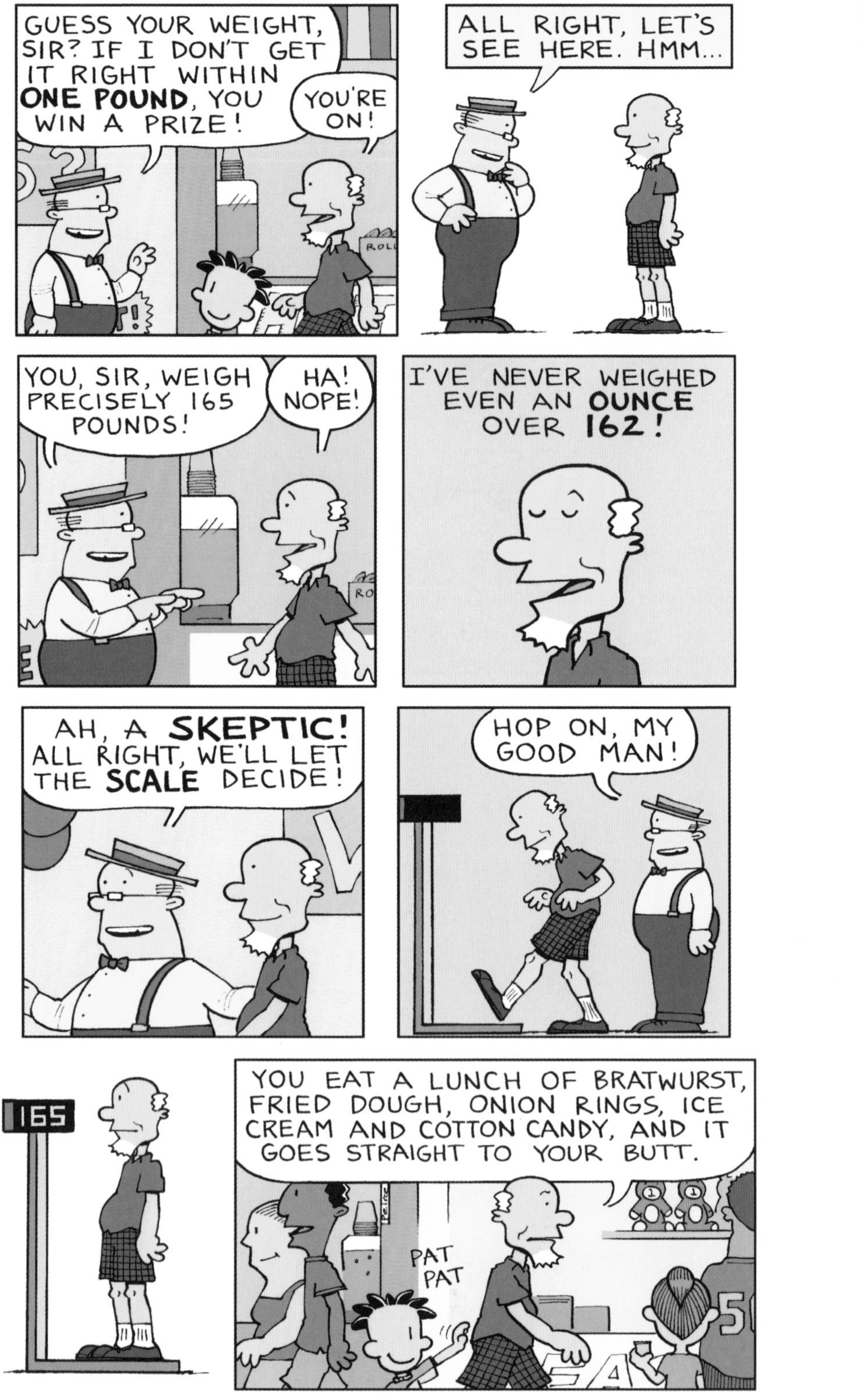
GUESS YOUR WEIGHT, SIR? IF I DON'T GET IT RIGHT WITHIN **ONE POUND**, YOU WIN A PRIZE!
YOU'RE ON!
ROLL
ALL RIGHT, LET'S SEE HERE. HMM...
YOU, SIR, WEIGH PRECISELY 165 POUNDS!
HA! NOPE!
I'VE NEVER WEIGHED EVEN AN **OUNCE** OVER **162**!
AH, A **SKEPTIC**! ALL RIGHT, WE'LL LET THE **SCALE** DECIDE!
HOP ON, MY GOOD MAN!
165
YOU EAT A LUNCH OF BRATWURST, FRIED DOUGH, ONION RINGS, ICE CREAM AND COTTON CANDY, AND IT GOES STRAIGHT TO YOUR BUTT.
PAT PAT

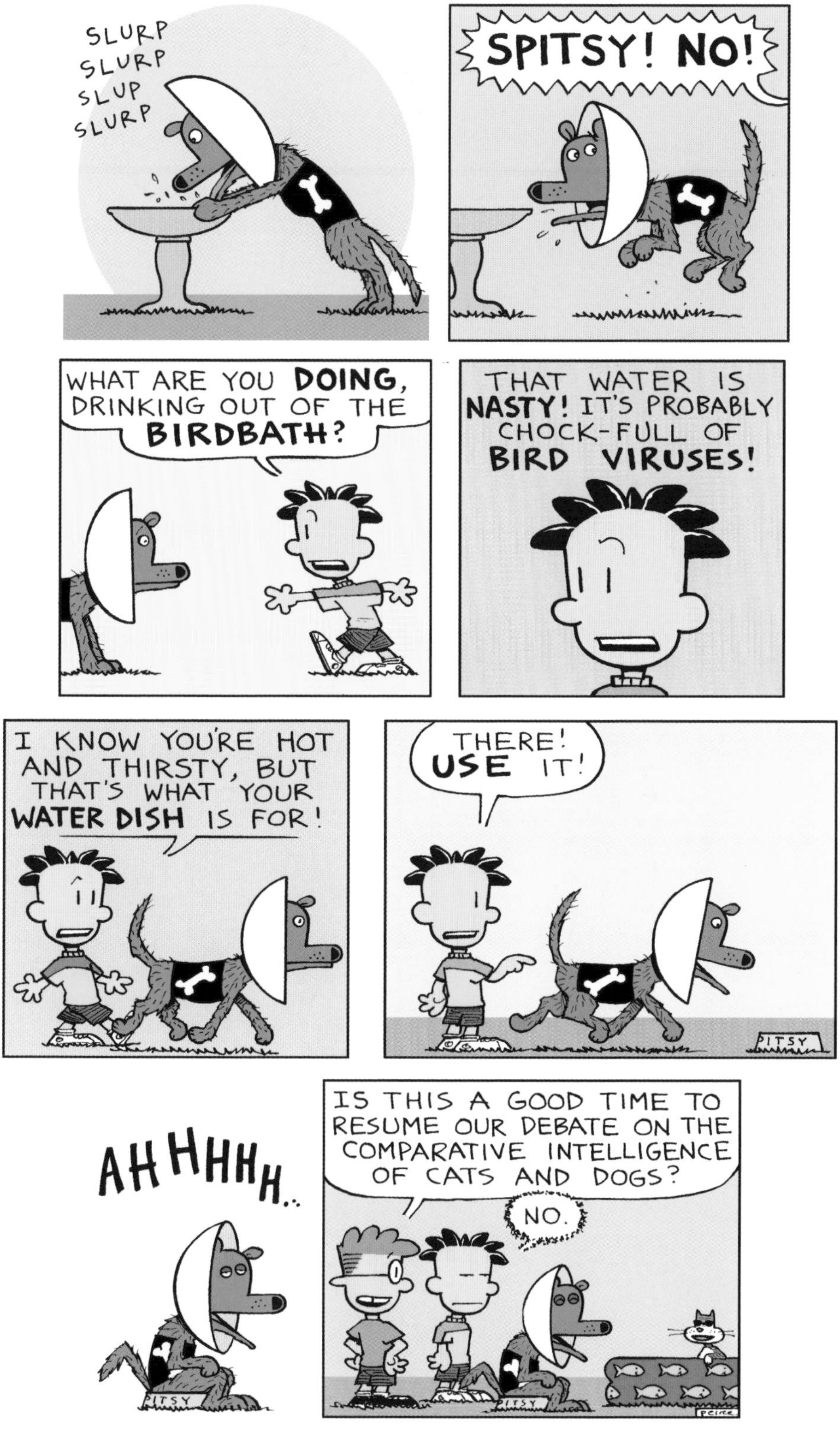
SLURP
SLURP
SLUP
SLURP
SPITSY! NO!
WHAT ARE YOU DOING, DRINKING OUT OF THE BIRDBATH?
THAT WATER IS NASTY! IT'S PROBABLY CHOCK-FULL OF BIRD VIRUSES!
I KNOW YOU'RE HOT AND THIRSTY, BUT THAT'S WHAT YOUR WATER DISH IS FOR!
THERE! USE IT!
PITSY
AHHHHH...
PITSY
IS THIS A GOOD TIME TO RESUME OUR DEBATE ON THE COMPARATIVE INTELLIGENCE OF CATS AND DOGS?
NO.
PITSY
peirce

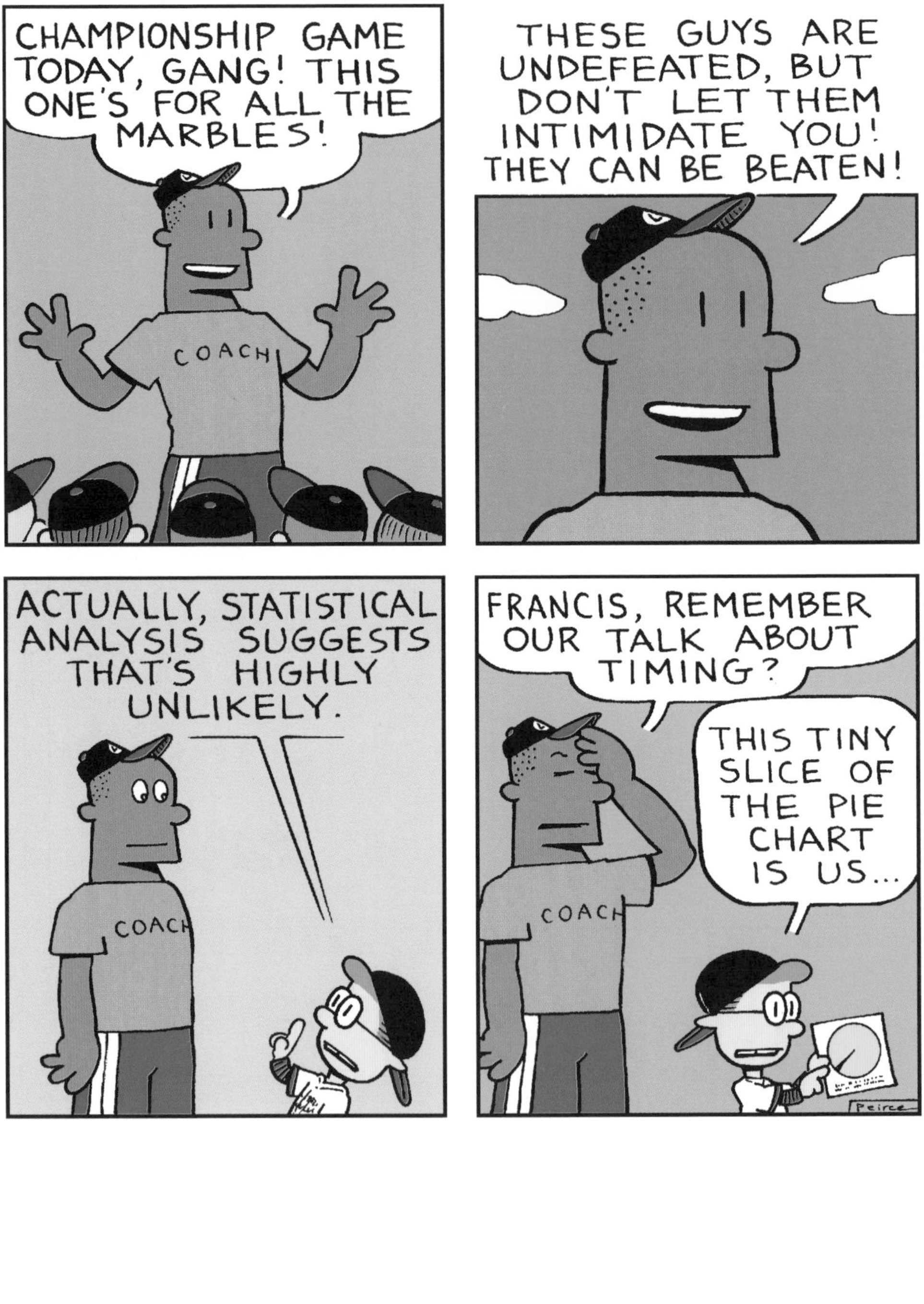
CHAMPIONSHIP GAME TODAY, GANG! THIS ONE'S FOR ALL THE MARBLES!
COACH
THESE GUYS ARE UNDEFEATED, BUT DON'T LET THEM INTIMIDATE YOU! THEY CAN BE BEATEN!
ACTUALLY, STATISTICAL ANALYSIS SUGGESTS THAT'S HIGHLY UNLIKELY.
COACH
FRANCIS, REMEMBER OUR TALK ABOUT TIMING?
THIS TINY SLICE OF THE PIE CHART IS US...
COACH
Peirce

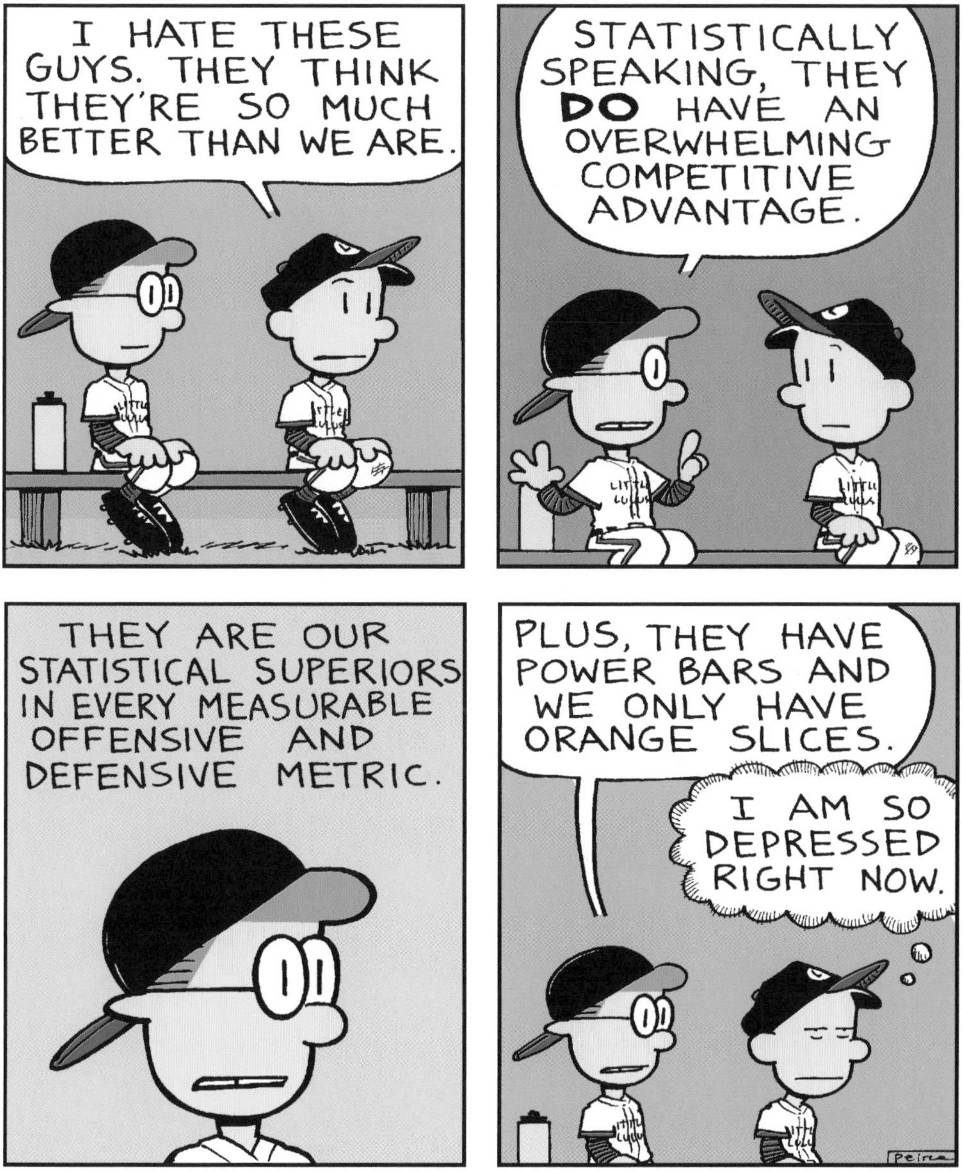
I HATE THESE GUYS. THEY THINK THEY'RE SO MUCH BETTER THAN WE ARE.
STATISTICALLY SPEAKING, THEY **DO** HAVE AN OVERWHELMING COMPETITIVE ADVANTAGE.
THEY ARE OUR STATISTICAL SUPERIORS IN EVERY MEASURABLE OFFENSIVE AND DEFENSIVE METRIC.
PLUS, THEY HAVE POWER BARS AND WE ONLY HAVE ORANGE SLICES.
I AM SO DEPRESSED RIGHT NOW.
peirce

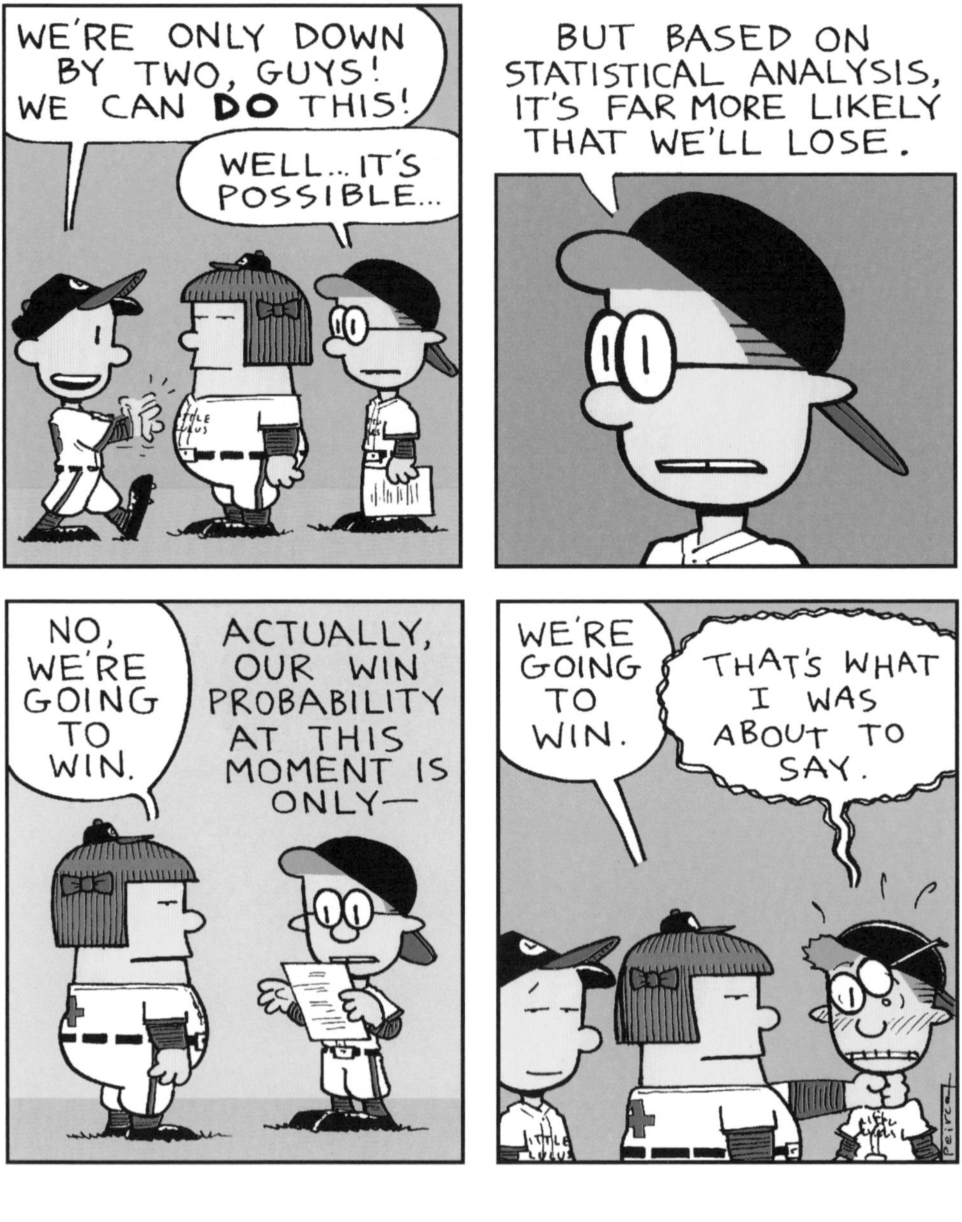
WE'RE ONLY DOWN BY TWO, GUYS! WE CAN **DO** THIS!
WELL... IT'S POSSIBLE...
BUT BASED ON STATISTICAL ANALYSIS, IT'S FAR MORE LIKELY THAT WE'LL LOSE.
NO, WE'RE GOING TO WIN.
ACTUALLY, OUR WIN PROBABILITY AT THIS MOMENT IS ONLY—
WE'RE GOING TO WIN.
THAT'S WHAT I WAS ABOUT TO SAY.

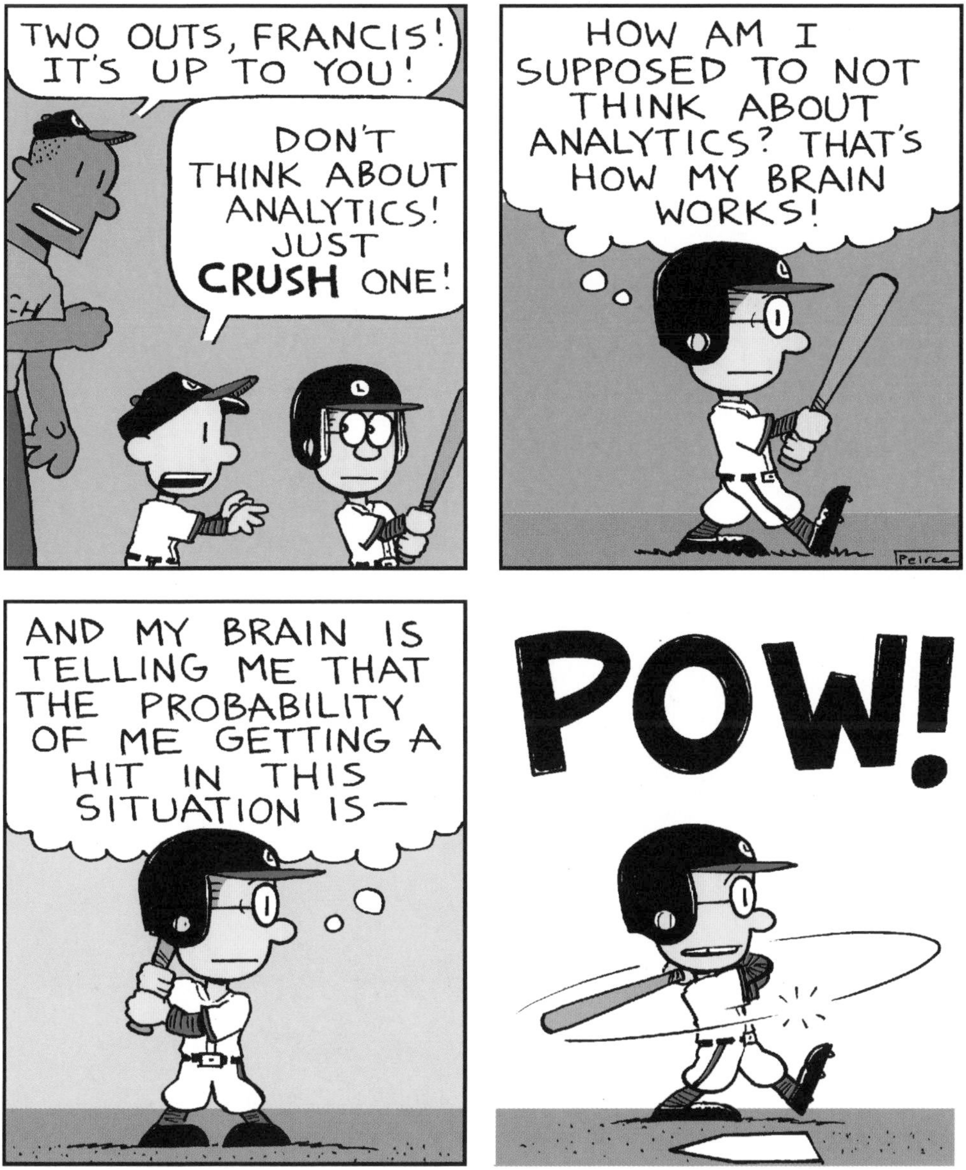
TWO OUTS, FRANCIS! IT'S UP TO YOU!
DON'T THINK ABOUT ANALYTICS! JUST **CRUSH** ONE!
HOW AM I SUPPOSED TO NOT THINK ABOUT ANALYTICS? THAT'S HOW MY BRAIN WORKS!
Peirce
AND MY BRAIN IS TELLING ME THAT THE PROBABILITY OF ME GETTING A HIT IN THIS SITUATION IS—
POW!

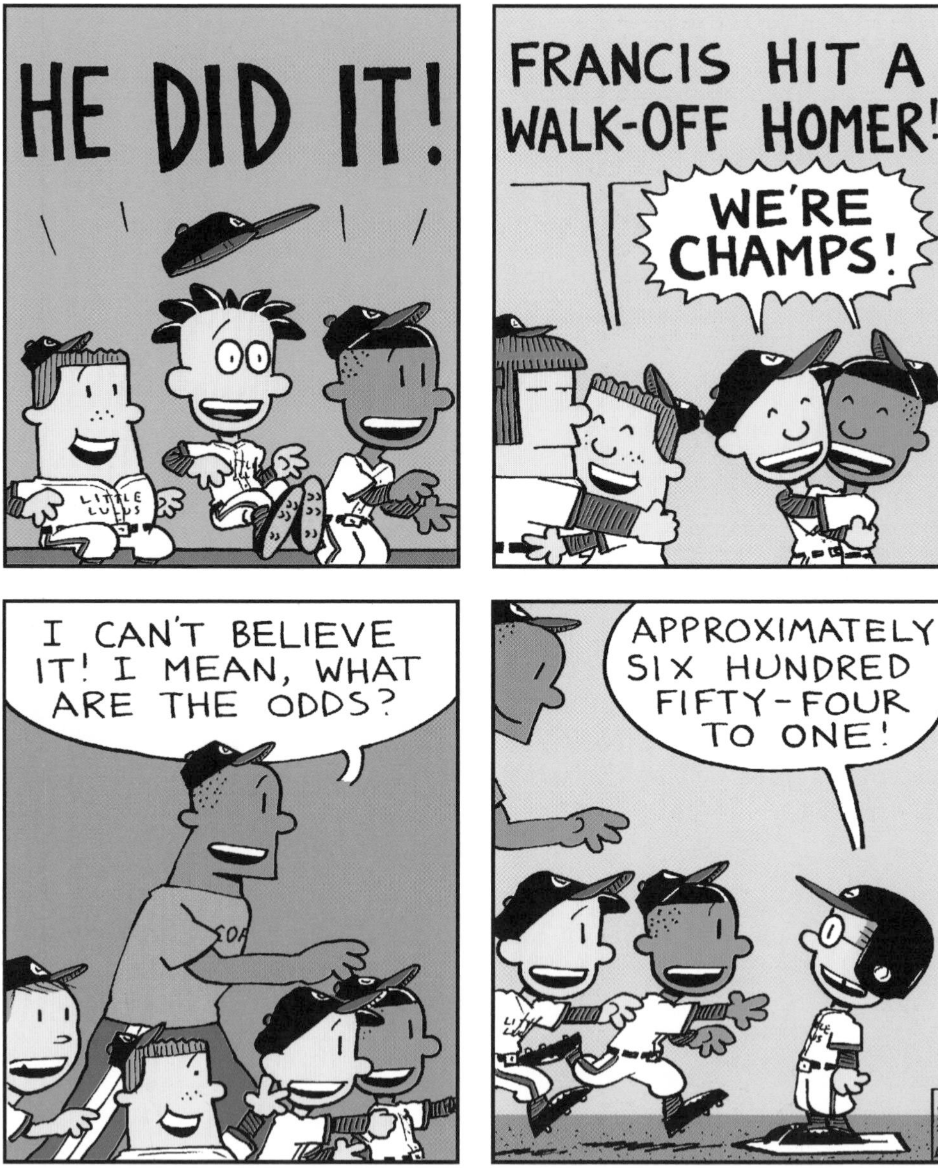
HE DID IT!
FRANCIS HIT A WALK-OFF HOMER!
WE'RE CHAMPS!
I CAN'T BELIEVE IT! I MEAN, WHAT ARE THE ODDS?
APPROXIMATELY SIX HUNDRED FIFTY-FOUR TO ONE!

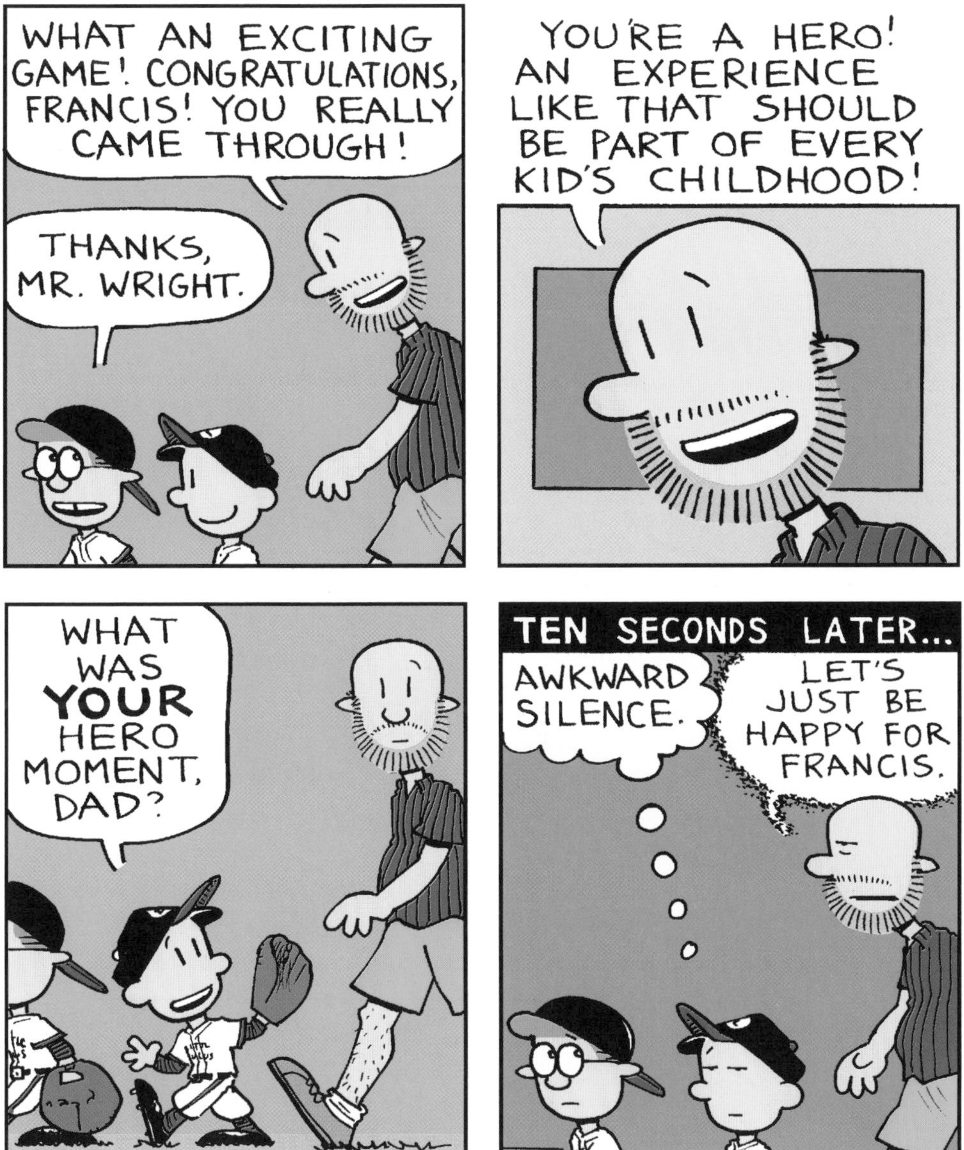
WHAT AN EXCITING GAME! CONGRATULATIONS, FRANCIS! YOU REALLY CAME THROUGH!
THANKS, MR. WRIGHT.
YOU'RE A HERO! AN EXPERIENCE LIKE THAT SHOULD BE PART OF EVERY KID'S CHILDHOOD!
WHAT WAS **YOUR** HERO MOMENT, DAD?
TEN SECONDS LATER...
AWKWARD SILENCE.
LET'S JUST BE HAPPY FOR FRANCIS.
PEIRCE

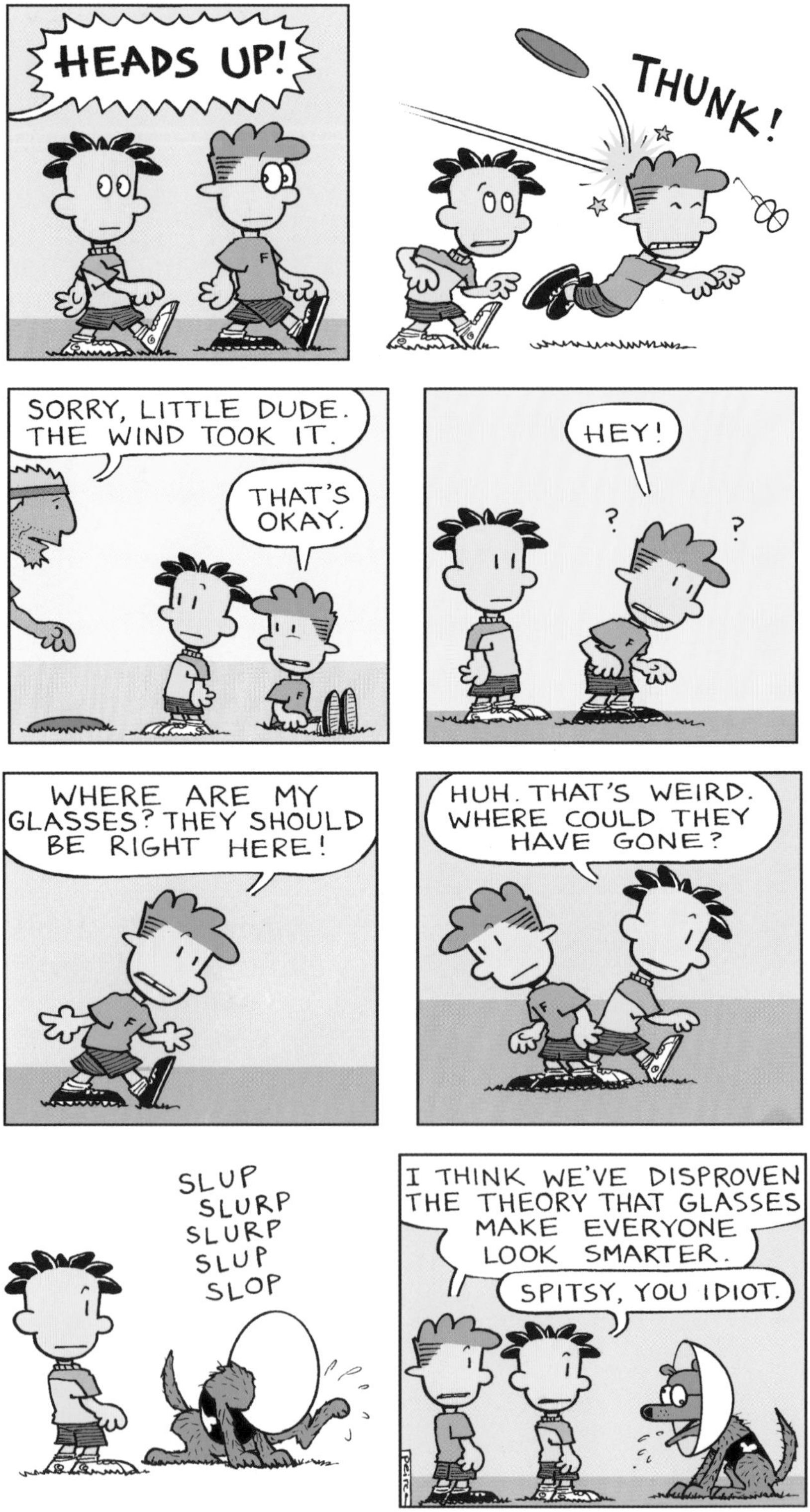
HEADS UP!
THUNK!
SORRY, LITTLE DUDE. THE WIND TOOK IT.
THAT'S OKAY.
HEY!
? ?
WHERE ARE MY GLASSES? THEY SHOULD BE RIGHT HERE!
HUH. THAT'S WEIRD. WHERE COULD THEY HAVE GONE?
SLUP SLURP SLURP SLUP SLOP
I THINK WE'VE DISPROVEN THE THEORY THAT GLASSES MAKE EVERYONE LOOK SMARTER.
SPITSY, YOU IDIOT.

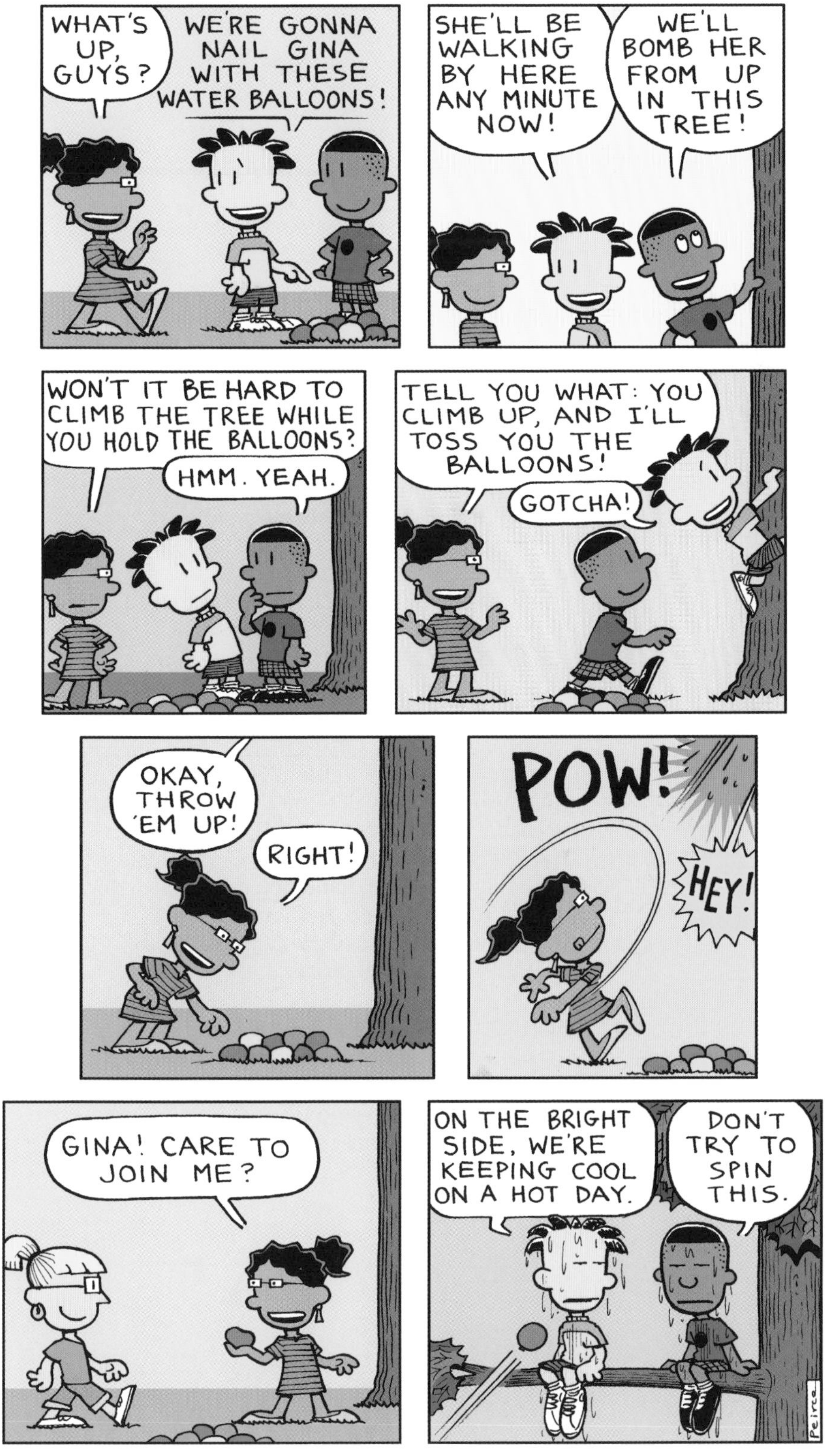
WHAT'S UP, GUYS?
WE'RE GONNA NAIL GINA WITH THESE WATER BALLOONS!
SHE'LL BE WALKING BY HERE ANY MINUTE NOW!
WE'LL BOMB HER FROM UP IN THIS TREE!
WON'T IT BE HARD TO CLIMB THE TREE WHILE YOU HOLD THE BALLOONS?
HMM. YEAH.
TELL YOU WHAT: YOU CLIMB UP, AND I'LL TOSS YOU THE BALLOONS!
GOTCHA!
OKAY, THROW 'EM UP!
RIGHT!
POW!
HEY!
GINA! CARE TO JOIN ME?
ON THE BRIGHT SIDE, WE'RE KEEPING COOL ON A HOT DAY.
DON'T TRY TO SPIN THIS.
Peirce

Big Nate is distributed internationally by Andrews McMeel Syndication.

Big Nate: This Means War! copyright © 2024 by United Feature Syndicate, Inc. All rights reserved. Printed in China. No part of this book may be used or reproduced in any manner whatsoever without written permission except in the case of reprints in the context of reviews.

Andrews McMeel Publishing
a division of Andrews McMeel Universal
1130 Walnut Street, Kansas City, Missouri 64106

www.andrewsmcmeel.com

24 25 26 27 28 SDB 10 9 8 7 6 5 4 3 2 1

ISBN: 978-1-5248-8749-0

Library of Congress Control Number: 2023943211

Made by:
RR Donnelley (Guangdong) Printing Solutions Company Ltd
Address and location of manufacturer:
No. 2, Minzhu Road, Daning, Humen Town,
Dongguan City, Guangdong Province, China 523930
1st Printing – 10/30/23

ATTENTION: SCHOOLS AND BUSINESSES
Andrews McMeel books are available at quantity discounts with bulk purchase for educational, business, or sales promotional use. For information, please e-mail the Andrews McMeel Publishing Special Sales Department: sales@amuniversal.com.

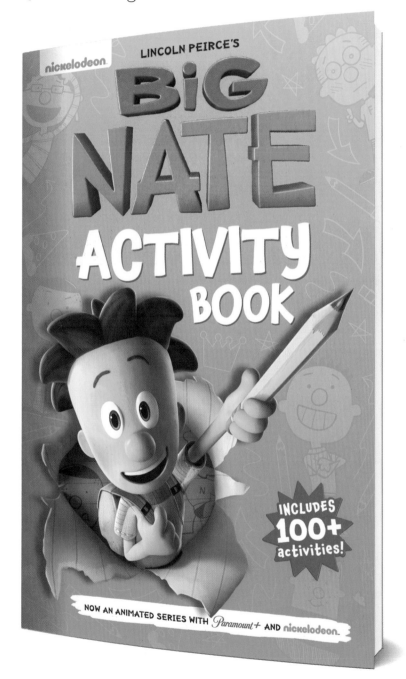

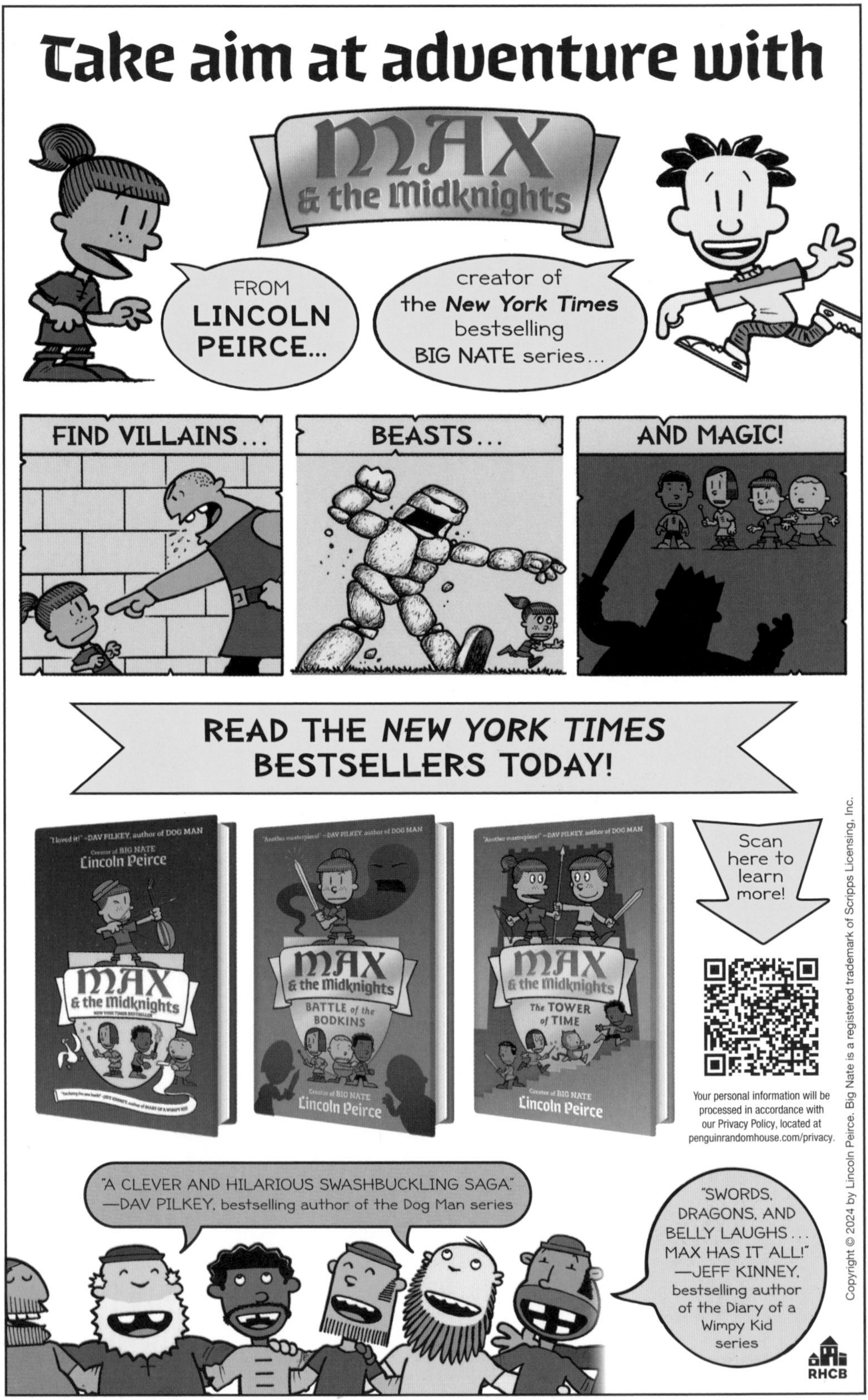
Take aim at adventure with
MAX & the Midknights
FROM LINCOLN PEIRCE...
creator of the New York Times bestselling BIG NATE series...
FIND VILLAINS...
BEASTS...
AND MAGIC!
READ THE NEW YORK TIMES BESTSELLERS TODAY!
Scan here to learn more!
Your personal information will be processed in accordance with our Privacy Policy, located at penguinrandomhouse.com/privacy.
"A CLEVER AND HILARIOUS SWASHBUCKLING SAGA." —DAV PILKEY, bestselling author of the Dog Man series
"SWORDS, DRAGONS, AND BELLY LAUGHS . . . MAX HAS IT ALL!" —JEFF KINNEY, bestselling author of the Diary of a Wimpy Kid series
Copyright © 2024 by Lincoln Peirce. Big Nate is a registered trademark of Scripps Licensing, Inc.
RHCB